THE FRONTIERS SAGA
EPISODE 7

THE
EXPANSE

D1706655

Ryk Brown

CHAPTER ONE

Captain Nathan Scott walked the corridor of the command deck on his way to the captain's mess. Over the last few weeks, the Aurora had been under repair at the Takaran shipyards. During their downtime, Nathan had renewed his tradition of sharing breakfast with his friend and chief engineer, Lieutenant Commander Vladimir Kamenetskiy. When they had still been in the orbital assembly platform high above Earth, he and Vladimir had shared meals in the ship's mess with the rest of the crew. However, they had been ensigns at the time, and only a third of the ship's standard complement had been aboard as well. Now, with the ship fully crewed and the mess hall constantly busy, Nathan and his friend were forced to take their meals in the captain's mess in order to have an open conversation.

During the last few weeks, both the ship's executive officer, Commander Cameron Taylor, and the ship's chief of security, Lieutenant Commander Jessica Nash, had also become regular attendees for the morning breakfast in the captain's mess. It was a time that Nathan had grown to relish. Over their morning meal, he was not the captain; he was just Nathan. He was hanging out with his three friends. He could relax and be himself, as could they all.

There was something therapeutic about their

meals together. After all they had been through during their adventures in the Pentaurus cluster, a little therapy couldn't hurt. In fact, Doctor Ahlitara, a behavioral psychologist on loan from Corinair, had recommended such interactions among the senior staff. He had warned that the crew needed an outlet, a way to release the stress and tension that had been building up, even during their post-battle downtime in the Pallax shipyards.

Commander Taylor's idea of therapy was different. She kept the crew busy. Those not participating in repairs spent most of their time in training, as she was determined to make them into a proper crew. Nathan had wondered if it was worth the effort, as there was every chance that, once they arrived back at Earth, the lot of them would be replaced by more qualified officers and crew. The members of his crew hailing from the Pentaurus cluster would undoubtedly be returned to their homes as soon as feasible, which, depending on the current situation on Earth, could be some time. It hardly seemed fair, especially considering what they had sacrificed for not only their own worlds, but for the Aurora and, by association, the Earth itself. Without them, the Aurora and her few remaining crew would surely have perished, and the Earth would have been left with inadequate defense against the Jung.

Nathan finished the short trip from his quarters to the captain's mess, passing only a few members of his crew along the way as they made their way to their duty stations to start their shifts. The crew had settled into a familiar routine, which also helped to ease their frazzled nerves. A few 'morning, sirs,' and his brief journey was complete.

"Good morning, Lieutenant Commander," Nathan

said as he entered the captain's mess.

"Good morning, sir," the 'Cheng' answered. Vladimir's tone was more formal than expected, which alerted Nathan of someone else in the room. He looked about the compact dining room and saw no one. The Cheng darted his eyes toward the galley, and as if on cue, one of the ship's cooks carried out a tray and placed it on the table.

"Good morning, Mister Collins," Nathan greeted the cook. Mister Collins had been assigned as the captain's personal cook by the galley chief. The young Corinairan had left culinary school and volunteered for duty aboard the Aurora after the Yamaro had attacked his world. While his culinary talents were evident, the galley chief did not feel that the young man had the right skill set for the volume of cooking required to feed an entire crew. Cooking for the captain and his senior staff seemed the perfect assignment for the eager young recruit. Over the past few weeks, the young man had memorized most of the senior staff's culinary likes and dislikes. He had even learned to cook a few of their favorite recipes from Earth, especially those of Lieutenant Commander Kamenetskiy, who always seemed willing to spend an hour in the kitchen educating the young chef on the art of Russian cuisine.

"Good morning, sir," Mister Collins responded in accented English. Along with his studies of Earth cuisine, he was also working on his English skills. His English still carried the heavy brogue so common to the Corinairan version of English they called 'Angla.'

"It will just be the two of us this morning," Nathan said, noticing that the cook had set out the usual four place settings.

"The ladies will not to be joining you this morning?"

"I'm afraid they have other duties to attend to this morning," Nathan told him.

"Yes, sir," Mister Collins said, immediately removing the extra settings.

"No ladies?" Vladimir said. His face drooped with disappointment.

Nathan looked at him funny as the chef left the room and returned to the adjoining galley. "We're talking about Cameron and Jessica here, Vlad, not a couple of hot nurses."

"Just because I am not trying to sleep with them does not mean I cannot enjoy their company," Vladimir argued. "After all, they are women, even if they are not susceptible to my obvious charms," he added with the slightest hint of sarcasm.

Nathan smiled as he took his first sip of morning coffee, or what the Ancotans had provided as a substitute. It was bitter, more so than the coffee on Earth, and required a considerable amount of sweetener to make it palatable for the small Terran portion of the crew.

"Where are they?" Vlad asked.

Nathan winced slightly at the bitter flavor as he set his cup down and began to add more sweetener. "Cameron is down on Corinair. They're giving her a final deep scan to ensure that all the nanites have left her system."

"I thought they were gone weeks ago," Vladimir said.

"So did I. Apparently they just wanted to be sure before she left the Pentaurus cluster for good."

"What about Jessica? What's her excuse?"

"The shuttles bringing the crew back from Corinair

are arriving this morning," Nathan explained. "She wanted to oversee their check-in."

"Doesn't she have staff that can handle such details?"

"You know Jess," Nathan said as he took another sip, finding the level of bitterness more tolerable, "still the one to do it herself whenever possible."

Vladimir chuckled softly as the cook placed a plate of the Corinairan version of bacon and eggs on the table in front of him. "It was not so long ago that you and I were much the same way, my friend." Vladimir began devouring his breakfast in earnest as he spoke. He paused, taking notice of the weary look on Nathan's face. "Still not sleeping?"

"Not much, no," Nathan admitted as he took his first bite. "At least not as much as I'd like. To be honest, I'm really looking forward to getting back to Earth and handing everything over to Fleet. Perhaps then I can get some sleep."

"Yes, I hear the beds in prison are quite comfortable."

"Funny." Nathan took another bite of his food, chasing it with a sip of the Ancotan coffee. He tried to ignore his friend's remark, fully aware of its sarcastic intent. However, the thought still haunted him to some degree, just as it had since the day he decided to form the alliance with the people of the Pentaurus cluster and share the jump drive technology with them. "You don't really think they will..."

"Pssht." Vladimir smirked as he continued to shovel food in his mouth. "You have done amazing things while in command, Nathan. You liberated billions of people and gained advanced technologies, but more importantly, you managed to save this ship and return her to Earth. You will be welcomed as a hero, my friend."

"Let's hope," Nathan said, unconvinced, "but we're not home yet."

"Pssht!"

"What? Did you spring a leak or something?"

Vladimir finished chewing his food and swallowed before continuing. "We survived four attacks, destroyed a dozen enemy warships, and invaded a technologically advanced empire." Vladimir scooped up another load of eggs, his loaded fork hovering at his mouth. "After all that, how hard can a thousand light year journey be?" Vladimir loaded his mouth up once again. "Trust me," he continued, his mouth again full of food, "you will become a legend on Earth, just as you are in the Pentaurus cluster."

"I think you're exaggerating again," Nathan said. "I'm not worthy of such status. You and I both know that most of it was just dumb luck."

Vladimir raised his finger to pause the conversation as he finished swallowing. "Legends are not born as such; rather, they are persons no different than you or I who accepted a role thrust upon them by fate and had the fortitude to live up to the challenge to the best of their ability." Vladimir smiled, obviously pleased that he had remembered the quote correctly.

"I've heard that somewhere before," Nathan said, a quizzical expression on his face.

Vladimir smiled even more broadly. "I too know something of history."

"Who said that?"

"That I do not remember," he admitted as he took another bite, "but I am sure he was Russian."

* * *

Lieutenant Commander Jessica Nash stood silently behind the security detail while they checked the credentials of each crewman as they stepped off the shuttle. Despite the fact that the Ta'Akar Empire had been defeated and the few remaining loyalists left on Corinair had all but disappeared, she did not intend to take chances. The identity of each and every person on board was confirmed with both retinal and DNA scans before they were allowed to leave the Aurora's main hangar bay.

Most of the Aurora's Corinairan crew had already returned from their two-day shore leave on their homeworld. At this point, the only crewmen left on Corinair were the two platoons of special forces troops that Corinari command had insisted the Aurora bring along. Captain Scott had been reluctant to do so, as he was already concerned about what would happen to his crew once they returned to Earth. Bringing an additional one hundred highly trained combatants might further complicate matters. However, Jessica had convinced her commanding officer that since there was still a lot of unknown space to pass through on their way home, there was nothing wrong with having some extra muscle on board, especially highly trained muscle. In the end, Nathan had agreed, with the stipulation that the platoons remained attached to her security command.

Jessica, of course, had no problem with the captain's stipulation. She was also trained for special operations, and having two platoons of similarly trained troops at her disposal made her feel better. They had already defended against three boarding actions, and with the Corinari spec-ops aboard, they would be more prepared for any other such attempts.

Of course, she expected nothing of the sort during their journey back to Earth. They had no idea if there would be any more inhabited systems along their course home other than the few known systems all lying within fifty light years of the Pentaurus cluster. The truth, however, was that neither they nor the people of the Pentaurus cluster knew exactly what lay within the vast expanse of space that separated the Pentaurus and Sol sectors. It was nearly nine hundred light years of unexplored space. As far as they knew, the Aurora would be the first ship from Earth to explore this area of the galaxy since getting back into space.

"Lieutenant Commander," Sergeant Weatherly said as he stepped up and saluted.

"Sergeant. Has Commander Taylor checked in?"

"Yes, sir, about an hour ago. She went down to the cargo bay with the chief of the boat to check over the food supplies that arrived from Ancot this morning."

"I guess Mister Soloman's old man came through after all," Jessica said with amusement.

"Yes, sir. I heard the Ancotans have been sending over as much food as they can fit in that heavy cargo shuttle the Corinairans fitted with a jump drive."

"Yeah. Last I heard they had three more heavy jumpers just about ready to go."

"Major Prechitt came back with the commander as well," the sergeant reported.

"I thought he was staying behind to oversee the rebuilding of the Corinari forces."

"I guess not. Commander Taylor told me to put

him back on the roster as CAG."

"I wonder who's going to lead the Corinari," Jessica said.

He shrugged. "You'd have to ask the major."

Jessica glanced at the sergeant's data pad. "How are we doing with crew check-in?"

"First platoon just checked in. All their bio and DNA scans matched, and they all scanned clean of contraband. Second platoon's in the transfer airlock pressure-cycling."

"How about their arms?"

"Came aboard last night," the sergeant reported. "Passed inspection by the weapons master."

"Yeah, I saw the report. Those boys carry some sweet gear," Jessica said.

Sergeant Weatherly smiled. "Yes, sir, they do."

"Any word on who they're sending as their company CO?" she wondered.

Sergeant Weatherly said nothing. Instead, he held up his data pad for her to see.

Jessica looked at the roster for the shuttle that was still in the transfer airlock waiting for the pressurization cycle to complete before it rolled into the main hangar bay. "You're kidding me," she stated as her eyes widened. "I thought he was still in the hospital."

"Says he cleared med and psych yesterday."

"I thought Waddell had family on Corinair," she said. "Between his family and his injuries, I assumed he'd be staying behind."

"His son was killed on Takara. Rumor is he and his wife are on the outs."

"Yeah, I heard about his son," she commented as the massive airlock door began to raise. "I didn't know about his wife, though."

"I guess there wasn't much left for him on Corinair."

The shuttle rolled to a stop twenty meters in front of them, and its boarding ramp began to deploy from its hull just below the main, port-side boarding hatch. A minute later, the hatch swung outward, and a flight tech stepped out onto the fully deployed boarding ramp, checking that it was locked securely in place before allowing the passengers to disembark.

The first man out of the shuttle was Waddell. He paused at the top of the ramp, taking a moment to scan the hangar. Jessica watched as Waddell stepped down the ramp. His face was different than she remembered. His scraggy blond hair was trimmed high and tight, so much so that its true color was almost indiscernible. His face was scarred from the thermal burns he had suffered when he had ordered the Aurora's fighters to bomb the staging area and destroy the Ghatazhak forces that were about to overrun his position. The nanite therapy used by the Corinairan doctors was impressive, but apparently they were not capable of repairing everything. She suspected that the scars of that day would be with him, in more ways than one, for a long time to come.

One other thing had changed about him. His eyes. They were cold, and his expression was unreadable. She had seen this before, back on Earth. Despite the sudden burst of prosperity and cooperation that had taken place over the hundred years since the discovery of the Data Ark, her world was still not without its own conflicts which had produced their own share of men with such scars.

As he approached, she also noticed the change in his rank.

"Major Waddell," she said. "Congratulations on your promotion."

"Thank you, sir," he responded, snapping a salute.

"I'm not sure you're required to salute me," she told him. "In fact, you may outrank me at this point. I'll have to check."

"Yes, sir," he answered.

"I see you're taking command of the spec-ops company. By order of the captain, your company will be attached to my command, at least for now."

"Very good, sir."

"You and your men will have to go through our check-in security screenings, just like everyone else."

"I wouldn't have it any other way, sir."

"Very well," Jessica responded. She had never been overly chummy with the man before, but he seemed more tense than she remembered. "It's good to see you well, Major. Carry on."

* * *

"What exactly are 'cantors'?" Commander Taylor wondered as she stared at the stack of food barrels.

"They are a type of bean," Master Chief Montrose explained, "that are grown only on Ancot. They are based on a bean from Earth, but they have been genetically modified to grow better in the soil of Ancot."

"Genetically modified, huh?"

"Only to grow better in the soil of Ancot. They are high in protein and are quite nutritious." The chief of the boat noticed the concern on the executive officer's face. "They have been consumed for several hundred years, Commander. I have never heard of any health issues due to the consumption of cantor beans, except possibly from eating too many of them," he added, blowing up his cheeks and sticking out his belly to simulate weight gain. Cameron's expression did not change. "Cantor beans have been a popular staple throughout the Pentaurus cluster since before I was born. The people of Ancot eat them on a daily basis, and they are some of the healthiest people in the cluster. Do you not have genetically modified crops on Earth?"

"We did," Cameron answered as she looked at the row of bean containers stacked four crates high along the wall of the cargo hold. "They were quite common before the plague. According to history discovered in the Data Ark, there were some problems associated with genetically modified crops in the late twenty-first century due to lack of government oversight of the industry. The problems were corrected, but the industry was never the same, at least not until faster-than-light travel was invented. Once humans started colonizing other Earth-like worlds, the practice increased in order to accommodate differences in environmental conditions."

"Just as they did on Ancot," the master chief pointed out.

"Yes. However, that knowledge was lost along with everything else when the bio-digital plague swept across the Earth and throughout her core worlds. When the Earth was eventually repopulated, the practice was never adopted again. Even when the methods were found in the Ark, it was deemed unnecessary, as the standard methods of agriculture were more than enough to feed the population of Earth. It became one of the many technologies that were considered better left alone, at least for the time being."

"There are reasons for genetic seed modification other than yield."

"True, but after the bio-digital plague, the people of Earth adopted a simpler attitude toward such things out of necessity. Technology scared them for many centuries after the plague. Many were vehemently opposed to our getting back into space." Commander Taylor paused as she counted the crates of cantor beans stacked to the ceiling of the cargo hold. "In retrospect, they may have been right."

"You do not truly believe that."

"No, not me," she assured him. "You can't hide from progress. Eventually it finds you."

"Quite true."

"Besides, had we not gotten back into space, we would have been sitting ducks for the Jung."

"Also true," Master Chief Montrose agreed.

"How many rows deep are these bean boxes stacked?"

"Four rows, I believe."

"What's behind them?" Cameron asked as she tried to see past the rows of crates to the back wall.

"Mostly crates of dehydrated food products and seasonings," the master chief reported. "We try to keep all the food products in the same area whenever we can, which has not been easy since we have been using every space possible."

"We are loaded to the rafters, aren't we?" Cameron admitted.

"If by that you mean from floor to ceiling, then yes, we are." After serving with Terrans for several months, he was becoming accustomed to their various turns of phrase, most of which he did not understand.

"We should make aisles through here going all the way back to the bulkhead so we can get to whatever is behind this without having to restack the crates in front."

The chief of the boat gestured to his men standing behind him, who quickly went to work with their anti-grav lifts to create the requested aisle. "Commander, it was my understanding that you requested what I believe you referred to as an 'administrative load'?"

"You are correct, Master Chief. But whenever possible, we need to make it flexible. We don't know what to expect during our voyage home. It pays to be prepared."

"Agreed."

"Think of it as a cross between an administrative and a tactical loadout."

"We may not have enough space to do as you ask," he warned.

"Be creative, Master Chief," she said with a smile. "And don't be afraid to shift things around as stuff gets used up and space is made available. Just keep good records as you change things around."

"Be creative, aye."

Cameron watched as the men finished shifting crates around and quickly created an aisle down the center of the stacks that led all the way back to the bulkhead. Only it wasn't the bulkhead at the end of the aisle; it was a large metal container. "What is that?" she asked, pointing at the container at the end of the newly created aisle.

"It is a shipping container," the master chief answered.

"I can see that." Cameron walked down the

aisle toward the container. As she grew nearer the container, she could see that it stretched from floor to ceiling and nearly from fore to aft of the hold. "This thing must be at least twenty meters long. How the hell did you get it in here?"

"It was a tight fit to be sure. We had to shift everything over to one side of the hold in order to load this container."

"What's inside?"

"I do not know."

Commander Taylor looked at the master chief, her eyebrows raising in disbelief.

"All I know is that it came from Takara," the master chief explained. "It has the seal of Prince Casimir, and the locks are coded for the captain only. I assumed he was aware of its contents."

"Well if he is, he didn't say anything to me about it." Cameron moved down the narrow space between the crates full of dehydrated foods and seasonings, making her way to the front of the massive Takaran shipping container. Once at the front of the container, she found the lock control panel. She placed her hand on the scanner pad. A moment later, a message appeared in red. It was in Takaran, which the commander could not read.

"It says, 'Unlock request denied. Access restricted to Captain Nathan Scott,'" Chief Montrose explained.

Cameron looked at the front end of the container. It was dark gray and polished just like the rest of the container's walls, and it had structural ribs along the outside spaced every meter. It was solidly built with the obvious intention of protecting whatever was stored inside. For a moment, she felt apprehensive. The container was from a world that only weeks ago had been their enemy. She couldn't help but wonder if the contents of the container might pose a threat. Many stories had survived the bio-digital plague, and the story of the Trojan horse had been one of them. Tug, or Prince Casimir, was a trusted ally who had laid his life on the line like everyone else, perhaps even more so than others. Still, not knowing what was inside bothered her. She was the ship's XO, and she needed to know. It was her job to know.

* * *

"As you were," Nathan announced as he entered the command briefing room. The trappings of rank and protocol never sat well with him, and he took every opportunity to avoid them whenever possible. Compelling them to remain seated before they even had a chance to stand had become habit with him, despite the constant objections from his executive officer. Nathan moved to his chair at the end of the table, the rest of his staff having already arrived for the morning briefing. As he took his seat, he noticed a late arrival coming through the hatchway. "Major Prechitt," he stated with surprise, "I thought you were reassigned by the Corinari. Aren't you supposed to be on the surface and in command of the Corinairan military forces?"

"I have been reassigned," the major said as he stepped up to the table.

"To where?" Nathan wondered.

"To the Aurora, sir, so that I may continue serving as your CAG, at least until you have safely returned to Earth—that is, if you'd still like me to do so."

"Of course, Major," Nathan said, gesturing for him to take a seat and join them. "Glad to have you back aboard."

"Thank you, sir," Major Prechitt said as he took his seat.

"Who's running the Corinari?" Jessica wondered.

"Commander Toral will be taking command," the major told her.

"I wasn't aware he had survived," Nathan said.

"His injuries were quite severe," Doctor Chen said. "In my care, he would not have made it. The Corinairan surgeons were able to stabilize him enough to get him back to a hospital on Corinair. He's been through several surgeries since then, as well as intensive nanite therapy. He will probably never regain full mobility of his legs, but last I heard, he was able to walk."

"Granted, he still has a long way to go in his recovery, but so do the Corinari."

"Wasn't he a lieutenant commander when he was injured?" Cameron asked.

"Yes, he was," Major Prechitt said. "There are others that might be more experienced and more qualified than Commander Toral, but the Corinari numbers are already depleted, and combat-ready officers are in short supply. Toral was an obvious choice, under the circumstances."

"I'm surprised they let you go," Nathan said. "I'm surprised they let any of you go, for that matter."

"They would have found it difficult to stop many of us," the major responded.

"How many did return?" Jessica wondered.

Cameron picked up her data pad and studied it for a moment before responding. "All but fifty-seven, most of whom were serving in noncritical positions."

"I suspect that many of them were swept up in the moment or did not want to be seen in an unfavorable light in the eyes of their peers," Major Prechitt said. "In addition, I know of several who, although they sincerely meant to stay aboard, were forced to remain on Corinair for family reasons. One of my own pilots was forced to remain when he discovered that his best friend's children had been orphaned as a result of the attack by the Wallach."

"We never expected everyone to remain and make the journey back to Earth with us," Nathan told him. "I consider us lucky that so many *have* returned." Nathan turned to Cameron. "How will the loss of fifty-seven crewmen affect our staffing?"

"Since most of them were noncritical positions, we still have three full shifts of operational crew. With a little cross-training, I can juggle them around a bit and make it work. We can even go down to two shifts if necessary. That would give us extra personnel to better cover sick calls. I will work something out and run it past you later today, sir."

"Very well." Nathan turned to Vladimir. "How's the ship looking, Lieutenant Commander?"

"Better than she did when we first left Earth," Vladimir said. "All flight systems are fully operational. Main propulsion, maneuvering, power generation, environmental: all are in perfect order. It is quite nice for a change."

"How about our jump drive?" Nathan asked.

"The jump drive is fully operational, Captain," Doctor Sorenson reported. "We also have two sets of emitters, guaranteeing us at least one full degree of redundancy. In addition, the Takarans upgraded all of the computers used by the jump drive and the jump plotting system. They also changed some of the basic algorithms to allow us to program a series of short local jumps. Now, you can create a preprogrammed series of jumps to quickly move the ship about during a tactical situation such as combat."

"Really?" Nathan didn't hide the interest in his voice. "That was good thinking, Doctor."

"It was the Takarans, actually. Captain Navarro, the captain of the Avendahl, was fascinated by the possibilities of using a jump drive during combat. I believe it was his idea."

"So, we could jump several times in rapid succession?" Cameron wondered.

"Yes. During our previous engagements, Captain Scott regularly made a series of short jumps in order to strike the same target from different angles. Because of the time required to calculate each jump in the series, it generally took several minutes for the Aurora to get into her next strike position. Captain Navarro was convinced that, if that time could be reduced to seconds, it would provide an even bigger tactical advantage."

"He's right," Nathan agreed. "The only delay would be our time to turn, which, if we were moving slowly enough, would only be seconds. A four-point turn could be done in less than a minute instead of a few minutes. If we were simply doing a one-eighty and jumping back in, it could be less than twenty seconds, assuming we were traveling slowly enough."

"The slower we travel when we jump in to attack, the easier it is for our opponent to strike back."

"True," Nathan said, "but it only takes us ten seconds to get a round of torpedoes launched and another five seconds to change course and jump away. If we jump in at just the right distance from the target, we can be long gone before their weapons reach us, even if they launch the moment we appear."

"Unless they're using energy weapons," Jessica warned.

"Do the Jung have energy weapons on their ships?" Nathan wondered.

"We haven't seen any evidence that the Jung possess them," Jessica admitted, adding, "yet."

Nathan thought for a moment. "Regardless, the concept is worth looking into further. Commander, why don't you and Lieutenant Commander Nash come up with some maneuvers that might be of use to us in a combat situation. You can start by analyzing the jump drive tactics we've used thus far that have been successful."

"Yes, sir," Cameron said.

"Feel free to throw in some ideas of your own," Nathan added, the slightest hint of a smile forming on his face.

"Count on it, sir," Cameron answered, also fighting the urge to smile.

Nathan had found it considerably easier to smile these days. While it was true that they were still a long way from home, they were no longer under threat and fighting for their lives. They also had a fully functional and properly supplied ship and nearly a full crew. Although he had grown accustomed to his role as captain as of late, he had no regrets at the thought of handing over command to someone more qualified upon their return to Earth.

"How are we doing on supplies, Commander?" Nathan asked, changing the subject.

"We're fully loaded, sir," Cameron told him. "In fact, I doubt we could fit much more. We've got enough food, water, and consumables to last us nearly a year at our current staffing levels. We're also carrying quite a bit of raw materials for the fabricators that the Takarans gave us, so we should be able to manufacture any spare parts we might need along the way."

"Hopefully that won't become necessary," Nathan commented as he turned his attention to Lieutenant Commander Nash. "How are we with weapons?"

"All sixteen mini-rail guns are operational," Jessica began, "and we're carrying full loads of both standard slugs and point-defense frag-rounds. The four quad guns are also operational, as are their translation rails, so they can be used from both our topside and our belly. The Takarans loaded us up with custom-manufactured rounds for the quads. We've got full loads of standard slugs, frag-rounds, and hull-piercing, delayed-trigger explosive rounds."

"What about torpedoes?" Nathan wondered.

"That was a little trickier. As you know, the Takarans aren't big torpedo users. They like missiles. They were able to scrounge up some older air-to-surface cruise missiles, the same kind they let the Corinari use. They were sitting in an ammo dump somewhere. They put fixed-yield tactical nukes in them and adapted them to be launched from our tubes. But again, they are point-and-shoot weapons with no maneuvering capabilities, as they were designed for atmospheric use, not deep space. However, they do some damage, just like the ones from the Corinari."

"How many?"

"Twenty-three."

"That should be more than enough," Nathan said. "I don't expect to get involved in any more rebellions on our way home."

"Let's hope not," Cameron agreed.

"What about shields?" Nathan asked. "Any word on that?"

Doctor Sorenson leaned forward to chime in on the subject. "It is possible, at least according to the Takaran scientists and technicians that are making the trip with us. The problem is power generation. In order for the shields to be effective, they need to have a dedicated power source."

"We have four antimatter reactors, Doctor," Vladimir stated. "Surely that would provide enough power."

"Of course," she agreed. "Even one of them would be enough. However, our reactors are designed to work together to provide huge amounts of power to the entire ship and to balance the loads across all operational reactors, are they not?"

"Da, that is correct."

"The design of the Takaran shields are such that strikes against them require massive energy surges from the reactors that supply them. For this reason, the Takarans always isolate the reactors powering the shields from those powering other systems. They also insist that at least one redundant reactor be available for the shields, again, in isolation from the rest of the ship."

"That would make it more difficult to recharge the jump drive in a timely fashion," Vladimir noted, seeing her point.

"What about the zero-point energy device?" Nathan asked.

"We are looking into that possibility as well," Abby assured him. "However, as you remember, the ZPED used by the Avendahl causes significant problems with our jump drive, even at lower output levels. We're hoping that we can implement the smaller ZPEDs used by the high-speed comm-drones to power the shields. Theoretically, they should provide sufficient power. However, we are not yet sure if they will have a similar effect on the jump drive."

"We'd have to drop our shields first," Jessica said. "Not an attractive requirement during battle, even if only for a split second."

"No, it's not," Nathan agreed. "Continue your research, Doctor. At the very least, I would think Fleet Command would want to incorporate the Takaran shields into future ship designs."

"Yes, sir."

"How about our jump range?" Nathan asked. "Any word on that yet?"

"Theoretically, the new emitters and improved energy storage systems should increase our operational safe jump range. However, we have only performed a few jumps with the new systems. We will need to conduct a few more before I have enough data to perform a proper evaluation."

"Care to make any guesses?"

"Not particularly, sir."

"Humor me, Doctor."

"Without using any power from the smaller ZPEDs in the high-speed comm-drones, we may get as much as twenty-five light years per jump. But again, that is only in theory."

"Still, that's quite encouraging," Nathan stated. "I mean, that would get us home in half the time. That's what... forty jumps instead of one hundred?"

"Give or take a dozen jumps or so, yes," Abby said. "Even if it proves to be true, I wouldn't push the jumps to the maximum range. It might be safer to make twenty light year jumps."

"Okay, fifty jumps then," Nathan corrected himself. "That's still only three weeks instead of six. Make that your priority, Abby. I want that increased range."

"Yes, sir."

"Doctor Chen?" Nathan said, inviting the young doctor that headed up the Aurora's medical department to give her status report.

"Medical is fully stocked and staffed," she reported. "The Takarans aren't any more advanced medically than the Corinairans. However, they have more experienced trauma surgeons and better procedures for dealing with wounded. One of the Takaran trauma surgeons has signed on, so along with the Corinairan doctor specializing in nanite therapy and Doctor Galloway who has been with us since the last boarding attempt, we have four doctors on board as well as several nurses and medical technicians. In addition, many of the Corinari security troops under Lieutenant Commander Nash have field medic training as well. I believe we are as prepared as we possibly can be, more so than when we attacked the Takaran homeworld."

"That's good to hear," Nathan said. "We'll do our best to keep your job as dull as possible."

"Thank you, sir. That would be appreciated."

Nathan leaned back in his chair, taking a moment before concluding the briefing. "Well, we're finally about to begin our journey home, people. It has taken a long time and a lot of sacrifice to get to this point. But make no mistake; we're not home yet. The Takaran star charts only cover the immediate sector. Once we leave the Pentaurus sector, we're looking at over eight hundred light years of unexplored space. The only knowledge we have of this expanse of space are observations made by our ancestors over a millennium ago. We'll conduct deep space scans along our course ahead during each of our layovers while we recharge the jump drive. Hopefully, that will be enough to ensure safe passage. However, as we do *not* know what *is* out there, we will operate under the assumption that there are threats out there waiting for us."

"Hope for the best and prepare for the worst," Jessica mumbled.

"Exactly," Nathan agreed.

"My father always says that," she explained. "Used to drive me nuts."

"We'll get under way at fourteen hundred hours after a final inspection of all systems and departments has been concluded." Nathan looked to each of their faces to see if anyone had something to add. Satisfied that they did not, he added, "Dismissed."

Nathan watched as his senior department heads filed out of the command briefing room to begin their final inspections prior to departure—all of them except for Cameron who remained in her seat, pretending to study her data pad while waiting for the others to vacate the room.

"Commander?" Nathan queried once they were alone.

"Sir, are you aware of a large shipping container sent over from the Takarans? One whose access is restricted to you and you alone?"

"Tug said he was sending me something special, something to make my life easier."

"Like what? A private shuttle?"

Nathan looked confused. "How big a container are we talking?"

"At least twenty meters long, four high, and four

wide."

Nathan looked even more confused. "I was expecting steaks or something. Or maybe some of that ale they served in the palace, but nothing that big; I assure you. Any idea what's inside?"

"Like I said, the locks are programmed to allow access to only you."

* * *

Nathan placed his hand on the scanner pad to the right of the entry hatch at the end of the Takaran shipping container. The digital display above the pad turned green. The words were in Takaran, but he assumed green was good. His assumption was confirmed a moment later when the six bolts on the hatch slid into the unlocked position with a loud clunk.

"Are you sure you want to go inside?" Nathan asked the commander.

"Try and stop me, sir."

Nathan swung the hatch open, revealing an inner airlock about three meters square, with another inner hatch on the opposite bulkhead. "Must be an airlock."

"On a shipping container?"

Nathan stepped inside the airlock, looking about. "Maybe this thing was designed to be carried on the outside of a cargo ship. There was a docking collar around the outside hatch."

"Perhaps, but we've seen more than a few Takaran cargo ships over the past couple of weeks. How many of them had containers on the outside of the hull?"

"Good point. This control pad isn't responding,"

he said after he repeatedly pressed what appeared to be the button to open the inner hatch.

Cameron pointed up at the red light over their heads. "It's an airlock, remember?" Cameron pulled the outer door closed and locked it. The overhead light turned blue.

"Still not working." A fine mist began to spray into the room from all sides.

"What the...?"

"I think we're being decontaminated," Cameron said as she looked around nervously.

The spray continued for several seconds, after which a ventilation fan in the ceiling quickly sucked the swirling mist up and away, clearing the room once again. The overhead light turned green.

"Ah, it's working now," Nathan said, activating the inner door.

The inner hatch sprung free, allowing Nathan to swing it slowly into the container. The inside of the container was dark except for hundreds of small lights along the sides close to the container's deck. Most of the lights were green, like status indicators on some control console. There was no interior illumination other than the pale green light spilling in through the inner airlock hatch, casting their shadows inward.

Nathan moved to one side, gesturing with his hand. "Ladies first."

"I'm not even cleared to be here, sir."

Nathan looked at her with surprise. "What happened to 'try and stop me'?"

"There could be some type of inner security features in there. It's probably safe for you, but for all we know, I might get blasted the moment I step through the door."

Nathan shrugged her off, unsure if she was serious. He pulled a small light out of his pocket and turned it on, shining the small narrow beam of light about the interior of the container. There were two levels inside with only a meter-wide passageway down the center aisle that ran all the way to the far end of the container. Along either side of the aisle, clear cylinders sat atop devices of some type. The devices at the bottom of the cylinders appeared to be some type of control mechanisms with numerous indicator lights on their small interface panels. At the top of each tube were complex, interconnected systems of pipes and conduit running the length of the compartment and connecting all the cylinders.

"What's inside them?" Cameron asked, peering around Nathan to get a better view of the interior.

Nathan focused his light on one of the closest cylinders, studying it for a moment. At first, he thought the clear tubes were filled with some type of gray liquid, but on closer inspection, it looked more like a heavy fog swirling slowly about within the cylinders. "I don't know, but I'm pretty sure it isn't steaks."

Cameron gently pushed him forward through the inner airlock hatch. The moment his boot touched the deck inside, pale, blue lights located above each of the clear cylinders began to flicker to life. First, the lights closest to them came on, followed by each one in succession until all the cylinders along either wall were lit.

"Whoa," Nathan mumbled as he continued forward. "I guess it knows we're here." He took a few more steps forward, looking at the cylinders more closely. "There's something in here, Cam." He turned back to her and noticed that she was still standing in the doorway. "Take a look at this."

Cameron entered the container, closing the inner airlock hatch behind her.

"What are you doing?" Nathan asked urgently as the hatch resealed automatically.

"Sorry. Habit I guess. Always close an airlock hatch behind you."

"Except when entering a mysterious shipping container full of..."

Cameron pointed behind Nathan, causing him to stop mid-sentence. Nathan spun around to see a hologram materializing into view in the middle of the aisle not more than a few meters in front of them. It blinked and flickered for a moment, finally resolving into such clarity that he could hardly tell it wasn't a live person standing in front of them.

That person was Prince Casimir, the new ruler of Takara, the man they knew as Redmond Tugwell, the leader of the Karuzari rebels that they had helped to defeat the Ta'Akar Empire. Nathan had dined with him on his last night on the Takaran system just three days ago.

"Wow, that's one hell of a hologram," Nathan said, taking a few steps forward and passing his hand through Tug's image as it stood before him adorned in the trappings of his new title as the leader of the Takaran system.

"Why do people always do that?" Cameron asked, rolling her eyes.

"What?"

"Pass their hand through the image like they were seeing a magic trick for the first time."

"I don't know," Nathan said as he withdrew his hand.

"It's not like you've never seen a..."

"*Captain Scott,*" Tug's image interrupted.

Cameron stared at Tug's talking image, feeling somewhat spooked by the realism of the hologram. "It's so real, it's creepy," she whispered.

Nathan gestured for her to be silent as Tug's image continued to speak.

"*I regret that I could not do more to help you prepare for whatever challenges you may yet have to face on your voyage home. Indeed, you and your crew have sacrificed much to help the people of the Pentaurus cluster. No one, not even I, would have seen fault in you had you chosen to abandon us and returned posthaste to help your own world defend against its foes. Had I been able, I would gladly have sent a fleet of warships with you to defend the world of our ancestors, the birthplace of humanity. But alas, it was not within my power, as what few ships we have left are needed to defend and help rebuild the very worlds that they once crushed at the behest of their previous leader.*"

Tug's image turned away from them and began to stroll casually down the center aisle of the container as it continued to speak. "*Soon you will be jumping your way across the vast expanse of unexplored space that separates our two sectors. None of us knows what you will find along the way. You may find nothing, or you may find dangers that make those we recently faced together seem like a squabble amongst children.*" Tug's image turned back around to face them once more. "*Hopefully, it will be the former. Nevertheless, I felt compelled to provide you with something... something to help protect you along the way. This was a difficult task, as the Aurora is probably now the most formidable ship in the entire sector, quite possibly the galaxy.*

There was nothing I could provide you that might equal the Aurora." Tug turned and started to stroll away from them again. "*So I chose to provide you with something else, something you did not have, either aboard the Aurora or on Earth. A weapon so powerful that its name strikes fear in the hearts of even the most seasoned warriors.*" Tug stopped and turned to face them once more. "*Captain Scott, my trusted and loyal friend and ally, to protect you and your crew should your situation become dire, I present you with...*" Tug raised his hands to shoulder height, his arms outstretched. "*...the Ghatazhak!*"

On cue, the gray swirling fog within the cylinders began to drain into the floor of each chamber, revealing their contents. Each cylinder contained a finely chiseled specimen of a man with broad shoulders and massive arms. Nathan and Cameron watched as the fog sank into the floor of each cylinder, slowly revealing each Ghatazhak warrior from the head down.

"Uh, is he going to suck all the fog out of those tubes?" Cameron asked, her face slightly reddening. "Because I'm pretty sure they're completely naked in there."

"They must be in some kind of stasis," Nathan commented.

"*Within these tubes are one hundred of the Ta'Akar Empire's mighty Ghatazhak warriors. As we all know from their attack on the staging point during the battle of Answari, only the fires of hell itself can stop the Ghatazhak from following the orders of the one they are programmed to obey. These one hundred warriors, Captain Scott, have been programmed to obey and protect you, as well as anyone you order them to protect. They have no fear, and they have no conscience. They are, quite literally, human killing machines. They have no hopes. They have no dreams. Their only wish is to serve and to die an honorable death in the service of their leader, which is now you, Captain Scott.*"

"You're right," Nathan whispered, "this is creepy."

Tug's image continued. "*It seems a gruesome and savage thing, these men who are bred only for combat, men without souls or self-determination.*" Tug hung his head down low for a moment. "*The Ghatazhak are an abhorrent thing to behold. The question of what to do with such creatures has not been an easy one. Our scientists are working on ways to deprogram these ruthless men; however, until we are certain that this can be done with one hundred percent certainty, we must keep them in stasis to protect not only the people, but the Ghatazhak themselves. There are more than one thousand of them in stasis on Takara under the absolute highest security. However, considering the unknowns that may lie ahead of you, keeping a platoon of such close at hand seems a logical step, should their need ever arise. Trust me, Captain. As absurd as it may sound, if such a need does arise, you will be thankful that these men are available to you.*"

Tug's image paused, straightening his attire before continuing. "*When you require the services of the Ghatazhak, place your hand on the command console here,*" Tug explained, his hologram pointing toward a control panel on one of the support pillars in between two cylinders. "*It will take one of your hours for them to be fully revived, at which point they will undoubtedly need to be fed...*" Tug smiled. "*A lot. Twenty-four hours later, they will be ready for action. Their combat armor and weapons are stored in the lockers above each cylinder and are keyed to each of the occupants. Additional supplies and ammunition are stored in lockers accessible at the rear of this container.*"

Tug's image took several steps toward Nathan and Cameron. "*Nathan, we can never fully repay you for all that you have done for us. Please accept this gift in the spirit in which it was intended. I only wish to see that you survive to achieve your goals, whatever they may be.*" Tug's image stood motionless as the hologram began to fade out. "*Good luck to you, my friend.*"

Nathan and Cameron stood in silence. He looked about at the two levels of tubes full of the deadliest men in the galaxy. He tried to imagine a scenario in which he might be forced to utilize such men. One word came to his lips. "Damn."

CHAPTER TWO

Loki turned his head slowly from side to side, checking to see if anyone was standing nearby. As he'd hoped, everyone on the bridge was busy attending to their respective duties as the Aurora prepared for departure. Satisfied that no one was paying him undue attention, he leaned to his right and spoke in a hushed tone. "Are you nervous?"

"What?" Josh replied with more volume than Loki would have liked.

Loki looked about again. "Are you nervous?"

"What is there to be nervous about? It's not like we haven't flown this ship before."

"But we're about to fly it to the other side of the galaxy."

"It's only a thousand light years, Loki," Josh reminded his friend, "and it'll take us less time to get there than it originally took you to get to Haven."

"Maybe, but still, we're leaving everything and everyone we know behind."

"Good riddance, I say."

"Easy enough for you; Marcus is coming, too. But I may never see my family again. And they don't even know I'm leaving."

"You sent them word, didn't you?"

"Yeah, through Tug, or Prince Casimir, or whatever we're supposed to call him these days.

The captain assured me that Tug would get word to them." Loki scanned his displays once more, sighing at the thought of never seeing his parents and his sister again. "I just wish I could have told them myself, I guess."

"Don't sweat it," Josh told him. "Considering the state of the cluster right now, you may be back before they even get the message."

"That's not helping."

"You know what your problem is, Loki? You think too much."

"I think too much? How does one think too much?"

"You're always thinking about all the little, related things. You need to be more like me."

"You mean charging through life at a million kilometers per second without any forethought?"

Josh grinned. "It is less complicated."

"No thanks. I'd rather think too much."

"Suit yourself," Josh said, "but all that thinking can get in the way. Trust me."

"How would you even know?" Loki wondered.

"I used to be just like you when I first started flying. Believe it or not, it was Marcus who set me straight. He taught me to use my instincts instead of trying to analyze the life out of everything."

"Is that what you think I do?"

"Pretty much."

"Well, one of us has to," Loki said, "or else you'd surely get us killed."

"Why do you think I fly with you?" Josh added with a wink.

* * *

"I see we're not taking a direct route out of the Pentaurus cluster," Nathan commented as he examined the departure course displayed on the wall-mounted display above the couch in his ready room.

"There are still quite a few inhabited systems between Darvano and the edge of the sector," Cameron said. "I thought it best to avoid contact with anyone else on our way out."

"Not a bad idea, Commander. How many jumps will that add?"

"Only four, sir."

"We're still sticking to jumps of ten light years?"

"For now," Cameron said. "Abby still isn't ready to try increasing our range. She expects she'll be ready by the time we clear the Pentaurus sector. However, the good news is that the upgrades installed by the Takarans have cut our recharge time in half. So the four extra jumps will only cost us twenty hours instead of forty."

"I've got no problem giving up a day to avoid extra complications," Nathan said. "I've had enough of those to last me a lifetime."

"Yes, sir."

"Then we're all set to depart?"

"We're still waiting on engineering. Lieutenant Commander Kamenetskiy wanted to make one last check of the backup fusion reactors that the Takarans installed."

"He still doesn't trust them, does he?"

"The Takarans?"

"No, their fusion reactors," Nathan said.

"I think he just doesn't completely understand them yet; that's all. Until he does, I don't think he *can* trust them."

"According to Vlad, the Takarans' knowledge of controlled fusion is centuries ahead of us. They've been using fusion reactors to power everything from homes to cars to ships," Nathan said. "Did you know they don't even have a power grid on Takara? Every building has its own little reactor to provide electrical power. They're self-contained, little units that require no service whatsoever. They just light them up, and they run for like a decade or something. Then they just swap them out and refurbish them for reuse. Can you imagine?"

"It does sound less complicated. I'm just not sure it's safe."

"That's because we're not used to such technologies."

"We'll have to make sure Mister Montgomery and his people share that knowledge with Fleet once we get home," Cameron stated.

"Yes, of course. Thank you, Commander."

Nathan returned his attention to the display on his desk. After a moment, he realized that Commander Taylor was still standing there. "Was there something else?"

"I was wondering what you're planning to do with Tug's little present."

"Nothing for now," Nathan said.

"Nothing?"

He shrugged. "What did you expect me to do with it? Send it back?"

"You're actually going to take a platoon of men programmed to kill everything in their path back to Earth with us?" she wondered. "Pardon me, sir, but do you think that's wise?"

"To be honest, I really don't know," Nathan admitted. "But I think Tug was right about one thing. If we ever find ourselves in a situation where we truly need them, we're going to be glad we have them."

"Nathan, they're a deadly weapon, one that we're not even sure we can control."

"And nukes on point-and-shoot torpedoes aren't?"

"That's not the same thing, and you know it."

"Look, Cam, I've been doing some reading on the Ghatazhak. They're not as much robots as people like to imagine. In fact, I'm beginning to suspect that much of that is myth, maybe even propaganda used by the Ta'Akar to instill fear in their subjects. Those are men, just like us..."

"You mean like you."

"You know what I mean. They're highly trained, fanatically dedicated to their code of honor, which is leader, code, brother, in that order. They're more akin to holy warriors than special forces, at least in their dedication. In their training, they make special forces look like recruits straight out of boot camp."

"So you expect to find trouble on the way home?" she asked.

"No, I don't. But after all we've been through, I'm not about to take any chances either."

"We do have our own platoon of Corinari on board, you know."

"Yes, I do. Speaking of which, it would be better if Major Waddell did *not* know about the Ghatazhak. In fact, I would prefer that it remain our little secret."

Cameron sighed, which was rare.

"Look, Cam, I hope to God we never have to wake those guys up. But they'd be in stasis either way, so why not park a few of them with us?" Nathan leaned back in his chair. "Hell, I wish he would've given us a whole company of them."

"*Captain, Comms,*" Naralena's voice called over the intercom on the work terminal on his desk.

"Go ahead."

"*Sir, Cheng reports the engineering department is ready for departure.*"

"Very well." Nathan clicked off his intercom. "I guess we're ready." He rose from his seat. "I assume the matter is closed?"

"Yes, sir," Cameron agreed, "for now."

"I'll take what I can get, Commander." Nathan noticed the look on her face, but he knew she technically had no say in the matter. He also knew that Cameron would continue to pester him about the Ghatazhak hiding in their cargo hold. That was fine with him, as she always kept him on his toes and thinking, which was a good thing. "Shall we?"

"After you, sir," she said, respecting his rank, as always.

Nathan strolled out of his ready room and onto the bridge of the Aurora, nodding at the guard as he passed with Commander Taylor following behind him.

"Captain on the bridge!" the guard announced.

The bridge had a completely different feel now that it was fully repaired. Gone were the burnt-out consoles and blackened conduits. The entire comm-center located along the aft end of the bridge between either exit had finally been completely replaced during their layover at the Takaran shipyards. Now there were two comm stations in use, making internal communications far easier to manage during combat.

All six of the stations that lined either side of the bridge had also undergone extensive refit. Their computer systems had been upgraded, as well as their software. In fact, there were only three things that weren't completely replaced during their time at the shipyards: the helm and navigation console located at the front of the bridge, the command chair in the center, and the tactical station directly behind it. Although they had received some enhancements, they were relatively unchanged.

Not only had everything been repaired, replaced or upgraded, but it had all been cleaned. For that matter, the entire ship sparkled from top to bottom, inside and out. They had even been given a few of the automated cleaning bots used by Takaran warships.

To Nathan, the Aurora felt like a whole new ship. It was still the same design and the same layout, but it felt new, like she had never seen combat. Still, he would have done anything for working shields similar to those used by the Takaran warships. He hoped that Abby and the Takaran scientists that had agreed to travel with them back to Earth would figure out how to make the ZPEDs work without interfering with the jump drive.

"Comms, notify the Corinairans that we are breaking orbit and heading home."

"Yes, sir," Naralena said.

"Well, that sure felt good to say," Nathan said to Cameron. "Helm, take us up to departure altitude, and break orbit as soon as we're on a general heading for the Sol sector."

"Aye, Captain," Josh answered. "Increasing power, climbing to departure altitude."

"Departure point in six minutes, sir," Loki announced after making some quick calculations on the new navigational computer installed by the Takarans.

"Very well. Once we break orbit, bring us on course and speed for the first jump."

"Aye, sir," Josh responded.

"Naralena, you'd better send a courtesy call to Karuzara to let them know we're departing as well."

"Captain," Commander Taylor interrupted, "the Karuzari disbanded more than a week ago."

"What did they do with their base?"

"They gave it back to the Corinairans. Now that FTL travel is no longer reserved for Takaran ships, the asteroid base is being hollowed out further and made into a spaceport."

"That's a good idea," Nathan said. "That will certainly help get them ready for interstellar travel more quickly. What about the Yamaro base?"

"They are expanding that one as well, increasing the interior space so that they can begin fitting interplanetary ships with jump drives once they start production."

"I have a feeling this entire sector is going to see a major change over the next decade."

"Indeed."

"Sir," Naralena said, "I have the Prime Minister of Corinair on comms. He wishes to speak with you."

"Put him on the main view screen," Nathan ordered.

A separate window appeared in the center of the main view screen that wrapped around the forward half of the bridge. In the middle was the Prime Minister.

"*Captain Scott,*" the minister began in a heavily accented brogue, "*on behalf of the peoples of the Darvano system, as well as all peoples in the Pentaurus cluster, I wish again to thank you and your most brave crew for all that you have done.*"

Nathan smiled at the minister's attempt to speak Angla, knowing that he must have practiced that poorly worded phrase repeatedly in order to personally communicate his sincere thanks. "Thank you, Prime Minister. I wasn't aware that you were learning Angla."

"*I am to trying most hard.*"

"You are doing quite well, sir."

"*Perhaps, when someday you are to return to Corinair, we will to have long conversations in your language.*"

"I look forward to it, sir."

"*Pleasant journey to you, Na-Tan. To all of you.*"

"Thank you, sir. Good luck with your rebuilding. The future of Corinair looks quite exciting."

"*Yes, yes. Goodbye, Captain.*"

"Goodbye, sir." Nathan turned and nodded at Naralena, who ended the communication.

"Breaking orbit in one minute," Loki reported.

"Ship-wide," Nathan said, gesturing at Naralena once more.

"Ship-wide, aye."

"Attention all hands. This is your captain. In less than a minute, we will break orbit and begin our journey back to the Sol sector. It will take us several weeks, perhaps even months, to reach our final destination. During this time, I am confident that each and every one of you will perform your jobs to the best of your ability. Most of you are volunteers on this mission, and for that I am deeply grateful. We know not what we will find when we reach Earth, but I promise that I will do everything within my power to get you all back to your homes once again."

"Coming up on departure point, Captain," Loki said softly.

"That is all." Nathan waited a moment for Naralena to kill the ship-wide broadcast, then took a deep breath and let it out. "Take us out, Mister Hayes."

"Aye, Captain. Breaking orbit." Josh increased power to the main engines once again, quickly accelerating the ship and causing her to break out of her high orbit above the planet Corinair. "Coming onto heading for the first jump," Josh reported. "Transferring helm to auto-nav."

Nathan felt a bit nervous, as it was the first time that the new jump navigation control system was going to take control of the helm and jump execution systems for a jump of maximum range. He turned to Abby, who sat at the starboard auxiliary console at the aft end of the bridge as she monitored the first long-range jump executed by the automated jump system. "The first jump is going to be nine light years, right, Doctor?"

"Yes, Captain. In fact, we won't begin experimenting with increased ranges until after we are clear of the Pentaurus sector."

"Any particular reason you want to clear the sector first?" Nathan asked, suspicious.

"No, sir. That's simply how many jumps it will take us to gather enough data to feel comfortable increasing our range."

"Very well."

"Auto-nav has control," Josh announced.

"Course and speed are in the green," Loki reported. "Auto-nav is making final adjustments. Jump point in ten seconds. Waiting for your word, sir."

"Jump the ship, Mister Sheehan."

"Jumping in three......two......one......jumping."

The bridge of the Aurora quickly filled with the blue-white flash of the jump fields despite the view screen's attempt to filter out the intensity of the light generated by the system's jump field emitters. An instant later, the flash disappeared, and the screen reverted back to normal.

"Jump complete," Loki reported.

"Position?" Nathan asked. As usual, he couldn't really tell any difference in the positions of the stars. Tug had been able to notice even the tiniest shifts in the positions of the stars after a max-range jump, but he had spent years piloting his FTL-equipped interceptor through deep space. Despite his current position, Nathan was still a neophyte in comparison.

"One moment, sir," Lieutenant Yosef reported as she verified the sensor operator's findings. She was one of the original crew from Earth and had come aboard as an ensign assigned as the Aurora's science officer. Past events had thrust her into the position of sensor operator, a role in which she had excelled. Now that there were nearly a dozen Takaran scientists on board, all of whom possessed considerably more scientific knowledge than she, Commander Taylor had offered Yosef the position of lead sensor operator. Since it had come with a promotion as well, Kaylah Yosef had accepted the new assignment, but only on the condition that she would be allowed to expand her scientific expertise under the tutelage of the Takarans during the journey back to Earth.

"Right on target, sir," Lieutenant Yosef reported, grinning widely as she turned toward Nathan. "You would not believe how close we came to the jump point."

"Try me, Lieutenant."

"Seven hundred thirty-eight meters, sir."

"You're kidding."

"No, sir."

"You're telling me that, after a nine light year jump, we came out only seven hundred meters off our target?"

"Seven hundred thirty-eight." She smiled.

Nathan turned back to Abby. "Nicely done, Doctor."

"Thank you, sir, but I wouldn't be too happy, not yet. It may not seem like a lot, but that is nearly a kilometer off target. If the error grows with distance, and if we had been jumping twenty-five light years, the error might have been considerably worse. We will have to become far more precise if we intend to significantly increase our jump range."

"How long until our next jump?" Nathan asked.

"Just over nine hours to recharge the energy banks."

"Very well. Helm, put us on course and speed for the next jump, and steady as she goes."

* * *

Major Prechitt slowed his stride slightly as he exited the service line in the mess hall. He scanned the room looking for a place to sit. Unlike the Takaran warships on which he had served as a young man, the Aurora did not have separate dining facilities for officers and enlisted personnel. The major liked the mixed arrangement, although there was naturally still some degree of separation within the mess hall itself.

After a moment, he spotted one of the Takaran scientists sitting in a corner alone. Understandably so, the dozen scientists and technical specialists on loan from Takara had found themselves more segregated than most. For the most part, they dined together in groups of four or more and usually at the very same table where the lone Takaran currently sat. The major wondered what it must be like for the Takarans, serving aboard a ship full of people who, until recently, had been subjugated by their former empire.

Of course, the Takarans currently aboard the ship were not of noble houses. They were commoners—well educated and well trained commoners, to be sure, and probably of at least moderate socioeconomic status on their worlds, all of them except their leader, Lieutenant Montgomery, the lone diner.

Major Prechitt found himself standing at the lone Takaran man's table, looking down at him. He could feel the eyes of the other Corinairans in the mess hall, all watching him to see what he would do. "Lieutenant Montgomery, isn't it?"

The lieutenant looked up from the data pad that he had been studying while dining, a look of surprise on his face. "Uh, yes," he mumbled. He instantly noticed the rank insignia on the major's uniform. "Yes, sir," he said more clearly, standing in respect.

"As you were, Lieutenant," Major Prechitt told him. "May I join you?"

"Uh, yes, of course, sir." The lieutenant looked even more confused. "Why?" he added in a more hushed tone.

"I figured I'd set an example for the rest of the men," Major Prechitt said, "give them something to think about."

"I appreciate the thought, sir, but it is not necessary. I understand how they feel about us, and

I do not blame them. I would feel similar were our roles reversed."

"That is exactly why it *is* necessary, Lieutenant," the major said as he sat. "It will take some time for the animosity between our worlds to subside. Better that the process is started sooner rather than later. We Corinairans must realize that it was the regime that was our enemy, not its people. That regime no longer exists."

"An enlightened attitude, to be sure," the lieutenant stated. "However, I served that regime willingly."

"Did you kill any of my countrymen?" Major Prechitt asked plainly.

"No, sir. I am a scientist, not a combatant. My rank is only for the purpose of leading others." The lieutenant looked at Major Prechitt with as honest an expression as he could muster. "However, had I been ordered to do so, I would have complied."

"Because you wanted to kill Corinairans, or because you were afraid of the consequences should you refuse that order?"

"Because it was my duty, sir. Those that kill out of desire are not honorable men; they are savages."

Major Prechitt looked at the lieutenant, studying him for a moment. "You don't sound like any of the nobles I met during my forced service to the empire."

"Not all of us believed in the babble that spewed forth from the mouth of our former emperor."

"Then what is it that the nobles are loyal to?" Major Prechitt asked. "Other than wealth and power, that is."

"I am not about to defend the nobles whose interests were focused on such concerns. I can only speak for the loyalties of myself and my house, which were to our society. Upholding it was the duty of every nobleman."

"One might call that a flawed system," Major Prechitt said. "However, I appreciate your honesty, Lieutenant, and I respect your sense of duty and honor as well." The major took a bite of his salad. "I suspect we have more in common than you might think."

"I might add, Major, that I am quite happy that the leader I currently serve is unlikely to ever give such an order."

Major Prechitt looked at the lieutenant, who was smiling. "As am I, Lieutenant. As am I."

* * *

"We have completed the analysis of jump eight," a Takaran scientist reported as he handed the data pad to Doctor Sorenson.

Abby looked at the information displayed on the data pad, mentally sifting through the numbers as her trained eye searched for the relevant data. The Takarans were technologically more advanced than the people from Earth, but at times, their methodology for presenting data left something to be desired. "This is very promising," she noted as she continued to study the information.

"It appears that the new emitters and energy banks are more efficient than originally expected," the young man reported with obvious pride. "I'm sure it is safe to begin practical test jumps of at least fifteen light years."

"Perhaps." Abby looked at the young man. "I apologize. I am very bad with names."

"Rinne," the man responded eagerly, "Pyotor

Rinne, and I am not at all insulted, Doctor. In fact, I am honored to be working with you."

"Thank you, Mister Rinne."

"What you have created is beyond description," the man began, stumbling with his words as he elaborated. "The possible applications for instantaneous interstellar transportation are staggering to say the least..."

"Thank you again, Mister Rinne, but I am not its creator. It was my father's vision, not mine, that brought the jump drive into existence. I was merely a facilitator."

"I did not mean to detract from your father's accomplishments, good doctor. He was a brilliant man. But do not discount your own contributions. I have read all of the project reports and journals. He may have had vision, but I believe that it was your guiding hand that led to his eventual success, as did your father."

"Pardon me?"

The young Takaran scientist noticed the Terran physicist's reaction. "I am sorry. I just assumed that it was permissible to read all of the documentation, including your father's journals." The young man was becoming more defensive as he continued. "There were no locks on his files, so I just assumed..."

"It's quite all right, Mister Rinne," Abby assured him, sensing his discomfort.

After an uncomfortable pause, the young man continued. "You have not read them?"

"No, I have not," Abby admitted as she studied the data pad.

"If I am not being too personal, might I inquire why?"

"I guess I've just been too busy since we left Earth."

Abby stopped, lowering the data pad. "Actually, now that I think about it, I've been too busy for much of anything for going on ten years now."

Mister Rinne noticed a look of sadness cast upon her face. "Do you have family back on Earth?"

"Yes, a husband and child," she said, "both of whom I fear I have not given enough attention."

"I am sure they understand," Mister Rinne assured her in his most comforting tone. "At least, they will once they realize what you and your father were working on."

Surprisingly, his comments made her feel better. "I hope you are correct, Mister Rinne," she said as she handed him his data pad, "about my family and your analysis. I will speak to the captain about increasing our jump range."

* * *

"Jump nine complete," Loki reported.

"Position verified," Lieutenant Yosef confirmed.

"Very well," Commander Taylor said from the command chair. "Begin full sensor sweeps of the area and start long-range scans of our next jump target. Time to full charge?"

"Nine hours twenty-three minutes," Loki said.

"Very well. Set course for the next jump point and maintain current speed, Mister Hayes," Commander Taylor ordered as she turned her chair slightly left and noticed Doctor Sorenson entering the captain's ready room at the aft end of the bridge.

"Setting course for jump point ten. Maintaining current speed, aye," Josh answered in a monotone voice.

"Getting bored, Mister Hayes?" Commander

Taylor asked as she turned her chair forward.

"Pretty much."

"Sorry that there's no one shooting at us," Cameron said.

"I'm not," Loki added.

"Sir?" Naralena interrupted. "The captain needs you in his ready room."

"Very well," Cameron answered as she rose. "Lieutenant Yosef, you have the bridge."

"Aye, sir."

Josh waited until the commander had left the bridge. "I don't know how much more of this I can take."

"How much more of what?" Loki asked.

"Jump, recharge, jump, recharge, jump, recharge... it's worse than flying recon," Josh complained.

"You really are an adrenaline junkie, aren't you?"

"I just want to do some flying; that's all."

"Isn't that what you're doing now, Mister Hayes?" Lieutenant Yosef stated as she took the command chair behind them.

"That's not what I'd call it. I'm just pushing buttons here. Hell, other than the simulators, I haven't had my hand on a flight control stick in weeks."

"Well, with all the time you've been spending in the simulators, I'd expect you to be rated for every ship the Aurora carries and then some," the lieutenant said.

Her tone carried more meaning than did her words; of that Josh was sure. He had been spending most of his spare time in the simulators, a fact that she had complained about on more than one occasion. Between her new responsibilities as a lieutenant and as head of her department and Josh spending all his off-duty time in the simulators, they had little time together.

"Yeah, maybe it's time to seek other forms of entertainment," Josh added with a sly smile. "Hey, I hear they've got a huge collection of old Earth vid-flicks in the database." He could feel the lieutenant glaring at him.

* * *

"You asked to see me, sir?" Commander Taylor stated as she entered the ready room. She was not surprised to see Doctor Sorenson sitting at the captain's desk, as she had noticed her entering earlier. "Doctor."

"Commander."

"Yes, have a seat," Captain Scott instructed. "Doctor Sorenson feels it is safe to dial our max jump range up to fifteen light years."

"That's good news," the commander stated as she took her seat. "Will it increase our recharge time?"

"Apparently not."

"How is that possible? I thought it was one hour per light year jumped."

"The Takarans replaced many of the jump drive's components during our repairs," Doctor Sorenson explained, "most notably, the emitters and the energy banks. The Takaran energy banks are capable of taking a charge at a much faster rate than our original energy banks—at least fifty percent faster."

"Then why are we still taking nine hours to recharge after each nine light year jump?" Commander Taylor wondered. "Shouldn't it be taking more like four and a half hours?"

"Because we lack the energy production capacity."

"We have four antimatter reactors," Cameron said.

"Each of which is designed to deliver a smooth, even flow of power. In order to charge the energy banks at a faster rate, much larger amounts of power are required. They are not designed to deliver large pulses of energy. The safety protocols won't allow it."

"And for good reason," Cameron said.

"Of course, Commander," Nathan said. "No one is suggesting that we attempt to do otherwise. However, Abbey has some ideas." Nathan turned to Doctor Sorenson.

"The Takarans have proposed a way to use the mini-ZPEDs to directly power the jump drive. This may or may not increase our range per jump. However, it would allow us to execute repeated maximum range jumps without recharging. Although at the time of our departure they had not yet attempted jumps of greater distances, theoretically, they should be able to reach a single jump range of at least fifty light years."

Nathan looked intrigued. "Imagine how quickly we could get home if we didn't have to recharge between every jump."

"A pair of mini-ZPEDs running as low as ten percent maximum output would provide enough energy for a twenty light year jump in a single pulse," Doctor Sorenson explained. "Energy banks would not be needed."

"Seriously? No recharge time?"

"Even if we were taking an hour to scan ahead as we calculate each jump, we'd still be home in less than a week instead of three."

"And that would be at twenty light years per jump. We do not yet know how high we could run the mini-ZPEDs without interfering with our own systems. It is entirely possible that we may be able to jump even farther."

Cameron could see that Nathan wanted this. She also knew that, when Nathan wanted something this badly, he had a tendency to take unnecessary risks. It was a bad habit that had been facilitated by his wealthy, well-connected parents during his adolescence. He had gotten better since leaving Earth, but that jump-first attitude was still in him. Cameron, on the other hand, was exactly the opposite, always analyzing the consequences and alternatives. It was why the Aurora's original captain had chosen her and Nathan as his flight team. "I thought the ZPEDs caused problems with the jump drive's operation."

"When used at higher outputs, yes," Doctor Sorenson admitted.

"Can our emitters even tolerate the higher energy?"

"No, they cannot. The emitters would have to be replaced."

"Can we even do that?" Cameron wondered.

"We have a redundant emitter network, thanks to the Takarans," Nathan reminded Cameron. "We could replace those emitters without touching the primaries."

"How long would that take?"

"We replaced thirty-some-odd emitters over Corinair in less than a day," Nathan said.

"Yes, and two men died doing so."

"That was because of the radiation levels in the Darvano system."

"I haven't run the numbers, as I am not really qualified to make such judgments," Abby said.

"I'll talk to Vladimir about it," Nathan said, "but I think it's worth considering, don't you, Commander?" Nathan looked at his executive officer.

"Considering? Yes. But perhaps it would be better to start with the basics and work our way up to fifty light year jumps," Cameron urged.

"Of course," Abby agreed. "Ideally, I would like to begin increasing our jump range by one light year per jump over the next five jumps. If there are not any problems, we can reassess the idea at that time."

"Sounds reasonable enough to me," Nathan said.

Cameron sat, holding her tongue. She did not care for the idea of using the Aurora, their only means of getting back to Earth, as a test ship. "That still doesn't shorten our recharge time. How were you planning on shortening that?"

"By using the mini-ZPEDs to assist in the recharge process and then powering them back down before the actual jump."

"I see." Cameron looked at Nathan, who appeared to be waiting for her approval. "What?"

"I'd like to know you're on board with this, Commander," Nathan stated.

"The idea of getting home in three days is, of course, appealing," Cameron admitted, "assuming that it all works as hoped. I'm just not comfortable taking risks with our only ship."

"Neither am I, Commander," Abby agreed. "But every jump we have made since we left Earth has been a risk. The fact that the jump drive has performed as reliably as it has is nothing short of miraculous. It was never intended to be used so extensively. After all, it was a prototype."

"That's a very good point," Nathan said.

"Yes, it is," Cameron agreed.

"Very well, Doctor," Nathan stated. "You may begin increasing the range by one light year per jump over the next five jumps. In the meantime, I'll discuss our idea for the hybrid drive with our chief engineer. Thank you."

"Thank you, Captain." Abby stood. "Commander."

Cameron waited for Doctor Sorenson to leave the ready room before speaking further. "Promise me you won't let yourself get carried away with this hybrid idea, Nathan."

Nathan was a bit surprised by her sudden, informal tone, but he had told her on more than one occasion to drop the formalities when they were alone. "Me, get carried away?"

* * *

Marcus scratched his head as he stared at the open end of a Corinairan troop shuttle. "It's not a mechanics problem, Major," Marcus argued. "It's a power problem. These here shuttles just don't generate enough power to give'm both shields and guns. They're only carryin' the standard fusion generators. Hell, the one in my hauler back on Haven was more powerful."

"If we're going to turn these into combat landers that can fly into a hot LZ, we're going to need both shields and guns," Major Waddell insisted, speaking loud enough to be heard over the noise of the Aurora's main hangar bay.

"I ain't arguing that point, but you're gonna have to choose one or the other."

"I need both," the major insisted. "Can we just use one at a time? Ride down with shields, then switch them off on final approach so we can start using guns to calm down the LZ just before touchdown?"

"Maybe, but if something goes wrong and you try to use both, you might cause an automatic shutdown of the reactors and fall from the sky. Not a pleasant thought. Besides, them reactors are so pitiful I ain't even sure they'll be able to handle any extra load beyond that of flyin' the shuttle."

"Excuse me," Lieutenant Montgomery interrupted from behind. "Perhaps I can be of assistance."

"Really?" Marcus asked. Like most of the crew, he wasn't comfortable with the idea of having Takarans on board, even if they were ones that Tug trusted.

"If I'm not mistaken, the fusion reactors in this model are very outdated by Takaran standards. It would be no trouble at all to fabricate upgraded reactors that would more than handle your power needs."

"Is that so?" Major Waddell asked. "Thanks, but we'll handle this on our own, Takaran."

Lieutenant Montgomery looked confused for a moment.

"I don't know, Major," Marcus mumbled. "Maybe we'd better take him up on his offer..."

"Dismissed, Lieutenant," Major Waddell said sternly to Lieutenant Montgomery, cutting Marcus off.

"Is there a problem, here?" Major Prechitt interrupted.

"No problem at all, Major," Waddell said. "I was just telling the lieutenant that he was dismissed."

"I think I'd like to hear more about the lieutenant's idea, Major. How about you, Senior Chief?"

Marcus's eyes darted nervously back and forth between the two majors. "Uh, I could go either way... sirs."

"No disrespect intended, Major, but this isn't really any of your..."

"Actually, since I am the CAG, and this is one of my ships, it is my business," Major Prechitt insisted. He turned to the lieutenant. "Lieutenant Montgomery, submit your proposal to the senior chief for review."

"Yes, sir," Lieutenant Montgomery answered.

"Senior Chief, once you have reviewed the lieutenant's proposal, comment on it and send it to my office for approval."

"Aye, sir."

"Major? Any questions?"

"No, sir," Major Waddell answered, his eyes locked on the lieutenant and full of rage.

Waddell's angry gaze did not go unnoticed by Major Prechitt. "Dismissed, Major," he stated with absolute authority.

Major Waddell said nothing further, turned, and walked briskly across the hangar deck away from them.

"Senior Chief, Lieutenant," Major Prechitt said calmly as he departed their company.

There was a moment of silence as neither the senior chief nor the lieutenant knew exactly what to say. Finally, the lieutenant broke the uncomfortable quiet. "I apologize, Senior Chief. I was only trying to help."

"Yeah, I know," Marcus said.

"If I had known that the major would react so..."

"Look," Marcus interrupted, "just because I ain't givin' you the evil eye don't mean that I like you any more than Waddell or any other Corinairan aboard this ship. Truth be told, I'd be happier if none of you were here. But you are, and there ain't shit I can do about that. So just go on about your business, and I'll go on about mine. You can send me your proposal for the reactor upgrades through the network." Marcus turned abruptly and walked away, leaving the lieutenant standing alone in the busy hangar bay.

* * *

"Thank you all for coming," Nathan stated as he entered the command briefing room and took his seat. They had been underway for nearly five days now, and for a change, things had settled into a comfortable routine on board the Aurora. By now, his senior staff knew better than to come to attention when their captain entered, having been told by him time and again that he considered such formalities a waste of time in the briefing room. He wanted more informal discussions to take place in this room so his staff would feel more comfortable expressing their opinions openly. He had learned how to turn up the formality as needed, and his staff had learned how to read such cues as well.

"Why don't you start us off, Doctor, since this meeting is primarily about the jump drive."

"As you know, sir, we began increasing our range by one light year per jump back with jump ten, carefully analyzing the data after each jump. We completed jump fifteen a few hours ago, and I'm happy to report that we have seen no problems with either the performance or the accuracy of the jumps, even during the last jump of fifteen light years."

"How are the mini-ZPEDs working out?" Nathan wondered.

"They are amazing devices," Vladimir exclaimed. "Thanks to Lieutenant Montgomery and his team, interfacing them with the jump drive's energy storage banks was not a problem."

"We have been running the ZPEDs at twenty-five percent of their maximum output in order to recharge the energy banks more quickly," Abby explained. "We estimate it will take just over seven hours to fully recharge after a fifteen light year jump."

"That's good news, Doctor," Nathan declared.

"Have there been any problems noted with the use of the ZPEDs?" Cameron wondered. "I mean, have they had any noticeable effect on the jump drive's performance?"

"None that we could detect," Abby stated. "However, we have been taking the ZPEDs completely offline prior to jumping, just to be safe."

"Any chance we can squeeze a few more light years out of the drive?" Nathan asked.

"Doubtful, Captain. We are going to try to overcharge the energy banks during this recharge cycle in the hopes that we will have at least enough power left for a short-range escape jump, maybe a light day or so. I do not believe that the energy banks can store any more power than that."

"Pity," Nathan mumbled, taking a deep breath.

"Something wrong, sir?" Cameron asked.

"I was secretly hoping for a bit more range; that's all."

"Perhaps now would be a good time to begin replacing the secondary jump field emitters," Vladimir suggested.

Nathan looked at Abby. "Doctor?"

"Before we commit to the idea, I would like to try running the ZPEDs at low levels during a standard jump being fed by the energy banks."

"How low?" Cameron wondered.

"Less than ten percent."

"How about less than one percent?" Nathan suggested. "And work your way up with each jump, as long as nothing goes wrong."

"It would take at least five percent output from a pair of mini-ZPEDs to power a ten light year jump without using the energy banks, Captain."

"I understand that, Doctor. However, I'm not convinced that it is safe to run them at all, at least not during a jump. Start with one percent and work your way up from there."

"As you wish, Captain."

"There's no reason we can't start manufacturing the new emitters while she is testing the effects of ZPEDs on the jump drive field generators," Vladimir stated.

"What if we don't end up using them?" Cameron asked.

"We will just make a handful for testing and validation. We won't start a full production run until we are sure that the hybrid drive project is approved."

"How long does it take to fabricate an emitter?" Nathan asked.

"About four hours using a single fabricator, and we have four of them," Vladimir explained.

"What about raw materials?"

"We have plenty of them in the hold, sir," Cameron told him. "In fact, we still have most of the ore from our time in the rings of Haven as well."

"Very well. Go ahead and start fabrication for

now. How many jumps will you need to collect enough data, Doctor?"

"Five jumps should suffice."

"What are you going to do with the additional power being generated by the ZPEDs?" Cameron asked.

"We will feed it into the ship's power grid," Vladimir explained. "It is not a problem."

"Will five jumps give you enough time to fully validate the new emitter design?" Nathan asked Vladimir.

"It should be plenty," Vladimir assured him.

"Very well, Doctor. You may begin the next phase of testing."

"Anything else we need to talk about?" Nathan looked around the room. "Very well, dismissed."

* * *

"Lieutenant Commander," Major Waddell greeted as he entered the security office.

Jessica turned away from her display to face Waddell from behind her desk. "Major Waddell."

"You asked to see me?"

"Yes, take a seat, Major." She waited as the major pulled up a chair and sat down on the opposite side of the desk from her. "Commander Taylor has asked me to deal with a particular problem."

"What problem might that be?"

"It seems that there is friction between some of the Corinairans and the Takaran specialists on board."

"That's to be expected, is it not? We were at war with them only a month ago."

"Perhaps, but not with any of these men. They

are all civilians."

"Not all of them," Major Waddell corrected.

"Lieutenant Montgomery's rank was administrative. He was never a combatant."

"He wears the uniform of the Ta'Akar..."

"Maybe you haven't noticed, Major," Jessica interrupted, "but the patch has changed. It's not the uniform of the Ta'Akar he wears; it's the Takaran Defense Force."

"Same military, different name."

"No, it's not. Not even close. Different agenda, different philosophy, different leaders..."

"Same colors, same arrogance, same..."

"Perhaps I'm not making myself clear, Major," Jessica stated, the tone of her voice becoming more formal. "You are to treat the Takarans no differently than you would treat any Corinairan, or Terran for that matter. Is that clear?"

"Forgive me, Lieutenant Commander. I haven't had the time to study up on the ranking system of the Terran military, or how it compares with that of the Corinari..."

"Then let me make it crystal clear for you, Major. I'm the head of security on this ship. Your unit is attached to my command. You are under my command. That makes me your commanding officer. It doesn't matter if I'm an ensign or an admiral; I'm still your boss. Is that clear enough for you?"

"Yes, sir," the major responded smartly.

"Now knock the stupid, childish shit off and act your rank, Major, or you'll be relieved of your command, and you'll spend the rest of the voyage confined to your quarters. Is *that* understood?"

"Yes, sir." There was no emotion in the major's response.

Jessica stared at the major for several seconds. She could see in his eyes that her threats made little difference.

"Will there be anything else, sir?"

"No, Major. You're dismissed."

Major Waddell rose from his chair, came to attention, and raised his hand in salute, a gesture meant to demonstrate his understanding of his commanding officer's authority over him.

Jessica returned the major's salute and watched him depart in proper Corinari fashion, pivoting perfectly on his heel and toe. She knew that, although his behavior would probably change, his hatred of the Takarans would remain. She only hoped it wouldn't be a problem.

* * *

"Analysis of jump twenty is complete," Commander Taylor said as she entered the captain's ready room.

"And?" the captain asked from behind his desk.

"Everything looks good. According to Doctor Sorenson, running the ZPEDs at up to five percent during jumps did not result in any abnormalities."

"No changes in accuracy noted?"

"No, sir," Cameron assured him. "Abby is confident that it is safe to begin installing the upgraded emitters. She would like to continue jumping fifteen light years at a time with the ZPEDs running at five percent while we upgrade the secondary emitter array."

"Did she say why?"

"The more data the better, as I understood it. I think she would just feel more comfortable if she saw consistently positive results before attempting a ZPED-powered jump."

"Can't argue with that, can we?"

"No, sir."

"I talked to Vlad at breakfast this morning. He finished validating the new emitters last night."

"Then I guess we're all set," Cameron stated.

Nathan could hear the lack of commitment in her voice. "Something tells me you're less than enthusiastic about the idea."

"I'm just not sure it's really worth the risk, Nathan."

"I don't think there's as much risk as you think," he argued. "Abby's not the type to take chances, especially now that we're finally on our way home."

"Perhaps, but we're already jumping fifteen light years at a time. That's a fifty percent increase in range. As we are now, we could be home in just over two weeks without the additional risk."

"It's not just about the time it takes to get home, Cam. It's much more than that."

"Like making sure the benefits of the alliance are enough to keep you out of prison?"

"Funny, Cam. Very funny. Think of it... jumping twenty or more light years at a time without recharging. You could cross the galaxy in a matter of weeks. You could strike the Jung home world—wherever that is—in a few jumps, return to Earth, reload, then jump back, and strike again. You could deliver as much ordnance on a target as an entire fleet using just one ship. I think that's well worth the risk of a few test jumps along the way."

"I'm not disagreeing with you, Nathan. I'm just saying I wish we didn't have to take the risk, at least not now."

"Then you don't mind if I give Vlad the green

light?"

"What are you asking me for? You're the captain."

"Yes, I am. But I depend on you to keep me from going off the deep end, remember?"

"Hey, I was in a coma when you started that whole Na-Tan thing."

"I'll let Vlad know," he told her with a smile.

"I'll start organizing work crews," she told him as she headed for the exit.

"Hey, you don't really think they're going to toss me in the brig, do you?"

"Probably not," she admitted, "not with all the cool tech the Takarans are contributing." She paused at the hatch for a moment, then turned back to face him. "Still, for once, I'm glad you're the captain and not me."

* * *

"What are we having?" Jessica asked as she entered the captain's mess.

"I have no idea," Nathan admitted. "I stopped asking a week ago. I can never remember how to pronounce the names anyway."

"I don't care as long as it's meat and lots of it," Vladimir declared. "I have not eaten since breakfast."

"*You* skipped lunch?" Cameron asked in disbelief. "*You?*"

"We are very busy installing and testing the new emitters," Vladimir defended. "I am definitely earning my pay this week."

"I was watching those spidery-looking things you're using," Nathan said. "What do you call them?"

"We call them 'crawlers,'" Lieutenant Montgomery stated.

"That makes sense," Nathan agreed.

"They are used by exterior work crews on all Takaran warships. They are very efficient."

"And a lot more comfortable than wearing a pressure suit," Vladimir added as he watched the captain's chef place dishes of food onto the table in front of him. "They are safer as well."

"Yes, they offer significantly better protection against cosmic radiation than even the best pressure suits," Lieutenant Montgomery agreed.

"I haven't seen them yet," Major Prechitt stated with curiosity. "What do they look like?"

"Well, like spiders," Nathan stated.

"Spiders?" Major Prechitt was unfamiliar with the word.

"They have an oval pod in the middle of an oval ring. The pod holds the worker who can reach out using arms to perform work on the exterior of the ship. They move around using these long, articulated legs like a spider." Vladimir placed his hand on the table, walking his fingers around to mimic a spider walking.

"Ah, 'prycopa,'" the major declared. "Interesting. I would like to see them."

"They are operating from the starboard cargo airlock," Vladimir explained. "Both of them are in use during the recharge cycle, but they come in to be recharged for about an hour during each jump."

"We use something similar in the orbital assembly facility over Earth," Nathan explained, "except ours sit on the end of a single, long, articulated arm that connects to a trolley on a track that runs the length of the assembly structure. Workers could spend an entire shift inside one of those things."

"How is the refit progressing?" Major Prechitt

wondered.

"Slightly behind schedule," Lieutenant Montgomery admitted. "After all, this would best be done in port. However, I am confident that we will finish in a few days."

"It would be faster if we had a few more crawlers," Vladimir admitted.

"Why don't you just fabricate more?" Jessica suggested as she loaded her plate.

"All the fabricators are busy making emitters," Vladimir told her as he began eating.

"Crawlers are rather complex machines," Lieutenant Montgomery explained. "Fabricating them would take considerable time and would tie up all four fabricators. Perhaps later, when there is room in the fabrication schedule."

"Sounds like we should fabricate some more fabricators," Nathan stated.

"Are any of these dishes meat-free?" Cameron asked.

"Yes, sir," the cook answered. "I prepared these two especially for you."

"Thank you."

"I guess there are vegetarians on Corinair as well," Nathan commented as he began eating.

"How can you not eat meat?" Jessica wondered.

"How can you eat it?" Cameron responded.

"Like this," Jessica stated, placing a chunk of meat in her mouth.

"Classy. It's my great-grandmother's fault, really. She grew up in northern Europe during the bovine plagues. So many died from tainted beef that people just stopped eating meat period. No beef, no fowl, no fish. Her parents organized a neighborhood farm where everyone helped cultivate their own food, so they could be sure it was safe."

"Seems a bit drastic," Major Prechitt commented.

"Perhaps to you and me," Cameron admitted. "However, there were people dying by the thousands then. It was nearly one hundred years ago, and the knowledge from the Data Ark had yet to reach everyone, especially the smaller villages."

"It seems so impossible," Lieutenant Montgomery admitted. "There has not been a case of tainted food products of any kind on Takara for centuries."

"A hundred years ago, our people were just reinventing propeller-driven aircraft," Nathan explained. "After the bio-digital plague nearly destroyed humanity, we had to relearn everything. We had to reinvent things that had been used for hundreds of years."

"I'm confused," Major Prechitt stated. "How did you get from airplanes to starships in only one hundred years?"

"The Data Ark," Nathan stated.

"What is a Data Ark?" Lieutenant Montgomery asked.

"Someone more than a millennia ago, before the great plague, decided to create a database to contain all the history, science, culture, and religion of humanity. When the bio-digital plague hit, the Ark was closed down to protect its contents. In the chaos of the following decades, the Ark was forgotten. It was discovered nearly nine hundred years later in a sealed facility in the Swiss Alps. Once the people of Earth figured out how to get it running again, we had access to all the information stored inside. Because of that information, we were able to jump ahead technologically more than three hundred years in only a century."

"Amazing," the lieutenant muttered. "What type of information did it contain?"

"Everything."

"A sudden influx of such scientific knowledge seems like it would be dangerous," Major Prechitt observed.

"Very true," Nathan agreed. "Luckily, the people that discovered the Ark realized this early on. An international commission was formed in order to prevent just such a mistake from being made. It was quickly realized that the application of the knowledge had to be carefully chosen and monitored to prevent another catastrophe like the bio-digital plague. In fact, many people objected to accessing any of the data, claiming we weren't ready."

"Seems a valid argument," the major said. "Odd that you chose to develop a space program over preventing tainted foods from reaching the population."

"It didn't go quite that way," Nathan chuckled. "Once we learned that humanity had once colonized other worlds, we were curious to learn if they, too, had recovered. When we discovered that an empire known as the Jung had risen up and conquered most of the core and fringe worlds, we became concerned and decided we needed to be able to protect our world. Hence, we needed to be in space."

"But to go from airplanes to starships in a single century," Lieutenant Montgomery stated in awe, "it seems impossible, even with fabricators."

"Funny you should mention fabricators," Nathan said. "We use a similar technology called 3D printing. It is nowhere near as advanced as your fabricators, but it was a lot better than the old methods of die-casting."

"But a space program requires a huge industrial base."

"We had plenty of industry," Nathan said. "It just wasn't high-tech at the time. Computers were the first thing to be produced using the information from the Data Ark, since it was a computer, after all. What resulted was an overnight renaissance of science, technology, and manufacturing. Within seventy years, we were building the Defender class ships in orbit."

"Defender class?" the lieutenant asked.

"Very big, very slow," Vladimir said.

"The Defender class ships are sub-light vessels used to patrol and defend our home system. We built four of them over the last twenty years. They may be slow, but they are heavily armed."

"Why didn't you construct faster-than-light ships?" Major Prechitt asked.

"The technologies required for FTL-capable ships were a bit more advanced, and we didn't want to wait that long to get some type of defensive capabilities in place," Nathan explained. "In addition, there were many who feared that building FTL warships might appear a provocative act to the Jung, forcing them to attack before we were ready to defend ourselves."

"A reasonable point of view," Lieutenant Montgomery said.

"Perhaps, if you know the size and strength of your enemy, which at the time, we did not. We did eventually build a few small FTL ships for the purpose of reconnaissance."

"What did your people learn?" Major Prechitt wondered.

"That the Jung were far greater in number than we had originally estimated, and that their wave of domination was headed our way. In fact, the Sol system is now the last of the original core worlds that is not under the control of the Jung."

"Do the Jung have jump drives as well?" the lieutenant wondered, concern for his own world obvious on his face.

"Not to our knowledge," Nathan told him. "All our intelligence indicates that the Jung still use linear propulsion systems that are similar in capabilities to your own."

"Then surely your people have a tactical advantage over them, and an enormous one at that," Major Prechitt observed.

"If we can get back to Earth, yes," Cameron said. "As far as we know, our jump drive is the only operational prototype in existence."

"According to Doctor Sorenson, all data concerning the jump drive program is contained in the computer systems on this ship. Without us, the Earth has no jump drive. They can't even build another one."

"That still doesn't make sense to me," Jessica mumbled. She noticed that Major Prechitt and Lieutenant Montgomery were staring at her as if they wanted her to elaborate. She looked at Nathan, who didn't seem to object. "I mean, why? Why put everything and everyone in one place, especially when testing a prototype? Don't scientists usually hide in a bunker somewhere and press a button remotely?"

"She has a point, Captain," Major Prechitt agreed.

"You have to understand, Major," Nathan explained. "The Earth is under incredible stress. Our industrial complex is strained to its limits. The international economies are spending money they do not have on spaceships, and the sons and daughters of every country on Earth are going through training to crew those ships. The governments of Earth still can't agree on how to handle the Jung: with diplomacy or force."

"It still doesn't make sense," Jessica said.

"Captain," Abby interrupted, "if I may?"

"Of course, Doctor."

"Fleet has been aware of Jung operatives on Earth for some time."

"I knew it!" Jessica declared, dropping her fork on her plate. "It *was* an ambush!"

Major Prechitt was looking directly at Nathan. "An ambush?"

"On the first test jump, we found Jung gunboats lying in wait. Captain Roberts suspected an ambush. We fought, one of their antimatter reactors overloaded as we tried to jump away, and we ended up in the Pentaurus cluster being fired on by the Campaglia."

Both Major Prechitt's and Lieutenant Montgomery's eyes were wide open in astonishment. "Incredible," the major declared. "The odds of your ship jumping a thousand light years across the galaxy and ending up at that point in space at that particular time... Quite frankly, Captain, I don't think astronomical adequately describes those odds."

"There may be a reason that we came out of the jump where we did," Nathan said, "but that's another story."

"The project was kept under the tightest security, with only a few key people in Fleet Command and the government aware of the nature of our research. There was much deception involved, including moving our facility about from time to time. I believe they even had decoy teams at one time, but I cannot be sure. Exactly why they chose to put all of the researchers and our data into the prototype vessel, I cannot be certain. However, I suspect they feared that our facility was about to be discovered by Jung operatives."

"You think they were about to attack?" Jessica wondered. "That they were going to try to take the research?"

"Maybe even the researchers," Abby added.

"There's one other possibility," Nathan said. "They may have been worried that the Jung were about to attack the Earth in force, and they didn't want to run the risk of the research falling into their hands." The captain's mess became silent. "Think about it," Nathan continued. "If the Jung had jump drives, I doubt they would be satisfied with just the core worlds. They'd eventually dominate the entire galaxy."

CHAPTER THREE

"Jump thirty-one will be two light years with the ZPEDs directly feeding the jump drive at one percent of their combined maximum output," Abby explained from her place at the starboard auxiliary console on the bridge.

"How's the road ahead?" Nathan asked.

"Open space forward for at least sixty-eight light years, Captain," Lieutenant Yosef answered. "The closest star system along our path will be more than ten light years to port and above us."

"Very well, as soon as you're ready, Doctor."

"Course is already plotted and locked, sir," Loki announced.

Nathan looked at Cameron who was standing to his right. Despite her concerns over the use of the ZPEDs to directly power the jump drive, she appeared as calm as ever. "Nervous?" he asked with the slightest hint of sarcasm.

"No," she answered rather quickly. "You?"

"Nope," he lied. "Mister Sheehan, execute jump thirty-one."

"Jumping in three......two......one......jump."

The bridge momentarily filled with the flash of the jump drive, subdued just enough by the view screen's filter to prevent the flash from overpowering their eyes.

"Jump thirty-one complete," Loki reported.

"Verifying position," Lieutenant Yosef announced.

"Did that look different to you?" Nathan asked Cameron.

"Did what look different?"

"The jump flash," Nathan said. "Didn't it have more blue in it before?"

"I think you're imagining it, sir," Cameron said.

Nathan turned and looked over his shoulder at Jessica.

"Looked the same to me," she told him.

"Position verified," Lieutenant Yosef announced. "In fact, we came out less than two hundred meters off target."

"Two hundred meters? That's all?"

"Yes, sir."

"Not exactly accurate for a combat jump," Cameron said.

"Combat jumps are not done from two light years, Commander," Nathan said.

"Captain, we were also a few hundred meters downrange of our target," Abby said.

"Is that a problem?"

"Not unless it becomes worse at higher outputs, no."

"Any reason not to increase the range with the next jump?" Nathan wondered.

"No, sir. We are still well within safety parameters for the given jump distance."

"Very well, let's make the next jump four light years."

"Aye, sir," Loki acknowledged. "Calculating jump thirty-two at four light years."

"And no recharge," Nathan said with controlled excitement. Cameron shot him a disapproving glance, which he ignored. The idea of being able to jump around the galaxy at will fascinated him. He had never imagined himself an explorer, as the idea of sitting in a ship waiting months or years to reach a destination seemed incredibly boring. If they could jump repeatedly without recharging, exploration of even the most remote regions of the galaxy suddenly seemed a possibility, and an intriguing one at that.

"We could be making history here," Nathan told Cameron.

"We've been making history since we left Earth."

"True enough. You know, I've read a lot of history books. I never thought that I would be in one."

"Oh, you're going to be in them; that's a given. Let's just hope you aren't portrayed as a villain."

"Jump thirty-two plotted and locked," Loki reported.

"Doctor?" Nathan asked.

"ZPEDs are running at two percent. All jump systems show normal. The ship is ready to jump."

"Execute jump thirty-two."

"Jumping in three......two......one......jump."

Again the bridge filled with the jump flash. Despite the filters, Nathan always found himself squinting.

"Jump thirty-two complete," Loki reported.

"Verifying position," Lieutenant Yosef announced.

"Any reason we even have that dumb thing on when we jump?" Nathan asked. "It's not like there's anything out there for us to see."

"Vladimir has programmers working on it," Cameron told him. "He plans to devise a more appropriate set of data displays for you to choose from as needed."

"That would be nice. I still can't believe that the

designers thought the forward exterior view should be the default."

"It's not like the people of Earth have a whole lot of experience designing starships, Nathan," Cameron said.

"I'm not an engineer; I'm a history major, and I figured it out."

"You're also a qualified starship pilot."

"They didn't have any pilots advising them?"

"Position verified," Lieutenant Yosef reported. "Two hundred fourteen meters to port and eight hundred sixty meters downrange."

"That's an increase of more than five hundred meters in our downrange variance," Abby noted, concern in her voice.

"What does that mean?" Nathan asked.

"Two jumps doesn't give us enough data to reach any conclusions, sir," Abby told him.

"Care to make a guess?"

She furrowed her brow. "Not really, but my first concern would be the decay rate of the exterior jump field."

"Are we feeding the correct amount of energy into the fields?"

"According to my data, we are," Abby assured him.

"Recommendations?" Nathan asked.

"I recommend we proceed with the test jumps, continuing to increase the range with each jump. If there is a pattern, the additional jumps will help us to determine both the pattern of variation and possibly the cause. Even if we cannot correct it, we may be able to compensate for the variance."

"Is it safe?"

"As long as the downrange variance increases at

a predictable rate. It isn't like we're going to run into something if we go a few kilometers past our target at this point."

"Kilometers?" Nathan wondered. "I thought we were talking about meters, Doctor."

"Based on the results of the first two jumps, the next jump will put us either eight hundred or sixteen hundred meters downrange of our target. On an astronomical scale, neither of those distances are significant."

"Very well," Nathan relented. "What range shall we set?"

"We should stay true to our previous pattern in order to accurately compare the results. The next jump should be six light years at three percent power."

"Very well. Mister Sheehan, you heard the Doctor."

"Aye, sir. Plotting jump thirty-three for six light years."

Nathan looked at Cameron, raising his eyebrows momentarily, yet still getting no response from the implacable commander. He turned further around to face Jessica. "How's the threat board, Jess?"

"Are you kidding? I haven't seen a contact since we left the Pentaurus sector twenty jumps ago."

"You think we'll come across any more inhabited worlds along the way?" Nathan wondered.

"There are only eleven G-type stars within ten light years of our course, sir," Lieutenant Yosef commented. "According to the catalog, only three of them have potentially habitable planets. However, none of them have been explored, at least to our knowledge."

"Which is considerably limited," Nathan added.

The lieutenant nodded her agreement. "Still, it would be nice if there were."

"I'll be perfectly happy not seeing any one else until we reach Earth," Cameron said.

"Makes for a boring journey."

"Exactly."

"Jump thirty-three plotted and locked," Loki reported.

"ZPEDs at three percent. All jump systems show normal," Abby reported.

"Execute jump thirty-three," Nathan ordered.

"Jumping in three......two......one......jump."

Nathan took a deep breath and let it out slowly as the jump flash cleared.

"Jump thirty-three complete," Loki reported.

"Verifying position," Lieutenant Yosef announced.

Nathan waited silently for the lieutenant to complete the verification process. It normally only took seconds to verify their position. However, he knew that the lieutenant was triple-checking her findings in this case.

"Position verified," Yosef reported. "Four hundred meters to starboard, thirty-two hundred meters downrange of target."

"Thirty-two hundred meters?" Nathan said. "I thought you said sixteen hundred max."

"It appears that the problem is amplified at a much greater rate than anticipated, sir," Abby admitted. "To be honest, I'm as surprised as anyone."

"Sir," Cameron interrupted, "perhaps it would be best if we terminated the tests, at least for now, to give Doctor Sorenson time to analyze the jump events."

"We need to continue through to ten light years, Captain," Abby insisted. "Otherwise we will not have enough data to figure out what is causing the problem, let alone how to correct it."

"That was a three-kilometer error, Abby," Nathan said.

"Still not significant on an astronomical scale, Captain. The increasing errors in the actual range have not put the ship at any additional risk."

"Captain," Cameron interrupted, "I have to disagree with Doctor Sorenson. The very fact that we do *not* know why the errors are occurring is *more* than enough reason to discontinue the tests."

"Which is precisely why we need to complete the tests, Commander," Abby defended, "so that we can figure out and resolve the problem."

"She is right, Commander," Nathan argued. "Three, thirty, or three hundred kilometers. It's still..."

"I know," Cameron interrupted, "it's astronomically insignificant. Did you notice that the lateral position relative to target has also been off, sir?"

"It takes time to calibrate a new emitter system, Captain," Abby stated. "We went through the same process after we replaced the emitters back at Corinair."

"I'm inclined to agree with Abby on this one, Commander. We need the last two jumps in order to figure this out. However, if the next jump is wildly off the mark, I will terminate the testing. Fair enough?"

"Yes, sir."

"Jump thirty-four, Mister Sheehan. Eight light years."

Loki looked at Josh who, for once, appeared just as concerned as he was. "Aye, sir. Plotting jump thirty-four at eight light years."

Nathan looked at Cameron again. He could tell by the look in her eyes that she wasn't happy about his decision. He also knew that she was aware that she had come extremely close to being insubordinate. However, she had only been doing her job, looking after the well-being of the ship. Furthermore, she was doing exactly what he needed her to do, which was to keep him thinking as much as possible.

"Jump thirty-four plotted and locked," Loki reported.

"ZPEDs at four percent," Abby reported. "All jump systems show ready."

"Mister Sheehan, execute jump thirty-four."

"Aye, sir. Jumping in three......two......one...... jump."

Nathan closed his eyes this time, again breathing out slowly as they jumped.

"Jump thirty-four complete," Loki reported with a hint of relief in his voice.

"Verifying position," Lieutenant Yosef announced again.

Nathan looked at Abby, then at Cameron, both of whom looked tense.

"Position verified," Yosef reported. "Fifty-seven meters to port, slightly high." The lieutenant paused as if she didn't want to report the next number. "Twenty-five point four kilometers downrange."

The bridge was silent. Nathan again looked at Abby. The physicist was not usually a confident looking person, but this time her face radiated confidence. Cameron, on the other hand, looked like she was about to scream, which was completely opposite from her usual demeanor. For a moment, Nathan worried how she would react to his next command. "Mister Sheehan," he began calmly, "plot jump thirty-five. Ten light years."

Loki swallowed hard, his only solace being the knowledge that this was the last jump in the test series. "Aye, sir. Plotting jump thirty-five at ten light years."

The bridge remained silent while Loki plotted the next jump. Finally, Cameron stepped closer to the command chair as if to speak.

"Don't," Nathan told her in a hushed tone before she could say anything.

"Jump thirty-five, ten light years, plotted and locked," Loki reported.

"ZPEDs at five percent, Captain. All jump systems show normal."

"Execute jump thirty-five," Nathan ordered calmly.

"Jumping in three......"

Nathan thought about all the things that had happened to them since they had left Earth on what should have been a day trip.

"Two......"

No matter how difficult things had become, his instincts and a bit of luck had managed to find a way to come out on top.

"One......"

He only hoped they weren't about to fail him.

"Jump."

For a split second, as the bridge filled with the jump flash, he wondered if Cameron was right.

"Jump thirty-five complete," Loki announced with obvious relief.

"Verifying position."

Nathan looked at Cameron. He couldn't tell if she was relieved or disappointed that nothing had happened to prove her right. He dismissed the urge to toss an 'I told you so' look in her direction.

"Position verified," Lieutenant Yosef announced. "Two hundred twelve meters to port, fifty-seven meters below, one hundred eighty-seven kilometers downrange."

Nathan looked back at Cameron. Her look turned a bit more smug. "Take the ZPEDs offline and shut down the hybrid jump drive," he ordered as he stood from the command chair. "Plot jump thirty-six for fourteen light years using the standard emitter array and jump when ready, Mister Sheehan."

Cameron breathed a sigh of relief.

"Aye, sir. Plotting jump thirty-six for fourteen light years using the standard emitter array."

"Doctor Sorenson, I suggest you get busy on your analysis. I want a full report as soon as possible."

"Yes, sir."

Nathan stepped down from the command platform, passing Cameron. "You have the bridge, Commander," he ordered as he headed aft toward his ready room. Abby also rose, exiting the bridge to starboard.

Cameron took a seat in the command chair, trying to maintain her composure. She noticed Josh as he turned around slightly and peeked at her over his shoulder. "Exciting enough for you, Mister Hayes?"

Josh just turned back around and stared at his console.

* * *

"I'd like to conduct at least one training exercise during each recharge layover," Major Prechitt stated.

Nathan looked surprised. So far, the morning briefing had been the same old mundane operational details, just like every morning. He was beginning to wonder why they had these morning briefings. "Is that necessary?"

"Yes, sir, I believe so," the major insisted. "Although most of my pilots are veterans of the Takara campaign, several have never even launched through the tubes and have only experienced one shipboard landing. If we're to be expected to maintain a combat-ready state, we need to maintain our basic skills."

"What about the simulators?" Cameron asked.

"The simulators have been most helpful," Major Prechitt admitted, "but they are no substitute for actual flight time."

"Simulators are good for running 'what-if' scenarios," Master Chief Montrose stated, "but pilots need to fly to stay sharp, especially the new ones."

"Can't argue with that logic," Nathan admitted.

"Since we do not know the state of affairs between the Earth and the Jung Empire, we should maintain a high state of readiness. That is why my pilots came along, is it not? To protect this ship?"

"No, you're quite right, Major," Nathan said. "Jump thirty-eight is less than an hour away. After that, you'll have your first opportunity for your pilots to get out and stretch their legs a bit." Nathan turned to Cameron. "Does that sound good to you, Commander?"

"I would suggest we limit the sortie windows to three hours to ensure that all spacecraft are safely aboard and the flight deck is red before jumping. Will that be enough time for your training flights, Major?"

"That would be plenty, Commander. I'll start with my least experienced pilots in order to bring everyone to an even state of readiness."

"Very well." Nathan turned to Abby who had been sitting quietly at the opposite end of the table throughout the briefing. "Doctor? Have you anything to report?"

"Yes, sir. We have completed our analysis of the range variation problem we experienced while testing the hybrid jump drive system. I believe that we can compensate for the problem."

"Care to elaborate?"

"The ZPEDs themselves create a rather odd field when running at higher outputs. Its effects are similar to that of a strong gravity well. It's as if the vacuum point created by the module has mass, even though it does not."

"But our ZPEDs were only running at five percent," Cameron said.

"Yes, which is why we did not detect this field. We know of its existence because of the data from our encounter with both the Campaglia and the Avendahl."

"If the ZPEDs act like gravity wells, wouldn't that affect ships around it, pulling them in toward the ZPED?" Nathan asked.

"As I said, it's like a gravity well, but it isn't one. We can detect and measure the field, but it doesn't seem to have the physical effects that one might expect. It does, however, affect other fields around it. The Takarans get around this problem in two ways: in their larger ships, they encase the entire ZPED reactor in a container made of a special, multi-layered, shielded alloy. This reduces the effect enough that it does not cause problems with other systems within the ship, like her exterior shields. This containment system allows them to run their

ZPEDs at near maximum output."

"What about in their comm-drones?" Nathan asked. "How do they get around the problem in them? There's nowhere near enough space for such a containment system."

"Correct. Their solution was rather simple: they keep their output at low levels—below twenty percent, I suspect. Even at a lower output, the mini-ZPED is more than powerful enough to run the high-speed comm-drones."

"Forgive me, Doctor," Cameron said, "I don't mean to challenge your assumptions, but if this field isn't detectable at lower output levels like those we were using during our test jumps, how can you be sure this was the cause of the range variance we experienced?"

"During the test jumps, we had reports of variations in the ship's artificial gravity," Vladimir announced. "These anomalies occurred in the decks around the mini-ZPEDs. It took some time to make the connection."

"The variation patterns of the artificial gravity plating in the affected decks matches the expected patterns that would be generated by the ZPEDs at higher outputs," Abby elaborated, "thus leading us to believe that the effect is still present at lower outputs, even if it is not enough for us to detect. This also explains why there were minor surges in power in the emitters nearest the ZPEDs themselves. The effect caused small surges, which the system compensated for by adding additional power to the remaining, unaffected emitters. The result was a longer jump than expected."

Nathan rubbed his eyes. "This is all very interesting, but what exactly does it mean to us from an operational standpoint?"

"It means, Captain, that we can calculate the effect and adjust our power output to the emitters to compensate for the surge created by the ZPED fields. In fact, if we took apart the other two comm-drones and ran four ZPEDs at even lower outputs, we might be able to jump even farther and at even lower power outputs... again, without recharging."

"That would leave us without working models for Fleet to reverse engineer when we get home," Cameron pointed out.

"The commander is right, Doctor," Nathan agreed. "We're doing enough already. Best we hand over the last two mini-ZPEDs to Fleet R and D. I'm sure they'd love to get their hands on them."

"As you wish, Captain. It shouldn't take me more than a day to create and validate the new algorithms," Abby promised.

"Doctor," Cameron said, leaning back in her chair as she cast an accusatory look toward Abby, "can you guarantee that the new algorithms will work as intended?"

"No, I cannot. However, if we start with shorter jumps at lower outputs and work our way up with each successful jump..."

"Until what? Until we have a problem?" Cameron interrupted as she leaned forward. She turned her head toward Nathan. "Sir, I'm not sure the risk is worth the potential gains here. Maybe if Doctor Sorenson took a little more time, ran the numbers some more..."

"Running the numbers further will not accomplish anything," Abby protested. "Without practical testing we cannot be sure..."

"That's what I'm worried about," Cameron

interrupted. "We can't be sure. Sir, we're nearly halfway home already. Why take the additional risk?"

"A jump drive with greater range and without the need to recharge would be a significant tactical advantage," Nathan reminded her as he leaned forward and placed his hands, folded, on the conference table.

"I'm not arguing that," Cameron said. "But let Fleet R and D worry about that instead of risking the only jump-capable ship the fleet has."

Nathan took a deep breath, letting it out slowly. "I'll take everything discussed here under consideration and give you my decision in the morning. If there is nothing else…" Nathan looked about for a moment to give everyone a chance to bring up another topic if desired. "Dismissed, everyone."

Cameron sat patiently as the others made their way out of the briefing room, expecting to have a few words with her captain in private. However, unlike most days when Nathan would stay behind for a moment, today he, too, departed the room with haste, leaving Cameron alone without a word.

* * *

Cameron entered the captain's ready room full of determination. She was going to have her say, regardless of military protocol.

"Captain," she announced as she closed the hatch behind her.

"Commander," Nathan responded, his eyes still on his desktop display. He glanced up momentarily and noticed that she was closing the hatch. "Something I can do for you?"

"Permission to speak freely, sir?"

Nathan leaned back in his chair. "Since when do you need permission, Commander?"

Cameron paused for a moment as she considered how to best address her concerns. Nathan, at times, was difficult for her to read. When they had first left Earth, she thought she'd had him all figured out. For the most part, she had been correct, but the last few months had changed him considerably. There were times when he was his old, arrogant, condescending self, confident that he could do no wrong. However, these days, he seemed more pensive, taking more time to consider his decisions. Still, she could not help but question his decision to continue the testing of the hybrid jump drive. He was the captain, and his decision would stand. She knew she had no grounds to override him on the matter. She did, however, have an obligation to protect the ship, even from her captain. She would have her say; she would challenge his decision in private. After all, he had granted her that right months ago.

"Speak your mind, Cam."

"Are you seriously considering allowing Abby to continue testing the hybrid drive concept?"

"Yes, I'm seriously considering it."

"Why, Nathan? Why are you so focused on getting that thing to work?"

"It's simple, really. Being able to jump farther and without the need to recharge would be a huge step forward and would provide an even greater advantage than the original prototype provides."

"I don't see it as that great an advantage," Cameron argued. "At least, not so much that it's worth risking the ship."

"How am I risking the ship?"

"Every jump is a risk, Nathan. You know that. For God's sake, when we jump we're literally plowing through space at unimaginable speeds and arriving in the middle of a completely unexplored region. That alone is a risk."

"Granted."

"At least with the prototype we have experience and an abundance of performance data. This helps us reduce the risk associated with jumping about the galaxy."

"How so? Just because we haven't yet had any problems associated with the prototype? We're still jumping into unknown space every time. How is using the ZPED-powered hybrid any more risky?"

"Because of the range variance error..."

"Which is why I stopped the previous testing once we had accumulated sufficient data," Nathan said, interrupting her. "Now Abby believes she has figured out how to compensate for the effect of the ZPED's field disturbance. I'm inclined to give her a chance to test her theories."

"At the risk of this ship."

"Tell me how I am increasing the risk to this ship by any significant degree," Nathan demanded calmly.

Cameron paused to regroup. "It's not the level of risk that I object to, Nathan. I admit that Abby has done everything possible to mitigate the risk. My objection is to the use of this ship as the test vehicle. Under other circumstances, I might agree that the additional effort is worth it. However, we have an obligation to get this ship back to Earth."

"We have an obligation to *protect* the Earth," Nathan corrected. "I'm trying to make sure we're as prepared as possible to do just that."

"And how exactly does putting this ship at additional risk help protect the Earth? We're going to be home in less than two weeks, Nathan, even without the ZPEDs. We don't *need* to experiment with them..."

"People died for those ZPEDs!" Nathan declared, sitting forward again with such determination and speed that it startled Cameron. "So you can be damned sure I'm going to try to find a way to use them!"

"Is that why you're so hell-bent on getting the ZPEDs to work? They didn't die so that we could have ZPEDs, Nathan. They died defending their world."

"They died because I couldn't leave well enough alone!"

Nathan took pause to gather his thoughts, leaning back in his chair again as he regained his composure. "From a practical standpoint, it makes sense to conduct further tests of the hybrid jump system. Should it prove usable, it might allow us to jump right past Jung-occupied space, giving us a better chance of reaching Earth without further incident." Nathan looked Cameron directly in the eyes. "That's the reason I'm 'hell-bent' on getting the ZPEDs to work, Commander, and that's the only reason. I don't want any more of us to die, not if there's a way to prevent it. The ZPEDs are our best hope, Commander. For us *and* the Earth. Is that understood?"

"Couldn't leave well enough alone. Aye, sir, I understand *that*," Cameron retorted, feeling confident that she had gotten to the bottom of Nathan's reasons for pursuing the ZPEDs so fervently. "Then you've decided?"

"No, I haven't, Commander," Nathan stated, returning to his previously calm demeanor. "But rest assured that your comments *will* have some bearing on my decision."

After a long silence, she dipped her chin down slightly, trying to look into Nathan's eyes. He had the amazing ability to go from enraged to dead calm in seconds. It was one of the traits that had surprised her early on. "Are we good?"

Despite his best efforts to conceal it, a smile started to form at the corner of his mouth. "We're good, Commander."

"Just checking." She took two steps backward, maintaining eye contact long enough to see that he had relaxed a bit. Satisfied that they truly were okay, she began to turn toward the hatch.

"Hey, Cam," Nathan called. She stopped and turned back toward him. "If Captain Roberts were still alive and in command, and you were his XO, would you be asking him the same questions?"

"If he was thinking about doing the same stupid thing? Hell yes."

Nathan's smile broadened. "Just checking."

* * *

Nathan walked across the main room of his quarters to the entrance hatch. He swung the hatch open and found Vladimir smiling on the other side.

"Did I wake you?" Vladimir asked. "Of course not," he added with a laugh, "you don't sleep."

"Not from lack of trying," Nathan said as he closed the hatch and followed Vladimir into the main room.

"Sorry I could not join you for dinner," Vladimir said as he went to Nathan's kitchenette, looking for a snack. "Abby had my entire department installing special sensors in the decks around the mini-ZPEDs. That woman..." Vladimir stopped mid-sentence, thinking. "How long have we been gone?"

"From Earth?" Nathan asked, plopping down on the couch.

"Of course from Earth."

"I don't know exactly. I kind of lost track. Four months, maybe?"

"Four months, and that woman is still a pain in my popa."

"Your what?"

"Popa. You know." Vladimir stopped searching the kitchenette long enough to point at his butt. "Don't you have anything to eat around here?"

"I have my own cook, remember? I think there are a few of those meal bars in the cupboard over the sink."

"Oh," Vladimir declared with glee, "I love these things. I thought Cameron returned them all to the escape pods."

"I guess she missed a few."

"I find that hard to believe." Vladimir took a bite of one of the bars and took a seat on the opposite end of the couch. "She doesn't miss anything."

"You don't have to tell me," Nathan said. "She's been riding me nonstop about my wanting to let Abby test the hybrid jump drive."

"Why?"

"She thinks it's an unnecessary risk."

"What risk? We have sensors everywhere. Not a single electron flows without our knowing it. The worst thing that can happen is that we jump a bit farther than we planned."

"I guess she sees that as a risk."

"Nathan, she does know that we are in the middle of nowhere, right? It's not like we are going to run into something. I mean, the odds of that happening are so..."

"Don't talk to me about odds," Nathan said, grimacing. "I have a bad habit of proving them wrong, remember?"

"My point is that we are no more likely to run into trouble using the hybrid configuration than we are using the original one. In fact, if you think about it, we are less likely, as we would be making fewer total jumps to get home."

"Now why didn't I think of that argument?"

"Because you are not as smart as I am," Vladimir declared as he opened a second meal bar, "or as pretty."

"The word is 'handsome.'"

"Ah, yes. Handsome. I get those two words mixed up sometimes."

"Then you don't think I'm making a mistake?"

"Of course not. You are my best friend, Nathan, so trust me on this... If I thought you were doing something terribly stupid, I would tell you."

"Isn't that what Cameron is trying to do?"

"Perhaps. But what does she know? She is an administrator. She knows nothing of the jump drive or our power systems. And she definitely does *not* know anything about the ZPEDs."

"Do you?"

"No," he admitted, taking a swig of water from a half empty bottle sitting on the end table, "nothing at all." Vladimir laughed. "According to what I know of physics, they should not work at all."

"Then how can you be sure I'm not putting the ship at risk?"

"I can't," Vladimir said with a shrug, "but the Takarans *do* know something about ZPEDs, and they do not seem worried." Vladimir took another long drink, emptying the bottle. "Besides, Abby knows everything about the jump drive."

"She doesn't completely understand how it works," Nathan reminded him. "She has said as much in the past."

"Even the Takarans do not completely understand how our jump drive works. She knows enough, Nathan. She is a very smart woman, that one. Just do not tell her that I said this. She will never forget."

"Yeah, I don't understand half the techno-babble that comes out of her mouth."

"Nathan, you don't understand half the babble that comes out of *my* mouth."

He chuckled. "True enough."

"Do not worry my friend. Everything will be fine; you will see."

"I don't know, Vlad. Cameron is really dead set against it. I'm beginning to wonder if she might be right."

"She is not a risk taker like us," Vladimir said as he rose and headed for the hatch.

"You sure you don't want something else to eat?" Nathan asked. "I think I have some stale crackers lying around somewhere."

"No, I must go. I have much work to do." Vladimir made his way to the hatch. "We might be testing experimental drive tomorrow, and I must be sure we do not explode!"

"Funny."

"Get some sleep, my friend!" Vladimir ordered as he closed the hatch behind him.

"Even funnier!"

* * *

"Captain on the bridge!" the Corinari guard at the hatch announced as the captain entered. Nathan paused momentarily, noticing the tension on the faces of his bridge staff. After which, he turned and headed into his ready room.

Before he reached his chair behind his desk, the chief of the boat, Master Chief Montrose, entered. "Captain? A moment of your time, sir?"

"Come in, Master Chief." He stood behind his desk, watching as the master chief closed the hatch and entered the room. "Uh, oh. Are you going to chew me out as well, Master Chief?"

"I'm afraid so, sir," Master Chief Montrose told him. "I'm just not sure how to adequately express my concerns in English. I haven't been speaking it that long."

"You're doing fine, Master Chief. You've even started using contractions."

"Let's see if I remember this correctly," the master chief said. "Captain, what the fuck are you thinking?"

Nathan chuckled. "You've been talking to Lieutenant Commander Nash, haven't you?"

"She does have a colorful vocabulary. Quite spirited in its breadth, I'd say."

"Definitely."

"Seriously, sir," the master chief continued, "what *are* you thinking?"

"I assume you're referring to further testing of the hybrid jump drive concept?"

"Yes, sir. Pardon me for saying so, but you're being stupid, Captain. Stupid and childish."

"Really?" Nathan took his seat, crossing his hands in his lap.

"Your crewmen are all volunteers, sir. They're willing to give their lives for this ship. However, if you want them to continue to be willing to give their lives, they've got to know that you're always going to do your best to keep them safe. Risking our lives just so you can make your sword a bit sharper is, well, it's just stupid, Captain. Fucking stupid, it is."

"You're getting a lot of mileage out of that word, aren't you, Master Chief?"

"It's more useful than I thought it would be, sir. It sends a strong message, doesn't it?"

"Yes, it does. Keep it up, and you're going to fit in nicely with the other chiefs in the fleet," Nathan added with a smile. "Just be careful who you use it with. Some folks don't appreciate its use as much as others."

"Yes, sir. Sorry, sir."

"No problem, Master Chief," Nathan said as he rose from his chair. "Come on, we've got work to do."

The master chief's eyes widened slightly as the captain brushed past him on his way back to the bridge. He made his way down to his command chair, which Cameron immediately vacated. "Good morning, Commander," he greeted as he took his seat.

"Good morning, sir."

"Threat board?" he asked.

"Clear, sir," Jessica answered.

"How's the road ahead, Lieutenant Yosef?"

"Nothing on our course for at least thirty-seven light years, sir."

"Doctor Sorenson, what's our current maximum jump range using the primary array?"

"Fifteen point four light years, Captain."

"And the estimated max range using the secondary array with the ZPEDs at no more than ten percent?"

"Twenty light years."

"Can you guarantee that range is achievable without any range variance issues?"

"No, sir, not without further testing."

Nathan looked at Cameron and the master chief standing beside her. He also looked at the faces of Josh and Loki sitting at the helm in front of him. "Mister Sheehan, what jump are we at?"

"Forty-five, sir."

"Plot jump forty-five for fourteen light years using the primary emitter array."

"Yes, sir," Loki responded, smiling as he spun around to face his console.

"Sorry, Doctor, but further experimentation using the ZPEDs will have to be done by Fleet R and D. Take the ZPEDs offline for now. You can use them to speed up the recharge of the energy banks, but I want them throttled down to far below safe levels whenever we jump."

"As you wish, Captain," Abby answered, offering no reaction to his orders.

Nathan couldn't tell if Abby was relieved or annoyed at his orders, but he didn't care. He had done what was best for his ship and his crew, as well as for his primary mission, which was to get home in one piece. "Comms, inform the Cheng that we're proceeding using the primary array."

"Yes, sir."

"Doctor, am I correct in assuming that the new emitters on the secondary array will still work in the standard configuration?"

"Yes, sir," Abby confirmed. "However, we still

need to conduct calibration testing of the entire array, as it has yet to be used in the standard power configuration."

"Very well."

"Jump forty-five plotted and locked, sir," Loki reported.

"Execute jump forty-five, Mister Sheehan."

"Activating auto-nav," Loki reported. "Jump point in ten seconds."

Nathan smiled at the master chief who looked rather pleased with himself. "It was a nice speech, Master Chief, but I had already decided not to continue the tests before you entered my ready room."

"Yes, sir."

"Jumping in three......two......one......jump."

The bridge filled momentarily with the blue-white jump flash.

"Jump forty-five complete."

"Verifying position," Lieutenant Yosef announced. "On target, no significant variance."

"Time to jump forty-six: seven hours and four minutes," Loki reported.

"Very well." Nathan turned to Cameron. "Commander, if you're not too busy, would you mind taking the bridge? I haven't been sleeping well lately, and I think a nap is in order."

"Those big decisions are tiring, aren't they?" Cameron said, the barest hint of a smirk.

"Very." Nathan stood.

"You might try a workout first," Cameron suggested. "Helps me when I can't sleep."

"Good idea. You have the bridge, Commander."

* * *

Nathan looked down at his shackled hands, the weight of the heavy irons digging into the base of his thumbs. A chain led from the wrist irons down to those around his ankles. People were yelling at him, their voices familiar, yet unknown, many of them in languages he did not understand. A man, an elder man in a uniform among many similarly dressed men, sat in judgment of him, confident that Nathan had committed heinous crimes against his people. A voice stood out amongst the others in the crowd, his father's. *"Why did you do it, Nathan? Why?"* He looked toward his father's voice, but saw only the smiling face of his older brother, Eli. *"Who's the favored son now?"*

Nathan squinted, trying to see through the haze in the room. There was a sharp sound, a gavel striking its wooden base in rapid succession. Screams of pain and suffering continued to emanate from all around him, punctuated suddenly by his mother's voice. *"Nathan, don't worry; we'll fix it. Everything will be fine."* Nathan felt a sudden sharp pain in his head, his hands raising to his face in response. *"You'll have to find your own way out of this one, Nathan,"* he heard his father say. *"It's time you stood on your own two feet."* A panic swept over him. He felt alone, abandoned. *"How could you do this to us?"* someone cried. He pulled his hands away from his face. They were wet, covered with blood. *"How could you..."*

Nathan opened his eyes. He was on his back, his hands and feet free of restraint. He sat quickly upright, his head spinning. He glanced at his hands, finding them clean. He looked around and realized he was in his quarters on board the Aurora, sitting on the floor next to his bed. His head hurt. He touched his forehead, eliciting more pain. There was blood on his fingers now, apparently from a wound on his head.

There was a sudden thud. The room shook without warning. *"General quarters. General quarters,"* Naralena's voice announced over the ship's loudspeakers. *"All hands, man your stations."* Nathan scrambled to his feet and made his way shakily to the main room. He stumbled as the ship shook violently again. *What the hell is going on? Why aren't the inertial dampeners working?*

Nathan made his way into the corridor and immediately headed forward at a jog. The ship shook again and again, threatening to knock him off his stride each time. He reached out to steady himself against the walls as he continued forward, passing crewmen in the corridors as they all headed for their posts.

"Captain on the bridge!" the guard called out as he clung to the hatch frame to stay on his feet.

"Report!" Nathan bellowed as he stumbled over to the tactical station, grabbing onto Jessica's shoulder to stay on his feet as the ship seemed to suddenly jerk sideways under him.

"We've jumped in too close to the event horizon of a black hole!" Cameron said. There was uncharacteristic fear in her voice.

"Well get us out of here!" Nathan ordered, his pulse pounding as his own fear began to build.

"We're trying!"

The ship shook again, nearly knocking Nathan to the deck. "Why aren't the..."

"Inertial dampeners keep cutting in and out," Cameron said, anticipating his next question.

"Kill all secondary systems and channel power into the main drive!" Nathan ordered.

"Vlad's already working on it," Cameron said.

"I'm assuming we're at full power on the mains."

"Aye, sir," Josh reported.

"And we're steering away from the black hole?" Nathan asked. It felt like a stupid question, yet it also seemed important enough to ask.

"Aye, sir," Josh answered.

"We turned away as soon as we came out of the jump but got picked up by its gravity well," Cameron reported as something else struck the ship and jostled them about.

Nathan suddenly felt himself become lighter. For a split second, he felt as if his feet would come off the floor. A confused look came across his face. "Is it affecting our artificial gravity?"

Cameron shrugged her shoulders as she rose from the command chair. "What happened to your head?" Cameron asked, noticing the blood.

Nathan plopped down in the command chair, happy to get off his feet. "I fell... must've hit my head." Nathan wiped the blood away from his forehead again. "I'll be fine. Loki! Are we making any headway?"

"Negative, sir! We're barely holding position as it is!"

Another thud. "What the hell is hitting us?" Nathan keyed his comm-set. "Cheng, Captain! How much more can you push the reactors?"

"*Captain, Cheng,*" Vladimir answered. "*They are already at one hundred percent, all four of them. I can push them to maybe one ten.*"

"Give us one ten on all four," Nathan ordered.

"*Aye, sir.*"

"All decks are reporting minimal power usage," Master Chief Montrose reported from his position near the ship's systems console. "Getting reports from all over the ship, sir. Variations in artificial gravity and a lot of shaking."

"Engineering reports all reactors at one ten, sir," Naralena reported.

Nathan turned his attention back to the helm. "Any progress?"

"Not yet," Loki said, shaking his head.

"Put up the aft camera," Nathan ordered. The screen immediately switched, displaying the view from the aft end of the ship facing directly astern. The screen was normal, showing nothing but distant stars, except that they were only on the periphery. The middle of the screen was pitch black.

"Is that it?" Nathan wondered, seemingly disappointed.

"It's a black hole, Nathan," Cameron quipped. "What did you expect, a light show?"

"I don't know," he admitted. "Where did it come from?"

"Unknown, sir," Lieutenant Yosef admitted. "I haven't been able to get a fix on our position yet. The gravitational lensing from the black hole is distorting everything."

"We're beginning to make a little headway," Loki reported. "It's not much, sir. Maybe a few meters per second."

Something dark and mysterious suddenly passed across the view screen extremely close to their stern. "What the hell was that? Do we have external lights on our stern?" Nathan asked.

"We have lights all over the place," Jessica told him.

"Light up everything directly behind us."

Nathan watched the main view screen as the stern lights snapped on. A faintly lit ring of dust and debris appeared around the outer edges of the dark circle that filled the screen. The objects flickered as the Aurora's stern lights reflected off of them. They swirled slowly inward toward their eventual demise. Large, closer chunks of rock occasionally passed by at a range close enough for them to see surface detail.

"Were we jumping into a system?" Nathan asked.

"No, sir," Loki answered as another rock struck the ship, shaking them from side to side. "We should have jumped into open space."

"That's a lot of debris for open space," Cameron commented.

"At least we know what's hitting us," Nathan stated. "Cheng, Captain," he called over his comm-set.

"*Go for Cheng.*"

"Vlad, any chance you can push the reactors to one twenty? We're making a little headway, but it's not enough."

"*No, sir. One ten is already at the red line.*"

"I need one twenty..."

"*We can die now in an antimatter explosion, or we can die later in a black hole,*" Vladimir responded with irritation. "*The choice is yours, sir.*"

Nathan exhaled in frustration. "Understood."

"Captain, at this rate, we'll run out of propellant long before we get clear of the event horizon," Loki reported.

The ship rocked several times in succession as more debris stuck the hull.

"That's what I figured," Nathan told him. "Abby,

can we jump out of here?"

"We don't even know where *here* is, Captain," Abby told him.

"I don't care where *here* is, Abby. I just want to be somewhere else."

"We can't calculate a jump plot away from *here* if we don't know where *here* is," Abby said.

"It doesn't have to be perfect, Doctor. We just need to move a few million kilometers."

"The jump fields won't even form in the presence of the event horizon's gravity well," Abby said, exasperation in her voice. "Even if they did, there's no guarantee that they'd all work properly, which means that..."

"Part of the ship might not jump," Nathan finished for her. "Any other ideas, Doctor?"

Abby thought for a moment as the ship was again rocked by debris impact. "We could try the ZPEDs," she suggested.

"I thought you said the jump fields wouldn't form," Cameron stated.

"Not for the jump drive," Abby explained. She got blank stares from both Nathan and Cameron. "Our engines use electricity to accelerate propellant as thrust. That's why you wanted more power from the reactors, to further accelerate that propellant, thereby increasing our thrust. The ZPEDs could give us that extra power and then some."

"Is it safe?" Cameron asked, suspicion in her voice.

"Is staying here?" Abby countered, her face defiant.

"Do it," Nathan ordered without hesitation.

"Captain..." Cameron began to argue.

"Objection noted," he stated, effectively

dismissing her concerns.

"It may take some time," Abby warned. "The ZPEDs are currently wired into the jump drive's power grid, not the main engines."

"How long until we run out of propellant, Loki?"

"Forty-eight minutes, sir," Loki reported.

"That should be plenty," Abby said.

"Just because we have forty-eight minutes of propellant left at full throttle doesn't mean I want you to take forty-seven minutes to get ready, Doc. I'd like to have enough propellant left to get home."

"Of course."

"Get with Vlad. Use whoever you need."

"Yes, sir," Abby answered as she rose from her seat.

"COB, go with her. Be a motivator. The clock's ticking."

"Aye, sir," Master Chief Montrose acknowledged as he rose from his seat and followed Doctor Sorenson out of the bridge.

Another chunk of debris struck the hull, shaking the bridge again.

"We've got to be taking some exterior damage from all these hits," Nathan stated.

"We're lucky we jumped in where we did," Lieutenant Yosef reported.

"How so?" Nathan wondered.

"The closer to the event horizon, the greater the gravity and the smaller the debris. Farther out, that stuff is probably a lot larger."

"I hope we get a chance to prove you're right, Lieutenant," Nathan said.

"Lieutenant Commander," Abby called out as she,

Lieutenant Montgomery, and Master Chief Montrose entered the auxiliary power room, "we must wire both ZPEDs into the main power..."

"I know," Vladimir said. He pointed to the two Corinairan technicians that had come with him. "We are prepared to start as soon as you power down the ZPEDs."

"Of course, I'll do so immediately," Abby said, moving toward the control pedestal that sat in between the pair of ZPEDs.

"Wait!" Lieutenant Montgomery warned, grabbing Abby by the arm to stop her. "You cannot shut them down."

"We must," Abby said. "It is too dangerous..."

"If you shut them down, they may not reinitialize," the lieutenant warned, "not this close to the event horizon."

"Why not?" Vladimir asked.

"The gravity well from the black hole may prevent the devices from establishing their vacuum points."

"I don't understand," Vladimir said.

"The devices must create their own stable microgravity wells in order to..."

"We do not have time for a physics lecture," Master Chief Montrose insisted, cutting off the lieutenant mid-sentence. "Can we perform the necessary tasks while the devices are running? Yes or no?"

"It is very dangerous," Lieutenant Montgomery warned. "Even at the lowest potential output settings, there are enormous amounts of energy contained within the main power transfer trunks. One slip and..."

"Yes or no, Lieutenant?" Master Chief Montrose repeated calmly as the ship shook at another impact.

Lieutenant Montgomery stared at the master

chief, reluctant to answer. "Yes, it is possible if you install a bypass line, one that feeds directly into an energy sink of some kind."

"Like a power cell," Abby said, "like the ones the jump drive uses."

"Yes, yes, that might work," Lieutenant Montgomery agreed.

"We still have the original cells," Vladimir told them. "We saved them after your people upgraded all the energy banks for the jump drive."

"We must wire them into the junction points between the ZPEDs and the transfer trunks," Lieutenant Montgomery told him. "They will drain most of the energy away from the lines. This will reduce the electrostatic field around the lines to safe levels so that we can disconnect them from the jump drive transfer junction and reconnect them to the ship's main power grid. It will still be very dangerous, but you will be able to handle them. Just be careful. You must use non-ferromagnetic implements, and you must be well insulated from the..."

"I understand," Vladimir insisted, eager to begin the work. He, too, was aware of the amounts of propellant that they were burning with each passing minute. "I have changed a few light bulbs in my day," he joked as he turned to begin their work.

Lieutenant Montgomery grabbed Vladimir's arm. "This is not a light bulb, Lieutenant Commander," he said, his face grim.

"It's okay," Abby said. "It was just an expression." She looked directly into the lieutenant's eyes. "He knows what to do. They all do."

"Bring us one of the old energy cells!" Vladimir instructed one of Abby's jump drive technicians,

"*Buistra!*" Vladimir turned to the Corinairan technicians that had come with him.

"You will need two cells," Lieutenant Montgomery told them.

"Okay, I now have stupid question," Vladimir said. "Why two?"

"We must connect both ZPEDs, not just one," the lieutenant told him.

"Now I have another stupid question," Vladimir said.

"The devices are currently running in phase," Lieutenant Montgomery explained. "That is probably why they are still able to function in the presence of the black hole's gravity well."

Abby turned to her technician who was still waiting for clarification. "Two," she told him, "we need two cells."

"Prepare two short trunk lines," Vladimir ordered. "We will use them to connect the energy cells," he said, pointing as he spoke, "here and here. I want the lines ready by the time they get back with those cells."

"The electrostatic fields in the trunks will spike as soon as we connect them to the junctions," one of the Corinairan technicians reminded him. "We will not survive the discharge."

"I have a plan," Vladimir insisted. "Mister Donahue," he called over his comm-set, "I need two REMS-poles in the ZPED room, quickly!"

The Corinairan technicians and Vladimir pulled two bundles of thick, heavily insulated cables from the storage locker along one wall of the room. The cables themselves were as big as a man's arm and several meters long. Using special self-tapping plugs, the men quickly prepared each end of the pair of cables with quick-connect plugs that would fit into the receptacles in the junction boxes. Working in pairs, they slid the plug over the end of the wire, activated the clamps, and pulled the levers located on each side of the plug up and over, forcing the prongs deep into each side of the inner conductive material.

"Will the cables be long enough?" the lieutenant asked. "The cells must be as far apart as possible."

"These should reach to either side of the room," Vladimir explained. "We have longer trunks, but we will have to bring them from elsewhere on the ship, and they are not light."

"These should suffice," the lieutenant agreed.

"How are you going to do this?" Abby wondered.

Vladimir appeared annoyed. It was not the first time the doctor had insisted on an explanation of the most basic, technical procedure. "We will connect the transfer trunks to the cells, positioned on either side. Then we will use the REMS-poles to push the plugs at the free ends of the trunks into each of the ZPED junction blocks, all from a safe distance."

"How long are these poles?" Master Chief Montrose wondered.

"Four meters."

"I would not call that a safe distance," the master chief stated.

"Did I say safe? I meant safer," Vladimir admitted.

"What is to prevent the electrostatic energy from transferring through the poles?" Lieutenant Montgomery asked.

"REMS-poles are used to remotely manipulate EM field emitters within the outer containment bottle on the antimatter reactors," Vladimir explained. "They are designed to prevent the electrostatic energy from reaching the handler at the far end."

"How do they accomplish that?"

"We do not have time for a REMS-pole mechanics lecture." Vladimir smiled. "Trust me; they will work."

The ship shook again as another piece of debris struck the hull. Caught unexpectedly, the violent motion nearly toppled the Takaran lieutenant. "I trust you," he insisted.

Several men pushed two carts carrying energy cells larger than themselves into the room. "One on each side," Vladimir instructed. The men maneuvered the carts into position and prepared to unload them. "Leave them on the carts," Vladimir insisted. "It will take too long to unload them."

"They should be grounded to the deck," one of the jump drive technicians said.

"In the locker behind you," Vladimir said, "connect one end to the ground terminal on the cell. Strip the other end bare and wedge it between the deck plates to secure it. That should be enough."

The jump drive technician looked at Doctor Sorenson for some sort of a visual cue that it was all right to do as the Cheng had ordered. "What are you waiting for?" she asked him.

As the jump drive technicians began grounding the cells, the Corinairan engineers connected the energy transfer trunks to the cells in preparation for connecting them to the ZPEDs. As one of the technicians attempted to push the massive plug into the side of the cell, another piece of debris struck the hull, shaking the ship and knocking him over.

"I don't suppose there is anything we can do about that," Master Chief Montrose wondered aloud as he helped the technician back to his feet to continue his work, "like perhaps increasing power to the inertial dampeners?"

"They cannot spare the power," Abby warned. "We would risk slipping closer to the event horizon."

"Pity," the master chief exclaimed, "as all this shaking is not helping matters."

Another impact shook the ship, forcing Abby to grab the control pedestal to steady herself.

"The cells are grounded, Doctor," one of the jump drive technicians reported.

"Good, clear the room," she instructed the four technicians.

"We have prepared the junctions," one of the Corinairan engineers informed Vladimir. "We are ready to connect the drain trunks to the ZPEDs."

"Position the REMS-poles," Vladimir ordered. Several Corinairan engineers scrambled to unfold the tripods used to steady the REMS-poles. They placed them in position about two meters away from each of the ZPED junctions, coming from opposite sides of the room so as not to interfere with one another. Two men on each side placed the REMS-poles on top of the tripods, securing the poles to the mounting heads on top, while another man checked that the legs of the tripod were connected firmly to the deck plates.

"Do as I do," Vladimir ordered the team on the other REMS-pole. He picked up the control box for his REMS-pole while two Corinairan technicians took hold of the distal end of the pole and began moving it, raising the other end up off the deck. The pole was well balanced and easy to manipulate, even with the ship being tossed about by frequent debris impacts. As the end nearest the plug raised up off the deck, Vladimir manipulated the clamps on the end of the pole with his remote.

"Cheng, Captain," Nathan called over the comms.

"Gospadee!" Vladimir exclaimed in annoyance. "What is it, Nathan?"

"If we're going to have enough propellant to get home, we're going to need to wrap this up sooner rather than later. How's it going down there?"

"Soon, Nathan, soon."

"What's taking so long?"

"Would you like me to talk or work?" Vladimir snapped. He suddenly remembered that everyone was listening to him and that, despite the fact that the man he was speaking with was his best friend, he was also the captain of the ship. He quickly added, "Sir."

"Carry on," Nathan answered before closing the channel. Vladimir knew he would catch an earful from the XO later. He shrugged it off and continued his work. "Are you ready?" he asked the other team. They indicated their readiness to proceed by nodding. "Okay then. We must connect both ZPEDs to their respective energy cells at the same time, da?" he asked, looking to Lieutenant Montgomery.

"That is correct," the lieutenant confirmed, "or you risk knocking them out of phase with one another. They must remain in phase for both to be connected to the main power grid."

"Understood." Vladimir looked at the Corinairan technician manning the remote on the other REMS-pole. The man nodded back to Vladimir, indicating he, too, understood the situation. "Move the pole heads to the plugs," he instructed as he remotely opened the clamps at the end of his pole. The two men manipulating the REMS-pole slid it forward in its mount, pushing the claw at the far end up against the plug lying on the deck. Vladimir activated the clamps, taking a firm hold on the plug itself. "Clamps secured," he announced. He looked at the other operator who nodded that he had also completed the same step. "Lift the plug."

The two men manipulating Vladimir's REMS-pole slowly lowered their end, causing the other end to lift the plug off the floor. The servos in the REMS-pole kicked in, humming as they exerted additional lifting force to compensate for the weight of the plug and the heavy trunk line connected to it.

"Activating field opposition," Vladimir announced as he pressed the button on the remote. "Advancing the plug."

The men again moved the arm, sliding it farther forward. The ship shook again as another piece of debris struck the hull. The men stopped their advance momentarily as they steadied themselves.

"*Chort,*" Vladimir cursed under his breath. "Forward," he urged.

The men continued advancing the pole, moving the plug closer to the receptacle on their ZPED's junction box.

"One hundred centimeters," Vladimir reported as they continued to advance the plug. He glanced at the other remote operator. The man was concentrating on his display as well. Vladimir assumed that he was matching their rate of advance centimeter for centimeter as best he could. "Seventy-five centimeters," he continued. "Fifty..."

A loud pop accompanied a blue-green arc of electrical energy jumped from each of the ZPED's junction boxes to the poles on the plugs that dangled from the end of the REMS-poles.

"*BLIN!*" Vladimir looked at Lieutenant Montgomery, his eyes wide with fear and uncertainty.

"It is all right!" the lieutenant declared. "The energy jumped, and the connection was made when you closed within fifty centimeters! This was to be expected!"

"It was?" Vladimir exclaimed. "Thank you very much for warning me!"

"I apologize," the lieutenant told him. "You are now connected and in phase."

Vladimir looked over at the technician near the energy cell on his side of the room. The technician checked the indicators on the cell, then turned back and nodded at Vladimir.

"*Gospadee*," Vladimir mumbled as he regained his composure. "Continue advancing and make contact," he ordered.

The men continued sliding the pole forward, moving the plug all the way up to the socket and slowly inserting it into its receptacle on the ZPED's junction box as the blue-green energy sparked and jumped about.

The ship shuddered from another, even larger impact, knocking Vladimir to the floor. One of the technicians manipulating Vladimir's REMS-pole also lost his footing and fell into the pole, knocking the technician on the other side over and away from him. The clamps on the end of his pole broke free from the force of the suddenly shifting pole and slid across the top of the partially inserted plug, making contact with the edge of the receptacle. Blue-green energy leapt up the pole, blowing past the limiters at the tripod mounting head with ease and finding the technician still clinging to the pole for balance. A gurgled cry of pain erupted from the man's mouth as the massive amount of energy generated by the idling ZPED surged through his body. Had most of the energy not been channeled directly to the energy cell, the technician's body would have been instantly vaporized. Instead, he stood there frozen, clinging to the electrically charged pole and unable to release his grip.

The remote control exploded in a shower of sparks in Vladimir's hands as he quickly released it. He looked at the technician not more than a meter in front of him, his face frozen in pain and terror. "*Bozhe moi.*"

"We must free him!" one of the Takarans exclaimed as he charged toward the frozen man.

"NYET!" Vladimir cried out, but it was too late.

The Takaran ran at the Corinairan technician, momentarily adding himself to the conductive circuit and knocking the Corinairan free from his death grip on the electrified REMS-pole. There was a flash of blue-green light as the Takaran made contact and the energy invaded his body as well. A moment later, both men lay on the floor just beyond the smoking remote control unit that Vladimir had dropped. Faint smoke lingered around them, slowly rising from their bodies.

Vladimir scrambled to his feet to help the injured men, his face recoiling in disgust at the smell of burnt flesh.

"Medical emergency in the ZPED room!" Master Chief Montrose called over his comm-set. "Two men down! Repeat! Medical emergency in the ZPED room. Two men down!"

"The plug!" Lieutenant Montgomery yelled. "It is not inserted all the way."

Vladimir stopped and looked at the plug, then at the bodies of the two men as others rushed to their sides. He looked back at the lieutenant, his eyes pleading as the ship was rocked by another impact.

"If that plug falls out and is knocked beyond fifty centimeters, the ZPEDs will be out of phase!"

"Quickly!" Vladimir ordered the other REMS-pole team. "Move over here! We must secure that plug!"

"Med teams two and four are en route!" the damage control officer's voice reported over the master chief's comm-set. *"ETA two."*

"We must be quick!" Lieutenant Montgomery urged. "We only have a few minutes before the energy cells will be filled to capacity and the transfer trunk will again be too dangerous to handle."

Abby and the other members of her jump drive team rushed to the sides of the fallen men.

"Turn them over," Abby ordered, her voice calm. "Get them on their backs and remove their shirts." She turned to the technician nearest her. "Go to the next compartment and get the med-pack." She moved to the wall as the man left the compartment and took the med-pack for that compartment off its wall mounts. She dropped it on the floor beside the injured Takaran. As the others finished removing his shirt, she quickly opened the box, pulled out a small device, and placed it on the floor next to him. She then pulled the two leads out, stuck them onto the Takaran man's chest, and activated the unit. *"Analyzing. Analyzing,"* the mechanical voice announced as she checked the man's neck for a pulse. *"Stand clear. Stand clear."* Abby pushed a button on the device. *"Shocking."* The Takaran's body twitched slightly as the device delivered a precise electrical stimulus intended to restart his heart.

"Buistra!" Vladimir urged his engineers as they detached the REMS-pole tripod from the deck.

"Move, move, move!" he added as the four of them picked up the entire apparatus in one piece and carried it across the room. Two other technicians disconnected and removed the damaged REMS-pole and tripod.

The other jump drive technician rolled the injured Corinairan over. He gasped at the sight of the man's charred face and hands. "Oh, God!" he said, recoiling from the sight.

"Get his shirt off!" Abby ordered as the other technician returned with the med-pack from the next compartment.

"*Analyzing. Analyzing,*" the device connected to the Takaran again instructed. "*Stand clear. Stand clear.*" Abby pressed the button again. "*Shocking.*" Again the Takaran's body twitched.

"Do you know what to do?" Abby asked the other technician.

The man was already pulling the leads out of the device from the second med-pack. "I know! I know!" he exclaimed as he attached the leads to the Corinairan's burnt chest. He activated the unit.

"Reconnect the tripod to the deck," Vladimir ordered as he switched on the power for the second REMS-pole using its remote. Two of the technicians scrambled to secure the feet of the tripod as the other two began moving the head of the pole into position.

The ship shook as another chunk of the debris being pulled toward the black hole's event horizon struck the hull of the ship. The tripod began to topple over as one of the technicians scrambled to keep it upright until it could be secured to the deck.

Lieutenant Montgomery had his eyes fixed on the massive, half-inserted plug as it nearly fell out of its socket while the ship bounced. "It is coming out!" he cried. If it fell to the floor, the plug would be more than fifty centimeters from the socket, and the energy transfer would cease, taking the two ZPEDs out of phase and forcing them to shut down. If that happened, he doubted they would be able to get them restarted.

"*Analyzing. Analyzing,*" the cardio unit attached to the injured Corinairan technician announced.

"Come on!" the jump drive technician tending to the injured man yelled impatiently.

"*No shock indicated.*"

The jump drive technician's face sank.

"*Analyzing. Analyzing,*" Abby's device reported. "*Stand clear. Stand clear.*"

Abby pushed the button one last time.

"*Shocking,*" the device reported a third time. The Takaran's body twitched once more.

"*Analyzing. Analyzing,*" the device announced. "*No shock indicated. Begin resuscitation efforts.*"

"Pokkers!" Abby swore in her native tongue as she bent over the Takaran's face.

"The tripod is secure," one of the technicians announced.

"Advance the pole!" Vladimir ordered. He looked about the room, praying that the ship stayed steady. Another bounce at the wrong moment could end their efforts and, in essence, all their lives. He watched the monitor on the remote as the two technicians steadied the pole on the tripod. Vladimir adjusted the claws on the end of the pole, raising them slightly in order to line them up. His fingers ached, their tips burnt by the electrical current that had transferred through to his remote when the first REMS-pole made contact with the ZPEDs output socket. He could barely feel the controls on the remote. "Forward, slowly, slowly..." The ship bounced again as another piece of debris struck the hull. "*Gospadee!*" He looked around again, then checked the alignment on his screen. It was still good. "Forward," he prodded his men on the pole.

Abby adjusted the injured Takaran's head, pulling his chin upward to open his airway and pressed her lips around his open mouth, blowing forcefully into his lungs. She watched as his chest rose and fell with each breath, turning her head away momentarily as she filled her own lungs with fresh air between each rescue breath. After three breaths, she moved over and began chest compressions, her arms rigid and her hands locked over one another as she rocked downward. "Start resuscitation!" she ordered the technician operating the device connected to the Corinairan man.

"But the cardio unit said..."

"I don't care what it said! Start resuscitation!"

"Yes, ma'am," the technician responded as he moved to the head of the injured Corinairan to deliver rescue breaths.

"Contact!" Vladimir declared as the clamps touched the plug. He squeezed the trigger on the remote's control stick, causing the clamps at the end of the pole to close tightly on the plug. He paused as the ship violently shook again, then ordered, "Push!"

The two technicians slid the pole forward a bit more, pushing the massive plug firmly into the ZPEDs output socket. Vladimir twisted the control stick, causing the clamp to rotate the plug, locking it in place. "It's in!" he announced as he released the clamps. "Withdraw the pole quickly!"

After another round of chest compressions, Abby

121

repeated the rescue breaths once more. As she returned to the Takaran man's chest to continue with another round of compressions, she looked over her shoulder at Vladimir as he and his team retracted the REMS-pole and shut it down.

With both energy cells securely connected and drawing most of the idling ZPEDs power away, Vladimir and his men scrambled to quickly connect the ZPEDs to the ship's main power grid before they ran out of time. It would take only a few minutes for the energy cells to become fully charged, after which they would no longer be pulling energy away from the ZPEDs and their transfer trunk lines. If the transfer trunk line became fully charged before they were clear, there would be more dead men lying on the deck.

"ZPED room, Captain! Report!" Nathan's voice called over the comm-set. His hails repeated several times but continued to go unanswered.

The first medical team arrived and immediately relieved Abby of her resuscitative efforts. A minute later, the second medical team arrived and began their assessment of the severely burnt Corinairan man. It took them less than a minute to determine that there was nothing they could do for the man, and they joined the first team in their efforts to save the Takaran.

Abby leaned back against the wall, slowly sliding down until she was in a sitting position on the floor, her arms wrapped around her legs as she watched the medical teams work.

"What the hell is going on down there?" Nathan wondered.

"I'm sure they're busy," Cameron said.

"Naralena, have the med teams reported in?"

"Only that they were on scene, sir," Naralena answered.

"How much time do we have until we no longer have enough propellant to get home?" Nathan asked.

"Ten minutes, sir."

"Technically, if we steer a straight line for Sol, we could just do one short burn and jump along that line all the way home," Cameron said.

"No maneuvering? No course adjustments to steer around black holes or God knows what else?" Nathan said. "What are the odds that would work?"

"Pretty much zero, I suppose," Cameron agreed as she steadied herself against the force of another impact.

"*Captain, Cheng!*" Vladimir called over the comms.

"Go for Captain!" Nathan answered.

"*ZPEDs are hooked in and ready to go. Doctor Sorenson is ready to begin throttling up their output as needed.*"

"Outstanding!" Nathan exclaimed. "One percent at a time, if you please. I don't want to run them any higher than necessary to get out of here. No use in taking any chances," he added, looking at Cameron and smiling.

"*Da, da, da,*" Vladimir answered. "*Starting at one percent.*"

"Loki, channel that extra energy into the mains," Nathan ordered.

"Aye, sir. Channeling ZPED power into the mains."

"Anything?" Nathan asked. The ship shook again. Loki stared at his console for several seconds, waiting for an indication in the change of their rate of separation from the black hole's event horizon. "It's helping," he reported with some degree of hesitation. "Barely, but it's helping. I think it's going to take a bit more than one percent, though."

Nathan looked at Cameron. "Sometimes, you just have to take a chance, Commander."

Cameron smiled slightly.

"Vlad, take the ZPEDs to ten percent and stand by."

CHAPTER FOUR

"Our preliminary analysis indicates that we were somehow pulled off course during our last jump by the black hole's gravity," Abby said. She looked about at the faces gathered around the conference table in the command briefing room.

"How is that possible?" Nathan asked. "Our jump plot should have taken us well beyond the reach of that gravity well."

"Yes, you are correct; it should have," Abby admitted.

"Even now, we're considerably closer to the black hole than our original jump plot would've taken us," Cameron added.

"It appears that our jump drive is somehow attracted to massive gravity wells," Abby said. "A ship traveling in normal linear fashion would not have been affected by the black hole's gravity well, at least not when following the course we had plotted. However, somehow, our jump drive interacts with relatively nearby gravity wells, creating an attraction... one that can literally curve our jump path toward the gravity well pulling at us."

"How does that work?" Nathan asked.

"As you know, we still do not fully understand how the jump drive works." Abby thought for a moment, in obvious frustration, not only at the task of trying to explain complex physics to laypersons, but also at the fact that she herself did not fully understand the physics involved. "Imagine you have a powerful electromagnet. An object composed of a magnetic material, if placed close enough to the electromagnet, will be pulled toward it. However, if placed a sufficient distance away, the object will be unaffected. Now, instead of a simple magnetic object, place another powerful electromagnet at the same distance. The attractive force created by both electromagnets together is enough to overcome that same distance, thus drawing the two objects together."

"But we've been around large gravity wells before," Nathan said.

"In comparison to even a small, stellar mass black hole like the one we just escaped, anything we have encountered previously has been insignificant. Except for one."

"Which was?" Nathan wondered, a little annoyed that he had to ask.

"The Campaglia."

"The Campaglia was a ship, Doctor. I'm pretty sure she did not carry a significant gravity well about her," Cameron argued.

"The Campaglia's ZPED was massive compared to the miniature versions we have been experimenting with. If you remember, during testing of the hybrid jump drive concept, we experienced an effect that simulated that of a massive gravity well, even at relatively low outputs."

"The problems with the artificial gravity plating in the decks around the mini-ZPEDs," Vladimir added.

"Yes. Although the devices do not actually produce gravity, they have a similar attractive effect. This is why they caused problems with our jump drive."

"That's why we jumped into the middle of that battle?" Nathan asked.

"All the evidence seems to indicate such, Captain," Abby admitted. "The act of passing through the Campaglia's outer shields caused our jump fields to fail. Had they not done so, we would have collided with the Campaglia at unimaginable speeds."

"Then we just have to avoid black holes," Nathan said.

"Captain, there are thousands of stellar mass black holes out there," Lieutenant Yosef stated. "We only know the location of a handful of them."

"How many of those are between us and Sol?" Nathan asked.

"None, that we know of, that is. But we didn't know about the last one, either, and that's the point," Yosef said.

"Perhaps we should be looking for them along our course?" Cameron suggested.

"We were, sir," the lieutenant defended. "But we're looking forward from light years away. When a star collapses, a stellar mass black hole can form in an instant. The one that we just encountered could have formed years ago, or minutes ago."

"So you believe that it was the result of a collapsed star?" Cameron asked.

"That would explain the debris," Nathan said. "It would've broken up whatever planets were in orbit and sucked them in."

"I believe it was a system designated as B157-12087 in the fleet star catalog," Lieutenant Yosef stated.

"How do you know?" Nathan asked.

"Because it's not there, sir, and the black hole is.

That singularity is right where B157-12087 should be. Now there's just a black hole and a lot of debris."

Nathan took a deep breath. "So, now we have to try to avoid black holes, possibly ones that we don't even know of."

"We could adjust our course in an attempt to keep as much space between us and any system that we know has the potential to form a black hole," Abby suggested.

"I doubt that's going to make much of a difference," Nathan stated.

"Not to mention that it's bound to take longer," Lieutenant Yosef added.

"We have another matter to consider, Captain," Cameron said. "Propellant. We used more than three-quarters of it escaping the black hole. We have enough to get home as long as we keep our maneuvering, acceleration, and deceleration to a minimum. However if we run into a similar situation..."

"We won't have enough propellant to escape a second time," Nathan said, finishing her sentence for her. "We need to find more propellant. We have processing facilities on board, don't we?"

"No, sir. They were not installed prior to departure. The systems weren't even loaded. I guess Fleet didn't consider that aspect of our design as a priority."

"Any chance we can fabricate the components needed to rig something up ourselves?"

"Assuming you have all the specifications in your database, it is possible," Lieutenant Montgomery stated. "However, it would take some time, probably more time than it would take to get back to Earth."

"Not a lot of options, here," Nathan sighed. "How

far are we from reaching the fringe?"

"Based on the state of the core and fringe worlds of Earth at the time that the Data Ark was sealed up to protect it against the bio-digital plague, we should reach the outermost edges of the fringe in about ten to twelve jumps," Cameron reported.

"Maybe one of those worlds can spare some propellant," Nathan said.

"That's a really big maybe, sir," Cameron stated. "We have no idea if any of those outer worlds survived. Even if they did, are they controlled by the Jung? Do they have a compatible propellant? Are they willing to provide us with a significant amount? How are we to pay them?"

"I get the point, Commander. It's a long shot at best."

"I have another idea," Abby said. "It won't solve the problem, but it might extend the potential range of our current propellant stores."

"I'm all ears, Doctor," Nathan said as he looked across the briefing table at her.

"We could use the ZPEDs to achieve greater acceleration with smaller amounts of propellant."

"That might work," Vladimir agreed, sitting forward in interest.

"Does anyone have any objections to this idea?" Nathan asked the others in attendance. Nathan leaned back in his chair for a moment, contemplating his options as he waited for opposition from his staff. "Very well, Cheng, use the ZPEDs to get maximum thrust at minimal propellant cost."

"Yes, sir," Vladimir responded.

"Captain," Cameron said, "we should be careful not to use up too much propellant during the rest of our journey, if possible. We will need the propellant when we reach Sol."

"At that point, if we're out of propellant, I'm sure Fleet can send us a bit more to get us safely into port," Nathan commented with a smile. "Lieutenant Yosef, while you keep an eye out for black holes and other threatening anomalies, also look for signs of civilization. Maybe we'll get lucky and find someone willing to top us off."

"Yes, Captain," Lieutenant Yosef responded.

"Even if we make contact with another civilization," Cameron said, "we risk using valuable propellant just making orbit to investigate."

"Point taken, Commander," Nathan said. "However, it won't cost us any propellant to keep our eyes and ears open."

"I'm only saying that it might not be worth the course change."

"We'll make that decision if and when the time comes, Commander."

"Of course, sir."

"Lieutenant Montgomery," Nathan said as he turned toward the Takaran lieutenant sitting at the far end of the table, "go ahead and work out the details of creating our own propellant production capabilities. I'd like to know for sure if it's even an option. We're still a long way from Earth. Who knows what might happen along the way?"

* * *

Nathan sat in his ready room, studying his daily reports. It had been two days since they had escaped the black hole at B157-12087, and after five jumps, Nathan was beginning to relax a bit. Vladimir had incorporated the additional power created by the mini-ZPEDs into the ship's propulsion and maneuvering systems, which had improved their potential energy to maneuver the ship. Nathan still preferred to locate another source of propellant if possible. Having little room for maneuvering one's way out of an emergency was an unpleasant position in which to be.

"Captain?" Commander Taylor called from the open hatchway.

"Commander," Nathan responded. "What's up?"

"Lieutenant Montgomery would like to speak with you," she stated as she entered the ready room.

"Bring him in," Nathan urged.

The commander turned around and signaled for the lieutenant to enter.

"Lieutenant Montgomery," Nathan greeted. "My condolences on the loss of your fellow countryman."

The lieutenant looked slightly confused by the captain's terminology but surmised its meaning nonetheless. "Thank you, Captain. We appreciated your kind words at the memorial service."

"They were both fine men who gave their lives for this ship. As a captain, I cannot ask for more than that."

"They were both volunteers," the lieutenant stated. "I believe they both died serving a cause they believed in, as do we all."

"How can I help you?" Nathan asked, changing the subject as he motioned for the lieutenant and the commander to be seated.

"You asked me to investigate the possibility of creating onboard propellant production capabilities."

"Indeed I did. What have you learned?"

"As I originally suspected, it is not a small undertaking. Even using our more advanced systems

131

rather than those detailed in your database, it would take time and a great deal of effort. It simply is not an alternative given the amount of time available."

"You didn't need a personal meeting with me to tell me that it can't be done, Lieutenant," Nathan stated with suspicion. "Was there something else?"

"Yes, sir. While I was investigating the viability of onboard propellant processing, I took notice of some other systems on the Aurora that I believe we could improve upon using Takaran technologies."

"Such as?"

"As you know, we cannot provide you with shields that would not interfere with your jump drive fields as well."

"Yes, that's why we chose not to delay our departure in order to install the shield emitter arrays," Nathan told him.

"We could begin the installation process during our recharge layovers," the lieutenant suggested, "the same way that we upgraded the secondary jump field emitter array... using the crawlers."

"Wouldn't that take considerable time as well?" Nathan wondered.

"Yes, it would. However, we could do it a section at a time. Perhaps if we concentrated our efforts on strategic locations, such as the bow..."

"An interesting idea," Nathan admitted.

"There's more," Cameron said.

"There are two other projects that you might be interested in, sir. We could replace your missile battery with a plasma cannon. It would be similar to but smaller than those that defended Answari."

"Aren't they relatively short-range weapons?" Nathan asked.

"Correct. Their effective range is only about five

hundred kilometers. Beyond that the bursts begin to dissipate. However, their destructive power is far superior to that of ship-to-ship missiles."

"Then why don't Takaran warships use them?"

"Because they wouldn't be able to get in close enough," Cameron added, "not with everyone else using long-range missiles."

"Like taking a knife to a gun fight," Nathan said.

"Exactly," Cameron agreed. "Getting in close is our biggest strength."

"A plasma cannon, when used at the ranges that the Aurora regularly employs, would be quite formidable," Lieutenant Montgomery said.

"We wouldn't have to worry about running out of ammunition, either," Cameron added, "and plasma shots can't be taken out with point-defense systems."

"But they can be repelled with shields," Nathan said.

"To some extent, yes," the lieutenant explained. "However, if targeted directly at the location of the shield emitters, repeated fire can quickly overheat the emitters and cause failure, thus weakening the shield. Take out several shield emitters within close proximity to one another and you can collapse an entire segment of the enemy's shields."

"I think it's a good idea," Cameron said.

"What about the power requirements?" Nathan wondered.

"A single mini-ZPED would produce more than enough energy to power the weapon."

"How long would it take to make the change?"

"The entire conversion can be done within the pressurized compartment that houses the missile battery. The weapon itself can be fabricated within a week and installed within a day, assuming the missile battery has already been removed while the weapon is being fabricated."

"Could the weapon be mounted externally on the hull instead of replacing the missile battery?" Nathan asked.

"Yes, sir. However, leaving it out in the open during transit greatly decreases its operational lifetime."

"Same reason all our weapons are made to retract when not in use," Cameron said.

"I'm hesitant to take a working weapons system offline in order to experiment with a new one, even if it is more formidable." Nathan looked to Cameron, his XO. "Commander, I'm assuming you and the lieutenant have had a lengthy conversation about this idea?"

"Yes, Captain," Cameron answered confidently. "Risks, resources, personnel, the usual. I believe it is an interesting idea, in concept. However, I, too, would prefer not to trade in one weapons system for another. Perhaps we could fabricate the weapon, then mount it externally for testing purposes prior to using it to replace the missile battery. After all, we still have a full load of missiles. I see no reason to take them out of our arsenal."

"Good idea, Commander," Nathan agreed. "Would that be possible?" he asked the lieutenant.

"I'll speak to Lieutenant Commander Kamenetskiy. I am certain he will have an idea of where to mount the weapon."

"Very good. You may begin fabrication," Nathan said.

"Yes, sir."

"You said you had two ideas?" Nathan asked.

"Your torpedo tubes," the lieutenant continued,

"they could easily be converted to fire energy plasma shots as well. Although they would be at the disadvantage of having to fire along the same line as the ship is pointed, their destructive force would be easily one hundred times that of a plasma cannon shot. In addition, you could convert only one or two of your six torpedo tubes to fire plasma shots, leaving the other tubes to fire your existing torpedoes."

"What would the range be?" Nathan asked.

"At least that of the plasma cannon," the lieutenant promised.

"That's still better than our current torpedoes," Cameron said.

"Not much," Nathan said. "After all, most of our torpedoes are armed with nukes."

"But they do not travel at the speed of light," the lieutenant added with a smile.

Nathan smiled back. "Tubes two, four, and six, Lieutenant Montgomery. They're all yours."

* * *

"Still nothing, Mister Navashee?" Nathan asked as he strolled around the bridge.

"No, sir. Sorry," the sensor operator answered.

"We're only six or seven jumps from the outer edges of the fringe," Nathan said. "That's less than one hundred light years. You would think we'd find somebody this close to home."

"The files in the Data Ark only indicated that people were fleeing the core worlds to escape the plague," Cameron said. "They didn't say how far out they went."

"The Takarans were a thousand light years out."

"Perhaps they were the exception rather than the rule," Cameron suggested.

"Perhaps. One thousand light years is a long journey, even for sleeper ships. What was the top speed back then?"

"About five times light for a cargo ship, I believe."

"It would've taken them a couple hundred years to get that far out. You're probably right, Commander. Still, I expected to find someone by now."

"It could just be our course," Cameron said. "A few degrees in any direction could yield entirely different results."

"Doubtful, sir," Mister Navashee corrected. "We'd still pick up their emissions. They would be weak and difficult to pick out of the background radiation, but they would still be discernible."

"Point is we might just be traveling through the most sparsely populated region beyond the fringe," Cameron said.

"Mister Riley, are we ready to jump yet?"

"We'll be fully recharged and ready for jump fifty-two in one minute, sir," Mister Riley, the B-shift navigator, reported.

"Look at it this way, Captain," Cameron said, "if we don't run into anyone on our way home, we probably won't run into any trouble either."

"Jump drive is fully recharged, Captain," Mister Riley reported. "Jump fifty-two plotted and locked."

"Execute jump fifty-two," Nathan ordered.

"Transferring helm to auto-nav," Mister Chiles, the helmsman, reported.

Nathan sat back in the command chair and waited as the jump drive's automatic navigation system programmed by the Takarans took over the helm of the Aurora and made subtle adjustments to her course and speed in order to execute the jump at a precise point in space, on an exact course, and at an exact speed. The difference in the result of the accuracy of the jumps was substantial, especially at their new maximum operable range of fifteen light years. Nathan still insisted that all jumps be limited to fourteen light years, preferring to keep a little energy left in the jump drive for an emergency escape jump, which was usually pre-calculated prior to each jump.

"Jumping in three......two......one......jump." As Mister Riley announced the jump, the bridge filled momentarily with the blue-white flash as the two fields formed and collapsed into one another, causing the Aurora to transition instantly from one point in space to another, fourteen light years away. The entire process happened in less than a second, always culminating in the same blue-white flash of light that was automatically subdued by the ship's view screen. Nathan had long ago grown weary of the exterior view of the seemingly motionless stars offered by the viewer, finding no appreciable use for the display. The only reason he left the exterior view up during the jump was for the psychological confirmation that it seemed to have on his crew. Anyone who witnessed the act of jumping was awestruck. Even after seeing it dozens upon dozens of times, he, too, never ceased to be amazed by it.

"Jump fifty-two complete," Mister Riley reported. "Beginning recharge cycle."

"Position verified," Mister Navashee announced. "Beginning long-range scans."

"Your shift doesn't actually start for another thirty minutes, Captain," Cameron said. "You might as well get something to eat before you start your day."

"I already ate," Nathan told her. "I got up early and worked out before breakfast. Doctor Chen says I'm out of shape, that I've put on a few pounds. I didn't last as long in the gym as I thought I would. I guess the doc was right."

"It's all that meat," Cameron told him. "But don't feel bad. Doctor Chen told me that much of the crew has put on a few pounds. I think it is the Corinairan food everyone is eating. It's designed for a Corinairan lifestyle, which is far more physical than life aboard a starship."

"Perhaps you should institute mandatory physical training," Nathan suggested. "Maybe ask Jessica to put together a program for the crew."

"I'll speak to the master chief about it," Cameron said. "I'm sure the Corinari had considerable PT."

"Good idea," he said. "You know, you can take off early if you'd like."

"That's all right. I intend to have a few words with Mister Hayes when he comes on duty."

"Has Josh been a bad boy?" He knew that not a day went by that the Aurora's lead helmsman didn't do something to irritate the XO.

"Nothing big, just the usual tug on the leash of an overly exuberant puppy," the commander stated with a determined smile.

"I think I'll skip that show," Nathan said as he stood. "Perhaps I'll take a walk around the ship before I officially start my shift. That qualifies as exercise, doesn't it?"

"In some circles, I suppose."

* * *

"Jump fifty-three complete," Loki reported. "Beginning recharge cycle."

"Position verified," Lieutenant Yosef announced. "Beginning long-range scans."

"Tactical, set the deck green," Nathan ordered.

"Green deck, aye," Jessica answered smartly.

"Tell me again why you're here?" Nathan asked as he rose from his command chair and turned to walk toward his ready room at the aft end of the bridge.

"We only have two other tactical officers," Jessica said.

"That's why we're all working twelve-hour shifts, Lieutenant Commander," Nathan reminded her.

"Yes, and it wears on a person," Jessica said. "I like to give them a day off once in a while."

"You're just bored. I saw you playing around with the console just before the jump," he teased.

"I wasn't playing around, sir. I was running tactical simulations using a plasma cannon and plasma torpedoes as part of the arsenal. I got the specs from Lieutenant Montgomery."

"Oh, really?"

"You'd be surprised at the results I'm getting," Jessica stated. "If those plasma shots are half as powerful as Montgomery claims, we could do some serious damage to Jung ships. You might want to reconsider replacing the missile turret."

"Yeah, I saw the results of your simulations from the ready room," Nathan said. Jessica looked surprised. "Hey, the captain sees everything. Anyway, I was talking to Vlad about the idea. He thinks we could convert all three science labs into cannon bays. They were designed to hold stellar observation equipment and the like. They've even got working retractable ceilings and outer hull doors. Vlad thinks it would be possible to adapt the lift system to work with the Takaran cannon design. The hard part is routing sufficient power to them. The power trunks to those sections can't handle the amounts of energy needed to run those guns. We'd have to run new lines. There's also the problem of heat dissipation. Those lines will get hot during combat."

"A lot of work, then," Jessica said.

"According to Vlad, yes. But it would give us three plasma cannons, each with independent targeting systems."

"I'll volunteer to pull cable through the access tunnels," Jessica stated, "if it means we get three of those plasma cannons."

"Careful what you wish for, Lieutenant Commander. According to Vlad, those tunnels are awfully dirty."

"What's a little dirt?"

"Flight Ops reports they're launching a training flight of eight Talons, Captain," Naralena reported.

"Understood," Nathan said. "I'll be in my ready room, Lieutenant Commander," he told Jessica. "You have the..."

"Captain," Lieutenant Yosef interrupted, "I'm picking up a signal."

"What is it?" Nathan wondered.

"It's organized, in patterns," the lieutenant explained. "Very faint, but definitely manmade." Lieutenant Yosef turned to face the captain. "I think it's a comm signal, Captain."

"From who?"

"Unknown. I can't make it out. The signal keeps dropping in and out, mixing in with background radiation and other stellar noise. It might be a beacon, maybe an automated one."

"Is it in motion?"

"Also unknown," the lieutenant told him. "I'll need to gather more of the signal before I can tell you anything further."

"How long will that take?"

"Thirty minutes, maybe?" the lieutenant guessed. "It depends on how much interference the background stellar noise causes."

"Naralena, wake up the XO. Tell her to report to the bridge in thirty minutes."

"Aye, sir."

"Can you tell where it's coming from?" Nathan asked Lieutenant Yosef.

"Yes, sir, sending location to tactical."

Nathan moved closer to Jessica, watching as the tactical display quickly plotted the location of the signal source.

"System designation is BD+25 3252. It's about six light years away from our current position," Jessica noted. "Thirty-two degrees starboard of our course, eleven up relative."

"A single jump," Nathan contemplated.

"Database shows it as an F-eight star: six gas giants with a lot of moons," Jessica said. "Also two rocky planets, one listed as potentially habitable. According to the Data Ark, it was never colonized."

"Yeah, I wouldn't think so," Nathan said. "We're still too far out. Even the fringe worlds weren't more than thirty-five to forty light years from Sol."

Jessica looked at the captain. He could tell by the look in her eyes that she was hoping he would order them to investigate. Other than their near fatal jump near the event horizon, the process of jumping their way back home had been uneventful. For his security chief, the occasional dispute between Corinairan and Takaran crew members had been the only source of excitement. He was sure the only reason she was on the bridge was to break up the monotony of her daily routine.

"Mister Sheehan," Nathan began, "plot a course for that signal…"

"Yes," Jessica whispered to herself.

"I want propellant consumption reports for a hop to that signal, and then back on a course for Sol. Give me two possible profiles: one for deceleration to an orbit around an average moon orbiting a gas giant, and another for a full stellar orbit at approximately two hundred million kilometers. I want to know how much propellant we're likely to use by investigating the signal." Nathan looked at Jessica. "I'll consider going if the numbers are right *and* if Lieutenant Yosef can figure out exactly what that signal is." Nathan turned and headed for his ready room. "You've got thirty minutes, people."

* * *

"According to the files from the Data Ark, the star was part of a search for potentially habitable worlds," Nathan explained from behind his desk. "It was on the list of worlds to be further studied to determine habitability."

"Yes, I read up on it on the way," Cameron told him, holding up her data pad. "An F-eight, ninety-seven point two light years from Earth. Six gas giants, two rocky inner worlds, one in the system's habitable zone." She looked at him as she took a seat, noticing the intrigue on his face. "You want to go, don't you?" She rolled her eyes. "Why?"

"Yosef thinks it's a ship or a satellite of some kind," Nathan said.

"Thinks?"

"The signal is still pretty broken up. There's a Doppler component to the signal as well. Yosef believes it—whatever *it* is—is orbiting a planet approximately one point four Earth masses."

"How many hours until we could jump there?"

"About two and a half to jump. Seven to a full charge."

"Have you looked at the propellant consumption data yet?" she asked.

"Minimal for pre- and post-jump course corrections. A little more than I'd like, *if* we end up parking in a stellar orbit in the target system. I had Loki plot a coast-through course. That way, if we find nothing of interest, we won't waste any additional propellant putting ourselves on station."

"Well, it's too far beyond the fringe to be a Jung-occupied world, at least according to Fleet's limited intelligence," Cameron said. "So why bother wasting any propellant at all?"

"It's not like we don't have enough, Commander."

"I know. I just don't like the idea of waste," Cameron said. "So what do you expect to find?"

"I don't know. Another colony founded by people who escaped the plague a thousand years ago?" He grinned. "Perhaps with a big propellant factory," he added.

"Another thousand year-old colony?" Cameron said. "You really love those long odds, don't you?"

"What can I say? I'm an optimist."

"It's more likely an old survey probe," Cameron said. "They launched hundreds of them during the twenty-third century right after they developed mass-canceling fields."

"I thought about that," Nathan said, "but weren't those probes designed to go from one system to the next, ad infinitum? Those probes would be several thousand light years out by now."

"Perhaps something malfunctioned and it's stuck there."

"Come on, Cam; don't tell me you're not at least curious."

"Yes, of course I'm curious," she admitted, "but I am also practical. I did some calculating of my own. If we jump halfway there, we should be able to get a strong signal, possibly even an ID on the source. Then, if it turns out to be a waste of time, we can make our turn back to Sol earlier and burn a little less propellant in the turn."

"Is it really going to make that much of a difference?"

"No, but every little bit counts, Nathan. Besides, it's only prudent to get as much intel as possible before we go jumping into the target system. If that signal is coming from a ship, it parked itself in that system for a reason. I'd like to have a better idea of what that reason might be before we jump in close."

"Agreed," Nathan said, "but I'd like to jump in halfway as soon as possible and continue recharging the jump drive while we collect more of the signal."

* * *

"Jump fifty-five complete," Loki reported.

"Position verified," Lieutenant Yosef reported. "Scanning for signal source."

"Green deck," Nathan ordered.

"Green deck, aye," Jessica answered.

"I've reacquired the signal, sir. It's coming in strong and clear now, Captain," Lieutenant Yosef reported.

"Flight reports two Talons are away," Naralena reported.

"I have the contact," Jessica reported. "It's coming from the second planet."

"Transfer the target data to the Talons," Nathan ordered.

"Aye, Captain," Jessica responded, "transferring target data to Talons."

"It's definitely a ship, Captain," Lieutenant Yosef reported. "It's transmitting an automated distress beacon. I'm getting an ID string. Searching the database now."

"What's our flight time to the target?" Nathan asked.

"Six hours eight minutes at present speed," Loki reported, "but we're not on an intercept course, Captain. We'll pass well clear of her gravity well. Shall we alter course to intercept and make orbit?"

"Not yet, Mister Sheehan," Nathan said. "Let the Talons take a look at the target first. Helm, maintain course and speed for now."

"Aye, sir," Josh acknowledged, "maintaining course and speed."

Major Prechitt adjusted the beam width on his Talon fighter's forward scanner array, focusing it on the area specified by the targeting data transmitted to him by the Aurora.

"*See anything, Major?*" his wingman asked from his fighter as it followed off the major's starboard side.

"Stand by," the major told him. A shape began to resolve on his scanner display, but no information about the ship appeared. "Got it, I think. There's no data on the target, though. It must not be in our database."

"*This far from the Pentaurus sector, I'm not surprised,*" his wingman said.

"I'm sending you its position now," Major Prechitt told his wingman.

"*Let's go check it out.*"

Major Prechitt pushed his throttle to the wall, pushing him gently back into his seat as his fighter's inertial dampening system compensated for the sudden acceleration. "Aurora, Talon One," he called over the comms. "Contact acquired. Vectoring to intercept. We have no data on the target, no ID on the target."

"*Talon One, Aurora. We copy. We're searching our databases now. Stand by.*"

"Talon One copies. Time on target: sixty-seven minutes."

"I found a match, Captain," Lieutenant Yosef announced. "In an old ship registration database from the Data Ark. It took a while to find it, as it wasn't an active ship at the time. I found it in a list of decommissioned ships."

"Decommissioned?" Nathan wondered. "Then what's it doing out here?"

"It was a cargo ship, the Jasper. Launched from the Alpha Centauri shipyards in 2257. She was designed to run cargo between Alpha Centauri and Earth."

"She's a long way off course, then," Nathan said.

"The Jasper was registered to one of the old Earth interstellar shipping companies," the lieutenant continued, "in service on the Earth-Centauri run for sixty-eight years until she was decommissioned."

"How does a decommissioned, old freighter end up ninety-seven light years from home?" Nathan mumbled.

"Maybe someone bought her and fixed her up," Josh said as he turned back toward the captain.

Nathan had a look of surprise on his face at Josh's theory. Not that it didn't make sense, it just seemed odd coming from someone who, only a few months ago, didn't even know Earth existed.

"I've been reading up on the history of spaceflight," Josh explained, noticing his captain's look of surprise, "mostly about the Earth's expansion phase. A lot of the old decommissioned ships were later sold to small independents looking to make a living running cargo between fringe worlds. The big ships mostly serviced the core worlds, so there was a lot of opportunity for captains with small cargo ships to earn a living running freight around the fringe."

"Those worlds were up to a decade apart, even at FTL speeds for the time," Nathan said.

"They used sleeper pods," Josh explained. "To them, it was only a week per trip. Some of them had their whole family living on board."

"So they all traveled forward through time together," Nathan said, "only aging a few days while the rest of the universe aged years." Nathan shook his head. "An odd way to live."

"A few trips and their ship would become antiquated," Jessica said.

"It was antiquated when they bought it," Nathan corrected. "Any details about the ship?" he asked, turning to Lieutenant Yosef.

"Top speed of two point five light. Crew of eight. Probably using suspended animation systems during the bulk of the journey."

"What kind of cargo did she carry?"

"She was a container ship, so she could carry just about anything."

"Any other emissions coming from the target?"

"Just faint energy and very low thermal images."

Nathan took a deep breath. "Comms, convey what we know to Talon One."

"Odd world for a cargo ship to orbit," Major Prechitt commented as his flight of two Talon fighters approached the target. They had settled into orbit just behind the target, rather than intercepting her head on. Although the contact didn't appear to be a threat, caution seemed prudent. It was also a good opportunity for his wingman to get some orbital intercept practice.

He gazed out his canopy at the planet below. It was cold and desolate in its appearance, its gray-blue oceans broken up by barren, mountainous terrain along its middle latitudes. Both poles were covered with ice caps that extended considerably toward the planet's equator. "Doesn't seem very habitable to me."

"*Neither does Lonjetta,*" his wingman stated over the comms, "*but we all go there for vacation every year.*"

"Corinairans go to Lonjetta for the hot springs, not the climate."

"Don't forget the all-day night life."

Major Prechitt smiled. He had stopped vacationing at the resort on one of the many moons orbiting Darvano's largest gas-giant. That was a place for younger men.

He turned his gaze forward once more, picking out his distant target against the background of stars along the planetary horizon ahead. "Visual contact. Time on target: one minute."

"Still think it's an Earth ship?" his wingman asked.

"The configuration matches the one the Aurora sent us."

"Think there's anyone still living on that thing?"

"Negative, but we'll pass on opposite sides, just in case."

"Yes, sir."

Major Prechitt watched as the distant, gray-white dot rapidly grew in size, changing its shape into that of a ship as they grew closer with each passing second. "Twenty seconds. Beginning deceleration for rendezvous."

They had been coasting as they approached, and now both fighters applied deceleration thrust to gradually decrease their closure rate until they were traveling only slightly faster than their target, allowing them to overtake her slowly. As a precaution, the major had armed his weapons systems, knowing that his wingman would detect his actions and do the same. "Ten seconds."

Major Prechitt stared out his canopy at the freighter as they approached from her stern, glancing down at his instrument console every few seconds as he maneuvered his fighter in closer. "Recording," he announced as he activated his data recorders.

"Man, this thing is bigger than I thought," his wingman exclaimed.

The cargo ship was long and slender with three main sections located at her bow, midship, and stern. Each section was connected by long trusswork, within which were tunnels, piping, and conduit of all sizes. Along the exterior were large cargo containers neatly parked in rows along all four sides of the trusses, both fore and aft of the midship section. All but one of the cargo containers were missing from the forward truss. However, all of her aft containers were still affixed to the trusswork that joined the midship section to the drive section at the ship's aft end.

"She's definitely seen better days," Major Prechitt commented as they coasted past her mid-section on their way forward. He pivoted his fighter, keeping his nose on her as they passed. "Look at all the external damage."

"She looks fried, sir."

"And battered," Major Prechitt added, noting the various holes in her hull and the numerous broken truss sections. "She's taken more than a few debris hits in her day." He looked down at his instruments. "She's still got power," he announced. "Her reactor is still hot."

"She's got more than one, sir," his wingman reported. *"I'm picking up a few dozen fusion signatures."*

"Are you sure they're not just echoes of the same reactor?"

"No, sir, they're separate sources. Very faint, but definitely separate."

"Telemetry coming in from Talon One, sir," Lieutenant Yosef reported. "They confirm it's the Jasper. Transferring to viewer."

Nathan and the entire bridge crew watched as the data feed from Major Prechitt's fighter displayed on the main view screen in three separate windows. The visual feed was displayed in the center as the fighters performed their flyby. On the left was their flight data and course projections, and on the right was their sensor data.

"Initial reports indicate that, although she has suffered a lot of external damage, many of her internal systems are still operational."

"Well, she's still got power," Nathan said. "That alone is pretty impressive, especially after a thousand years."

"Why is she still heavily loaded?" Cameron asked.

"What?"

"Her cargo pods," Cameron added, pointing them out on the viewer for Nathan. "Her aft section is completely loaded. If she were delivering cargo to the planet below, she'd be empty, wouldn't she?"

"Assuming the planet was her destination," Nathan said. "Maybe she was bound for someplace farther out and had to stop here due to mechanical problems."

"For a thousand years?"

"Only one way to find out," Nathan turned toward Jessica at the tactical station behind him. "Think you can access her through one of her hatches?"

"If not, we'll blast our way in using the breach boxes," Jessica said with a constrained grin, "just like we did on the Loranoi."

Nathan smiled. He was finally giving his security chief something exciting to do. "Take a security team and some engineers with you."

"Yes, sir."

"Mister Sheehan, if we maintain our present course and speed, how long before we are too far past for a shuttle to catch up to us?"

"We'll be passing the planet in five and a half hours, sir." He paused for a moment as he ran the numbers. "It will take us about fourteen more hours to reach the shuttle's max return range—so about nineteen hours and thirty minutes, sir."

"Let's play it safe and say eighteen hours," Nathan said to Jessica.

"We'll be back in half that," Jessica announced as she turned to exit.

"Eighteen will be fine, Lieutenant Commander."

"We're not going to make orbit, then?" Cameron wondered.

"Unless they find some compelling reason to hang around longer, I don't see the need," Nathan said. "Every drop counts, eh, Commander?"

* * *

"Good seal," The shuttle's flight technician reported.

"How's that possible?" Sergeant Weatherly wondered. "It's a thousand year-old cargo ship, and a busted up one at that."

"It's probably because our docking collar is designed to create its own seal, independent of the target," the shuttle's Corinairan flight technician explained. "We're just lucky the ship's designers thought to make her hull smooth and flat around her boarding hatch."

The sergeant nodded. "At least we don't have to

blow our way in."

"I rather like blowing our way in," Jessica said, grinning.

"Not me," Sergeant Weatherly admitted. "I hate loud noises."

"You're a Marine," Jessica stated with amusement. "Man, did you pick the wrong job." Jessica turned to face the boarding team behind her. "Face plates down and sealed, gentlemen," she ordered as she dropped the face plate on her suit helmet and activated the sealing mechanism. All exterior noise suddenly left her ears as the helmet sealed up and the suit adjusted its internal pressure, becoming its own little environment. "So why did you enlist, Sergeant?" she asked over her suit comm.

"*I liked the pretty uniform,*" he joked, "*thought it would get me laid more.*"

"Did it work?"

"*Worked great with your sister,*" the sergeant jeered.

"I don't have a sister," Jessica answered, "just brothers."

"*My mistake. Must have been your mother.*"

Jessica shook her head inside her helmet. She sometimes missed the bravado of her old special operations unit, and the sergeant was a good substitute at times. "Check your weapons: low power, safeties on. This old wreck has already got enough holes in her; let's not make any more."

The internal lighting in the shuttle dimmed. "*Adjusting lighting to match the interior of the Jasper,*" the flight tech reported.

Jessica waited a moment for their eyes to adjust. "Stay dark until I light up." She turned to the flight tech, who had also donned his helmet and sealed up his suit. "Open her up."

The flight tech cracked open the shuttle's inner hatch, revealing the Jasper's midship boarding hatch on the other side. A thick layer of dust, collected over centuries in orbit, swirled up from the Jasper's hatch, pulled free by the slight suction created by the movement of the shuttle's inner hatch as it swung inward. Jessica stepped forward and brushed the dust off the control panel alongside the Jasper's hatch.

"It's in English," she stated without surprise. English had become the universal language long before the bio-digital plague had nearly destroyed humanity across the core. Even after the people of Earth had become separated and people had reverted to their native tongues, English had always been taught alongside whatever primary language the locals had spoken. She also spoke a derivative of Spanish common to the lower regions of the Florida peninsula on Earth.

Jessica activated the boarding hatch. A ring of dust around the hatch jumped outward, propelled by the small amount of pressure still present inside the Jasper's boarding airlock. The hatch motor seemed to struggle at first, the result of not having been activated for a millennium. After a moment's hesitation, the hatch retracted slightly inward then began to swing smoothly on its hinge, opening away from them and into the Jasper's airlock.

Jessica leaned forward, peering into the dark, empty airlock. She pulled out a small, handheld light and reached into the airlock, releasing the light as far inward as she could. The light hung in the airlock, floating in place. "No gravity in there," she announced as she retrieved her light and returned it to her suit pocket. "Have to use the mag-boots," she explained as she activated the electromagnetic gripping system built into the soles of her suit boots.

She stepped through the hatch and made her way across the airlock, feeling the resistance of the magnets in her boots release their grip on the deck with each step. She reached the inner hatch control panel at the other end of the airlock and attempted to activate the inner hatch. "It won't allow me to open the inner hatch while the outer hatch is open."

"*Wouldn't both hatches normally be open when docked?*" the sergeant asked.

"My guess is that it would be receiving a good seal signal from the docked ship, and we're not sending one. Besides, even if we were, I doubt this ship speaks Corinairan." Jessica stopped and turned around, looking over the airlock. "I think there's enough room for all of us in here. Everybody squeeze in," she ordered over comms. "Last man in, close and lock the outer hatch behind you."

One by one, the other seven members of the boarding party entered the airlock, their mag-boots tugging at the deck with each step. Sergeant Weatherly was the last one in, closing the Jasper's outer hatch behind him.

"*Outer hatch is secure,*" the sergeant reported.

Jessica returned to the inner hatch's control panel. The indicator light was now green. She punched the open button for the hatch. A moment later, the inner hatch seal released, and the hatch cracked open. "That did it." Unlike the outer hatch, the inner hatch was manually operated. She pushed the hatch inward, peering into the darkness beyond the hatch. She reached up and turned on her helmet light, casting a brilliant beam of light into the interior of the Jasper's boarding deck. The beam appeared thick as it cut through the floating dust that appeared to be everywhere. She stepped through the inner hatch and into the boarding area, signaling for the others to follow and stepping cautiously as the beams of light from those behind her danced about the Jasper's inner spaces ahead of her.

"*Where is all the dust coming from?*" Sergeant Weatherly asked.

"There are a lot of holes in the hull," Jessica explained. "This ship is basically open to space."

"*Seems kind of funny,*" Weatherly commented, "*since the inner door wouldn't open until the outer door was closed.*"

"I guess they didn't expect the inside to ever be opened up to space."

"*Or to survive a thousand years.*"

"Yeah, I'm surprised the hatches even worked." Jessica stopped as she came to the Jasper's central corridor. She looked to her right, her helmet light shining down the long corridor. At the far end was a closed hatch. She turned around and looked aft, seeing the same. "Three teams," she ordered. "Sergeant, you take two techs aft. I'll take forward. Last two, stay here and check out the midship area."

"*Aye, sir,*" Sergeant Weatherly answered.

"Most of the compartment hatches will be closed because of hull breaches. You'll have to manually override them. There should be some kind of override mechanism on the side."

"*Copy that.*"

"Maintain radio contact," Jessica advised. "If you lose contact, return here until you reestablish." She looked at the time display on the data display on the inside of her helmet visor. "The Aurora will be passing us in about three and a half hours, so let's be out of here in four at the most. I don't want to have to chase them across the system."

"*Yes, sir,*" the sergeant answered.

"Move out."

* * *

Vladimir entered the captain's ready room unannounced, unceremoniously dropping himself onto the couch along the wall.

"Can I help you?" Nathan asked from his desk.

"Nyet, I am good," Vladimir said as he stretched out. "I just need to relax a bit."

"You don't have a bed?"

"I don't need to sleep, just relax." Vladimir turned his head toward Nathan. "Am I bothering you?"

"Not at all," Nathan answered. "Am I bothering you?"

Vladimir looked at him, puzzled. "What?"

"I am the captain, and this is my ready room."

Vladimir looked around the room. "There is no one here but you and I," he announced. "Therefore, you are just Nathan, and I am just Vladimir."

"Of course." Nathan smiled. "Sorry, I forgot."

"That's why you have me," Vladimir explained, "to prevent unlimited expansion of your ego."

"What would I do without you?" Nathan mumbled. "How go the upgrades?"

"Everything is on schedule," Vladimir told him. "They have finished fabricating the parts for the cannon turret and have begun fabrication of the parts for the first torpedo tube conversion."

"How long will it take them to assemble the turret?"

"A few days, then another few days to install it for testing. We have already run the energy trunks to the compartment."

"You're making good time. You must be working hard."

"I'm not doing anything at all," Vladimir admitted, "at least, not in these projects. It's all the Takarans, and a few of the Corinairans."

"Then they are working together after all."

"The technicians seem to be fine with it. It's the down-in-the-dirt, Corinari types that get all ruffled up whenever there is a Takaran nearby. It is very amusing."

"Not according to Jessica."

"She worries too much. She has been spending too much time with Cameron." Vladimir sat up suddenly. "Hey, how is she doing over there on that ship?"

"They haven't reported anything since they boarded more than an hour ago. I guess they haven't found anything worth reporting."

"I really wanted to go on the boarding party," Vladimir said. "Can you imagine, a thousand year-old spaceship? From Earth no less. That would have been fascinating. Like being in a museum."

"A museum full of holes," Nathan reminded him, "ones that open the ship up to space."

"I have worn a spacesuit before."

"I can't send my chief engineer on dangerous assignments, Vlad; you know that."

"You could have fired me, at least long enough to go on the mission."

"It doesn't work that way."

"*Captain, Comms,*" Naralena's voice called over the comms.

"Go ahead," Nathan answered.

"*Sir, I have Lieutenant Commander Nash on comms. She needs to speak with you.*"

"Put her through." Nathan waited for the telltale crackle that told him Naralena had connected him with the lieutenant commander currently on the Jasper. "Whattaya got, Jess?"

"*You're not going to believe this, Nathan.*"

"Try me."

"*It's a colony ship,*" she reported over the comms. "*Or at least, that's how she was loaded out. And get this: there are still about three hundred colonists in stasis pods.*"

"*Bozhe moi,*" Vladimir exclaimed.

"Are they alive?" Nathan asked.

"*No, sir, most of the pods malfunctioned a long time ago. Probably due to power loss. There's only a trickle of energy coming out of the ship's reactor right now.*"

"You said most of the pods malfunctioned."

"*Three of them are still functioning, sir. And their occupants may be alive, we can't really tell.*"

Nathan stared at Vladimir for a moment as the wall-mounted display screen behind Vladimir's head came to life, showing an image feed from Jessica's helmet camera as it scanned the rows of pods, finally settling on the three that were still functioning. "You're right, Jess."

"*About what?*"

"I don't believe it."

"*What do you want me to do, sir?*"

"Tell her not to touch anything!" Vladimir insisted.

"Don't touch anything," Nathan ordered her. He looked at Vladimir, shrugging his shoulders.

Vladimir looked uncharacteristically grim. "If those people are alive, and if they were escaping the bio-digital plague, how do we know the passengers and their electronics are not infected?"

Nathan's face paled suddenly. "Lieutenant Commander," he called over the comms in a more official tone, "you and your team are ordered to withdraw to the shuttle and await further orders. Do not touch anything. Do not interface your suit electronics with that of the ship or any of its electronic equipment, and do not open your suits, even when you are back in the shuttle. You are all under quarantine until further notice. Understood?"

"*Understood, sir.*"

"We'll make orbit in about an hour. Sit tight until then."

"*Yes, sir. Nash out.*"

Nathan killed the comm channel. "Risk assessment?"

"Assuming the virus is present? If they do *not* open their suits, they should be fine. We can decontaminate them before they return. It isn't a problem."

"And their electronics?"

"We have been using Corinari suits for all EVAs," Vladimir explained. "Their software and comm systems are completely different than ours, or that of pre-plague Earth. We had to create translation algorithms in order to link the Corinari suits up with our own data systems. Those algorithms do not exist on that ship, so they should be safe. However, I would wipe the suits and reload their cores before using them again, just to be safe."

"Then the risk to the ship and crew is minimal at this point?"

"I am no doctor, but I think so."

Nathan nodded his head in agreement as he keyed up his comm-set. "Helm, change course to make orbit above the second planet, and rendezvous with the Jasper and our shuttle. Minimal propellant consumption."

"*Aye, sir,*" Josh answered over the comms.

Nathan quickly switched calls. "Comms, Captain. Wake up the XO and tell her to report to my ready room. Then contact Doctor Chen, Doctor Sorenson and Lieutenant Montgomery, and have them meet us in the command briefing room in half an hour."

"*Aye, sir.*"

Nathan looked at Vladimir. "I guess you're going to have a closer look at that ship after all."

"*Gospadee,*" Vladimir exclaimed. "I am not sure I want to, now."

* * *

"Are we sure there's no risk of infection?" Cameron asked.

Everyone at the conference table in the briefing room had been wondering the same thing ever since the meeting had started.

Nathan looked at Vladimir.

"All data that we have on the bio-digital plague indicated that while it could be transmitted over the air, it did require an open comm-system running compatible protocols. Most digital infections occurred over hard connections. However, many infections also occurred via wireless connections, such as those used for short-range data connections,

161

like in port. As our comm-protocols are based on those in the Data Ark from that period, had we been wearing our standard issue EVA suits, we might have been at risk of exposure, assuming the Jasper is infected."

"What about the ship?" Nathan asked. "Our computer and comm-systems are also closely integrated. We also have short-range data-comm systems that are used in port or in ship-to-ship links during rendezvous."

"Yes, that would make the ship susceptible as well," Vladimir agreed.

Abby shook her head. "No, it wouldn't."

"She is right, Captain," Lieutenant Montgomery agreed. "So many of your computer systems were damaged during the battle of Takara that it was easier to replace them than it was to repair them. Your ship is using Takaran computers and Takaran operating systems. We simply wrote translation algorithms to interface with various hard-coded components still functioning within your ship."

"That had not occurred to me," Vladimir said, looking sheepish. "They are correct, Captain. The translation program needed to link the ship with Earth data-comm systems has yet to be written. It was considered a lower priority, since we were so far from home at the time."

"Great, then the ship is safe." Nathan turned to Doctor Chen. "What about the crew?"

"No cure was ever created for the biological version of the plague," Doctor Chen explained. "Those few million that survived did so through a natural immunity. The biological version of the plague was bred into extinction over time."

"The digital version died out on Earth when her

industry collapsed and the last power plants went offline," Abby added.

"Correct," Doctor Chen agreed. "If the plague exists on this ship, in either version, the ship and anyone infected must be destroyed... completely."

The room went quiet for a moment.

"Doctor, we have eight people at risk over there," Nathan said.

"Nine," Cameron corrected, "the shuttle crew chief."

"Twelve if you count the three still alive in stasis on board the Jasper," Doctor Chen added. "I am well aware of that fact, Captain. But we are talking about a plague that nearly destroyed the entire human race. We're talking upwards of three hundred billion people, sir."

"What about the Corinairans?" Cameron asked. "Their medical technology far surpasses ours."

"I've talked about the plague at length with them," Doctor Chen said. "There was considerable documentation about the biological version stored within the Data Ark before they realized there was a digital component, and they locked the Ark down to protect it." Doctor Chen sighed. "However, it is not enough for them to tell if they could develop an antidote. They would need a live sample."

"Can we at least detect it?" Nathan asked.

"Yes, sir. I believe we know enough about it to be able to detect its presence," Doctor Chen assured him, "at least the biological version."

"And the digital version?"

"Yes," Vladimir answered. "Fragments of the base code were discovered in electronic components found in archaeological surveys on Earth. It should be enough for us to detect its presence in the Jasper's computer systems."

"With one hundred percent assurance?" Cameron asked.

"Nothing has one hundred percent assurance," Vladimir said with a shrug, "except never powering the potentially infected system up to begin with. Ninety-eight, ninety-nine, maybe ninety-seven..."

"Which is it?" Cameron asked.

"High nineties, to be sure."

"Problem, Commander?" Nathan asked.

"I can't help but wonder why we are even taking the risk."

"Besides the obvious ethical reasons?" Nathan asked.

"Obviously, we have to try to recover our own people, but do we have to rescue the survivors?"

"I think we do," Nathan said. "At least, we should do our best to determine if there even *is* a risk."

"I'm not sure I agree with you, sir," Cameron stated, "not when the stakes are this high."

"*There's another reason,*" Jessica called over the comm-channel.

Nathan felt guilty, having forgotten that Jessica was listening into the meeting from the shuttle docked to the Jasper via the comms. She had not taken active participation in the discussion because of the few second comm-lag that still existed as the Aurora approached the planet.

"*This ship's comm-array has been up and running for centuries,*" Jessica continued over the open comm channel. "*She's been recording incoming signals the whole time. That's a lot of signals intelligence.*"

"And a lot of post-plague history," Nathan added. "She's right." Nathan turned to Vladimir. "Would it be possible to access those comm-logs without connecting them to this ship?"

"We could pull the equipment from the Jasper, assuming it is still functioning, and set it up here. We just have to completely isolate it, not even connect it to the power grid. We'll have to set up a battery system or a small generator for it."

"What about those three stasis pods?" Doctor Chen asked. "Those people might survive the revival process. Can we bring them over as well?"

"That's a bit more difficult, but it is possible," Vladimir told them. "They were designed to be portable. The better ones even had their own backup power supplies that could run them for months."

"We can't revive them there?" Cameron wondered.

"The entire ship is open to space, remember?" Nathan said.

"Can we patch up and repressurize that one section?" she asked.

"Welding in zero gravity is hard enough," Vladimir told her, "let alone in a pressure suit."

"We have full quarantine capabilities within medical," Doctor Chen assured Nathan. "We should be able to tell if they are infected before reviving them."

Nathan sighed, looking at the time display on the bulkhead over the hatchway. "We'll reach the planet in approximately twenty-eight minutes. We'll start with retrieving our own people. If they pass decon and post-mission medical and are free of the bio-digital plague, we'll proceed with the rescue of the three survivors, as well as the recovery of the ship's logs. If our people are infected, they will remain in quarantine until they are cured or until other arrangements are made, and the Jasper, her logs, and her survivors will be destroyed." Nathan looked at the others, pausing for additional comments from his staff. "Everyone take the necessary steps to prepare. Dismissed."

Cameron remained seated, as usual, as the others cleared the briefing room.

Nathan looked sternly at her. "I'm not leaving her behind, Commander."

"I know, Nathan. Jessica and Sergeant Weatherly are immune."

"But the Corinairans and the Takaran on that team are not," Nathan stated, the guilt evident on his face, "and that's on me."

"Nathan..."

"I should have thought of that," he said, cutting her off. "I should have insisted the team be Terrans only. As soon as we ID'd that ship, I should have considered the possibility of it carrying the BD-plague."

"It's a cargo ship, Nathan, a thousand year-old cargo ship that was supposed to be decommissioned. You couldn't possibly have known that there would still be someone alive on board. I mean, what are the odds that a stasis pod would last that long?"

"I'm a student of history, Cam. I knew about all the refugees that fled the core to escape the plague. They did so in all manner of ships, legally operated or not. I should have connected the dots."

Cameron took a deep breath, letting it out slowly, then rose and left the briefing room without another word. She could tell by the expression on his face that there was nothing more to say.

Nathan sat there thinking for several minutes. He had made mistakes in the past, ones that had cost hundreds of thousands of lives, maybe even millions. He had let others convince him that, in the end, his actions had saved billions from oppression and suffering, and quite possibly extinction. But this time, his mistake could put billions of people at stake.

He never did like being captain.

CHAPTER FIVE

Nathan stood in the corner of the quarantine bay of the Aurora's medical section, watching as Vladimir and his engineers finished their scans of the three stasis pods brought over from the Jasper. As long as they remained unconnected from their systems, they posed no threat to the ship. The occupants of those pods, however, were another matter. If even one of them was infected, over two hundred of his crew would be at risk.

The Corinairan and Takaran members of the original boarding party, as well as the shuttle's crew chief, were all being held in another quarantine bay, awaiting the results of their own blood tests and those of the three survivors of the Jasper currently in stasis.

The Jasper itself was also an issue. Once they had arrived in orbit and rendezvoused with the old cargo vessel, Vladimir and his few Terran engineers had managed to connect batteries to the Jasper's comm-systems, allowing them to download the ship's entire database and comm-logs onto several data pads; this allowed them to view the contents on the portable device back on board the Aurora without further risk to the ship.

"I find no evidence of infection in any of the pods' systems," Vladimir announced as he approached

Nathan.

"Are you sure?"

"Nyet, there is no way to be sure. But it is of no matter. We simply do not connect them to our systems. Once the occupants are revived, we dispose of the pods. No risk at all."

"One of my favorite terms," Nathan said.

"You worry too much," Vladimir told his friend, noticing his expression. "How is Jessica doing with the Jasper's comm-logs?"

"They got back about an hour ago. She's going through the logs now, trying to find out who owned the ship, their mission, their launch date, and so on. It may take some time."

"Well, even if she does not learn anything of value, at least there was enough propellant on the Jasper to replace what we used getting to her."

"Yeah, that will at least keep Cameron off my back," Nathan said. "Are we going to be able to use that propellant?"

"It's not exactly the same as ours, but the Takarans can use it to synthesize a working substitute."

"How is that possible?"

"I do not know," Vladimir admitted, "but they assure me it is not difficult."

"Are we clear to begin our examinations?" Doctor Chen interrupted.

"Yes, of course, Doctor," Vladimir answered.

"Everyone will have to clear the room," she told them.

"Why?" Nathan wondered. "We're all immune, aren't we?"

"Rule number one when dealing with virulent pathogens: do not take unnecessary risks. You may watch from outside if you like."

"I guess I can't argue with that logic," Nathan admitted.

"No, sir, you cannot," she said as she motioned for them to exit.

* * *

Jessica entered the captain's ready room without warning, flopping down on the couch as usual.

"Does anyone realize this is the captain's office?" Nathan wondered aloud.

"A moment of your time, sir?" Jessica asked as she relaxed on the couch, her eyes closed.

"What's up?" As with Vladimir and Cameron, when they were alone in the room, he preferred to drop the formalities of rank.

"I thought I'd let you know what we've learned so far."

Nathan leaned back in his chair. "I'm all ears."

Jessica sat up as she began. "The Jasper's flight logs only go back to 2370. I suspect that's when she came out of retirement. All her previous logs must have been wiped by the new owner. Best we can tell, her new captain, Alan Dubnyk, was also her new owner. There's nothing about how much he paid, transfer of title, or new registry."

"So he was a rogue operator running an unregistered cargo ship," Nathan said.

"He only shows four runs in over eighty years. The first three were all long-haul smuggling stuff, running contraband out to the fringe worlds. His logs show that he and his crew spent most of their time in stasis, coming out occasionally to check on the ship and her course."

"What about the fourth one?" Nathan asked,

figuring it was the one that had eventually brought the Jasper to BD+25 3252.

"In 2454, he took on an unsanctioned colony mission. He picked up the job in Mu Herculis, one of the fringe systems about twenty-seven light years from Earth. A full load of refugees, with all the equipment and supplies they needed to start a new colony."

"How many refugees?"

"Five hundred and eight."

"Did he have a manifest or a passenger list?"

"Not exactly. It was more like a list of what order he was to deliver the cargo containers in once they reached their target world."

"Anything else?"

"Like what?" Jessica asked, closing her eyes and leaning back again.

"Like why only half his cargo containers were unloaded, or why three hundred refugees never made it down to the surface."

"We've only just started. I'm sure there will be something explaining all of that in the ship's log."

"Not much to go on," Nathan said with a slight frown.

"Actually, it's more than you realize. Think about it, Nathan. Mu Herculis was a fringe world. The fringe worlds were the last to become infected. The first reported case of the bio-digital plague on Earth was in 2435. A year later, the digital version showed up, and they locked down the Data Ark. The Jasper's last mission was only eight years later. Considering the distance between Mu Herculis and Earth, and the fact that the fringe worlds didn't have regular transport or comm-runs, the plague might not have even reached them by 2454. Those people might have left just in time. That ship might be clean."

"I hope you're right," Nathan said, "but we'll continue to play it safe just the same."

"Can I at least tell the guys still in quarantine?" Jessica asked. "They're going nuts down there. A little hope might go a long way."

"Go ahead, but don't lay it on too thick. Sometimes false hope is worse than no hope at all."

"Jesus, Nathan, you sound like my father."

"There's still one other question," Nathan said. "Where are the other two hundred refugees?"

* * *

"All their blood work came back clean," Doctor Chen reported.

"So no signs of the plague?" Nathan asked as he stared at the three stasis pods.

"None at all, Captain."

"What about the away team?"

"They're clean as well. We even used the Corinairan diagnostic scanners on them which, as you know, are far superior to our own. However, the three people in those pods do have some problems. They've been in stasis for a very long time. Those systems were designed to maintain the human body in stasis for decades, maybe even a century or two, but not for a millennium."

"Why not?" Nathan wondered. He knew very little about stasis technology other than the fact that it was widely used during interstellar travel before the bio-digital plague struck.

"Most people think stasis is the same thing as suspended animation, a complete suspension of cellular activity. It's not; it's just an extreme decline in the level of activity. The body still ages, just at a greatly reduced rate. Gases are still exchanged, waste is still generated and eliminated. There were even different levels of stasis, primarily long and short term."

"I read those files as well, Doctor. I'm pretty sure these are long-term stasis pods."

"They are, but again, they were not designed to last a thousand years."

"Cut to the chase, Doctor," Nathan said. "What's wrong with them?"

"Two of them are suffering from severe muscular atrophy. I believe the muscle stimulation systems in their pods stopped working long ago."

"So that would make them weak, right?"

"Very. Their hearts may not be strong enough to support a body running at normal metabolic rates. They will probably find it difficult to breathe as well. We'll have to keep them in a reduced gravity environment until they become stronger. That could take months."

"What about the Corinairans? Could they use their nanites?"

"We've discussed that option, and they would definitely help if they survive the revival process."

"So if we wake them, they could die, and if we don't they will definitely die, only later." Nathan sighed. "What are the odds that they'll lead normal, healthy lives if we revive them now?"

"Better than if they are revived later," Doctor Chen told him.

"You said two of them are weak," Nathan realized. "What about the third one?"

"He has some atrophy as well, but his pod was in much better shape than the others. According to

Lieutenant Commander Kamenetskiy, his pod was of a much better design, with multiple redundancies. He has the best chance of surviving out of the three of them."

Again, Nathan sighed. He shook his head from side to side. "I can't imagine what it would be like to wake up to an entirely new galaxy—everything they knew, every person they knew, all gone." Nathan stared at the pods for a few seconds, then turned back to Doctor Chen. "You know, they came here to start a new colony. They brought equipment, supplies, everything they needed to give them a fighting chance. Something must have gone wrong."

"Have you learned what it was?" Doctor Chen asked.

"Jessica is still studying the Jasper's logs. They must have gone down to the surface. Where else could they have gone?"

"Has anyone checked?" Doctor Chen asked. "The surface, I mean."

"We've been scanning it for hours but haven't found anything yet."

"So, what do you want me to do?" Doctor Chen asked.

"This isn't a medical decision?" he asked, hoping to pass the decision off on her.

"I'm afraid not. Even in their current state, as long as their pods keep working, they might survive longer than any of us."

"Well we can't leave them behind," Nathan said. "Their ship is full of holes, and their reactor core is nearly depleted. We also can't leave them sitting in thousand year-old stasis pods that were only designed to last a century or two. For all we know, those things could stop working at any moment."

Nathan looked at Doctor Chen, hoping for some advice.

"Captain, it seems to me that we only know two things about these people: they wanted to escape the plague, and they only intended to remain in these pods until they reached their destination. They certainly didn't intend to remain in them indefinitely."

"Good point," Nathan admitted. He suddenly felt much better. "Wake them up."

"Yes, sir," Doctor Chen said, turning back toward the pods.

"Doc," Nathan called after her. Doctor Chen turned back around to face the captain. "Thanks."

* * *

Nathan sat in his command chair on the bridge, waiting. It had been several hours since he had ordered Doctor Chen to revive the three survivors from the Jasper, yet there had been no word from medical about their disposition. He knew that, even if they did survive, it might be some time before any of them would be able to speak, let alone answer questions. Nathan had read everything he could find in the Aurora's database about stasis technology from the twenty-fourth century. The longer the subject was in stasis, the longer it took for them to become fully functional. Most interstellar crews were revived on a monthly basis during their journey in order to maintain their ship and reduce the recovery time needed at the end of their voyage when they were to off-load their cargo and take on the new. In such cases, it took no more than a few hours to recover. The longest stasis period on record was ten years, and that had been an accident. The occupant had required months of rehabilitation to become normal. He had even suffered some degradation in his motor skills that had taken years to regain. There was just no telling how long the survivors of the Jasper might take to recover, if ever.

While in orbit, there was little for him to do on the bridge. He sometimes grew tired of sitting in his ready room reading reports and operational manuals. Even after being captain for months, there was still so much about his ship and his command that he did not know. He often wondered why he even bothered to learn everything. In just over a week, they would be home, and his command would finally be over. He wondered how he would be judged by Fleet Command. Would action be taken against him? Would his father end up intervening yet again?

His father. By now the elections were over. If he had won, he would be the leader of the entire American continent and would be on the fast track to being appointed leader of the United Earth government when the current leader resigned. If he had won, his position alone might offer Nathan some consideration in judgment of his actions. He did, after all, complete his mission and get the Aurora back home safely. He even improved her and brought allies.

The more he thought about it, the more he was sure Fleet Command would approve of his performance as the de facto captain of the Aurora. He doubted he would be welcomed as a hero, and there would certainly be no parade, especially not if his father had been elected. Senator Scott's opinions of the fleet were quite clear.

"Captain," Jessica called as she entered the

bridge, "I know where the other two hundred refugees are." She moved to the tactical station, pushing Mister Randeen aside.

"Care to enlighten us?" Nathan asked.

"Just as we thought, they went to the surface to start the new colony," she explained as she punched coordinates into the tactical systems targeting scanners. "They went down in small groups, establishing a base camp and expanding the settlement a little at a time so as not to overwhelm themselves."

"What are you doing?" Nathan wondered.

"I'm using the optical targeting sensors to find them," she explained. "I'll put it up on the main viewer."

A moment later, the image popped up on the forward section of the spherical view screen that wrapped around the front half of the bridge. The image slowly zoomed in, giving the impression that they were falling from the sky toward the planet below. It finally stopped about one hundred meters above the ground.

"There!" Jessica exclaimed, pointing at the view screen.

"Where?"

"Right there, to the right of the ice shelf."

"All I see is ice," Nathan said, squinting. "Ice and snow."

"Look at the shape of that snow hill just below the ice shelf. It's rectangular."

"She's right," Mister Randeen agreed. "There are several more as well," he added, "to the right and above."

"Mister Navashee, scan that area for any signs of life. Thermal, electrical, fusion signatures, anything that would indicate someone is down there."

"Scanning now, Captain," Mister Navashee acknowledged from his station.

"Why didn't we find this before?" Nathan wondered.

"We were looking in the temperate areas closer to the equator," Mister Randeen explained. "We never thought to look in the frigid areas."

"Why would they set up their colony in such extreme conditions," Nathan wondered, "especially when they have habitable temperate zones available nearer the equator?"

"Maybe it's too hot in the lower latitudes?" Jessica said. "Or maybe the cold weather is seasonal?"

"I don't think that is seasonal, sir," Mister Navashee reported. "That snow is fifty meters thick in some places, and I'm pretty sure the edge of the polar ice sheet is only one hundred kilometers north of them."

"Anything?" Nathan asked.

"No, sir. No electrical, radiological, electromagnetic, or fusion signatures. And if there's anything warm under there, all that snow is masking it. They may have been there once, but I don't think anyone is there now."

Nathan thought for a moment. "It will take a few more hours to finish off-loading the propellant from the Jasper. Since we have the time, the only ethical thing to do is to check for survivors." He turned toward Jessica at the tactical station. "Put together a landing party, cold weather gear and full arms. Go down there and check out that site. I doubt there are any survivors, but maybe we'll at least learn what happened to them."

"Yes, sir," Jessica responded.

* * *

"The first two did not survive the revival process," Doctor Chen stated solemnly. "As we feared, the amount of tissue degradation was too severe. They suffered massive heart failure long before the nanites could sufficiently repair the degraded cardiac tissue."

"What about the third one?" Nathan asked as he stared at the last stasis pod.

"We learned quite a lot from the first two attempts," the doctor explained. "We have reprogrammed a batch of nanites so they can work in a patient who is in a reduced metabolic state."

"Reduced?"

"We've brought the last survivor up to half of the normal metabolic rate, like half-stasis. We're hoping that, by reducing the stress on the patient's organs, this will give the reprogrammed nanites enough time to repair the patient's degraded cells in the most critical areas before we attempt to fully revive him."

"Will that work?"

"We do not know," she admitted with a shrug. "The nanites normally depend on the patient's metabolic functions to support their activities and provide the base materials they need for reconstruction or repair. These nanites have been programmed to cannibalize those materials from nearby, less important tissues. The trick is not to damage those other tissues to the point that they become a problem as well."

Nathan shuddered at the idea. "Doesn't sound like fun. In fact, it sounds painful."

"I doubt he will feel it," Doctor Chen assured him. "Nevertheless, the patient will be unconscious during the process."

"How long will it take?"

"A few hours before we can attempt to revive him."

"Will he be able to speak?"

"I doubt he will regain consciousness anytime soon after being revived. He may not regain consciousness at all," she reminded him. "Remember, he has been in stasis far longer than these systems were designed to keep the human body alive."

"So you're saying he may have deficits," Nathan said.

"I'm saying he may come out in an irreversible comatose state."

"You're not painting a very rosy picture, Doc."

"It isn't one. Any idea who he is?"

"Lieutenant Commander Nash is still digging through the Jasper's logs, but it's slow going since she has to use data pads. Besides, she's on her way down to the surface right now to see what happened to the two hundred people that left."

"Is that wise?"

"Probably not," Nathan said, "but I think we need to be sure there are no survivors alive down there before we move on."

"And if you do find survivors?"

"We'll cross that bridge when we come to it, Doctor," Nathan stated. He paused a moment, taking a deep breath. "Keep me informed."

* * *

The wind howled as it swept across the frozen, gray-white landscape of the second planet in the BD+25 3252 star system. Waves of falling snow were blown laterally as they fell, creating a rippling effect on the surface as the snow was tossed about like grains of sand.

The waves of snow hitting the forward windshields of the shuttle sounded more like tiny rocks than snowflakes. Visibility outside was so poor that neither of the flight crew bothered to even look out the windows. Everything they needed to know to land the shuttle safely was displayed on the consoles in front of them, and the constant buffeting by the violent winds outside required their complete concentration during their descent.

Jessica held onto the flight harness that secured her tightly to her jump seat in the cargo area of the small shuttle. The six seats on either side of the shuttle were all occupied, all twelve of them needed for the mission on the surface.

She scanned the faces of her landing party. They were all clad in special thermally regulated cold-weather gear provided by the Corinairans. The outfits were thick and well insulated, and the hoods sealed up around a face mask that covered the entire face and chin.

The Corinari security team that accompanied them sat calmly in their jump seats, unconcerned with the violent shaking of the shuttle that had been going on ever since they first hit the atmosphere more than five minutes ago. The other three civilian personnel—two Corinairans and a Takaran—did not appear as calm.

There was no conversation between the members of the landing party as they continued their controlled fall from the sky, bouncing about at the whim of the violent air currents outside. Jessica smiled at the Takaran scientist, Mister Taves, who seemed to be having the most difficult time dealing with the descent, and gave him a thumbs up sign. She smiled again when he did not understand her gesture and looked up at the overhead, wondering what she was pointing at.

The shuttle came in low over the ice shelf, its engines barely audible above the icy winds. As it cleared the edge of the elevated shelf, it descended quickly, slipping under the path of the wind and into calmer air.

The shuttle drifted sideways as it continued forward, finally coming to a hover a few meters away from the first rectangular snow hill. As it lowered, its jet wash blasted several meters of snow away from the surface, revealing the level terrain detected by the shuttle's sensors. The shuttle settled gently onto the frozen ground, having blasted the snow away in an oval around them.

"*Touchdown,*" the pilot's voice announced over Jessica's comm-set. "*Give us a minute to shut her down before you crack the hatch.*"

"Copy that." Jessica unfastened her harness and rose from her jump seat along the port side of the shuttle's cargo area. "Everyone, check your mask seals and breathing systems. Remember, although the air is breathable, it is very thin, and it is damned cold. Without the mask, you're unconscious in a minute, dead in eight."

"Then how could anyone have survived here?" Mister Taves asked.

"That's what we're here to find out. To be honest, I don't expect to find anyone alive, but you never know." Jessica turned to Major Waddell. "Major, I trust your people will secure the area while we dig our way inside."

"Yes, sir," Major Waddell responded. He turned to face his men. "First team secures the LZ. Second team secures the perimeter. Nobody loses signals with the man to either side of them. Radio checks on the five." He turned back to face Jessica. "There will be no surprises while you're inside, Lieutenant Commander."

"Very well."

The shuttle's crew chief stepped up to the port side hatch and activated the exterior boarding ramp. "Pilot says we're all shut down and ready for exit."

"Mask up!" Jessica barked. She pushed her mask snugly against her as she pulled the harness up over the back of her head, wiggling it a bit to ensure it was seated properly. She pressed a small switch embedded in the side of the mask that activated the data display on the inside of the mask in the upper corners. The display allowed her to see where everyone on her landing party was located as well as keep track of her own position in relation to the shuttle and the nearby buildings buried in the deep snow. She pulled her hood up over her head and secured it to the edges of the mask. The hood felt warm and cozy, already heated by the cold-weather suit's built-in thermal control system. As long as her suit was working, she would remain at a normal temperature, despite the freezing cold outside.

Jessica turned around to check that the rest of her team was ready to go, then turned forward and gave the crew chief a thumbs up signal. Although the Takarans did not yet understand the gesture, most of the Corinairans on the Aurora's crew had long ago learned its meaning.

The crew chief pulled his hood in place and activated the hatch controls. The hatch slid open, allowing a gust of wind and miniature pebbles of frozen water to come blasting into the shuttle's cargo bay. The entire landing party braced themselves against the sudden rush of wind and ice, a few of them stumbling to avoid a fall.

Jessica moved aside as Major Waddell and the first team of Corinari charged down the ramp like they were charging into battle. Jessica found it a bit odd, since the Corinari knew full well that no signs of life had been detected: no thermal signatures, no electromagnetic emanations, not even a working battery pack. However, she was not one to discourage being overly cautious, especially in unfamiliar territory. She peered out the hatch after them as they bounded down the ramp and across the freshly blasted terrain which was already becoming covered over by the drifting gray-white snow. Within moments, they disappeared from sight, swallowed up by the haze of swirling snow and dust. She watched the data display on her visor as the men fanned out in four different directions. After a minute, they all came to a stop. She listened over the comms in her head gear as each member of the first squad reported in to Major Waddell, confirming that each of their stations were clear of threats.

"*LZ secure*," Major Waddell reported over the comms. Despite the masks, she could hear the wind howling over his comm-set. "*Second squad, move out.*"

Jessica stepped back once more, making room for the next four men to exit the shuttle. She felt out of place as she watched them also disappear into the swirling haze. Charging off into the face of danger was something that she was not only trained to do, but also enjoyed. Unfortunately, that was

Major Waddell's role in this situation. He and his men were trained for ground combat and security operations. They had gone along on the journey back to Earth to help protect the Aurora's crew in just such a situation, and Jessica was confident that Waddell and his men were up to the task.

Minutes later, Waddell reported that the perimeter had been secured. Jessica motioned for the other three members of her team to follow her out, and she headed down the ramp.

The wind was not as fierce as she had expected. The ice shelf that rose to their aft provided a natural wind block for them. In its shadow, the wind was less direct and swirled about aimlessly instead of blasting from one side to the other.

The first thing she noticed as her boots touched the surface was that the snow was not snow at all. It was the same tiny frozen pellets that had come blasting into the cabin when they first cracked the hatch open. It crunched under her boots in a peculiar way, allowing her feet to sink into the snow pellets. On the areas of the LZ that had been blasted clean, the little pellets that were gathering in an effort to once again cover the LZ rolled slightly under her feet, making the surface seem slippery at first. "Watch your step!" she called over the comm-set, warning the others coming down the ramp behind her. "This stuff is slippery." As soon as the four of them were down the ramp, they moved in a group toward the first rectangular hill only ten meters away.

As they headed into the deeper snow, she noticed that the little frozen pellets didn't clump up the way snow usually did. That made it easier to plow through the deepening drifts. Soon, however, they were up to their waists in the frozen pellets. After a few moments, the going became far more difficult.

"Is there any way to get through this?" Jessica asked Mister Taves behind her.

"*Give me your weapon,*" the Takaran responded.

"What?"

"*Your weapon.*"

Jessica handed him her energy pistol, butt first.

Taves adjusted the settings on the weapon. "*Stand aside,*" he ordered. Jessica stepped back as he'd asked, allowing the Takaran to take her place at the front of the line. He pointed the weapon and squeezed the trigger. Instead of a bolt of energy leaping out of the barrel, a conical beam flashed from the weapon in short bursts. The waist deep drifts of icy pellets in front of them sizzled, instantly melting and turning into steam under the superheated beam of the weapon. The steam instantly disappeared, joining the swirling ice pellets in the air above them. Jessica was sure she could see the steam immediately turning back into ice and being scattered by the wind due to the extremely frigid temperatures.

The trick worked, and the team began to advance toward the first rectangular snow hill at a brisker pace. Mister Taves continued firing the adjusted weapon, melting the ice in front of them with each blast. Within a few minutes, they found themselves at the edge of the rectangular snow hill.

"That was slick," Jessica said to the Takaran. "Think you can use it to clear a way inside whatever is under this hill?"

"*I can try,*" Taves answered over the comms. He turned back around to face the hill before them and began blasting away with the adjusted weapon. He started near them, sweeping from side to side and progressively upward. After clearing each meter, he would start the process again at the bottom, working his way back up and away from them. After a few minutes of carving away the snow hill, he suddenly stopped.

"What's wrong?" Jessica asked.

"*If I go much deeper, I may damage whatever is underneath the snow. I am afraid we must dig the rest of the way.*"

Jessica looked at the two Corinairans standing behind her. "You heard the man; start digging."

All four of them began digging at the wall of icy pellets standing in front of them. They scooped with their gloved hands, carving away at the snow for several minutes until, finally, one of them found something solid.

"*I found something!*" one of the Corinairans announced. "*I think it's a wall.*"

The rest of them concentrated their efforts in the same location, quickly revealing a stone wall.

"There's got to be a door around here somewhere," Jessica said. "Stand back," she ordered the Corinairans. "Start firing again that way," she instructed Mister Taves as she pointed to the right of the uncovered section of wall, "parallel to the wall. Cut us a path about two meters wide. If we don't find a door by the time we reach the corner, we'll go back the other way."

"*As you wish,*" Taves answered. He stepped up and began firing Jessica's adjusted weapon once more, carving away at the snow. He soon learned to cut only a few centimeters away from the wall and allow the remaining snow to fall away of its own weight. Within minutes, they reached the corner of the wall without finding a doorway.

"Let's go back the other way," Jessica said.

"*Lieutenant Commander,*" Taves began in his most diplomatic fashion. "*We do not know what wall the entrance would be on. It could be around this corner for all we know.*"

"Good point," Jessica agreed. "Waddell," Jessica called over the comms, "send me one of your guys from the LZ, and make sure he's carrying an energy pistol."

"*Understood,*" Waddell answered.

"As soon as he gets here, adjust his weapon the same way," Jessica ordered. "I'll have him cut back the other way while you keep cutting this way, around the corner. One of you has got to uncover a door sooner or later."

"*Good thinking,*" the Takaran agreed. "*That will be much more efficient.*"

* * *

"Why aren't you eating with Vlad today?" Cameron asked.

"He's busy overseeing the installation of the first plasma torpedo cannon." Nathan picked at his salad. He had already eaten the small chunks of meat that the chef had added on his request. "You really eat only vegetables?"

"For the most part, yes."

"What if you were starving, and there was nothing but meat?"

"Then I'd eat it. I may be a vegetarian, but I'm not stupid."

"What about bread?"

"I eat bread on occasion."

"On occasion? I don't think I could survive

without bread."

"You and Vlad were made for each other, you know that?" Cameron said. "That man eats nothing but meat, potatoes, and bread."

"Yeah." Nathan pushed his unfinished salad away, leaning back in his chair. "The first thing I'm going to do when we get back to Earth is get myself a nice big steak."

"I thought we had plenty of steaks on board."

"Dollag steaks," Nathan corrected. "It's not the same thing; trust me."

"I'll take your word for it."

"What are you going to do when we get home?"

"New clothes and some fresh sea air," Cameron said. "I've been wearing the same three sets of uniforms forever, and I miss the sound of the ocean." She sighed at the thought. "But I imagine we'll all be quite busy writing reports about what happened." She glanced at Nathan, noting the quizzical look on his face. "I mean, a lot has happened. Over sixty of our crew died, including the entire command staff. We engaged in hostile actions with not only the Jung, but another previously unknown interstellar power. We even formed an alliance and initiated attacks. I imagine we are all going to have a lot of explaining to do."

Nathan stared at her for what seemed like forever. "You think it's that bad?"

"I don't know," she admitted with a shrug, "but there have got to be investigations. There are always investigations, especially when people die."

"You think we're in trouble?"

"I'm pretty sure *I'm* okay," Cameron stated. "I know the regs pretty well, and so far, nothing you've done *required* me to override you and take command.

Not even the forming of the alliance."

"Then I'm probably okay as well." The day-to-day activities, as well as the discovery of the Jasper, had managed to distract him from such thoughts. Now, he was starting to become nervous again.

"I wouldn't be so sure. Whenever something bad happens, someone always needs a scapegoat."

"And you think it'll be me," Nathan said.

"You would be the logical choice. The captain of a ship is responsible for everything that happens under his command. I don't think they'll toss you in prison or anything, but they may ask you to resign."

"I think I can handle that," Nathan said. "I think I've had enough excitement and adventure to last me a lifetime."

"Still, I'd consider an attorney if I were you," Cameron added. "Surely your father knows a few good ones."

* * *

The snow wall on their left suddenly collapsed, revealing a short tunnel that led into the stone wall.

"Stop! Stop!" Jessica ordered. Mister Taves deactivated the weapon. "I think this is it!" She looked about at the snow still piled up around the entrance to the tunnel. "Clear all of this. That snow piles up fast, and we don't want to get buried inside."

As Mister Taves continued using the weapon to melt the snow away from the entrance, Jessica and the two Corinairans proceeded into the tunnel. The tunnel darkened as they approached the far end. Jessica switched on the chest-mounted lighting panel, casting a pale white glow in front of her. Her light revealed a large wooden door built of vertical strips of heavy lumber. The strips were held together with rusted, iron straps, with heavy hand-forged rivets holding them in place. The door reminded Jessica of the old fortresses built by the early villages that formed in the first century after the bio-digital plague back on Earth. She had seen the images in school in the holo-suites used to educate children in groups. From the Data Ark, they had learned that such fortresses had been built by humans on Earth a thousand years before the great plague.

"Should I be recording this?" one of the Corinairans asked.

Jessica turned to look at him, taking note of the name on his helmet. "What do you think, Mister Soutter?"

"I should be recording this."

Jessica turned back around to face the door as Mister Soutter's chest-mounted lighting plate also snapped on, casting its own pale, white light in addition to Jessica's. She stepped forward and pulled at the great door, but it did not move. She pulled again and again, but it was stuck.

"The hinges are probably frozen shut," Mister Taves commented as his own light panel came to life.

"Or rusted in place," Jessica added. "How are we going to get it open?"

Taves held up the weapon that he had been using to carve away the snow. *"This weapon has many useful settings,"* he proclaimed with no small amount of pride. He stepped forward and made several more adjustments to the weapon's power settings and the tip of its barrel. He took aim and fired at the door, this time sending a narrow, precise beam of red light that burned a clean line through the heavy door. The tunnel began to fill with smoke. Mister Taves struggled to see clearly, hoping to avoid the uppermost metal strap for fear of collapsing the entire door. Within minutes, he had completed a clean cut across the door at about shoulder height just below the uppermost iron strap. After another minute, he'd managed to cut through the iron strap at the bottom. *"Give me a hand,"* he said as he handed the weapon back to Jessica.

Mister Soutter and his fellow Corinairan, Mister Kilbore, stepped up on either side of the Takaran. Together, they pushed inward on the cut door timbers, slowly forcing them to move until they finally fell inward.

Jessica crouched down and leaned inward through the shoulder high opening. She shined a handheld light about the space on the other side. There appeared to be several pieces of equipment, all in various states of disrepair. The room was dusty and frozen with icicles hanging from the beams as well as from points on various pieces of equipment where they had once leaked fluid.

"This place hasn't seen light in years," Mister Soutter commented as he peered from behind Jessica.

"More like centuries," she corrected as she advanced through the opening, stepping over the fallen door timbers. "Waddell, Nash. I'm stepping inside. How do you copy?"

"Loud and clear, Lieutenant Commander."

"I'll check back with you every few minutes."

"Understood."

Jessica slowly made her way deeper into the dark room, followed closely by her three team members.

"It looks like an entry chamber," Mister Taves

said. "*There are stalls along that wall, as if to hold cold weather gear,*" he explained, pointing to the far wall. "*And those appear to be tool lockers.*"

"*If those are cold weather gear stalls, where is the cold weather gear?*" Mister Soutter wondered.

"Maybe this is just some sort of outpost?" Jessica said. She came to another door at the far end of the room. "If you're right, then this must be the inner door."

Mister Taves examined the second door. "*Its construction is similar to the outer door, only smaller. Odd that there are no latches or other mechanisms for securing the doors.*"

"*The wind blows inward from the outside,*" Mister Soutter noted. "*They probably didn't need a way to secure the doors.*"

Jessica ignored their debate, pulling the door outward. Its hinges creaked and moaned as the door resisted her efforts. Finally, it gave in and opened. Jessica moved through the inner doorway, confirming her connectivity with Major Waddell and his security teams on the outside as she made her way forward. She paused just after stepping through the doorway, shining her light both left and right. "It's a corridor," she told the others. "It goes off nearly perpendicular to the right and at about a forty-five degree angle to the left."

"*It must connect with the other buildings,*" Mister Taves said. "*There were at least five more rectangular hills in the overhead optical scans of the surface.*"

"Taves, with me," Jessica ordered. "Soutter, Kilbore, head right. Check in every five minutes."

"Yes, sir," Mister Soutter answered.

Jessica watched for a moment as Soutter and Kilbore headed down the right corridor, their suit lights quickly fading into the darkness. She turned and started down the corridor to their left, shining her light from side to side. She did not care for the illumination provided by the panels on the chest of her cold weather garment, as the light was pale, which made it difficult to pick out details.

The corridor was long and featureless other than the pattern of stones that formed the walls. There were light panels every five meters, interconnected by conduit that ran along the upper edges of the wall. The floor appeared to also be made of stone. However, it was smooth and seamless as if cast as one long piece. The colonists must have had considerable technology available to them at some point, as well as the knowledge to use it.

After a few minutes, they came to another door, this time with a sign on the wall next to the door. The sign was carved out of wood, the letters filled in with some type of dye.

"Control room," Jessica announced.

"*What?*" Mister Taves asked.

Jessica pointed at the sign. "I thought you guys already learned how to read Angla."

"*That is not Angla,*" Mister Taves objected over the comm-set. He studied the sign further. "*However, it does bear some resemblance.*"

Jessica opened the door and entered the control room. Inside, there were several consoles. They did not appear to be designed specifically for the space, but rather, they looked as if they had been scavenged from a ship of some type and installed here. It occurred to her that most of the technology she had seen so far could easily have been scavenged from a spaceship. She moved deeper into the room, approaching what appeared to be the main console on the far side. She came up behind the high-backed chair in front of the console, slowly turning it around to face her. In the chair sat a middle-aged man huddled in a heavy parka. His hands were clad in gloves and several strips of cloth. His legs were covered by several blankets, each wrapped tightly around his lower extremities. His eyes were half open, and his mouth slightly agape. His skin was pale and ghostly with a fine layer of gray-white ice crystals covering every surface of his body. "I've got a body," Jessica stated calmly.

"There are two more over here," Mister Taves stated over the comm-set. *"They appear to be frozen."*

"Lieutenant Commander Nash, this is Soutter," Mister Soutter called over the comm-set. His voice had a twinge of panic in its tone.

"Go ahead," Jessica answered.

"We've got bodies over here," he announced over the comm-set. *"There are at least ten of them so far. They're all frozen, sir."*

"Copy that. We've got some as well," Jessica answered. "Keep pushing forward, and keep a body count as you go, and record everything, Mister Soutter." Jessica turned to Mister Taves. "See if you can find a data core or something. There's got to be a log file around here somewhere."

* * *

Nathan stood in the main hangar deck as the landing shuttle rolled to a stop and began cycling down its engines. The shuttle looked weather beaten and worn, as did the landing party as they disembarked still clad in their cold weather gear with their hoods back and their air masks dangling from their necks. Jessica separated from the group, veering over to her captain with a case in her left hand.

"Lieutenant Commander," Nathan greeted.

"Sir."

"Rough trip?"

"I've had rougher."

"Well?"

"They're all dead, sir. It wasn't pretty."

"Were they from the Jasper?"

"I'm not sure," she admitted. "Maybe, or maybe their descendants."

"What's that?" he asked, pointing to the case in her left hand.

"We pulled what we think is a data core. I don't know if it still works."

"Give it to Cheng's people," Nathan instructed.

"Mister Taves offered to take a crack at it," Jessica told him.

"Give it to Vlad first. I suspect it's closer to our technology than the Takarans' anyway."

"Yes, sir."

Nathan noticed Jessica wasn't herself. She seemed emotionally drained. "You okay?"

"Like I said, it was not pretty."

"Care to talk about it?"

"Not really, Nathan," she told him, "at least not now. Maybe later, after a long hot shower and some chow." Jessica pulled a data module from the chest piece on her cold weather suit and handed it to Nathan. "We recorded everything we saw."

Nathan looked at the data module in his hand, wondering what was stored on the device.

"Those people never had a chance down there," Jessica told him, "not in that cold."

"Makes you wonder why they even went down there to begin with," Nathan said.

"Yes, sir, it does."

"Take some down time, Lieutenant Commander. I'll take a look at the recordings, and we'll talk later."

"Yes, sir."

* * *

Nathan sat in his ready room, transfixed by the images shown on the large view screen built into the forward bulkhead. Emaciated humans with sunken eyes and cheeks, wrapped in layers upon layers of well-worn clothing and blankets. There were many signs of technology: electrical, electronics, even a fusion generator. However, many of these items appeared to have been scavenged from systems not intended for use on the surface. They were too diverse, and in many places had been joined together in haphazard fashion. Nathan was sure that most of the components had come from one or more shuttles, possibly the one that had brought them down to the surface.

The worst images were those of the carcasses of the dead, most of which had been carefully butchered as if to be consumed. When he first saw the carcasses, Nathan couldn't believe it. He was sure his eyes were playing tricks on him. There were so many of them. They had been so desperate that they had abandoned all decency, leaving the carcasses lying in a cold room where they would quickly freeze and not smell. In the end, they must have fallen deeper into despair as they no longer bothered disposing of the carcasses, leaving them lying about. Perhaps they were too weak to drag

197

them into storage. Nathan could only hope that had been the case.

"Captain?" Cameron called from the hatchway.

Nathan paused the video playback. "Yes, Commander?"

"Medical has finished with the tissue samples brought back from the surface. There were no signs of the plague."

"Well, we didn't expect any. The biological version cannot survive in sub-zero temperatures. That much we do know." Nathan sighed. "What about the data core?"

"Vlad is working on it now. He's going to link it up with a data pad instead of our own systems, just to be safe."

"Very well."

"Is everything all right?"

"These people didn't die of the plague, Commander. They were alive long enough to build heavy stone shelters. They were able to make use of technology from disabled shuttles; at least, I think that's where they got it. When they died, they were cold, starving, and desperate. You can see it in their frozen expressions. What I don't get is why they settled in such an unforgiving environment. Why not closer to the planet's equator where it's warmer?"

"Yosef says there's evidence of heavy lava flows all over the central latitudes. She thinks there was considerable volcanic activity some time ago."

"Then why not settle on the edge or a few hundred kilometers away from the flows? It would still have to be warmer."

"Maybe the site was more habitable when they landed," Cameron theorized. "It is in the middle latitudes."

"Well tell Vlad to get on that core," Nathan urged. "I want to know what happened to these people."

"Why is it so important to you?" Cameron wondered.

Nathan jumped the paused video image back a few frames, stopping on a shot of one of the neatly carved bodies. "These people were forced to eat each other, Commander, while everything they needed was sitting in orbit above them."

"Understood," Cameron answered. "In the meantime, we've finished off-loading what usable propellant was left on the Jasper. Perhaps we should be moving on."

"How's our propellant level?"

"Twenty-two percent of capacity," Cameron answered. "We gained about ten percent by coming here."

"Very well. Make way as soon as possible."

"Aye, sir." Cameron glanced at the horrible image on the screen, quickly turning her head away to exit the ready room.

Nathan continued watching the video playback, feeling compelled to witness what the passengers of the Jasper had gone through. He was enraged at what had happened on the surface below him so many centuries ago. He was also frustrated that there was nothing he could do about it. Those people died, perhaps needlessly, and there would be no one to hold accountable for their deaths. It made him wonder, in the end, who would be held accountable for all the deaths both on the Aurora and in her wake.

CHAPTER SIX

"Cheng," Nathan greeted as he entered the port torpedo room. "Something to show me?"

"Yes, Captain," Vladimir stated. "Lieutenant Montgomery and his team have completed the first tube refit. Torpedo tube number two is now configured to fire plasma cannon shots."

"Wonderful," Nathan answered, albeit with some skepticism in his voice. "How does it work?"

"Well, our final design was a bit different than our first conceptual drawings," Lieutenant Montgomery explained. "To make a long story short, we had to make the cannon a bit smaller in order to fit it inside the existing outer tube sleeve. While this does decrease the potential strike power of the weapon to some degree, it gives us room to gimble the cannon within the tube."

"This means we no longer have to be pointed exactly at the target when firing," Vladimir elaborated. "We just have to be pointed in the close vicinity of the target."

"How close?" Nathan asked.

"The more distant the target, the less accurately the ship needs to point," Lieutenant Montgomery explained.

"And this weapon will work?"

"We will need to conduct a series of test shots

at targets positioned at exact locations in relation to the weapon in order to calibrate the targeting systems," Vladimir told him. "However, the weapon is ready to fire, sir."

"What did you say the effective range of the weapon is?" Nathan asked.

"Five hundred kilometers," Lieutenant Montgomery answered. "After that, the plasma shot begins to spread out and weaken rather rapidly."

"Tactical, Captain," Nathan called over his comm-set.

"*Captain, go for Tactical,*" Mister Randeen answered.

"Threat board?"

"*All clear, sir.*"

"Do we have any training flights out?"

"*No, sir. They landed ten minutes ago. We're at red deck.*"

"Very well. We're about to fire a test shot of the plasma cannon out of the number two torpedo tube. Please track the flight path and intensity of the shot. Send the results to the port torpedo room."

"*Aye, sir.*"

"Gentlemen, you may take a test shot," Nathan announced.

"Very well, sir," Lieutenant Montgomery responded. "If everyone will please clear the chamber, we will proceed."

Nathan and the others turned and withdrew to the next compartment, after which, the large door that separated the torpedo tube chamber from the main torpedo room lowered into place.

"Charge the weapon to ten percent," Lieutenant Montgomery ordered his crew.

"Only ten percent?" Nathan wondered.

"There is no need to fire at full power on the first shot," Vladimir said. "That would be an unnecessary risk."

"Of course," Nathan said, trying not to appear as dumb as he felt.

"Tube room sealed," the Takaran technician reported. "Tube two charged at ten percent. Outer doors are open. All systems report weapon is ready to fire."

"Fire the weapon," Lieutenant Montgomery ordered.

"Firing weapon."

A muffled hum sounded from the tube room on the other side of the heavy door. The hum quickly grew in intensity but, within a second, was replaced with a *thwang* that shook the room and would have been deafening had they not been separated from the weapon by the heavy door. As the weapon fired, Nathan was sure he felt every hair on his body tingle for a moment.

"Firing cycle complete. Charge expended. Taking the weapon offline," the technician reported.

"Vent and scrub the chamber," Lieutenant Montgomery ordered.

Nathan looked at Vladimir. "When the weapon fires, it vents toxic gases into the chamber," Vladimir explained. "The compartment must be ventilated to space and repressurized before anyone can safely enter the chamber."

"That doesn't seem like a good idea," Nathan said.

"These cannons were not designed to be used in an enclosed space," Lieutenant Montgomery reminded them. "Accommodations will have to be made."

"Will this interfere with our regular torpedoes?"

"Currently, yes," Vladimir answered. "Since we do not have auto-loading systems, no one would be able to enter the chamber to load conventional torpedoes. However, assuming the weapon passes all tests, we have plans to install a secondary bulkhead to allow us to manually load conventional torpedoes while using the plasma cannon."

"You're going to add a wall?" Nathan wondered.

"It is not as difficult as it sounds," Vladimir assured him.

"Data is coming in now," the technician reported.

Nathan stepped up to the display, noticing the potential energy of the shot. "That was at ten percent power?" he asked, pointing at the display.

"Yes, sir," Lieutenant Montgomery answered proudly.

"Nice," Nathan congratulated. "Very nice indeed. How long do you need to prepare for calibration?"

"A few hours," Vladimir answered.

"We jump in one, then you'll have a seven-hour window in which to calibrate that thing. Assuming that it works, how long will it take to install the other two tubes?"

"About a week for each," Lieutenant Montgomery stated.

"Excellent. Carry on, Lieutenant," Nathan ordered.

* * *

"I believe it's safe to revive him now, Captain," Doctor Chen said.

Nathan looked at the old man lying on the medical bed. His hair was long and gray, and he had a rough, untrimmed beard. He was thin and appeared frail, which Nathan understood to be the result of the failing neuromuscular stimulation systems in the man's stasis pod.

"I wonder how he'll react," Nathan said. "I mean, he's been in stasis for eight hundred years." Nathan turned to the doctor. "Do you think he'll react badly?"

"If by badly you mean with a lot of emotion and disbelief, then yes," Doctor Chen answered. "However, he is still under selective muscular paralytics. They were necessary to keep him still while the nanites repaired damage to his major organs and skeletal muscles." She paused and looked at Nathan. "Shall I?"

"Yes." Nathan watched as Doctor Chen administered the stimulant into the patient's intravenous line.

"It should only take a moment or two to take effect," she announced as she put away the syringe.

"Imagine, this guy was around during the plague," Nathan said in amazement. "He witnessed the collapse of civilization."

"You are such a history geek," Jessica mumbled, rolling her eyes.

The old man's head moved slowly from side to side as his eyes began to squint at the bright lights in the room. Doctor Chen quickly turned off the overhead examination light, making the illumination in the room considerably less bright. The old man's left eye cracked open wider, looking at Jessica. "Either I'm dreaming..." he mumbled as he closed his left eye again. His head rolled back to the right as his right eye opened to the sight of Nathan and Vladimir. "... or it worked." The old man's head rolled back to the left and both his eyes opened. He looked Jessica up and down for a moment. "Well, since you're not naked, I guess I'm not dreaming." Jessica smiled as the old man's eyes closed and his head rolled back to center. "What year?"

"What?" Nathan asked.

The old man coughed. "What year is it? I just came out of stasis; what the hell did you expect me to ask?"

"3472," Nathan answered.

The old man opened his eyes, looking directly at Nathan. "Bullshit."

"Why would I lie?"

"Then you're not bullshitting me?"

"No, sir, I'm not," Nathan assured him. "The year is 3472."

"I knew it might take a while, but I didn't expect 3472." The old man tried unsuccessfully to raise his left hand. "Hey, why can't I move my arms? Or my legs for that matter?"

"You were given targeted paralytics to keep your body immobile during regenerative treatment," Doctor Chen explained. "They will wear off soon, and you will be able to move again."

"You must be the doctor, then," the old man surmised.

"Yes, sir, I am Doctor Chen, the ship's chief medical officer."

"Ship? What ship?"

"You're on the United Earth Ship, Aurora," Nathan tried to explain.

"United what?"

"United Earth..."

"The only thing united about the people of Earth was that they were all on the same hunk of rock," the old man objected. "Where's the captain?"

"I am the captain," Nathan stated, "Captain Nathan Scott of the Earth Defense Force."

"Defense? Defense against what?"

"Sir, try to relax," Doctor Chen urged. "You've been in stasis for a long time. A lot has changed."

The old man closed his eyes again as he tried to deal with the onslaught of information. Finally, he opened his eyes again and looked at Nathan. "You don't look old enough to be a captain."

"Yeah, I get that a lot. This is my chief engineer, Lieutenant Commander Kamenetskiy, and my chief of security, Lieutenant Commander Nash."

"Chief of security?" the old man asked in disbelief. "You're too hot to be in security."

"Lulls my adversaries into a false sense of security," Jessica answered with a wink.

The old man chuckled. "I'll bet it does at that." He coughed again. "What about the others?" he asked. "Did any of them make it?"

Nathan's expression turned grim. "I'm afraid not, sir. I am sorry."

The old man closed his eyes and mumbled softly, "Damn."

"It is a miracle that you survived," Doctor Chen commented, trying to ease his pain.

"Ain't no miracle about it, Doc," the old man insisted. "I chose to survive. I was just lucky enough to have the tools to do so."

"May I ask your name, sir?" Nathan's tone had become more serious.

The old man looked at Nathan. "Percival, Jonathon Percival."

"Do you feel up to answering some questions, Mister Percival?"

The old man closed his eyes again. "Perhaps your questions could wait, Captain. I seem to be under the influence of your futuristic medications at the moment."

"Of course, Mister Percival. I will check back with you later." Nathan looked at the others, gesturing for them to follow him out of the room.

Nathan waited until Doctor Chen closed the door behind them before speaking. "Doctor, how long until he's more himself, mentally that is?"

"There's no telling, Captain. We don't know what his normal mental state was, so we have nothing to compare it to. I suspect that after the paralytics wear off and he's had time to clean up a bit, he will feel more up to conversation."

"Sir," Jessica interrupted, "if I may make a suggestion?"

"Go ahead."

"Don't interrogate the man. After all, as far as we know, he hasn't done anything wrong."

"Three hundred people died in their stasis pods while the others died on the surface," Nathan argued. "Someone did something wrong."

"For all we know, he knows nothing about it," Jessica defended, tilting her head back toward the medical treatment room where Mister Percival rested.

"Then why didn't he ask specifically about the mission?" Nathan said. "He asked about the others, but not the colony or the mission. He knew something went wrong."

"He could have surmised that by the fact that he is on another ship and not in the colony where he expected to wake up."

"And why didn't he seem more surprised that

he'd been in stasis for so long?" Nathan asked.

"He did accept that fact rather easily," Vladimir added.

"All I'm saying is that there is a better way to go about this. If you start asking him questions, he's going to become defensive."

"What do you suggest we do?"

"Invite him to dinner," Jessica suggested with a sinister grin.

"I can make Golupzi," Vladimir said.

"We want him alive," Nathan jeered.

"Let him get cleaned up and put on some fresh clothes. Give him some self-respect. People are more relaxed when they're eating; they're more likely to talk. Get him to talk about himself, the mission. It worked on Haven."

"She's right," Vladimir admitted.

"Very well, invite him to dinner in the captain's mess at eighteen hundred hours. I'll have my cook find something from his time period in the Ark files."

"No Golupzi?" Vladimir asked.

"We're inviting him to dinner, Vlad, not torturing him." Nathan turned to look at Vladimir. "Shouldn't you be installing some plasma cannons or something?" He turned back to Jessica. "All right, we'll try it your way. Senior staff and Mister Percival. Meanwhile, search the Ark files and see what you can find out about Jonathon Percival."

"I'll take a look, but don't hold your breath. I don't think they have records on every single human being that lived in the core."

"Try anyway," Nathan instructed Jessica. "And you invite him. He seems to like you better."

"Doesn't everyone?"

* * *

"Jump fifty-nine complete," Loki reported.

"Position verified," Lieutenant Yosef added. "We are now fifty-seven light years from Sol."

Nathan smiled at the lieutenant. She had been announcing their distance from home ever since they left BD+25 3252. They had been jumping their way home for more than two weeks now, and the knowledge that the Earth was now only a handful of jumps away was having a positive effect on morale, at least for the Terran members of the crew.

For Nathan, it was a mixed bag of emotions. On the one hand, he dreaded the endless documentation and questioning that he and his crew were sure to undergo, but on the other hand, the idea of turning over the ship and all the responsibilities that went with it created an overwhelming feeling of anticipated relief. He had never wanted to be in command. Unlike his father, Nathan did not see himself as a leader. There had been times during his tenure as the Aurora's de facto captain that he had enjoyed his role, but those times had been few and far between. The decisions he had been forced to make and the lives that had been sacrificed as a result would haunt him for years to come, most probably for his lifetime. He could justify each and every one of them quite logically, but logic did not help him sleep at night.

"Captain, I'm picking up the same transmissions as before," Lieutenant Yosef reported.

"Those from the last layover?" Nathan asked. As they had grown closer to the core worlds, they had begun picking up various signals. However, thus far, they had been too weak to decipher with any certainty.

"Yes, sir, but they're stronger now. I think I might be able to make them out this time."

"How long?"

"I can tell you where they are coming from now. 72 Herculis. It's a G-type system located forty-seven point eight light years from Earth. It's about ten light years from our current position."

"72 Herculis is listed in the Ark as a fringe settlement," Jessica added from the tactical station. "The fourth planet was settled and named Tanna."

"What do we know about the settlement?" Nathan asked.

"At the time the Ark was locked down, the Tanna settlement was only twenty-two years old. Population of seven thousand, mostly miners and their families as well as infrastructure support personnel. It was a corporate colony started by one of the interstellar mega-corps. It was intended to be an industrial base to support colonization efforts farther out in the fringe."

"Put the local star map up," Nathan ordered. A moment later, a three-dimensional view of the core and all her worlds appeared on the main view screen.

"At forty-seven light years, isn't it already pretty far out, even for a fringe world?" Lieutenant Yosef wondered.

"Just before the bio-digital plague struck, the mega-corps were preparing for another colonization push. A few hundred habitable worlds had been cataloged, some as far as two-hundred light years out. With improved FTL drives on the horizon, the mega-corps were betting on another wave of eager colonists willing to sell their souls for a chance to start a new world. An industrial base on the edge of the fringe would have made a lot of money, as it would have gotten goods out to the new worlds faster and cheaper than hauling them out from the core worlds." Nathan examined the star map on the main view screen, taking note of the relative positions of all the stars along their route back to Sol. "Any updated data on the settlement?" he asked.

"No, sir," Jessica told him.

"Captain, I'm looking at multiple signals here," Lieutenant Yosef announced, "civilian comm, navigation, entertainment broadcasts. I'm also picking up transmissions on Jung frequencies."

"Ship-to-ship?" Nathan wondered.

"No, sir. I'm pretty sure they're automated navigational transponders."

"Then we can assume that it's a Jung-controlled system," Jessica stated.

"According to Fleet intel, they all are, except Sol," Nathan reminded her.

"Fleet's intel on the influence of the Jung is based mostly on limited signals intelligence, sir. They had only a dozen or so FTL recon flights prior to our departure. 72 Herculis has never been reconnoitered."

"Think we should check it out?" Nathan asked his security chief.

"We should at least send the Falcon on a coast-through," Jessica suggested. "If we're lucky, there might even be a Jung ship or two in port there."

"If we're lucky, there won't be," Nathan commented.

"Captain, Fleet has only seen eight actual Jung warships to date, not including the gunboats that jumped us in the Oort. Three of those were the same design. Knowing how spread out their ships actually are could be extremely valuable information. Don't forget: we still don't know exactly where the Jung homeworld is located."

"That's what's worrying me," Nathan admitted. "What if it's 72 Herculis?"

"Doubtful, sir. All indications are that their homeworld is on the other side of the core based on the density of signals collected by Earth thus far."

"Be even better if we could get boots on the ground for a few days."

Nathan turned and looked at Jessica who was smiling. "Don't even think about it, Lieutenant Commander." Nathan turned back to his flight team sitting at the helm in front of him. "Wake up your relief team, boys. You've got a recon mission to fly."

"Hell yeah," Josh exclaimed.

Loki rolled his eyes. "I thought you hated recon flights?"

"Anything is better than this jump-wait-jump crap."

"We'll see if you still feel that way after fourteen hours sitting in a cold, cramped cockpit," Loki mumbled.

* * *

"I'm just not sure it's a good idea," Cameron stated as she took her seat at the dining table in the captain's mess. "It takes about fifteen hours to do a coast-through recon pass. That's a long time for us to sit in one place waiting for them to return."

"They're going to meet us at the next jump point," Nathan told her. "That way, we won't lose any time."

"And if they are detected? Wouldn't that alert the Jung to our presence in the area?"

"It might alert them to a presence in the area, but there's nothing on the Falcon that screams Earth technology."

"Except the jump drive," Cameron reminded him.

"They are well aware of their responsibilities in the matter, Commander."

"Are they, Nathan? It's not like they swore an oath or anything."

"Not everyone requires an oath to make them do the right thing, Cameron. Josh and Loki know the stakes. I'm confident they would be willing to sacrifice themselves rather than be captured. I shouldn't have to remind you that they've both demonstrated their willingness to put their lives on the line on more than one occasion."

"It's just that Josh takes such great risks without even thinking about them."

"Actually, I don't think he does," Nathan defended. "I think he's confident in every maneuver he makes. He doesn't see the risk, because he knows it will work. It's a gift, really."

"Or a curse," Cameron added.

"That's why he and Loki make such a great team. Loki sees the risk and reminds Josh of it when necessary. You might say Loki is Josh's Cameron."

"Is that how you see me: unwilling to take risks?"

"Not at all," Nathan said. "I tend to make decisions based on instinct; you tend to fully analyze your options before deciding. I think that's why Captain Roberts put us together to begin with. He knew that your analytical side would properly balance my instinctive side. Whenever you question my decision, it makes me think twice. If you agree with me, then I'm that much more confident that I'm doing the right thing."

"Because I'll call you on it if you're wrong," Cameron said.

"Exactly. I can count on you to tell me when I'm wrong."

"Well, rest assured, sir, I'll always be there to tell you when you're being stupid."

"I said wrong, not stupid."

Cameron picked up her glass of water, concealing the smile on her face.

"What did we miss?" Jessica asked as she and Vladimir entered the captain's mess.

"Nathan was just telling me that it was my job to tell him when he's wrong," Cameron announced.

"Sounds like too much work," Vladimir said.

"Where's the guest of honor?" Jessica wondered.

"He'll be here shortly," Nathan answered. "Did you find anything about him in the Ark files?"

"Nothing," Jessica answered as she took her seat. "The Ark doesn't contain information about individuals unless they did something noteworthy."

"Then we'll have no way to validate whatever he tells us," Cameron noted.

"Other than repetitive questioning, no," Jessica admitted, "and that will only take us so far."

"What is it you're hoping to discover?" Vladimir asked.

"What went wrong," Nathan answered. "Why were more than half of the cargo containers still in orbit? Why weren't the remaining colonists revived and moved down to the surface? What happened to the colonists that did go down to the surface?"

"If he was in stasis the whole time, he probably won't have any of those answers."

"Yeah, I'd thought of that," Nathan said. "Well, at the very least, he might be able to shed some light on what happened after the Data Ark was sealed off. There is still so much we don't know about the fall of the core worlds and the Earth itself. He actually lived through it."

"How is that going to help us in our current situation?" Jessica wondered.

"It won't," Nathan admitted, "but it is interesting."

The conversation was interrupted when the door opened and Mister Percival was wheeled in by one of Jessica's Corinari security officers. His hair had been trimmed and tied back, and his beard shaved. He sported a basic day uniform without any rank insignia or service patches.

"Mister Percival, welcome." Nathan seemed a bit taken aback by the wheel chair. "If you're not up to this, we can postpone..."

"No need, Captain," Mister Percival insisted. He struggled slightly to rise to his feet and walked the two meters from his wheelchair to his place at the captain's table. "I am well enough to dine and partake in some light conversation. I'm just not yet strong enough to walk from the medical center to your dining cabin, at least not according to young Doctor Chen."

"If you're sure then."

"Yes, I'm sure. Besides, I haven't eaten in a thousand years."

"Not a statement you hear every day," Nathan noted. "I hope you don't mind, but on the advice of Doctor Chen, tonight's menu will be on the bland side."

"Yes, I have been instructed to eat lightly until my digestive system returns to normal."

"Very well then. Shall we eat?" Nathan motioned to Mister Collins, his personal chef, to begin dinner service.

Mister Percival looked at Cameron.

"Oh, my apologies," Nathan offered, realizing that Mister Percival and Cameron had not yet been introduced. "This is my executive officer, Commander Cameron Taylor."

"A pleasure to meet you, ma'am," Mister Percival said.

"The pleasure is all mine, sir," Cameron answered politely.

"You have a fine ship, Captain," Mister Percival began, "from what little I have seen of her. What type of vessel is she?"

"The Aurora was built primarily as a ship of exploration and diplomacy," Nathan explained.

"Your personnel do not appear to be explorers, Captain."

"As we are a member of the Earth Defense Force, we are also a ship of war. Recent events have required us to take a more aggressive stance in terms of security."

"What type of events?"

"It's a bit complicated," Nathan said, sidestepping the topic, "and perhaps a matter better discussed later."

"Of course. I assume your ship is FTL capable."

"In a manner of speaking, yes." Again, Nathan was avoiding answering Mister Percival's question directly.

"Another matter best left for later?" Mister Percival wondered aloud.

"Probably, yes. For now, let's just say that the Aurora is capable of moving about the galaxy more quickly than most ships."

Mister Percival took a small bite of the salad

placed before him, chewing slowly as he savored the taste and texture of the unfamiliar leafy vegetables. "This is quite tasty. However, I am unfamiliar with this vegetable."

"We obtained it during our journey," Nathan stated. "I can inquire as to its name if you'd like."

"It is not necessary," Mister Percival stated as he took another bite. He chewed another moment, watching the others as they also worked on their meals. All eyes seemed to be upon him. "Perhaps we should skip the pleasantries and get to the heart of the matter. I am sure you all have many questions of me. I am more than willing to answer them to the best of my knowledge."

"Tell us about your mission," Nathan said. "Your ship was last listed as decommissioned. According to your logs, your ship began service again in 2370 under the command of Alan Dubnyk."

"Yes, he was our captain."

"Captain Dubnyk was an independent hauler dealing in questionable cargo, and doing so in an unregistered and unregulated vessel. He was hardly the type one would hire to transport a colonization mission."

"Quite true, Captain. But his price was right, and pickings were slim at the time. That made the decision rather easy."

Nathan looked puzzled. "You speak as if you have firsthand knowledge of the transaction."

"I was the mission's benefactor, Captain. I was the one that hired him."

"You were the mission's benefactor," Jessica said in disbelief.

"I was not its sole source of finance," Mister Percival explained, "just its largest contributor.

Every passenger paid for their passage, as well as their basic supplies. I paid for the stasis pods and the colonization packages that would ensure the success of the settlement."

"Still, a sizable and somewhat risky investment," Nathan stated.

"It was a crazy and horrific time, Captain. You might be surprised how little normal logic applied to day–to-day life back then."

"Still, we're talking billions of credits, Mister Percival. You must have been quite wealthy."

"Actually, it was more like millions. As I said, each passenger had to pay their own way. And much of the equipment needed was available on the black market, one of the many benefits of mounting such a mission from the fringe instead of the core."

"It doesn't sound entirely legal," Cameron said, her face revealing no underlying emotions.

Mister Percival laughed. "There was very little about the mission that was legal, Commander. Then again, there was very little that was legal about *most* refugee missions. Like I said, it was a crazy, horrific time."

"Still," Nathan said, "I can't help but wonder why you invested such a disproportionate amount of your own money into the expedition."

"I was trying to save my own life."

"Wasn't everyone?" Cameron asked.

"No, you don't understand," Mister Percival explained, shaking his head. "In the beginning, there were many evacuee colonization expeditions, each of them fully licensed and properly registered with the appropriate authorities. But I could not buy my way into any of them because of medical problems."

"What type of medical problems?" Nathan asked.

"I have an incurable degenerative muscular disorder called Minnian's disease. This precluded me from being a member of legitimate colonization missions. The only way I could see to survive the plague was to fund my own expedition. It was well known that unregistered expeditions were leaving fringe worlds on a regular basis, so I traveled to 26 Draconis where I met up with Captain Dubnyk. Together, we assembled an expedition of five hundred evacuees with all the appropriate equipment and supplies needed to guarantee their success."

"That still would not save your life," Vladimir stated. "It would only prevent you from succumbing to the plague."

"The pod," Nathan realized. "You intended to stay in it until a cure was found."

"Correct," Mister Percival admitted.

"Couldn't you have done that at home?" Jessica wondered.

"The predictions were dire," Mister Percival stated. "It was all over the news. Civilization in the core was headed for complete collapse. It seemed safer to have my pod taken elsewhere for safe keeping."

"That's why you funded the expedition," Cameron said.

"My only requirement was that my pod be kept safe and functioning. It was designed to last for hundreds of years, even without human supervision. If and when a cure for my ailment was discovered, I was to be revived and cured."

"That's why you chose BD+25 3252," Nathan realized, "because of its location."

"It was not too far out, in case some of the fringe worlds managed to survive, and it was not too far off the flight path of many other expeditions that had already launched."

"Hedging your bets," Jessica commented.

"In a manner of speaking, yes." Mister Percival put down his fork. "Captain, other than funding an unregistered expedition, I did nothing wrong. In fact, I gave five hundred evacuees a chance that they otherwise might not have had. It is unfortunate that it did not work out for them."

"We aren't here to pass judgment on you, Mister Percival," Nathan assured him. "We just want to know the truth. As you have said, those were difficult times. You are incredibly lucky to have survived them."

The room went silent for several minutes as they dined. Both Nathan and Jessica watched Mister Percival through discreet glances. Although his story made sense and lined up with what little they knew about the time of the great plague, there was something about the man that didn't sit right with Nathan.

"Captain," Mister Percival said, breaking the tense silence, "I have been made aware that the others on the Jasper did not survive, but no one has told me what happened to them."

"We don't really know for sure," Nathan admitted, "at least, not yet. All we know is that about two hundred of them went down to the surface, along with nearly half of their cargo. We found the Jasper, just over half her cargo, and three hundred passengers who passed away in their stasis pods—except for you, of course."

"What happened to those who went to the surface?" Mister Percival asked.

Nathan noticed a lack of hope in the man's voice.

"I'm afraid they did not survive either. Apparently, the winters were more harsh than originally anticipated."

"The second planet of the BD+25 3252 system was considered habitable," Mister Percival insisted, "borderline, due to the fact that two-thirds of the world was covered by ice, but habitable nonetheless. Any idea what caused their demise?"

"All we know is that they appeared to have starved and frozen to death."

"Was there any information in the colony logs?"

"We are working on retrieving the colony logs, as well as those from the Jasper. We were hoping you might know something about their demise."

"I'm sorry, Captain. I was placed in stasis before departure. I never even met the other passengers, only Captain Dubnyk and the flight medic."

Another uncomfortable silence fell on them as they continued to dine. "I cannot help but wonder how many of them actually made it," Mister Percival stated, breaking the silence once again. His eyes rose from his plate to meet Nathan's. He noticed a puzzled look on the captain's face. "I'm sorry; I was speaking of all the other expeditions. There were so many in the end, some well prepared, some not so much. I wonder how many of them survived or even thrived and grew into fully industrialized worlds."

"We have come across a few," Nathan admitted. "You said there were many such expeditions?"

"Yes, indeed. Perhaps thousands." Mister Percival paused for a moment. "But surely, being from Earth, you know all of this."

"We have no records pertaining to the collapse of the core. The records in the Data Ark end just as the digital aspect of..."

"The Data Ark? The collapse?" Mister Percival wondered. "What are you talking about, Captain? What collapse?"

"I'm sorry, Mister Percival. I assumed you knew," Nathan said.

"How bad was it? I mean, the predictions were grave, but we always figured it was because they wanted to sell more colonization packages."

"I'm not quite sure how to tell you this," Nathan began. "I cannot speak directly about any of the core or fringe worlds, but the bio-digital plague killed ninety percent of the population of Earth. All civilization fell into ruins, as there simply weren't enough people to keep everything running: no power, no government, no industry. Those that survived converted to a primitive existence. The Earth fell into a technological dark age that lasted over seven hundred years."

"But you are here, in this ship. Surely you did not go from sticks and stones to starships in a mere three hundred years."

"About three hundred years ago, we began a second industrial revolution. But we had to rediscover most of our science and technology, as everything had been stored digitally. We had just entered the age of flight when we discovered the Data Ark."

"The Data Ark?"

"A vast digital ark stored in a vault buried in the Swiss Alps. It was powered by geothermal energy and had been designed to operate in standby mode for centuries, even millennia if need be. It contained all of humanity's science, technology, culture, and history from before the plague. We used the data from the ark to jump ahead three hundred years technologically in only a century. But the Data Ark had been sealed up once the digital component of the plague was discovered. So you see, we know very little about what happened other than what our archaeologists have been able to piece together."

Mister Percival appeared somewhat pale. "Ninety percent?"

"Are you all right, Mister Percival?" Cameron asked.

"And what of the core worlds? And the fringe? What became of them?"

"We don't know for sure," Nathan admitted. "The people of Earth have only just gotten back into space. In fact, this ship is the Earth's first FTL capable starship other than a few small test ships used to develop FTL capabilities."

"But if you have come this far out, surely you must know something of the core worlds?"

"I'm afraid we do not."

"But how?"

"It's complicated. Our best guess is that the core and fringe worlds suffered a similar fate. The Aurora was designed to seek out and make contact with the lost worlds and to reestablish diplomatic relations. Unfortunately, we learned that many, if not all, of the core and fringe worlds are under the control of the Jung Empire."

"The Jung? Who are the Jung?"

"We know very little about them, just that they are ruthless and take what they want by force."

"How many worlds do they control?" Mister Percival asked.

"It is our understanding that they control all of them," Nathan stated, "all of them except Sol."

Mister Percival pushed his plate away, his face

pale and his expression downtrodden. "Captain, if you'll please excuse me, I'm feeling a bit weak at the moment. This news is all a bit overwhelming. I think it might be best if I return to medical for the evening."

"Of course," Nathan agreed, motioning for the security officer to bring the wheelchair. "We can talk another time."

"Thank you for your hospitality," Mister Percival said as he moved to the wheelchair, "and for rescuing me. Unfortunately, it appears that my plan has not worked as well as I'd hoped."

Nathan and his staff watched as the security officer wheeled Mister Percival away. As the door closed behind them, Nathan continued his meal.

"He is lying," Vladimir said as he stabbed a mound of lettuce.

Nathan looked at him quizzically out of the corner of his eye. He also felt that there was much Mister Percival was holding back, but it was only a hunch; he had no evidence to back his suspicions. He was surprised that Vladimir had been the one to openly make the accusation, as the engineer never seemed to bother with such matters. Nathan would have expected suspicions from Jessica or Cameron.

Vladimir could feel Nathan looking at him. As usual, he did not wait until his mouth was empty to speak. "The log clock on his stasis chamber."

"What log clock?" Nathan asked.

"It is on the side, high on the right. It is small, easy to miss. It shows how long the occupant has been in stasis. It is a simple backup device in case the operational logs are corrupted. Medical personnel need to know how long the occupant was in stasis in order to properly revive them in case the automatic reanimation system fails."

"What about the log clock?" Jessica demanded impatiently.

Vladimir looked surprised at her reaction. "Am I the only one who finds interest in such details?"

"Why do you think he is lying?" Nathan asked calmly. He, too, was getting impatient, as Vladimir did tend to over-explain things.

"He said he was put into stasis before the journey began. That was over one thousand years ago, da?"

"Yes."

"Then why did the backup log clock show eight hundred twelve years?"

Nathan stared at Vladimir.

"I only realized this discrepancy when he was speaking," Vladimir defended, recognizing Nathan's expression.

"Jess?" Nathan said.

"I'll keep digging through the Jasper's logs," Jessica promised.

"And?"

"I'll have security keep an eye on Mister Percival twenty-four seven."

"Vlad?"

"I'll keep working on the data core from the surface."

Nathan took another bite of his salad.

"No instructions for me?" Cameron wondered.

"Nope. You're good," Nathan answered as he continued working on his salad.

"You know, it might be a good idea for Cam to buddy up to him," Jessica suggested.

"Buddy up?" Cameron inquired.

"You know, be his friend, make him think he has an ally."

"How am I supposed to do that?" she asked, a quizzical expression on her face.

"I don't know," Jessica fumbled. "Spend some time with him. Talk a bit... Oh! Give him a tour of the ship."

"Why?"

"The more he talks, the more he might let some information slip," Jessica explained. "He has to feel comfortable, like he knows and understands his surroundings."

"How am I supposed to remember everything he says? A tour could take hours."

"Leave your comm-set open. I can record everything," Jessica suggested.

"You know, I do have responsibilities," Cameron said. "I am the XO, after all."

"I'll cover you," Nathan offered.

Cameron sighed, resigning herself to the idea of becoming friends with Mister Percival. "Very well."

"Well, people," Nathan began, "it seems we have a few mysteries to solve. Who is Jonathon Percival, why did he lie about how long he has been in stasis, and what happened to the expedition? We're only about six or seven jumps from Sol, so we've got less than two days to figure it all out."

CHAPTER SEVEN

Major Prechitt entered the preflight briefing room, just as he had done at the conclusion of each jump cycle, in order to brief his pilots on the next training exercise. This time, however, he did not have a room full of dedicated, highly-trained fighter pilots. He had Josh and Loki.

As usual, he went straight to the podium. He looked out at the two young men: Loki sitting straight up and looking very attentive, and Josh slouching in his high-backed seat and looking like he was about to fall asleep out of boredom. At that moment, he changed tactics. He picked up his data pad from the podium, pulled a chair from the side, and took a seat directly in front of the two young men. "Do you guys know who I am?"

"Yes, sir, Major Prechitt," Loki answered immediately. "You're the commander of the Aurora's air group."

Josh made a faint kissing sound, meant only for Loki's ears.

"That's right, Loki," Major Prechitt answered, staring at Josh. "I'm the Aurora's CAG. Do you know why you're here?"

"You're going to tell us how to fly a recon mission, right and proper," Josh remarked.

Major Prechitt swallowed hard. He was used to

dealing with polished Corinari pilots, not punk kids with bad attitudes. "Actually, Josh, Captain Scott has high regards for your piloting skills. He insists the two of you are a great team, that you have a natural chemistry that balances one another's strengths and weaknesses."

"Then why are we here, sir?" Loki asked politely.

"The CAG is responsible for all spacecraft operations other than that of the Aurora herself. Until now, your recon flights have been under the direct control of Captain Scott. I've asked him to place operations of the Falcon under my control, where it should be."

"So you can tell us how to fly," Josh mumbled.

"This would be easier if you'd just give me a chance," Major Prechitt said, staring straight at Josh. "After all, that *is* what I'm trying to do for you."

Josh straightened up just enough to demonstrate compliance. "Sorry, sir. You were saying?"

Major Prechitt took Josh's change in posture as a positive step forward and continued. "I have no doubt that the two of you can fly the Falcon superbly. I saw what you did over both Ancot and Aitkenna. That took both skill and courage. But I've got a problem. I've got fifty well-trained pilots who know their own spacecraft inside and out. But they have never seen, nor do they know anything about, Jung fighters."

"Neither do we, sir," Loki reminded him.

"Yes, I know. But you are about to fly a recon mission into what we believe to be Jung-controlled space. If we're lucky, you might even be able to witness a few of them patrolling the system."

"If we're lucky, we won't," Josh corrected.

Major Prechitt smiled, understanding Josh's sentiment and appreciating that the young man wasn't foolish enough to desire such encounters, as many young pilots might. "If you do, take notes about everything: the speeds they travel during each maneuver, how sharply they turn, or how quickly they can accelerate. These are things that passive scans don't reveal. It takes a trained observer." The major leaned back in his chair. "You two have been thrice blessed. You have a unique spacecraft at your disposal, you have the skills to fly it, and you have a situation that demands its use. I can help you both become better pilots and a better flight team. All I ask is that you let me." Major Prechitt looked at Loki, whose face was enthusiastic and wide-eyed. Then he looked at Josh, who had straightened up a bit more. "What do you say, boys?"

Josh looked at Loki and his eager expression. "You've got my interest, sir."

"Good," Major Prechitt responded. "Now, first, we've added a few toys to your ship."

"Like what?" Josh asked with suspicion.

"Nothing that will change her flight characteristics, Josh. They're more like toys for Loki."

"Like what?" Loki asked with interest.

"We installed a pair of decoy drones. When you launch them, they emit both thermal and radiological patterns that mimic those of the Falcon. They are maneuverable and can be used to lure your enemy away from you."

"Sweet," Loki said. "How did you manage that so fast?"

"Such things are standard issue on Takaran fighters," Major Prechitt stated. "The Karuzari have been using them effectively for years. We just reprogrammed them to mimic the Falcon instead of a Takaran fighter."

"Nice," Josh said.

"We also installed a pair of comm-drones. They were emergency comm-drones for use on Takaran recon ships. We stripped the FTL out of them and installed mini-jump drives. When launched, they will carry a message all the way back to the Aurora's last known position by jumping in rapid succession."

"What happens if the Aurora isn't there?"

"If they know the Aurora's next jump point, they will go there. Otherwise, they will self-destruct."

"And they're only one-way?" Loki asked.

"For now, yes. We're hoping to make them two-way systems, but that involves rendezvous and docking, which is far more complicated to automate."

"How will we know how to use these new toys?" Josh wondered.

"Senior Chief Taggart will go over them with you on the flight line." Major Prechitt handed them each a data card. "These contain a list of things to look for if you do see their fighters in action. I figured, since you're going to have a lot of down time while you're cruising through the target system, you might as well review it then... give you something to do."

"Yeah, every little bit helps," Loki admitted.

"Very well, gentlemen," Major Prechitt said as he stood. "Good luck and good hunting."

Josh and Loki both stood, shaking the major's hand. Josh stuffed the data card into his flight suit hip pocket along with all the other data cards he had brought along to keep himself entertained for the mission. As they left the pilot's briefing room and headed down the corridor toward the hangar deck, Josh turned to Loki. "Someone needs to tell the major that a recon pilot's favorite thing to find is nothing."

* * *

Nathan made his way across the Aurora's main hangar deck. Over the weeks, the flight deck had changed considerably. Major Prechitt, the Corinari flight technicians, Senior Chief Taggart, and the Chief of the Boat, Master Chief Montrose, had all worked together—using the Aurora's flight operations manuals as a guide—to turn the Aurora's flight operations into a model of efficiency. As expected, their methods varied somewhat from standard Fleet flight deck operations, a necessity brought about by the differences in both spacecraft and roles. The Aurora had been designed as a ship of exploration and diplomacy first and as a warship second. Now, ninety percent of all flight deck operations were designed for combat operations. To this end, both the port and starboard transfer airlocks had been tasked for the recovery of fighter-craft only, while the larger, center transfer airlock was now reserved for the launch and recovery of cargo shuttles.

Even the Falcon, while much bigger than a fighter, was still small enough to fit on the forward elevator pads. It was no longer allowed to use the flight apron for operations. Instead, she launched and recovered via the forward elevator pads, which were designed to travel all the way up through the top of the Aurora's hull, thus becoming flight pads of their own once exposed to space.

Nathan walked across the hangar deck toward the Falcon as it sat on the port side forward elevator pad. As he approached, he could see Josh and Loki being given instructions by Marcus, the chief of the deck. "Gentlemen," Nathan greeted.

"Captain," Marcus responded, giving a less-than-perfect salute.

"I heard you got a few new toys," Nathan said.

"Yes, sir," Loki responded. "They're pretty cool, too. Marcus, uh, I mean, Senior Chief Taggart, was just going over them with us."

"Well, don't let me interrupt."

"I was pretty much finished, sir," Marcus assured him. His attention was suddenly taken away. "Hey! Dumbass!" he hollered at some distant Corinari flight deck technician. "Yeah! You! What the hell do you think you're doing?" Marcus turned back to the captain. "Excuse me, sir. I have to go slap someone."

Nathan laughed to himself.

"Come to see us off, Captain?" Josh asked, coming around the nose of the Falcon as he completed his preflight inspection.

"Something like that," Nathan said. "Listen, I don't know if you two realize this, but this flight, it's different. It's not like before, back in the cluster. Then, we already knew basically what was there. We knew what the risk was ahead of time. This place, well, no one from Earth has been there in over a thousand years. For all we know, it could be a hornet's nest of Jung ships."

"Yeah, the thought had occurred to us," Loki stated.

"Not to me," Josh said with a small amount of alarm. "Hey, what's a hornet?"

"Just, don't take any unnecessary chances; that's all. It's not worth the risk," Nathan said, "especially since..."

"Since we have a jump drive that we don't want to

fall into Jung hands," Loki finished for him. "Don't worry, Captain. We won't let that happen. If they're coming for us, we'll jump away fast."

"Good, but there's one other thing. You can't let them see you jump away."

"Why not?" Josh asked.

"We think the Jung already know about, or at least suspect that we have been developing, a jump drive. If they see us jump, they'll have confirmation. And that confirmation could provoke an attack on the Earth."

"But they've only got linear FTL, right?" Loki asked. "We'd still make it to Earth long before word of the jump drive got out."

"Yes, you're right," Nathan agreed, "but it would just escalate things. The Earth doesn't need that right now. She's not ready to defend herself, not yet."

"Right," Josh said. "Jump before they see us. I like that even better. If they haven't seen us, then they ain't shootin' at us."

"Good." Nathan handed Loki a data card.

"What's that?" Josh asked. "Another history book for me?"

"It's a message from me to Fleet Command on Earth. If for some reason we don't make it back to Earth and you do, this contains all of my reports. It's all encrypted, except for the first message, which you can transmit to keep Fleet from opening fire on you." Nathan looked at them with a serious expression. "We are all about to cross Jung-occupied space, gentlemen. One of us must make it through to Earth. One of us must get the jump drive technology back to Fleet Command."

"Captain, what are the odds that you're going to

run into another Jung ship between here and Sol?" Josh said. "I mean, space, it's really big, you know?"

"Just covering all the bases," Nathan told him.

"Bases?" Loki wondered.

"Oh, I got that one!" Josh yelled. "It's about baseball! I read about it the other day!" He turned to Loki. "It's a game, everyone on Earth plays it. I'll explain it to you on the way. It's really interesting."

"Don't worry, Captain," Loki said, ignoring Josh. "If we can't find you, we'll head straight to Earth."

"Good luck," Nathan told them.

"No worries," Josh stated with his usual confidence. They turned, ascended the boarding ladder, and climbed into the Falcon's cockpit, pulling their helmets on and locking them in place as they slid down into their flight seats.

"Sometimes, I can't tell how much of that boy's confidence is arrogance and how much is stupidity," Marcus stated as he stepped up behind the captain.

"A bit of both, I imagine."

Marcus looked across the flight deck, taking note of Commander Taylor and Mister Percival. "Who the hell is that guy?"

"Who, Mister Percival?" Nathan asked. "He's the guy we rescued from the Jasper."

"The one that was in stasis for a thousand years?" Marcus asked.

"That's him."

"Damn, he don't look much older than me. Whattaya suppose it's like? Going to sleep and waking up a thousand years later to a totally different galaxy. Everything and everyone you ever knew, dead and gone, turned to dust long ago."

Nathan turned to Marcus. "You know, you should ask him."

"What? Who? Me?"

"Yeah, you. We're trying to get him to open up, to tell us about how things were back before the plague, and what happened when the plague hit. Maybe you two would hit it off."

"If you think it's a good idea, I guess I could try. Maybe put a little ale in him first, just to lube up his tongue and all."

"You might want to ask the doctor about that first," Nathan warned. "And speak to Lieutenant Commander Nash first as well. She's got a list of things we're not to discuss with him just yet. Better yet, maybe you and the lieutenant commander can share some ale with him together. He seems to like her."

"Big surprise there," Marcus said, "what with all her attributes and such."

Nathan turned slowly and looked at Marcus, who immediately straightened up slightly.

"Uh, I'll speak to the lieutenant commander about it directly, Captain."

"Carry on, Senior Chief." Nathan returned the Senior Chief's salute as he watched the elevator pad raise the Falcon upward, disappearing into the bulkhead above.

"Canopy closed and locked," Loki announced. "Reactors are hot, running at one percent. All systems are online and ready for launch."

"Maneuvering is hot. Mains are hot. Jump drive is in standby. Weapons are safe." Josh glanced out the window as the walls of the elevator tube passed by them outside. Numbers indicating the distance remaining to the outer hull moved past them almost too quickly to read. "Topside in ten seconds."

"Flight Control, Falcon. Ten seconds," Loki called over the comms.

"*Falcon, Flight copies,*" the flight controller answered.

The elevator pad began to slow its ascent. Josh looked upwards as the outer doors parted down the middle, retracting to either side. A few moments later, the elevator came to a stop, locking into place and becoming one with the Aurora's outer hull.

"*Falcon, Flight. Pad one locked and ready for launch.*"

"Copy, Flight," Loki answered. "Falcon launching."

"Mag-locks, launching," Josh announced as he applied upward thrust. The Falcon lifted quickly up off the elevator pad, rapidly moving away from the Aurora perpendicularly.

"Flight, Falcon. Airborne."

"*Copy Falcon. Safe flight.*"

Josh pushed the throttles forward slowly, easing the ship forward at a leisurely rate.

"Not that I'm complaining or anything," Loki began, "but usually our departures cause the blood to drain out of my toes."

"I'm feeling a bit... *cautious* today," Josh said.

"Cautious?" Loki asked. "Turn around and look at me."

"Why?"

"I want to make sure it's you."

Josh slammed the throttles forward, instantly bringing the main drive to full power. Despite the interceptor's inertial dampening systems, the sudden acceleration pushed them both hard into the flight seats.

"Yup," Loki struggled to say, as his fingers and

toes suddenly became cold. "It's you."

Josh backed the throttles down, settling in the interceptor at twenty-five percent forward thrust. "Jump speed in five seconds. Coming on jump heading."

"Engaging auto-nav," Loki announced. "Jumping in three......"

"I hate the auto-nav," Josh complained as he felt the system take over the controls, leaving them dead in his hands.

"Two......one......jump."

Josh closed his eyes tight as the Falcon jumped away in a flash of blue-white light.

* * *

"Your ship is of an interesting design," Mister Percival commented as they left the hangar bay.

"An odd choice of words," Cameron responded.

"It is an odd situation." Mister Percival moved slowly down the corridor, taking each step with caution as he continued the process of getting used to using his legs again. Although he was able to walk on his own, he had to pace himself to avoid getting too fatigued. Commander Taylor had offered to push him about the ship in a wheelchair, but Mister Percival had immediately refused the notion, choosing instead to take periodic breaks in the tour.

"How so?" Cameron asked.

"I had expected to wake up in a future full of fancy, high-tech gizmos and gadgets, where everyone had perfect health and lived wonderful lives. Instead, the technology is similar if not inferior to what I knew, and the people seem to be struggling as much as before. The only difference, perhaps, is that humanity has spread farther out into the galaxy and has become more disconnected than ever before. It seems a bit sad, really." Mister Percival smiled. "To be honest, looking back, I feel kind of silly for believing it might be otherwise."

"Why do you say that?"

"I knew what was happening back in the core with the plague and all. Civilization was collapsing. Humanity was dying. Those that had somehow escaped infection were fleeing in droves." Mister Percival paused a moment and sighed. "I guess I wanted to believe that, somehow, it was all going to be all right, that civilization would manage to survive and continue to march forward, albeit at a more careful pace."

"It seems only natural for one to hope for the best," Cameron agreed.

"Hope, perhaps. But I knew better. Even though we were far from the last ones to leave the fringe, the writing was on the wall, so to speak." Mister Percival sighed again.

Cameron appeared somewhat confused by Mister Percival's choice of words.

"Maybe it was all for the best."

"Excuse me?"

"Maybe humanity needed to experience such a catastrophe in order to get us to change our ways."

"What ways do you speak of?" Cameron wondered.

"We are a reckless species, arrogant and self-centered, refusing to accept our own fragile nature until death stares us in the face. We want power without limitation, wealth beyond need, and freedom without consequence or responsibility. We also want someone else to blame when something goes wrong."

"I don't know about all of that," Cameron objected

politely, "but that last one sounds about right. Have you considered that perhaps humanity has changed over the last thousand years?"

"Humanity had not changed in the thousands of years before the plague, even in the face of countless atrocities. Why would I expect them to have done so now?"

"Anything is possible."

"Humans all have one thing in common above all others," Mister Percival declared, "the will to survive. To this end, we have the amazing ability to justify whatever we must do to achieve this goal. It is the blessing and the curse of the *Homo sapiens*— the proverbial double-edged sword, if you will."

"Yes, but that instinct and ability extends beyond ourselves to include the survival of those we care about: family, friends, even one's nation or entire species."

Mister Percival paused for a moment, looking at Cameron with considerable thought. "An excellent point, Commander. If only that were true of the majority of us."

"You made a comment before," Cameron said as they continued their stroll down the corridor on their way to engineering, "that 'maybe it was all for the best.' What did you mean by that?"

"Many people throughout history have espoused such views, believing that mankind had upset the natural balance of things by exceeding the carrying capacity of the Earth. Several radical groups even advocated a culling of the herd, claiming the need to drastically reduce the population in order to once again regain that balance."

"But if humanity is incapable of changing, as you say, wouldn't that only be a temporary solution?"

"Ah yes, the most common argument. If we can't fix it, let's not do anything at all."

"That's not what I meant."

"I realize that, Commander. Nevertheless, it was the common argument of the day. Did you know that there were even a few extremist groups that tried to orchestrate such events in the past?"

"No, I did not," Cameron admitted. "There is so much about pre-plague Earth history that most of us do not yet know."

"Was it not all contained within the Data Ark that your captain spoke of?"

"Yes, of course, but there is so much information in the Ark. They formed a committee to oversee the distribution of the data to the world. Early on, it was decided that releasing everything in an uncontrolled fashion might prove dangerous. There was a lot of technology in there that the people of Earth just weren't yet ready for. More importantly, some of the old Earth religions were in such opposition to their current versions... Can you imagine what trouble that might cause?"

"Surely, factual historical events posed no threat," Mister Percival said with a frown.

"It depends. For example, the people of my Earth do not see any race as inferior to another. We see differences, yes. We still tend to mingle with those more like us than not, but we don't look down upon those differences; we embrace them. The knowledge that at one point in humanity's history racism not only existed, but there was actual slavery based on those concepts, was considered a dangerous concept to be released back into the general public."

"So you think some elements of humanity's past arc better forgotten?"

Cameron considered the question as they headed down the ramp from the flight level to the engineering deck in the aft section of the ship. "In most cases, no. In fact, in the end, the history of racism and slavery was made public. However, I do agree that such things should be considered. Blindly revealing all knowledge of the past is just irresponsible."

"Some might call it being honest," Mister Percival argued.

"Perhaps," Cameron admitted. "It doesn't matter anyway. Once we discovered the Jung threat, all efforts were concentrated on developing technologies to get us back into space in order to defend ourselves. Since then, very little of Earth's pre-plague history has been revealed."

"Many preach that one must know history to prevent repeating the same mistakes," Mister Percival said.

"That's what the captain says. He studied history in college."

"A good discipline to be versed in when commanding a ship of war."

Cameron noticed Vladimir talking to a Corinairan technician as they passed the first reactor compartment. "Lieutenant Commander," she called to him as she motioned for Mister Percival to enter the compartment ahead of her.

"Mister Percival," Vladimir greeted, "Commander. How is the tour going?"

"Most interesting," Mister Percival responded.

"Lieutenant Commander Kamenetskiy, if you would be so kind as to show Mister Percival around engineering, I have a few things to attend to."

"But, I was..."

"Call me when you have completed your tour of

engineering, Mister Percival," Cameron said.

"Thank you, Commander."

Cameron turned back toward Vladimir. "Lieutenant Commander," she stated as she walked past him, pausing to add in a low voice, "remember your list."

"Sir," Vladimir responded, gritting his teeth at being saddled with the strange, old survivor. "Mister Percival, where would you like to start?"

"Here is fine. Is this your reactor?"

"It is one of four reactors," Vladimir stated proudly. If there was one thing Vladimir loved to talk about, it was the ship's systems, even with a thousand-year-old man.

"Seems a bit large for a fusion reactor."

"They are antimatter reactors," Vladimir corrected.

"Really? And you have four of them?" Mister Percival looked over the reactor. "I have heard of antimatter reactors. They were the latest thing in shipboard power generation in my day. But they were only being used by the military at the time."

"It is the same now. There are many fusion reactors being built on Earth. I believe that when we left, more than half the world's energy was being produced by fusion plants. Our sub-light warships use fusion reactors as well. The Aurora is the first new ship to utilize antimatter reactors."

"And it takes all four of them to run this ship?"

"The ship can run on one reactor, but it is normally run on a balance of two reactors."

"Then why the other two?"

"For redundancy and to power our FTL systems," Vladimir explained.

"Seems like overkill to me."

"We also have a pair of smaller fusion reactors as backups," Vladimir added.

"Now that is overkill." Mister Percival looked about. "Is there someplace we could sit for a few moments? I'm feeling a bit fatigued from all this walking."

"Of course, there is an office right over there." Vladimir led the old man into the office, pulling out a chair for him to sit.

"Would you like some water?"

"Perhaps. I could use a snack as well, if it's not too much trouble."

"I am always ready to eat," Vladimir agreed with a smile as he activated his comm-set. "Galley, Cheng. Send two fruit trays and two bottles of water to the office in reactor compartment one."

"So, you are Russian?" Mister Percival said.

"Yes, sir. Born and raised just outside of Moscow."

"I've never met a Russian before."

"Really?" Vladimir said with obvious surprise. "I thought they were everywhere on Earth during your time."

"I was born and raised in Stillwell."

"Where is that?"

"It's a small city on the main continent on Cetus, the fourth planet in the Tau Ceti system. I've never been to Earth, but from what I remember, a large segment of the Earth's Russian population migrated to the Russian national settlements in the 70 Ophiuchi system."

"Yes, I heard that as well," Vladimir said. "I have always wondered if they survived the plague." Vladimir leaned back in his chair, daydreaming. "I cannot imagine an entire planet of Russians. It would be amazing."

"I'm sure it would be," Mister Percival admitted. "I never got there myself. I took a job in the Sigma Draconis system as soon as I got out of the service. There was a new settlement starting up there, mostly Norwegians and such from Earth. There was a lot of money to be made there."

"It is hard to imagine. You speak of moving between the stars as we would speak of moving between continents."

"But you move between the stars," Mister Percival said.

"Yes, *we* do, but not the people of Earth. We only found out that we had once colonized other star systems a hundred years ago. We've only been back in space for about thirty years."

"I, on the other hand, cannot imagine humanity being restricted to a single planet."

"How many worlds had been colonized?" Vladimir wondered.

"I couldn't tell you for sure," Mister Percival admitted. "There was always some expedition setting off to colonize another world out in the fringe or farther. Every group that didn't like the way things were on their world would find a way to raise the capital needed to buy a colonization package and hire some ship to haul them out into space."

"What about those started by Earth?" Vladimir asked. "I know of the five core worlds, the biggest ones. But I've only heard of a few of the fringe worlds."

"Yes, the fringe worlds. Those are the ones that were the most exciting. They were beyond the control of the core governments. They were the new frontier, so to speak. Imagine stepping onto a clean, relatively unspoiled world with nothing but what you could carry, and being able to stake claim to whatever chunk of land you could find. That was the dream."

Vladimir smiled. "A very nice dream."

"But it was a very hard life for most," Mister Percival added. "Many did not survive."

"Yes, I can imagine."

"I don't think you can. It's not like on Earth. Most of these worlds weren't intended for humans to live on, nor were they made for growing Earth crops. Most fringe worlds were dependent on regular shipments of basic supplies from the core worlds and from Earth just to survive. It took the core settlements nearly two centuries to become self-sustaining, and they had massive support infrastructure from their sponsoring nations back on Earth. I can't imagine what the expeditions that went deeper out into space went through. I suspect most of them are long dead."

"Lieutenant Commander," the crewman announced as he stepped through the door carrying two small trays of diced fruit and two bottles of water.

"Thank you, crewman," Vladimir stated, taking the order from him and handing one to Mister Percival. He turned his attention back to Mister Percival. "Tell me more about the fringe worlds."

* * *

"I've got three contacts deep in the system," Loki reported.

"Are they Jung?"

"I have no idea. We're still eight light hours from the edge of the system. We're too far away to get any details. They're just thermal contacts that are in motion at this point."

"So they're moving," Josh said from the front seat of the Falcon. "Where are they moving to?"

"Two of them appear to be positioned farther out in the system," Loki explained. "The third one looks like it's on its way out of the system."

"Are you sure?"

"Not without watching them for a while to get more course and speed data. Even then, the information is probably about twelve to fifteen hours old."

"What should we do?"

"I say we sit for a few minutes to verify their trajectories as well as the trajectories of everything in the system before we plot our course. Then we jump in a little deeper and start our run."

"Sounds good to me," Josh agreed. "So, what did you think of Major Prechitt?"

"Seems like a good CAG."

"Please, you don't even know what a good CAG is," Josh sneered.

"And you do?"

"Haven't a clue nor a care."

Loki looked up from his console. "Well you should, especially if we're going to be under his command every time we fly this ship."

"It's just a formality, as I see it," Josh assured him. "The captain's still our boss, Prechitt's as well for that matter. He can't pull us from our primary duty to fly this thing without the captain's say so. So if you ask me, it's still the captain that's giving us the orders, even if they're being passed through the CAG."

"You know, it wouldn't take long for them to teach someone else how to fly the Falcon," Loki said.

"It's not like there aren't plenty of pilots on board."

"Yeah, but we're only a few days from Earth. Why would they bother?"

"At which point the Earth Defense Force will take possession of the Aurora and probably all of the spacecraft aboard. In a few days, we might very well be out of a job, my friend."

"The captain will look out for us," Josh said.

"I think you're placing too much faith in his power, Josh. He may be the captain now, but once we get back to Earth, he has to answer to Fleet Command."

Josh was beginning to become concerned. The thought of what would happen to them when they arrived at Earth had crossed his mind, but the scenarios that played out in his mind were far more favorable than those Loki was painting. "So what do you think they'll do with us? I mean, all of us as in those of us that are *not* from Earth."

"Best case, maybe they'll put us up until they get another jump-enabled ship built that can take us home. But that could take years."

"And the worst case?" Josh asked.

"They treat us with distrust and suspicion, detaining us and subjecting us to endless interrogations to learn as much as possible about the Pentaurus cluster."

"You're just being paranoid," Josh protested. "They ain't gonna lock us up and interrogate us."

"I admit it sounds paranoid," Loki agreed, "but people facing imminent invasion tend to be that way, don't you think?"

"Yeah, you could be right." Josh pondered the situation a moment. "Wait, isn't the captain connected or something? Isn't his father the president of something?"

"He was a senator for a very powerful continent. He was running for president when the Aurora left Earth."

"Well, maybe he got elected," Josh postulated. "That would be good for us, right?"

"Probably, yes," Loki agreed. "I'm sending you a course plot."

Josh looked down at his center console, examining the plot. "That's cutting it pretty close, isn't it?"

"If we're going to get close enough to get good images of the planet's surface, we need to get close."

"Yeah, but that's between the planet and her moons."

"If we come in on that trajectory, the sun will be on our backside from the planet, so we'll stay cold."

"How come we never had to pass this close before?"

"It's because of the planet's position on its orbit of the star," Loki explained, "that, and the position of the other planets. It's either that course, or we have to wait a few more hours to start."

"If we do that, we might miss our rendezvous with the Aurora, and I do not want to go jumping across the core sector all alone."

"Didn't you once talk about stealing this ship and going off to points unknown?"

"That was just talk, Loki, and I was talking about jumping around the Pentaurus sector, not someplace completely unfamiliar." Josh altered the interceptor's course, bringing it to the heading indicated on the course plot. "Coming on to course heading. Let's get this over with."

"Transferring flight control to auto-nav system," Loki announced. "Jumping in three seconds."

* * *

"Captain?" Jessica called from the hatch to the ready room.

"Yes?"

"I've pretty much finished up with the Jasper's logs," she told him as she entered the compartment, closing the hatch behind her.

"And?"

"It's not pretty, just as we suspected."

"Let's hear it," Nathan said, gesturing for her to take a seat. For once, Jessica sat in one of the chairs instead of making herself comfortable on his couch. That's when Nathan realized she wasn't kidding.

"To be honest, it seems like this expedition was doomed from the start. First, the ship wasn't really designed for this long of a haul. They outfitted her with additional propellant and such, and set up a rotation schedule for the crew to come out of stasis less often to conserve resources, all the standard stuff that you would expect them to do to stretch their range. But the plain fact of the matter was that the ship was already old and worn out when Dubnyk bought her on the black market. If the expedition had actually applied for a permit, they would have been denied solely on the inadequacies of the Jasper as the transport vehicle. Even the cargo containers they used were not rated for transporting consumables. They didn't have enough radiation shielding. The only new component on that whole ship was her fusion reactor. Luckily for the passengers, the stasis containers were properly rated. But none of that is what caused the expedition to fail."

"What was?"

"The first problem was their cargo shuttles. They weren't stored inside. They were docked outside the ship."

"For the entire journey?"

"All fifty-two years."

"I thought she had a top speed of two point five?" Nathan wondered.

"She was so heavily loaded that they decided to run at half speed to increase their range and still have enough propellant to decelerate and make orbit at the end of the journey. By the time they arrived, one shuttle was inoperable and the other one had some damage as well. They were able to scavenge parts from one to repair the other, but that left them with only one shuttle to move all the cargo and passengers to the surface."

"Well, it would take a lot longer, but one shuttle would still do the trick," Nathan said.

"Unless your one shuttle crashes before you've off-loaded even half your cargo," Jessica told him.

"You're kidding me."

"Like I said, doomed from the start. But wait, it gets worse. By that time, they had about two hundred people on the surface, and at least some of their equipment. The plan was for them to make do with what they had and try to repair the crashed shuttle. They realized that if given a few years, they might be able to get the shuttle flying again. But with winter approaching, they needed to concentrate on survival. Captain Dubnyk and his remaining crew went back into stasis to conserve consumables aboard the Jasper, with the system set to wake the captain in one year to check on the colonists. It would also wake him if something on the ship needed attention."

"So there were three hundred colonists, half their gear, and the Jasper's crew, all waiting in stasis in orbit," Nathan said.

"Yes, sir. The first winter was rough, far colder than they had expected based on the planetary survey performed a hundred years earlier by some corporate probe. About twenty people died. When the captain woke up a year later, he realized that it might take them longer than expected to repair the shuttle. He continued putting himself in stasis for a year at a time. This went on for about ten years. Every winter was brutal, but the colony survived. Birth rates were poor, and the colony was barely able to maintain their population, but they had managed to develop some basic refining and fabrication capabilities and were actually making some progress with the shuttle repairs. Then one year, Dubnyk came out of stasis, and nobody answered. He used the optical sensors to scan for the colony, but it was gone, wiped out by a massive lava flow. He found a message in the ship's comm logs from the colony. A massive volcano had erupted, forcing them to abandon their camp and move farther north. They promised to re-contact him once they established a new settlement."

"What about the shuttle? They couldn't have moved it?" Nathan asked.

"No, it was lost in the lava flows. They scavenged what they could, like sensors, a fusion reactor, and comm gear. But the shuttle itself was gone."

"Shit."

"Yeah. Dubnyk and the rest of them were stuck on the Jasper with no way down and not enough propellant to go anywhere else."

"So what happened to the colonists?"

"Dubnyk made contact with them the next time he came out of stasis, but the news was grim. They had moved as far north as they dared, but all the ash the volcano dumped into the atmosphere was changing the climate, making it colder."

"They were going into an ice age?" Nathan wondered.

"That's what Dubnyk thought. One of the colonists also thought that the planet might have already been on its way to a cold cycle, and the volcano just made matters worse. They built some pretty hefty shelters and survived for another decade. Dubnyk came out of stasis every year to check in on them, but he could see that their numbers were dwindling and their spirits were fading. Eventually, no one answered his calls. He could still see the energy of their fusion reactor at their northern colony site even though it was buried in the snow. So he switched to five-year cycles, hoping their comm-unit had simply broken. But every time he woke up and checked, it was the same thing: no messages, no signs of life. Only more snow. Once the fusion reactor's signal disappeared, he simply gave up. He activated the emergency beacon and put himself under indefinitely, to be awakened only when the ship needed his attention. Eventually, the ship lost pressure and the onboard systems refused to awaken anyone into a vacuum."

"Yeah, that would suck."

"Literally." Jessica sighed. "Like I said, doomed from the get-go."

"That must have been hard to watch, Jess. I'm sorry."

"Actually, there wasn't any video. The captain converted all his earlier videos to text reports once he realized he could be stuck there a long time, I guess to save storage space and power. All I did was read a bunch of short log entries. Depressing as all hell, but at least I didn't have to watch anyone freak out on video."

"So Percival knows nothing about this," Nathan commented.

"No, sir. As far as I can tell, he and the rest of the colonists were in stasis the entire time. The only contradictory information is the backup time log on Mister Percival's stasis pod, and that could just be a system failure. I mean, it was in operation for a thousand years. I'm pretty sure the warranty expired on it a long time ago."

"I've got Vlad looking into that, seeing if there's a way to make it drop a chunk of time or run more slowly—anything that would explain the two-hundred year discrepancy."

"Would you like me to tell him?" Jessica asked.

"That's okay. I should be the one to tell him," Nathan insisted.

"If there's nothing else, I'm going to take a shower and get some rack time. I've been staring at the damned data pad for so long I'm getting cross-eyed."

"Thanks, Jess." Nathan watched her exit, wondering how any one expedition could be so unfortunate. Many times he had thought their own string of events to be unfortunate, but they were still alive. They were also nearly home.

* * *

"Uh, Josh, we have a little problem," Loki reported. After a few moments, he reached forward over his console and tapped Josh's helmet. "Josh!"

"What?"

"We have a problem."

"What? I'm awake. What is it?"

"There are five moons orbiting the target world, not four."

"Wow, Loki, that is bad. What are we to do?"

"Don't be an ass," Loki chided. "There must of have been a fifth moon hidden behind the planet. It's my fault. We should have waited longer before plotting a course."

"So it's a fifth moon; big deal," Josh said. "Are we going to crash into it?"

"No," Loki admitted, "but we're going to fly uncomfortably close to it."

"How big is it? Is it going to pull us in?"

"It's pretty small, actually. It's probably an asteroid that was either trapped in orbit, or they parked it there."

"Like the Corinairans did?" Josh wondered.

"It's possible, but it seems a little big for that."

"The Corinairans hollowed them out before they parked them in orbit, right?"

"Yeah, so?" Loki wondered.

"If these guys do the same, then it won't have much mass. Maybe it won't pull us in."

"But if it does, we're going to need to do a burn to keep our distance. That close to the planet, someone is bound to notice the sudden thermal signature," Loki warned.

"Can we do a burn now and change course to stay away from it?"

"No way, we're still too close to that third ship, the one that is moving out of the system. They'd see us for sure."

"If they're even looking."

"Good point, but now that we're close enough to

use opticals on her, I'm pretty sure she's a warship, just like the two we passed on the way in."

Josh studied the plots on his display. "Okay, if we burn now we're screwed for sure. We'd have to make a run for it and try to duck behind something to jump away unseen."

"And we don't know what their maximum acceleration is or if they have fighters and what *their* maximum acceleration is," Loki reminded him.

"Yeah, so we don't even know if we can outrun them," Josh said. "So better we wait and do the burn at the last minute. Then if they do come after us, we're already in position to quickly put either the moon or the planet itself between us and them and jump away before they can catch up to us. Fast or not, it has got to take them some time to get up to speed, and we're already doing point three. Can you run that, Loki?"

"I'm doing it now," Loki announced as he keyed variables into his navigation computer. "The captain never has us going more than a quarter of our maximum sub-light speed through a system under normal conditions, right?"

"That's right."

"So I'll assume those ships do the same."

"Why?"

"Because it's all I've got to go on, Josh. You got any better ideas?"

"Nope."

"They're doing about point one right now. So let's assume they can go point four light. Fighters are usually faster, so we'll say twice that, or point eight."

"About the same as us," Josh commented. "Works for me. So how's it look?"

"Just a minute." Loki ran the numbers for both scenarios, double-checking each time. "If we burn now and my assumptions are correct, and assuming they react the moment our burn signature reaches their sensors, they could catch us. If we wait and burn later, they'd have to go FTL to reach us before we ducked behind the moon and jumped."

"Which they might," Josh said. "Either way, our chances seem better burning later, wouldn't you say?"

"Agreed. We burn as we approach," Loki said. "We might even be able to use the fifth moon's gravity to whip us around, which would require less of a burn."

"Making us less obvious on their sensors."

"Not really less, just for a shorter duration."

"Hey, less is less," Josh said, "and less is good."

"In this case, yes. In how long you collect data before you start a recon run, no."

"Don't worry about it, Loki," Josh told him. "At least, for once, it wasn't me that got us into trouble."

"Thanks, Josh, really. I feel so much better."

"How long until the burn?"

"Another eighty-seven minutes," Loki answered. "At least I'll have time to get a proper mass reading on that fifth moon."

"And a real good look at the planet," Josh added. "The CAG's gonna think we were in orbit."

"We practically will be, Josh."

* * *

"Jump sixty-one in one minute," Mister Riley announced. "Switching to auto-nav."

Cameron entered the bridge and made her way

down to stand beside Nathan.

"You're early," Nathan commented, noting the shipboard time.

"Always," she answered, noticing the worried look on his face. "What's wrong?"

"Nothing. I just hate jumping away without everyone on board."

"We've done it before."

"The battle of Takara?" Nathan asked. "That was different, and you know it."

"They'll be fine. They know where to meet us. It's not like they've never flown around deep space in that thing by themselves before."

"Yeah, but that was back in the Pentaurus cluster. That was familiar space to them. This is not. They can't even ID contacts out here."

"They have our charts for the core and all the same ships in their database that we have."

"We both know that the more times we jump without them, the less the chances are they'll successfully find us again."

"Captain, they could jump all the way back to Earth even faster than we could," Cameron reminded him.

"Through a sector full of Jung warships."

"Spread light years apart," she added. "You worry too much. You do realize that the two of them have more stick time than either of us. They even have combat stick time."

Nathan looked at Cameron, a little shocked by her defense of Josh's piloting skills. "That's Josh you're talking about, remember?"

"I still have my reservations about him flying this ship, but he is the perfect pilot for the Falcon. That much I will admit." Cameron looked at Nathan. "To you, not to him," she warned.

"Yeah, I guess you're right."

"Thirty seconds to jump," Mister Riley reported.

"Have you ever wondered what it would be like to jump around the stars in a ship like that? No crew to worry about, no responsibilities, just jumping about to whatever systems you felt like visiting."

"Seems like a boring existence," Cameron said. "Not to mention dangerous."

"Perhaps, but it's still an interesting thought."

"You're over-romanticizing it, sir."

"So you're telling me that you wouldn't want to do it?"

"No, I'm telling you it probably wouldn't be as much fun as you think."

"Really?"

"Look at that screen." She pointed to the view screen. "It's black, with a lot of little white dots. Most of those dots are galaxies, all of which are far too distant to explore. Of those that are stars, only ten percent of them have worlds orbiting them that are even remotely habitable, let alone hospitable. And as far as we know, only a couple hundred or so have been colonized. That makes for fairly bleak prospects as far as excitement and adventure go."

"Executing jump sixty-one in three......"

"Well, when you put it that way..." Nathan said.

"Two......"

"Like I said, you're over-romanticizing it."

"One......"

"Perhaps."

"Jump."

The bridge filled momentarily with the blue-white flash of the Aurora's jump drive as they instantly moved another ten light years closer to Earth.

"Jump sixty-one complete," Mister Riley reported.

"Verifying position," Mister Navashee announced.

"I guess I'm just a hopeless romantic at heart," Nathan admitted. "Isn't everyone?"

Cameron slowly turned her head toward Nathan, cocking her head down slightly and casting a questionable gaze his way. "Seriously?"

"Position verified," Mister Navashee reported. "We are now thirty-seven light years from Sol."

"Beginning layover sixty-two," Mister Riley reported. "Time to next jump: seven hours, eighteen minutes."

Nathan rose from his chair. "Very well, Commander, you have the bridge."

* * *

"Okay, this is just plain creepy," Josh declared as he watched the small, irregularly shaped moon pass on their starboard side. "Not only is that thing all shadowy and scary looking, but it's coming right at us."

"That's why we have to do a burn, Josh," Loki reminded him from his seat in the rear of the Falcon's cockpit, "to get out of its way."

"How long of a burn?"

"Fifteen seconds at ten percent on the mains is all we need."

"During which any half-assed sensor, telescope, or thermal goggles looking up at that moon will see us and go, 'Whoa, what the fuck is that?'"

"Probably, but even if they launched interceptors from the planet the moment they saw our engines light up, we'd still be able to whip around the moon and jump away on her far side long before they reached us."

"It just occurred to me, Loki; this is exactly what we are *not* supposed to do during a coast-through recon flight."

"That just occurred to you, did it?"

"Actually, it occurred to me a long time ago," Josh said. "I was just reminding myself."

"Twenty seconds to burn," Loki reported.

"Spinning up the reactors," Josh answered.

"Don't worry, Josh; in ten minutes, we'll be on the far side of that moon, jumping away to safety."

"That easy, huh?" Josh said. "Hey, since when are you Mister Calm?"

"Trust me; I'm not. This is just my new, more confident exterior," Loki told him. "What do you think?"

"I liked you better when you freaked out."

"Ten seconds."

"Reactors online and running at twenty percent. Spinning up the mains." Josh watched his systems display as the interceptor's main drive came to life. He looked outside again at the hunk of rock they were calling a moon as it moved closer to them with each passing second. "Yup, creepy."

"Five seconds."

"Mains armed," Josh reported. "Throttles at ten percent."

"Three......two......one......burn," Loki ordered.

Josh pressed the ignition button. The interceptor's main engines instantly came to life at a low rumble. Even though they were only at ten percent of their maximum output, without the inertial dampeners online, the sudden application of forward thrust pushed them back in their seats rather forcefully.

"Jeez!" Josh declared. "Maybe we should have

brought the inertial dampeners online first." He felt as if someone rather large were sitting on his chest, making it difficult to breath. He remembered the times as a child when Marcus, who couldn't stand to smack a child, would simply sit on him until he agreed to behave.

"Too much energy use," Loki answered as he, too, struggled to breathe. "Makes us even easier to track."

"It would be worth it."

"Five seconds to shutdown," Loki reported.

Josh struggled to get his finger back in position to kill the burn. "Ready."

"Three......two......one......shutdown!"

Josh pressed the button, and the mains instantly silenced, releasing them from the crushing force of acceleration. "Mains are off," he reported. He pulled the throttles back to zero. "Throttles at zero. Taking reactors off..."

"We're being scanned!" Loki announced, the panic beginning to sneak back into his voice. "Active radar!"

"From where?" Josh asked, his finger backing away from the reactor control panel.

"The fifth moon!" Loki answered.

"What?"

"The fifth moon! There's a base down there!"

"Why didn't we see any..."

"Missile lock!"

"I'm bringing the reactors to full power!" Josh announced. "Bring the inertial dampeners online fast, or we're gonna be piles of goo in our flight seats!"

"I can't until the reactors reach at least eighty percent, or we'll lose power to flight systems!"

"They're at forty!"

"Contacts!" Loki reported. "Four missiles inbound from the moon! Impact in twenty seconds!"

Josh quickly backed the reactors back down to one percent and shut off the mains completely. "Going cold! Pop decoys!"

A dozen small decoys shot out of the back of the Falcon and began emitting both thermal and radar signatures that approximated that of the Falcon. At the same time, Josh used the cold maneuvering jets to spin the Falcon around, flinging the decoys out around them. "Translating down!" Josh announced as he again used the cold jets to push the Falcon down and away from the spread of decoys.

"Ten seconds!"

"Come on," Josh mumbled as he continued to apply cold thrust to push them down and away from the decoys.

"Josh, you're going to use up the cold jets if you keep..."

"We need some distance from those decoys!"

"Five seconds!" Loki reported.

Josh watched the propellant level indicators for the cold jet maneuvering system the Corinairan engineers had installed before they had started recon flights of the Takaran system back in the Pentaurus cluster. Loki was right, it was dropping rapidly. Either way, in a few seconds, it wouldn't matter.

The cockpit lit up as all four missiles struck the decoys above them and exploded in rapid succession.

"Bringing the reactors back to full power!" Josh announced, skipping his usual celebratory cry. "Spinning the mains back up. As soon as the reactors are at eighty percent, start up the inertial dampeners! I need to be free to maneuver!"

"Got it!" Loki answered. "More contacts, slower ones, coming from the fifth moon again! Count four!"

"More missiles?" Josh wondered. He looked at the reactor panel. The Falcon's twin fusion reactors were only up to forty percent. He also didn't have enough cold jet propellant to pull the same trick a second time.

"Negative, they're maneuvering, moving into attack position." Loki swallowed hard. "They're fighters, Josh."

"ETA?"

"Forty seconds."

Josh looked at the reactor panel. "We're up to sixty. We'll be flying at full throttle before then."

"They're accelerating pretty quickly, Josh," Loki said, tension in his voice.

"That's okay; so can we." Josh was tuned in mentally, ready for the game. He had spent all his childhood playing in flight sims and everything after that bouncing around the rings of Haven in that old harvester. He knew how to fly. He also knew that, while he might be able to out-fly the enemy pilots, he couldn't out-fight them. Tug had taught him that. Tug had also taught him that no game could simulate real combat. Although he and Loki had been under fire and had returned fire, they had never engaged in a real dogfight. Josh was cocky and arrogant, but he wasn't stupid.

"Eighty percent!" Loki reported. "Spinning up the inertial dampeners."

Josh watched as the reactor's power levels continued to climb toward one hundred percent. He knew it would take a few seconds for the inertial dampening systems to spin up and balance before they would be effective. If he fired his flight systems—especially his main drive—too soon, he risked crashing the inertial dampeners before they stabilized. That would require a restart which would not complete before the incoming fighters were in attack range.

As much as he hated math, Josh was amazed at how many numbers flew through his head during such situations. Attack angles, turn rates, electrical energy loads, thrust levels, and acceleration curves; it was like his head was doing the math at a subconscious level. As he lit his main engines, it was as if he could sense the additional energy load the act placed on the reactors. He could even anticipate the millisecond lag between the movement of his throttles and the reaction of his engines.

"Inertial dampeners online!" Loki announced as Josh started easing the throttle forward. "Twenty seconds to intercept!"

"Mains coming up!" Josh announced. He glanced at the reactor control panel as the indicators reached one hundred percent. "We're outta here!" he declared as he slammed the throttles forward against their stops.

With the inertial dampeners now online, only enough force for the crew to feel their maneuvers was allowed to translate into the cockpit of the Falcon. "Bringing forward turret online."

"Why?" Josh wondered. "We're not going to be able to hit anything, not at this distance."

"Gives them something to think about," Loki argued. "Maybe it will keep them from coming to close."

"Doubtful." Josh looked at their trajectory around the moon. "Uh, Loki, this ain't gonna work."

"What's not gonna work?"

"The angles. We're never gonna get that moon between us and them."

"So?"

"Captain said not to jump if someone can see us!"

"Fuck, I almost forgot." Loki suddenly felt himself being pushed right as Josh rolled the ship to port and started a hard turn. "Where are you going?"

"Toward the planet," Josh answered. "I think I can put just enough distance between us and them that we can pull a hard turn around the planet and jump away when they can't see us."

"At this speed?"

"No, at a lot faster than this speed!"

"Are you insane?"

"Pretty much," Josh said with a chuckle.

"Josh, that's not physically possible, not even at half our current speed. Orbital velocity is..."

"I'm not trying to go into fucking orbit, Loki! I just want to put the planet between us and them. I never said it was gonna be pretty!"

"Okay! Okay! But let me run the numbers first. Maybe we don't have to go at full power all the way around!"

"Fine!"

Loki studied his console as he ran the numbers over and over, each time adjusting the speed of both the Falcon and its pursuers. A warning light began to flash, pulling his attention away from his calculations momentarily. "Shit. Four more contacts coming from the moon. No doubt more fighters. They're moving into formation and accelerating faster than the first four."

"What? How many fighters do they need to shoot

down one recon ship?"

"The first four were probably the ready flight," Loki surmised.

"The what?"

"The ready flight. Major Prechitt always keeps four fighters in the tubes with pilots in their cockpits ready to launch at a moment's notice."

"How do you know that?"

"I've been tracking flight ops during our jump layovers," Loki told him. "That's odd. The first four fighters haven't changed their rate of acceleration. In fact, they're matching our speed, accelerating as we accelerate."

"That's a good thing, right?"

"Back off on the throttles, Josh."

"Why?"

"I think I know what they're doing."

"How much?" Josh asked as he put his left hand on the pair of throttles.

"Try taking it down ten percent."

"Got it."

Loki watched as the Falcon slowed her acceleration. "They're slowing down as well."

"What about the second flight?"

"They're still accelerating, but they're not even at half the other flight's speed yet. They're going to try and catch us as we come around the planet," Loki explained, "from the opposite side."

"How did you figure that out?"

"The CAG had our fighters practicing the same maneuver a few jumps ago," Loki told him, "only they were using the Aurora as the planet."

"I've got to stop reading so much," Josh said.

"Is it just me, or does this conversation seem backwards?"

"Well, their plan is not going to work," Josh said with a smile. "As soon as the first flight loses sight of us, we flash out of here."

"Yeah, but they don't know that," Loki said. "This just might work, assuming they don't shoot us down first."

"They tried, remember? The missiles?"

"That might have been a knee-jerk reaction on their part," Loki said. "We suddenly appeared on their sensors, really close. They probably thought we were about to launch a sneak-attack. Drop a nuke or something."

"So what are they trying to do now?" Josh wondered. "Capture us?"

"Maybe? They're probably curious as to how we managed to get in so close without being detected. That would explain why they're launching so many fighters," Loki added, "to try and scare us into surrendering."

"Aren't they gonna be surprised when we don't come out around the other side of the planet?" Josh giggled.

"They're probably going to think we dove down into the atmosphere to hide. If so, they could be searching for days."

"That's fine with me," Josh said. "How long until we start our turn?"

"Two minutes."

Josh's comm-set suddenly crackled to life as an endless river of unintelligible words began to stream through his ear piece. "What the hell? Are you getting this?"

"Yeah," Loki answered. "I think they're trying to contact us."

"In what language?"

"I think they're repeating the same message in many different languages." Loki listened intently for several seconds as the message continued to replay, each time in a different language. "Wait!"

"...*immediately indicate your surrender, or we are to begin on hostile action.*" Loki backed up the recorded message a few seconds and replayed it. After a few unintelligible words followed by some static, he heard, "*You have aggressed into Jung space. Immediately indicate your surrender, or we are to begin on hostile action.*"

"Wow," Josh said. "Their Angla sucks."

"I'm pretty sure they hope to capture us," Loki said. "I'm sure they're in missile range by now."

"What's the second group doing?"

"They're still following the first group. They probably won't break off and change course to come around the other side of the planet until after we duck behind so that they don't tip us off on their little plan." The message began repeating, going through every language version again. "Should we answer them?" Loki asked.

"Yeah. How about, '*Fuck you. Open your eyes wide and check out our pretty jump flash*'?"

Loki chuckled. "They'll probably translate it as '*flash fuck your wide open eyes*' anyway. One minute to turn."

"Uh, I just thought of something," Josh said. "What if they are tracking us from the planet? Wouldn't they see us jump?"

"Yeah, I thought about that," Loki answered. "But we're going to be jumping from the dark side, so maybe everyone is asleep on that side. And so far, there are no tracking signals coming from the planet. Comm-signals, yes, emissions that would indicate tracking systems or sensors, no."

"You can't detect some junior-Junger looking at the night sky with his toy telescope."

"All we can do at this point is take the course of action that results in the least probability of our jump being witnessed," Loki explained. "The captain never said, *'Die before being seen jumping.'* He said, *'Die before being captured.'*"

"I'm with you on that one," Josh said.

"Twenty seconds to turn."

The two of them sat in silence for several seconds. Loki kept running his calculations over and over, making sure they were correct, while Josh stared out the window at the approaching planet, preparing himself for the nasty, high-speed turn he was about to attempt.

"Five seconds."

"Sure beats the hell out of jump-recharge-repeat, don't it?" Josh mused.

"Four......There really is something wrong with you."

Josh smiled.

"Two......one......start your turn."

Josh pulled the stick hard to port, slightly rolling the ship as he did so. Despite the inertial dampener's efforts, the force of his turn pushed them both hard to starboard, their bodies pulling against their flight harnesses. Josh peered out the left side as the planet started to move toward them more quickly. If he did the turn correctly, the planet's gravity would whip them around and accelerate them further, dropping them out of the sight of their pursuers just long enough for them to jump away unseen.

"Twenty seconds until they lose line of sight on us," Loki announced.

"Tell me you've already plotted our jump," Josh answered.

"Plotted and locked. Ten seconds."

"No fucking auto-nav this time, either."

"Wouldn't dream of it," Loki promised. "Five sec... SHIT!"

"What?"

"Contacts! Four more fighters, coming up from the planet, dead ahead!"

"Fuck!"

"They're painting us! They're firing! Four missiles inbound! Impact in fifteen seconds!"

"Shit!" Josh screamed in frustration. "I thought they wanted us alive!"

"They must think we're attacking the planet!" Loki responded. "Screw it, Josh! Let's jump!"

Josh looked at his tracking displays, then his flight data, and then glanced out the window at the planet below. There was a massive mountain range looming a few hundred kilometers below them. "I've got an idea!"

Loki's heart sank. Josh's ideas, although they usually worked, were usually wild rides that took years off Loki's life span.

"Charge up the reentry shields, and stand by to pop another dozen decoys." Without warning, Josh flipped the interceptor end over so that they were flying backwards, and then slammed his throttles back up to full power. Again, they were pushed back into their flight seats as the Falcon began to rapidly decelerate.

"Ten seconds to impact!" Loki called out.

The planet was now above them, sliding by from stern to nose. Josh eased the Falcon's nose toward the planet above, pitching the ship into a decelerating dive.

"Five......"

"Just a little more," Josh mumbled.

"Four......"

"Stand by decoys," Josh ordered.

"Three......decoys ready," Loki acknowledged. "Two......"

"Launch decoys," Josh ordered calmly.

"Decoys away!"

Another dozen decoys shot out the back of the Falcon as Josh pushed the nose straight into the planet and started a powered dive. Again, all four missiles struck the decoys and exploded.

The interceptor shook lightly for several seconds as the shock wave rippled through the planet's thin, upper atmosphere.

"If that had happened deeper in the atmosphere, we'd have been screwed!" Josh announced gleefully.

"Josh! You're in a powered dive at greater than orbital velocity!"

"Yeah, I'm gonna have to do something about that sooner or later, aren't I?"

"Sooner would be good."

"Where is that third group of fighters?" Josh asked.

"They're turning back into the planet to follow us," Loki answered, "two hundred kilometers and closing."

"Hang on," Josh warned. "You're not gonna like this."

Loki grabbed the handrails on either side of the cockpit and held on tight. Josh cut his engines, jerked back on the interceptor's nose, and pulled the ship level as they continued to fall toward the planet.

"Are you nuts?" Loki cried out. "A zero atmospheric entry angle?"

"Dump all power into the thermal shielding, Loki!" Josh barked.

"It isn't going to be enough, Josh! You're going to rip us to pieces!"

"It'll work! Trust me!" Josh yelled as the Falcon began to shake.

"Not in a million years, you psychotic, little shit!"

Josh laughed. That was the Loki he knew.

The Falcon continued its fiery descent through the planet's thickening atmosphere, the shaking becoming more violent with every meter they fell.

"Thermal shields are at maximum!" Loki announced. "Shield temp three thousand and climbing!"

Josh struggled to keep the interceptor's attitude perpendicular to their angle of attack. The more drag he created, the greater the rate of deceleration. But it also meant the greater the amount of heat their thermal shields were subjected to, and they had their limits as well.

"Altitude: ninety kilometers. Speed: fifty thousand. Shield temp: four thousand!" Loki called out. "Max shield temp is six, Josh!"

"I know!"

"Just sayin'."

Josh checked his propellant levels, quickly running the calculations in his head. They had used very little propellant thus far, having only made a few maneuvers since they had left the Aurora. In fact, they had used more propellant in the last five minutes than they had in the entire flight. "I need to know the escape velocity of this world," Josh said.

"One moment," Loki answered as he set to work

with the Falcon's scanners. "About fifteen thousand meters per second."

"So it will take us, what, about ten percent of our propellant to get off this planet?"

Loki again buried his attention in his display as he ran precise calculations.

"Loki?" Josh asked impatiently.

"Yeah, yeah. Eight point six eight! So ten gives us a nice margin. You're not thinking of landing, are you?"

"Not if I can help it," he proclaimed. "Just want to know where my point of no return is, propellant wise."

"Let's just worry about not burning up right now."

"Or slamming into the planet like a meteorite," Josh added.

"That too," Loki agreed. "Altitude: eighty kilometers. Speed: forty thousand. Temp: five thousand."

"Loki?" Josh asked as the ship shook violently. "What would happen if I did a half end-over right now?"

"Seriously?"

"Yeah, seriously."

"I'm not sure you could. The aerodynamics..."

"I was thinking about using my maneuvering thrusters."

"Uh, it might work," Loki said, "if the drag doesn't snap us like a twig."

"Could you run that for me?"

"Sure. Why not?" He glanced at the tracking display. "By the way, in case it matters, the third fighter group is still hot on our tail, albeit in a much more controlled fashion."

"I see them," Josh told him, glancing at his own tracking display screen. "But they're not overtaking us anymore."

"Hell no, they're not as crazy as we are," Loki declared as he ran simulations of the Falcon doing an end-over in their current situation. "It doesn't look good, Josh. We need to be down to at least half our current speed before we can even think about it. Even then, it's risky."

"So we'll be at, what, sixty kilometers by the time we get down to twenty thousand kilometers per hour?"

"Something like that. But we'll also be at seven thousand degrees on our shields," Loki added. "Failure is at six thousand three hundred."

"Bring the reactors up to one twenty and dump the extra into the shields."

"That won't work, Josh. It might keep the shield generators from blowing, but heat will get through, a lot of it!"

"So we'll be well-done," Josh said. "That's better than becoming ashes!"

Loki shook his head in dismay. "Passing seventy. Speed: thirty thousand. Temp: six thousand. Reactors at one twenty." Loki watched the thermal shield control display. "Thermal shields are holding. Shield temp is sixty-five hundred. Hull temp: fifteen hundred and climbing." Loki shook his head again. "Josh, it won't work. You can't shave off twenty-nine thousand KPH of speed in less than sixty kilometers. Even if you successfully end over without tearing us apart, the turbines just aren't powerful enough."

"We're not going to use the turbines!" Josh yelled. "Override the auto-drive selection and put all propulsion systems on manual activation."

"What?"

"Slave the turbines to my flight controls. Slave the main drive to yours."

"Oh shit! You are crazy!" Loki declared as he began to make the necessary changes. "Oh shit, oh shit, oh shit. I don't know if I can do this, Josh."

"You've got the easy part! I'm the one that's gotta try a half end-over and fly ass first at twenty thousand KPH!"

"Got it. I've got spaceflight. You've got aero!" Loki took a deep breath. "Twenty thousand kilometers per hour and falling."

"Here we go," Josh announced. "Roll forty-five right. NOW!" Josh and Loki simultaneously executed the same maneuver, Loki using the thrusters and Josh using the aerodynamic control surfaces. The ship snap-rolled forty-five degrees to the right, and they began falling starboard side first toward the planet below.

"Good!" Josh yelled. "Now we're going to yaw left forty-five. Got it?"

"Got it."

"Ready, NOW!" The ship yawed to port, shaking even more violently as the airflow was forced to change its path across the interceptor once again.

"Okay! Awesome! We're back in the slipstream again!" Josh announced as he struggled to hold the ship at its current attitude. The problem was it wasn't designed to fly tail first in the atmosphere. "Oh shit!" Josh cried out as he felt the interceptor slipping out of his control. "Loki! I can't hold it! The control surfaces are locking up! You're gonna have to take her!"

"Fuck!" Loki grabbed the controls again, twisting the stick from right to left, back and forth, side to side. Thrusters fired wildly outside as he tried to keep the ship falling smoothly tail first. "That's as smooth as I can get her!" Loki announced. "Firing mains!" he announced as he slammed the throttles forward.

Once more, they were slammed back into their seats as the main space drive that was designed to quickly accelerate them to near relativistic velocities used its might to quickly decelerate them.

"Passing fifty!" Josh announced. "Speed: eighteen! Shield temp: seven thousand! Hull temp: two thousand!" The idea of a rocket flying backwards suddenly appeared in Josh's mind. "Fuck me! It's working!"

"We're not there yet!" Loki yelled as he struggled to keep the ship at the proper attitude while they rode the massive tail of thrust coming from their main space drive.

"We just lost our deep-space comm-array," Josh announced. "Long-range sensors are offline as well."

"We're starting to melt," Loki mumbled as the interceptor continued to shake.

"Passing forty-five. Speed: fifteen thousand. Shield temp: seventy-two hundred. Hull temp: twenty-two hundred!" Josh tried not to giggle. It was working, but Loki was right; it wasn't over.

"I cannot believe I am doing this," Loki mumbled.

"Passing forty. Speed: ten thousand. Shield temp holding at seventy-two! Hull temp also holding at twenty-two! I told you!"

"Check tracking!" Loki yelled.

"They're still coming," Josh said. "Range: one hundred twenty kilometers and closing fast." Josh glanced at the flight systems display. "We're sucking up propellant awfully fast here. Passing forty. Speed:

five thousand. Temps are falling!"

For the first time in the last ten minutes, Loki was beginning to feel hope. They were still being pursued by at least twelve Jung fighters, all determined to destroy them, but they might actually avoid both crashing into the planet and burning up.

"Passing thirty! Speed: five thousand. Temps dropping." Josh checked the thermal shield control display. "Thermal shield temps are down to three thousand! I'm dialing the reactors back down to one hundred percent. Passing twenty-five. Speed: three thousand," Josh continued to report. "Speed down to two thousand. Passing twenty."

"Pitching over!" Loki announced as he used the thruster to perform another end-over. As the ship shuddered through the maneuver, Loki killed the main drive. "Mains at zero!" he announced. "Nose is coming down!"

"Spinning up the turbines," Josh announced as he grabbed the flight controls again.

"Killing thermal shields!" Loki announced as the view of the planet below filled their forward view once again.

"Turbines are hot!" Josh announced. "We're back in powered aerodynamic flight mode!"

"I'm reengaging the auto-flight system," Loki reported. His body went limp with relief, his head dipping forward for a moment. "Don't you fucking ever do that to me again!" he screamed.

"What? You were awesome!" Josh said as he began leveling the ship off. "Leveling off at five thousand meters. Speed at five hundred KPH."

"Four more contacts!" Loki announced. "Three o'clock low, about twenty kilometers out and closing fast. They're skimming the mountain tops."

"Loki, is this the hornet's nest the captain was talking about?"

"I expect so, Josh."

"Arm missiles," Josh ordered as he began a slow turn to starboard. "Target all four and prepare to fire."

"You're not really going to take them on, are you?"

"Don't have much choice, do I?"

"Missiles armed. Acquiring targets. Josh, I'm pretty sure stealth recon doesn't include engaging enemy targets in combat."

"Stand by on the nose turret as well, Loki," Josh ordered. "I'm pretty sure they're going to launch on us."

"Targets locked. Powering up the nose turret and acquiring targets."

The seconds ticked by as the Falcon closed on the four oncoming Jung fighters skimming along the edge of the mountain range that stretched out below them.

"Targets will be in missile range in five seconds," Loki announced.

"As soon as all four missiles are away, I'm gonna roll over and dive so that you can keep our gun turret on them. See if you can take out their missiles. We'll deploy decoys just before we duck down below the other side of the ridge line."

"Max range," Loki announced. "They're pitching up to fire."

"Firing missiles," Josh announced. "Four away."

"Four running hot and normal, locked on targets. Time on target: twenty seconds. They're firing."

"Rolling and pitching." Josh rolled the interceptor to port in a lazy arc, moving across to the opposite side of the ridge line as he did so. "Pitching down."

Loki tapped the nose turret's targeting screen with his finger, touching each of the symbols that represented the incoming Jung missiles. "Guns have acquired. Keep us on this attitude for ten seconds," Loki said. "Firing guns."

Long, angry, red bolts of energy leapt from the twin barrels of the Falcon's nose turret toward the incoming Jung missiles, firing in continuous succession. First one, then another, then a third missile fell to the assault.

"One missile left," Loki announced proudly.

"I can't hold this any longer, Lok," Josh declared. "I've gotta roll and level off, or we're gonna hit the mountains." Josh rolled the ship back over again, slipping down on the opposite side of the mountains from the oncoming Jung fighters.

"I've lost the contacts," Loki announced. "They're on the opposite side of the ridge."

"Pop decoys," Josh ordered as he pushed the Falcon down deeper into the valley below.

"The last missile is coming over the ridge line," Loki announced.

"Is it tracking us or the decoys?"

"Too close to tell," Loki said. "The decoys, I think."

"Pop the last batch," Josh ordered.

The last twelve decoys shot out the back of the Falcon, glowing red hot as they fanned out from either side in an irregular pattern.

"Decoys away. That's the last of them."

Josh watched as the oncoming missile streaked over their starboard side. "Shit! That was fucking close!" he declared as the missile struck the second set of decoys and exploded.

"Canyon narrows up ahead, Josh. Terrain

following sensors can't see past the next bend while we're below the ridge line."

"Any idea how many of those fighters are left?"

"Nope," Loki answered, "can't see them either."

"Damn."

"Wait," Loki said, "I've got one climbing. He's down a half loop," Loki decided. "I think he's gonna roll next to try and get in behind us."

"I like this guy," Josh said.

"There's another coming in behind him. Same maneuver."

"Fuck! Did we hit anything?"

"No one else. I think we got two of them." Loki watched as the two Jung fighters finished their roll and dove in behind them. "Yup, they're diving down, coming in behind us."

"It's on, baby!" Josh announced, pushing his throttle forward.

"Josh, we don't know the canyons ahead."

"Yeah, but they do, and they're not backing off. So they must be navigable. Just keep the nose turret pointed aft and take a shot whenever you can. Maybe we'll get lucky."

Several energy bolts streaked past them.

"I think they're trying to tell us something," Loki said.

"Like what?" Josh laughed.

"I think they're trying to tell us to stay out of the canyons."

"So say something back."

"Like what?"

"Like, 'Eat hot plasma, asshole.'"

"Okay." Loki opened fire, skimming his turret from side to side. For the most part, their rounds of energy were far below their pursuers, as the targets were flying at the same relative altitude and the Falcon's gun turret couldn't fire aft at an upward angle. "Bounce up a bit," Loki suggested. The Falcon suddenly rose upward a few meters, giving Loki a clean shot. He fire again, missing the targets but making them feel the heat of the plasma bolts as they streaked past the enemy cockpits. "That made them nervous."

"Here we go," Josh announced as he made a hard left around the first cliff.

Loki tried not to notice as the reddish-purple canyon wall passed uncomfortably close to port. Instead, he focused on his targeting screen, hoping to get a clean shot as Josh snaked back and forth through the narrow canyons.

The lead Jung fighter had the same idea, firing continuously as he weaved to and fro just a few hundred meters behind them. The Jung leader's wingman followed closely behind, taking a single shot at a time whenever his leader was out of the way and his sights were anywhere near the Falcon.

Josh couldn't tell the difference between the leader's shots and the wingman's, as his attention was focused on simply not crashing into the sides of the narrow, winding canyons. Every so often, the canyon would split, forcing him to make a split-second decision to the right or to the left with nothing more to go on than instinct. At any moment, he feared his choice might lead to a dead end, and their escape would fail in either a fiery crash or an unavoidable missile shot as they climbed out of the canyons.

"Missile!" Loki cried. "Jink right!"

Josh didn't hesitate, rolling the interceptor to the right once as the missile passed under their rising left wing-body. "Missiles! In here!" Josh cried. "I was wrong! I don't like this guy!"

Loki glanced at the systems displays. "We're burning propellant, Josh. That red line is coming up fast." A warning light flashed again. "Shit! Jink left!"

Josh glanced at his rear display and saw the incoming missile approaching on their starboard side. With a twist and a yank of his control stick, he pushed their tail down and yawed it to port, rolling the interceptor starboard at the same time. The missile passed right through the spot where their entire starboard side had been a second ago.

Loki watched the missile pass over them and streak ahead, slamming into the massive overhang that jutted out from the right side of the canyon ahead. The missile exploded on impact, cracking the reddish-purple rock and sending it tumbling down directly in their flight path. "WATCH THE ROCKS!" he screamed.

Josh glanced up from his console just in time to see the rocks falling directly in front of them. He stopped their roll, standing on their left side, passing between two massive chunks of the collapsing overhang, shooting safely out the other side.

The lead pilot was not as quick, trying to climb over the collapsing overhang. He skipped off the top, cracking his fuselage and catching fire, spraying burning propellant all over the wilderness below. His canopy blew and his ejection seat blasted him high up into the air. His wingman also climbed, managing to miss the collapsing overhang. He had to continue to pull up hard, going to full throttle to avoid slamming into his leader as he ejected.

With the lead Jung fighter down and his wingman in a climb with his belly facing the Falcon, Josh had his chance. He pulled hard to starboard at the upcoming split as Loki fired a few more rounds toward the climbing wingman.

"What are you doing?" Loki demanded. "Pitch up! Do a three-quarter loop and launch missiles while he's showing us his belly!"

"All we need is a short run of straight canyon while no one's on our tail, and we can pitch up slightly and jump away without anyone seeing us!"

"Well he can't see us now," Loki reported as the second Jung fighter fell off his tracking system, his line of sight to the target having been blocked by the canyon walls.

"We just need a kilometer or two of straightaway," Josh mumbled as he navigated the winding canyon. *Maybe the next turn*, he thought. "FUCK!"

As the Falcon came around the next turn in the narrow canyon, a massive waterfall appeared before them, cascading down from the top of the canyon on their left as they finished their turn to starboard. Unfortunately, their turn was swinging them wide to port, directly toward the massive falls.

"Hang on!" Josh yelled as he switched the automatic thrust vectoring system to manual, swung all four of the Falcon's turbine exhaust port straight down, and slammed the throttles to full power.

Loki looked up and saw the massive waterfall, his eyes opening wide as he watched the approaching water drop from what seemed like a thousand meters above them.

The Falcon slammed into the waterfall at over three hundred kilometers per hour. It felt like they had hit the side of the mountain, and for a split second, Josh was sure they had. The Falcon was suddenly pushed downward by the force of the water falling down upon them. Their turbines screamed at the additional load as they struggled to keep the interceptor aloft. For a split second, the Falcon was more submarine than aircraft.

That split second seemed an eternity to Josh, the sound of the pounding water deafening him even through his pressurized flight helmet. He wondered if this was one of those moments that warriors spoke about. Those moments in battle when everything seemed to go in slow motion. His eyes darted back and forth across his console. His altitude was dropping fast, as was his airspeed. Warning indicators were lighting up all over his cockpit, on his main console, and on either side of him. He thought he could hear the warning tones in his comm-set, but they were lost in the din of the waterfall. Out of the corner of his eye, he could see his canopy as it develop spider-web cracks along the port side. Another glance told him that they were rolling to starboard, already thirty degrees over. He instinctively adjusted his throttles, decreasing the lift on the port side to try to slow the roll, but it didn't seem to be working.

A second later, it was over. The Falcon burst out the other side of the massive waterfall with multiple alarms sounding in their comm-sets, just as Josh had thought. He switched the thrust vectoring back to automatic so that the ship would level itself.

"Multiple cautions and warnings!" Loki yelled, having no time to comment on what they had just done. "Port reactor is offline! Jump drive is offline! Turbine two is down. Turbine three is flooded and trying to restart! Inertial dampeners are offline! Trying to reinitialize!" Loki looked at the cracked canopy. "I'm not sure, but we might be losing pressure in the cockpit!"

"Slave the thrusters to my flight stick to compensate for the failing turbines, so I can keep her level until I can set down!" Josh ordered.

"Set down where?" Loki asked as he slaved the thrusters normally used to maneuver in space to Josh's flight stick.

Josh scanned his Terrain-Following Sensor display, looking for someplace to land. Something caught his eye, something on the wall of the canyon ahead. He looked out the forward canopy, bringing the ship to a sloppy hover about fifty meters above the massive river below. The canyon widened into a wide valley a few kilometers ahead. "Are missiles still working?"

"Yeah, but..."

"What about those new toys, the decoys and comm-drones?"

"They're still online, Josh, but..."

"Arm the missile warheads but not their engines. Prepare to drop all our missiles as well as all the drones on my mark," he ordered.

"What the..."

"Just do it!" Josh pushed the base of the stick forward, causing the ship to accelerate toward the valley ahead. "Don't arm the engines on the drones either!" he ordered as they accelerated.

Loki shook his head, having no idea what Josh was up to. "Missile warheads are armed. Drones are ready to drop."

"Drop everything!" Josh ordered. "Now! Now! Now!"

Loki opened the bay doors and released all four drones, followed by all four missiles. "Everything is away!"

Josh immediately stopped their forward acceleration, coming to a quick stop, again hovering precariously in the air as he struggled to keep the damaged ship aloft. He watched as the ordnance and the drones coasted ahead, slowly falling to the ground as they moved away from them. A few seconds later, they hit the ground, and the missile warheads exploded in a huge fireball that instantly vaporized hundreds of trees and left a massive crater in the ground. The blast ripped apart the drones, setting off the charges designed to blow the mini-jump drives and ZPEDs in the comm-drones. The ZPEDs flashed brightly, like miniature supernovas that burst into life and then died in a single moment.

Josh pulled the ship up and to port, turning around and heading back toward the waterfall as he slowly climbed.

Loki noticed they were turning around. He also noticed they were headed closer to the canyon wall. "What are you doing?"

"I just gave them a crash site," Josh said. "Now we have to hide."

"Where?" Loki asked as they turned around to face the waterfall. "We're not going back in there, are we?"

"Not exactly," Josh told him. "Look up to the right, just under that overhang. There's a small cave."

Loki trained the Falcon's sensors on the cave. "That thing's not tall enough for us to land in, Josh."

"It is if we don't use any landing gear!"

Loki just laughed in frustration. "Don't suppose there's anything I can do to change your mind."

"Hang on," Josh said. Josh pulled the ship up higher and turned into the canyon wall. The mist was heaving from the waterfall only one hundred meters away, and it made it difficult to see. Josh also knew that it would make the cave wet, and wet meant slippery. Slippery was good, especially when landing without landing gear.

"We're losing power on turbine four!" Loki warned.

"Just keep her running for ten more seconds," he begged. He fired the aft thrusters, sending them hurtling forward toward the cave. He added some upward thrust to compensate for the failing number four turbine.

"We're too high!" Loki said.

Josh ignored his warnings.

"We just lost four!" Loki's eyes widened as they began to fall from the sky as the overhang above the cave rushed toward them. He crossed his arms across his face to protect himself as Josh spun the interceptor one hundred eighty degrees. It slid below the overhang and into the cave, crashing into the cave floor. The ship bounced up slightly, its highest point striking the cave ceiling and breaking off large chunks of the reddish-purple rock that then rained down upon their ship. The ship slid several meters across the slippery cave floor, slamming into the back wall. Josh felt his head slam back against the inside of his helmet. The canopy shattered from the force of the impact, sending chunks of the clear canopy flying.

"Loki!" Josh yelled once the ship came to a stop. "Loki! Are you all right?!"

"Yeah, I'm fine, I think," Loki answered. "Fuck, Josh. Where did you learn to fly?"

"Self-taught, remember?"

"It fucking shows."

"Hey, we're alive!" he said. "Shut everything down, quickly! That other fighter will be flying over any second. We can't be hot!"

"We just flew through a waterfall a minute ago, Josh. How hot can we be?"

"Yeah, that worked out kind of nice, didn't it?" Josh looked at the canopy. The frame was jammed up against the ceiling of the cave. If the canopy itself had not shattered, they never would have been able to get out. "Jesus! The canopy is broken." He checked his helmet and suit, all of which appeared to be okay. "How's your suit, Loki?"

"Fine, never better."

"How are we looking back there?"

"I have no idea, Josh. I just shut everything down, remember?"

"Just tell me the self-destruct system still works."

"It's battery-powered. So yeah, it still works," Loki answered. "But can we get out first, before you blow it up?"

CHAPTER EIGHT

Nathan remembered how much he always dreaded going to medical. The cries of pain, the moans of those suffering bravely, the smell of open wounds and the ozone fields used to sterilize them. The worst was the sound of suction devices. The slurping made his stomach twist, threatening to reject its contents with only a moment's notice. The mandatory 'captain's rounds' as he had named them included going from bed to bed, offering the wounded words of encouragement from their de facto leader.

Despite the fact that he had been serving as captain for several months now, he still didn't feel like the true captain of the Aurora. In his mind, that would always be the late Captain Roberts. Some days were better than others, and he seemed to be able to perform his duties with at least enough skill to keep his XO from relieving him under some article or another.

Soon, however, the long performance would come to an end. They would dock the ship at the Orbital Assembly Platform in Earth orbit, and Fleet personnel would swarm all over the ship, relieving everyone and going through every nut, bolt, weld, and circuit. The Corinairan and Takaran specialists would be busy explaining the enhancements they had made, and no doubt those new technologies would keep the scientists on Earth excited for some time to come. That would make his non-Terran crew a bit of a commodity, which would probably make their extended stay on Earth a bit more pleasant. Still, he worried how long that stay might be. Those men had signed on to serve on the Aurora, not to sit on Earth and cool their heels, and especially not to wait out a war. However, try as he might, he could not envision a scenario in which Fleet could spare a ship, let alone a jump ship, to spend a month on a round trip to the Pentaurus cluster and back. Until the Aurora was inadvertently thrown across the galaxy, no one from his Earth had traveled more than twenty light years from home, at least not since the plague had struck a thousand years ago.

Nathan tried to tell himself that it did not matter. He had never promised anything more than he could deliver. He had only promised that he would do everything within his power to protect his crew and get them home again. Once they got back to Earth, that promise would have been fulfilled for just over ten percent of his crew.

Oddly enough, Nathan found himself hoping that his father had actually won his bid for the North American presidency. That might give him enough clout to get his non-Terran crew home sooner rather than later. At the very least, they might be given the resources to fabricate their own jump ship in order to get home. After all, a small production base with a single fabricator parked on a big enough asteroid might be all they needed—that, and enough consumables to keep them alive long enough to complete their task. And there were four fabricators on the Aurora. *Or were there three?* Nathan laughed to himself.

At least, now, medical was a different story. It was clean, quiet, and actually smelled pleasant. The Corinairan physicians—who were adamant about the effects of certain environmental factors when it came to healing—kept the place as relaxing as possible. They had even installed sound-dampening systems around each bed, allowing them to block out all exterior noise in order to keep the patient in a peaceful state. They had wanted to install a complex system that would create a holographic curtain around each bed. This would have allowed them to not only surround each patient with whatever peaceful setting they desired, but also to provide patient privacy. However, it would have required extensive reconstruction of the entire treatment area, hence it was given an extremely low priority.

Nathan made his way through the mostly empty treatment room. There were only two patients, both of whom were sleeping at the moment. His daily reports had told him of their conditions. One was being treated for a minor burn that occurred during the installation of one of the plasma cannons into a torpedo tube. The other inhaled some rather corrosive gas that had accidentally vented from one of the fighters in the hangar deck. He would be in for at least a week while nanites repaired damaged tissues in his lungs.

"Doctor Chen," Nathan called as he came to stand in the doorway to her office.

"Captain, how may I help you?"

Nathan entered her office and took a seat across from her. "I was wondering how Mister Percival was doing."

"Quite well considering how long he was in stasis.

The nanites have done a remarkable job of repairing his atrophied tissues."

"How strong is he?"

"Well, he managed to handle an entire day of touring the ship. Although, he is resting in his quarters now as a result."

"I meant, how strong is he emotionally?"

Doctor Chen shrugged her shoulders. "Hard to say. He seems fairly unaffected by what has happened. I mean, the collapse of humanity in the core didn't seem to affect him that much."

"But he knew that was coming before he went into stasis," Nathan reminded her.

"True enough, but he also took the death of the expedition pretty well. At least, I see no signs of depression or mourning on his part. No more than expected, anyway." Doctor Chen looked quizzically at Nathan. "Why do you ask?"

"Well, I need to tell him about what really happened to the Jasper expedition," Nathan explained, "and it isn't pretty."

"Death seldom is."

"Neither is despair," Nathan said, thinking of what the captain of the Jasper had gone through.

"I think you may be selling him short, Captain. Mister Percival was a self-made millionaire who worked in some extreme environments out on the fringe worlds. He faced his own terminal illness and developed a way to survive even in the face of the greatest plague in known history. I expect he has seen as much death and despair as any of us."

"I don't know, Doc. Between the two of us, I think we've seen more than our fair share."

Doctor Chen smiled. "I think you get my point, sir."

"Yeah, I do." Nathan leaned back in his chair. "Then you think it's okay to break the news to him?"

"Yes, I do," she assured him. "Besides, he is wearing a life-signs monitor. If he has an adverse reaction, we'll respond accordingly."

"Of course." This time it was Nathan who smiled.

* * *

"I count six," Josh said as he peered through the handheld view scope.

Loki sat leaning behind and against the same rock that Josh was peeking out over as he scanned the valley below. "I think the flight harness bruised my shoulder," he complained as he rubbed it.

"Including those two shuttles, that makes eight total," Josh added, ignoring Loki's complaints.

"How long do you think it will take them to figure out we didn't crash? There, I mean... because we did actually crash."

"Crash land," Josh said. "Big difference."

"Not according to my shoulder."

"I don't know," Josh answered. "It depends on how smart they are. Your average Takaran ground pounder would buy it in a heartbeat. A scientific type, not so much." Josh turned around and slid back down the rock next to Loki. "The big question is, will they start searching around the local area, or will they assume that we used the fake crash as a screen to fly away low out over the valley?"

"I caught glimpses on the sensors as you were fighting to stay aloft after we came out of that waterfall," Loki told him. "There are at least a few towns in that valley. I'm sure they heard the crash, and if so, they would have come outside to see what it was. If they ask them, they'll report that they didn't see anything flying away."

"And that will make them search the area between where they last saw us and the fake crash site," Josh concluded, "which is pretty much where we're sitting." He looked at Loki. Josh grimaced at his own aches and pains as the adrenaline of the chase and subsequent crash landing began to wear off. "What do you think? A few hours?"

"At the most."

"Then we need to bust ass and get the ship working," Josh declared.

"And do what? The canopy is busted, Josh."

Josh tugged at his flight suit. "Pressure suits, remember?"

"You want to fly across a few light years in an open cockpit?"

"You want to spend our days hiding from the Jung and every loyalist on this miserable planet?"

"It didn't look so miserable," Loki tried to convince himself. "I mean, it's got trees, rivers, waterfalls... and the mountains are an interesting shade of reddish-purple," he added, looking at the mountainside in front of him.

"Maybe the damage is minor," Josh said optimistically.

"We crashed into the side of a mountain, Josh."

"Crash landed. There's..."

"A difference, I know." Loki finished for him as he struggled to get his feet back under him. He remained in a crouched position behind their cover as he began to move away from the rock.

"Let's go take a look then."

* * *

"So, how was your tour of the ship?" Nathan asked Mister Percival as he entered his quarters.

"Very interesting," Mister Percival answered as he took a seat at his small desk.

"I'm sorry we couldn't provide better accommodations," Nathan apologized. "We're at one hundred and ten percent crew capacity right now. These rooms near medical were converted into extended recovery rooms during one of our previous battles. Since we had already doubled up and hot racked portions of the crew, we decided to keep these spaces available until we got back to Earth, just in case."

"Yes, your chief engineer alluded to your adventures in, what was it called, the Pentaurus cluster?"

"Yes, well, don't tell anyone else he told you, or my security chief is liable to kick his ass."

"Top secret stuff?"

"No, not really," Nathan said. "She just tends to be overly cautious."

"A good trait for a security officer, I suppose. Lieutenant Commander Kamenetskiy was quite talkative."

"Yes, he gets that way, especially when it comes to the ship's systems."

"Indeed. He seems to take great pride in them as well as the enhancements being made by your new crew. It should be quite a feather in your cap when you return."

"Perhaps."

"So, what may I do for you, Captain?"

"I'm afraid that I have bad news."

"About?"

"The Jasper expedition," Nathan told him, holding up a data card. "We finished reviewing the Jasper's logs—more specifically, Captain Dubnyk's logs."

"I see. And what did they reveal?" Mister Percival said.

Nathan noticed that Mister Percival seemed a bit apprehensive, which was to be expected. "The expedition experienced a number of mishaps, each of which contributed to their demise. A shuttle damaged during transit, the other one crashing before the ship was off-loaded, and finally a volcano that pushed their world into an ice age. I'm afraid the two hundred colonists that made it to the surface froze to death a few decades later." Nathan paused a moment, waiting as much to see if Mister Percival had any questions. Nathan was trying to judge how Mister Percival was handling the news.

Mister Percival cleared his throat. "And the other colonists?"

"They apparently died in their stasis chambers," Nathan stated as empathetically as possible. "They never knew of their own fate."

"And the crew of the Jasper?"

"I assume they did know," Nathan admitted. "However, lack of resources would have driven them back into their stasis pods sooner or later. Captain Dubnyk spent decades monitoring developments and coming out of stasis every so often to check on things. Eventually, the Jasper lost pressure, and the stasis systems refused to revive anyone. So I suppose they eventually perished in stasis as well." Nathan offered the data card to Mister Percival. "You may read the logs for yourself, if you wish. I must warn you, though; Captain Dubnyk's words can be quite moving, especially toward the end."

"Yes, I'm sure," he agreed, taking the data card. "I will read it later, in private."

"You can insert the card into any terminal," Nathan explained. "It will open the documents automatically."

"Thank you," Mister Percival said. He looked down at the card for a moment and let out a sigh. "Perhaps it is all for the best."

Nathan looked puzzled. "How so?"

"The galaxy, or at least the Earth's corner of it, does not appear to have become the advanced utopia many of us had hoped would evolve from the ashes of the plague."

"That seems a harsh judgment, Mister Percival," Nathan responded, a bit taken aback. "What did you expect?"

"Don't misunderstand me, Captain," Mister Percival said. "I understand that humanity has struggled greatly to survive. But you must understand something. Those of us that had to face that plague clung to the hope that it would lead to something better for the following generations. For many, what made them wake up every day and carry on *was* that hope: that maybe they might do something on that day that would contribute to whatever came after."

"I'm sorry if I seemed defensive," Nathan said. "I cannot imagine what it must have been like for the survivors, especially those that could not escape."

"Yes, they had it worse than most. Even before the end was in sight, before all hope had been lost, many millions had taken their own lives, having already given up on their futures. Only those with the means even dreamed of escaping."

"We have heard many references to expeditions

and colonization packages as if they were complete kits bought and sold."

"The only good thing about the plague, Captain, was its timing. It occurred at a uniquely opportune time in human history. Advances in FTL propulsion had just opened up deep space at far less expense than ever before. Travel times between core and fringe worlds had been reduced by fifty to seventy-five percent, and there were catalogs of star systems containing habitable worlds that had been surveyed by either remote probes or deep space observatories. There were literally thousands of potentially habitable worlds out there just waiting for colonization."

"But there were so many worlds close in that had already been colonized, most of which were nowhere near carrying capacity," Nathan said. "Why start over farther out, far away from additional help and resources?"

"Dreams, Captain. Dreams of creating something new, something unique, something better." Mister Percival leaned forward, looking directly at Nathan. "There are many indisputable truths about humans, the most common of which are that we are willing to kill to survive, we always want to know what is over the next hill, and we always think we can do it better than the other guy. Another one is that, as a people, we prefer to mingle with those more like ourselves."

"So you're saying that people wanted to settle worlds and populate them with their own kind?"

"Race, religion, political or economic systems... There were even those who wanted to live with only vegetarians, or people with blond hair and blue eyes. It was like a new fad. Get a thousand people to sell everything and buy into another attempt to create the perfect society."

"So they could buy kits to colonize other worlds?"

"It was more like a package or a program—all the equipment, supplies, and instructions needed to establish a settlement on a habitable, Earth-like world. All you had to do was supply the people and the transportation. You could even choose your world from one of several corporate catalogs."

"You can't buy and sell an entire planet," Nathan said.

"No, of course not, but you could buy what was called 'first stake,'" Mister Percival explained.

"What was first stake?"

"It was nothing more than an entry in a registration database by the company that had performed the planetary survey. It did not guarantee you exclusive rights to colonize that world, but it might dissuade others from attempting to settle there, especially if they were seeking an entire world for themselves. In addition, since these new worlds were so far away, they were not under the jurisdiction of any government. If you landed there second, and the original settlers did not want you, there was nothing to prevent them from using force to remove you."

"Really?" The bit about force surprised Nathan to some extent. "Weren't there any regulations about who could go off and start a new world?"

"Oh, of course," Mister Percival laughed, "but it was more like a way for governments to collect fees and impede the efforts of those who were not really serious about the idea. They knew that there was no way to stop people from going off and colonizing another world."

"Then why did people even bother applying for

permission?"

"Because most of the ships available for hire were owned by corporations that wanted to be able to continue doing business within the many different jurisdictions controlled by these governments."

"So how many of these expeditions were launched?"

"No one really knew," Mister Percival admitted, "not for sure. Based on the number that I heard of, which is a few dozen or so, I would guess a few hundred at least. And that's only the ones that were properly registered. There were many smaller expeditions, bootstrapped ones much like ours, that hired less than legal, owner-operated transports."

"How many of those were there?"

"Impossible to tell," Mister Percival admitted. "I suspect just as many if not more. And the last few years there were probably ten times as many, as everyone was trying to escape the plague."

"How far out do you think they went?"

"Again, there is no telling, but to be honest, I was surprised to learn that you encountered one such colony a thousand light years out. It must have taken them a century to get there."

"Amazing," Nathan said, shaking his head in disbelief. He noticed that Mister Percival seemed surprised by Nathan's reaction. "You have to remember, Mister Percival, I come from an Earth that has only just recently gotten back into space. A hundred years ago, we were just inventing the jet engine."

"Yes, a fact that is quite apparent in your strange mix of technology. I understand that it's the result of being forced to quickly pick and choose which technologies would have the greatest and most immediate benefit. I just can't help thinking that it's like cavemen with nuclear weapons. You know how to use them but don't yet understand the implications of doing so... no insult intended."

"You may not be far off the mark," Nathan admitted, remembering the many debates that had occurred back on Earth since the discovery of the Data Ark and the revelation of the impending Jung threat.

Nathan began to stand. "Well, I am glad to see that you are taking the news of your expedition's demise so well, Mister Percival."

"I have been called many things in my lifetime, Captain. Emotional is not one of them."

"Very well," Nathan said as he prepared to depart. "I'll leave you to rest."

"Thank you for coming to speak to me personally, Captain. The gesture is appreciated."

"It was my pleasure, Mister Percival." Nathan began to turn toward the exit, then stopped. "Oh, I almost forgot. You said you were put into stasis before departure, correct?"

"That is correct."

"That's what the stasis time display showed as well. However, the backup time display showed that you were under for only eight hundred years."

"That's odd," Mister Percival stated. "A malfunction, perhaps?"

"That's the first thing we thought," Nathan said, taking note that Mister Percival offered no obvious reaction to his inquiry.

"Like most things for the mission, it was purchased second-hand. My unit also underwent several modifications as well."

"Yes, well, Lieutenant Commander Kamenetskiy

is looking into the matter."

"I'm sure he will discover the cause of the discrepancy in due time." Mister Percival smiled. "No pun intended."

"Of course."

"Good night, Captain," Mister Percival said as Nathan stepped through the doorway.

Nathan stood in the doorway for several seconds, thinking. He had come to Mister Percival as the bearer of bad news and had, instead, been told that there might indeed be hundreds of unknown human colonies out there. There had been hints at such in the Data Ark itself, in fact. There had been a few dozen records of properly registered missions that included their destination worlds. Prior to learning of the Jung threat, the leaders of Earth had considered seeking out those lost colonies. Had they indeed survived and thrived, they were likely more advanced than the people of Earth, just as the people of Takara and Corinair had been. And now it appeared that Nathan had confirmation of those expeditions and possibly many more. He wondered how many of them had survived and even thrived over the last thousand years and what other wonders they might someday be willing to share with the people of Earth.

* * *

"I'm not finding anything wrong in here," Loki insisted. "What about you?"

Josh continued poking around the inside of the number three turbine on the opposite side of the Falcon with his flashlight. "Nothing, just a lot of water and a little debris in the intakes."

"You don't suppose that's what caused them to fail, do you?"

"What, water? No way," Josh answered, pulling his head out of the turbine compartment. "These things must be designed to fly through all kinds of weather, right? That should include heavy rains."

"Heavy rain, sure, but not waterfalls," Loki scolded.

"Look, for the last time, I didn't intend on flying through a waterfall. It was just suddenly there, and I had no way around it."

"I meant it's not designed to have that much water dumped into it at once," Loki explained. "Maybe it just fouled up the mixture, and that's why they failed. If we'd had a little more altitude under us, we might have been able to get them to restart once all the water was blasted out."

"You think?" Josh asked, finding it hard to believe.

"There's only one way to find out: clean out the water and debris and see if they light."

"You know, the canopy may be busted, and she may be banged up pretty bad on the outside, but all the space flight systems are fine," Josh reminded him. "If we can just get her in the air long enough to get out of this cave and tip our nose up toward the sky, we could jump the fuck outta here."

Loki looked at Josh, who had a big grin on his face. "If we turn on a single system while all those Jung ships are flying around, they'll zero in on us in seconds."

"How long do you think it would take us to fire up and blast our way out of this cave?"

"A lot more than a few seconds," Loki warned. "Even if everything was in perfect condition, a rapid launch sequence takes at least thirty seconds. It's a full minute to bring the jump drive online and ready to initiate."

"They'd blow us to hell as soon as we stuck our nose out," Josh admitted.

"Right," Loki agreed. "So we cross our fingers and wait, and hope that they don't find us."

"Exactly what I'm *not* good at," Josh complained, "waiting."

* * *

"We'll be fully charged and ready for jump sixty-two in ninety minutes," Cameron announced as she entered the captain's ready room.

"No word yet, huh?"

"No, sir."

"They're overdue, aren't they?"

"By half an hour," Cameron answered. Nathan said nothing, but she could see the worry on his face. "And if they still aren't back when we're ready to jump?"

"What are you asking, Commander?"

"You know exactly what I'm asking, Nathan," Cameron responded as she closed the hatch. "Are you going to be able to leave them behind when the time comes?"

"Don't you mean *if* the time comes?"

"Don't avoid the question, Nathan. You and I both know that you're closer to Josh and Loki than anyone else we adopted while in the cluster. I don't expect it to be easy to leave them behind and move on. It wouldn't be easy for me either."

"Is there any particular reason that we have to jump as soon as the drive is recharged?"

"Other than the fact that our captain's last orders were to get back to Earth as soon as possible?" Cameron reminded him. "Or that we're quite possibly the Earth's best shot at a defense against the Jung? Or that we've already been gone for..."

"I get your point, Cam," Nathan interrupted. "However, I don't think waiting an hour or so more will make that big a difference."

"Maybe not. But what if it does? And what message does it send the crew? That their captain isn't strong enough to make the tough calls?"

"That's not fair, Cam. I think I've already demonstrated the ability to make the tough calls, and more than once I might add."

"Yes, that's true, but every decision is a new test in the eyes of your crew, and a slip can send the wrong message."

"This isn't the classic 'lose the man or lose the ship' scenario, Cameron."

"No, it's not; that's true," she agreed. "But these considerations must be taken into account, Nathan. Sometimes it is very important for you to consider how the decisions you make will affect the lives of others."

"You're forgetting something, Commander."

"And that is?"

"The other message that waiting as long as possible for the men still out there might send to the crew, the message that the captain will do everything he can to protect them." Nathan stared at Cameron for several seconds, waiting for a response that never came. "Is there anything else, Commander?"

"No, sir."

"Dismissed."

"Yes, sir."

Nathan kept his gaze on his data pad as Cameron left the compartment in perfect military fashion. He knew she was only trying to help, but at times, he tired of her constant assumption that she knew better how a captain should act. It wasn't that she was wrong, and it wasn't that she didn't know more; it was just irritating.

Of even more concern, however, was the fact that his best flight team, and two of his favorite crewmen, were overdue. Nathan knew that a coast-through recon flight either went like clockwork, or it went all to hell. There were only three possible outcomes. They made it through without a problem, they were discovered and were pursued but still escaped, or they were unable to escape and they had to self-destruct. If everything had gone properly, they would have returned by now. Even if they had mechanical problems and were delayed, they could have sent word via their new mini comm-drones. They were in trouble. Either they were still trying to make it back, or they were already gone and waiting was pointless.

Or they had been captured before they could scuttle the Falcon, and now the Jung had both a jump drive and a couple of ZPEDs in their hands. The wave of nausea that washed over him reminded him of how much he hated being captain.

* * *

"I've got mine clear," Josh announced as he closed up the number three turbine compartment. "How are you doing over there?"

"There's still a lot of water in here," Loki answered. "It's going to take a while to scoop it all out by hand."

"If we could at least arm the batteries, we could blow it out with the turbo fans."

"Yeah, well, we can't, and these are the only tools we've got," Loki said, holding up his wet hands.

"Keep at it," Josh said. "I'll check the other turbines for water, just in case."

"Good idea." Loki's face crinkled. "Wait, what's that beeping sound?"

Josh's face also reacted as he grabbed for his pocket. "Shit, it's the proximity alert sensors we planted outside," he explained as he shut the receiver off. "Someone's coming up the trails." Josh grabbed his weapon and headed for the front of the cave. "Stay here. I'll check it out."

"What, are you going to fight them off yourself?" Loki asked, pulling his own weapon and following after Josh.

Josh suddenly stopped short of the front of the cave, spinning back around suddenly. "They're already here," he whispered, waving his hands. "Go back. Go back."

Loki spun around and ran around the Falcon with Josh hot on his heels. Falling to the cave floor as they got around behind the aft end of the interceptor, Loki pushed Josh toward the port side of the ship. "You take port; I'll take starboard," he instructed. Loki took up position tucked just behind the starboard drive's thrust nozzle, lying on his belly so he had a clear line of fire along the underside of the Falcon's starboard wing-body.

Josh scrambled his way over and took up a similar position behind the Falcon's port side thrust nozzle, peeking under the port wing-body, his eyes fixed on the point where the trail entered the mouth of the cave. He could hear the muffled voices of men as they came up the trail. There were several of them, to be sure. He could make out at least four distinctly different voices, maybe more. Despite the shadows cast by the setting sun, the men used no portable lights.

A face appeared, poking up from below the floor line of the cave. He held some sort of a weapon at his shoulder, aiming it forward as he cautiously advanced. He swung his weapon from right to left in sudden, quick motions. The man had training. Josh had seen the Corinari soldiers move in similar fashion.

The first man mumbled something back down the trail. Josh decided that he must be alerting the rest of his team that they had found the enemy ship. Another head appeared, and the two of them advanced farther into the cave, splitting to either side as they continued to sweep their weapons back and forth. As two more heads appeared, Josh rolled back over and crawled quietly over to Loki, the sound of the nearby waterfall masking the sound of his movement.

"You have the remote detonator?"

"Yes, why?" Loki asked, his color pale as ever.

"I'll challenge them and try to drive them back. If I'm lucky, I can push them back down the trail enough, so that you can jump in, fire up the ship, and get the fuck outta here."

"No way, Josh," Loki objected in hushed tones. "We go together or not at all."

"I don't have time to argue with you, Loki. When I open fire, you get your ass in that cockpit and get out of here. That's an order!"

"Since when do you give the orders?"

"I'm the pilot. The pilot is in charge of the ship.

Just promise me that if you don't make it, you'll blow the ship, them, us, and this whole fucking mountain to shit." Josh didn't wait for an answer, scrambling back to the port side of the ship and taking aim.

"Wait," Loki called after him.

Josh got to his feet in a crouch, then quickly stood up and took a step out to his left so that he could take aim over the port wing-body. "Stay where you are!" he warned as he flipped the arming switch on his energy weapon. The man on the left froze as Josh's pistol emitted an ascending whine, its systems quickly charging to fire. The man on the right tried to step farther over to put the Falcon's body between him and the charging weapon, but Josh spotted him and swung his weapon to the right while he took another step to his left to get a better angle on the second man. "Ack! You, too, asshole!" Josh could feel his body quivering, and he fought to keep his gun hand from shaking. Never in his life had he pointed a charged weapon at anyone, especially at men who were armed and well-trained. "Drop your weapons, now, or I burn you both!"

The third and fourth men, both of which had only barely shown their heads when Josh stepped out, had already taken cover, presumably moving back down the trail. It was just Josh and the two men pointing weapons at him, in a wet, shadowy cave on an alien world.

"If there is a Jung ship in range, your weapon will surely alert them to your location."

Josh looked around for the source of the voice, as neither of the two men he was threatening to shoot had spoken.

"Especially if you fire it," the voice added.

"Show yourself!" Josh ordered, his voice slightly cracking despite his best effort to sound as menacing as possible. A moment later, another head ascended from the floor line of the cave, and another man came walking slowly and confidently up the trail and into the cave between the first two men. The man had a neatly trimmed beard and long, dark hair tied back in a ponytail. He wore heavy clothing with splotches of colors that matched the trees and the mountains themselves, just like the other two men. However, he was not holding a weapon. He wore one on his hip, and Josh thought he had one slung over his shoulder so that it hung on his back. "That's far enough!" Josh warned.

"If you fire that weapon, you will bring your enemy to you in seconds. That is why we do not use energy weapons. They may have picked up the energy signature as your weapon charged already. Perhaps you would consider turning it off."

"Not a chance," Josh warned.

"Then we will take our leave," the man stated calmly. "If you wish to sacrifice yourself needlessly, that is your right. But it is our right not to go into the afterlife along with you." The man signaled with one hand for the first two men to withdraw, making a distinct clicking noise to alert them to his command gesture. The two men walked quickly backwards, staying on either side of the leader with their weapons still trained on Josh.

"Good luck," the man stated as he turned to walk away, demonstrating his confidence that he would not be shot in the back.

"Wait!" Josh called after him. "Who are you?"

The man stopped, turning back around. "I am not Jung, if that is what concerns you."

"That, and other things," Josh told him. "Why are you here?"

"The Jung tried to kill you, so it is a reasonable assumption that we are on the same side. The enemy of my enemy and all that."

"What?" Josh asked, unfamiliar with the expression.

"If you wish me to remain any longer, you must turn off your weapon."

"Okay, okay," Josh agreed. He glanced down at Loki to his right still hiding with his own weapon aimed under the other side of the ship. Loki shook his head back and forth violently. Josh switched off his weapon, its indicator light going dark as he pointed it up at the cave's low ceiling to show the status light to the man. "It's off!"

The man turned to the others and barked several orders, after which they disappeared back down the trail.

"Where are they going?" Josh asked.

"I told them to secure the perimeter and to contact the party we have monitoring the crash site. If the Jung picked up the energy signature of your weapon and are moving in, I would like to know."

"So who are you?"

"We are residents of this world, residents who oppose the Jung occupation."

"You're resistance fighters?"

"We prefer to call ourselves freedom fighters."

"Fuck me," Josh declared. "You're Karuzari!"

"I'm not familiar with this term. Perhaps you and your friend would like to come out and explain it to me." The man smiled, revealing a mouthful of dirty, fragmented teeth. It was not a pleasant sight, but there was something about the man's relaxed manner that made Josh want to trust him.

Josh turned to Loki. "Loki?"

Loki stood up slowly, waving at the man. The man waved back, again smiling.

"Where we come from, Karuzari means 'freedom fighter,'" Josh explained as he walked around the port side of the Falcon.

"On this world, Karuzara is the name of a very fast transport vehicle. They are very expensive; hence, not many are seen around these parts." The man extended his hand to Josh as he approached. "I am called Garrett."

Josh shook his hand. "Josh. That's Loki."

"Loki?" Garrett stated with surprise. "You carry the name of one of our most ancient gods."

Loki's eyebrows went up. "I had no idea."

"How did you know there were two of us?" Josh wondered.

Garrett pointed at the Falcon's cockpit. "Two seats."

"How did you know we were here?" Loki asked.

"We did not," Garrett admitted. "We come to this cave often to hide. The light shining on the mist from outside makes it nearly impossible for the Jung to see inside the cave unless they are at the perfect angle, which changes constantly as the sun moves across the sky. However, we can see out through the mist quite well. It makes for a good observation point." Garrett looked the Falcon over, moving to the port side for a better view. "I am amazed you found this cave, let alone managed to park your spacecraft inside it." He looked at Josh and Loki. "I am assuming you meant to do so."

"Of course," Josh answered.

"Interesting. You are either bold or crazy," Garrett

laughed. "How did you discover the cave's location?"

"I spotted it as we came out of the waterfall," Josh explained.

Garrett turned back to face Josh, a look of surprise on his face. "You flew *through* the waterfall?" Garrett laughed. "You *are* crazy. You are lucky only water fell upon you. This time of year, the river is very powerful. It carries away trees, rocks, livestock. You are lucky indeed." Garrett continued examining the Falcon. "I have never seen such a spacecraft. You must not be from a Jung-occupied world, for they surely would have copied its design." Garrett shook his head in approval. "It has a very purposeful look to its design."

"We like her," Josh said.

"So where are you from, Josh and Loki, and why have you come to our world?"

Loki opened his mouth to answer, but Josh beat him to it. "We are part of a great alliance who have come to rid this sector of the Jung threat," Josh said.

Loki looked at Josh like he was crazy.

"A great alliance, huh?" Garrett challenged, noticing the look on Loki's face. "And who are the members of this alliance?"

"Three great and powerful worlds," Josh boasted. "The Takarans, the Corinari, and the Terrans."

Garrett did not recognize the first two names, but he recognized the third. "Terrans? You mean the people of Earth?"

"Yes."

"But the Earth is long dead. It has been for a thousand years. It was destroyed by the great plague. It remains infected to this day. That is why it is off-limits." Garrett eyed the two of them, his hand slowly moving down toward his holstered weapon. "Have you been to Earth?"

"No," Loki interrupted, noticing Garrett's sudden apprehension. "We are on our way there now to join forces with those of the Earth. They are expecting us soon."

"Garrett," Josh began, "the Earth *was* nearly destroyed. Those that survived did so because they had a natural immunity to the disease. But the disease itself died away centuries ago."

"Then why have we not heard of them until now?"

"Their population was decimated, their civilization ruined. They spent centuries in darkness and despair as they struggled to survive in the aftermath of the collapse."

"Josh," Loki mumbled, "I don't think you're supposed to be telling them all of this."

"If they are against the Jung, then they are our friends. They should know that help is on the way."

"And the people of Earth, they are back in space?"

"They have only just returned to space in the last twenty years," Josh explained. "When they learned of the Jung, they immediately began building their fleet, and reached out to contact the lost colonies of Earth to ask for assistance."

"And you are from one of those colonies?" Garrett asked.

"Yes, we are from Takara. Our ancestors escaped the plague and set out to start a new civilization in the hopes of ensuring the survival of humanity."

Loki rolled his eyes as Josh spun his story.

"Then the people of Earth are very powerful?"

"Yes, but alone they are no match for the forces of the Jung. But our people have many advanced technologies that can help them, and you."

Garrett eyed them with suspicion. "If what you say is true, then it is wonderful news, yet it does not explain *why* you are *here* and in a single ship."

"Our forces are conducting reconnaissance of every system in the Sol sector to determine the location and strength of all Jung forces. Unfortunately, we were discovered and engaged before we could make our escape."

"But if your technology is superior to that of the Jung..."

"We are under orders not to reveal our identity *or* the capabilities of our technology to the Jung," Loki added, joining in on the charade. "We shouldn't even have revealed this to you," he added, casting a disapproving look at Josh.

"Then the crash site," Garrett realized, "it was a ruse?"

"We dumped everything we could to make it look like debris from our spacecraft."

"A clever deception, but it will not hold for long," Garrett told them. "What the Jung lack in intelligence they make up for with technology stolen from those they conquer. They will discover the truth, and the search will begin in earnest."

"How long do you think we have?" Loki asked.

"If you wish to keep your secrets safe from the Jung, you should destroy your ship and depart immediately."

"No, you don't understand," Josh told him. "We need to get the information we have gathered back to our leaders. They do not even know that there are people such as yourselves fighting against the Jung on their own. They need to know."

Garrett looked at the Falcon again. "But your ship, it is damaged."

"We still believe it will get us home," Josh stated confidently.

"Can you be sure of that?"

"No, we cannot, not until we try."

"And if you fail?"

"Then we will destroy our ship and ourselves with it."

Garrett looked at Josh, studying his face. "Bold words from one so young. How can I be sure that you speak the truth? How can I be sure that anything you have said to me this day is true?"

"You can't," Josh admitted. "But what have you got to lose by trusting us?"

"Your ship and all its technology," Garrett told him. "Do not for a moment believe that because I hide in the woods and maintain a disheveled appearance that I am technologically illiterate. I could kill you both in an instant without making a sound. In no time, I could figure out how to operate your ship..."

"And do what with it?" Loki interrupted. "Attack them on your own? One ship will not defeat the Jung. If you are as smart as you claim, you surely know that. Do you have the resources to take it apart, copy it, and build hundreds more? What about training the pilots? The ground crews?"

"It takes more to fight a war than weapons," Josh added. "It takes allies."

Garrett looked down, seeing that Josh had extended his hand in a symbolic gesture of friendship. "Your great worlds would ally themselves with a scraggily-toothed woodsman?"

"If he is an enemy of the Jung, yes," Josh said, casting his own smile back at the man.

Garrett reached out and took Josh's hand, shaking it and smiling. "Very well, young Joshua.

However, if you are deceiving me, it would be safer that we do not cross paths again."

"A fair warning," Josh said, trying to hide his nervousness.

"How long until you are ready to depart?" Garrett asked.

Josh looked at Loki.

Loki looked at his watch. "The Aurora jumps in about an hour. The sooner the better."

"How do you measure time?" Garrett asked.

Josh removed his own wristwatch and handed it to the man. "By the time this says nineteen hundred, we need to be gone. If not, we may never make it back to our ship."

Garrett nodded. "We have similar devices," he said, pulling his own timepiece from his jacket pocket. He held his timepiece face to face with Josh's wristwatch for a few seconds until it beeped at him. "I have synchronized one of my time channels with your own," he explained, handing Josh's wristwatch back to him.

"Keep it," Josh said. "If and when we make contact again, show them that watch to prove you can be trusted."

Garrett nodded, placing both devices back into his jacket. "How can we help?"

"We need a few minutes to fire up our ship in order to launch. I assume that when we do so, the Jung out there will detect us."

"Indeed they will."

"Then that's what we need help with."

Garrett thought on the problem for a moment. "We must draw them away from this valley, the farther the better. Their fighters are very fast. If they are within a hundred kilometers of you, they will pounce within minutes." Garrett continued thinking.

"We need a diversion," Loki stated.

"I can contact one of our cells in the next valley. If they can convince the Jung that you are there, that may be enough to pull their fighters away from here. Will that be enough?"

"I think so..."

"No," Josh said, interrupting Loki. "There can be no one within eyesight of our departure. We cannot allow the Jung to witness the nature of our propulsion technology. That is why we were unable to escape in the first place; we needed to be out of sight."

"This technology you speak of must be impressive," Garrett decided.

"It is; believe me."

"I will attempt to coordinate an attack against the ground forces investigating the crash site once the fighters have departed the area. They are mostly technicians and captured scientists. They will not present much of a fight."

"How will we know when it is safe for us to launch?"

Garrett looked at Josh's weapon. "What color does your weapon fire?"

"Uh, red." Josh looked at Loki. "Right?"

"Yeah, red."

"Give me your weapon," Garrett ordered Josh. "The Jung weapons are orange," Garrett explained as Josh handed him his sidearm. "When it is time, I will fire three shots in the air." Garrett pulled a knife from a sheath attached to his belt and handed it butt first to Josh. "Take this knife. It has been handed down through my family, from father to son, for generations. Anyone from your Alliance who wishes to prove themselves trustworthy need only present this knife. Any one of us will understand its significance."

"Uh, okay," Josh said, examining the knife. "Thanks."

"Good luck to you both," Garrett stated as he turned and headed back down the path in a jog, barking orders at his men outside as he departed.

"Garrett!" Loki called after him. Garrett stopped and turned back around. "Tell your men not to look toward the cave during the attack."

"Why?"

"Our propulsion system is very bright. Looking directly at it could blind you for several seconds."

Garrett cocked his head, smiling in amazement as he turned slowly back around and continued down the path.

Josh watched them go for nearly a minute before he turned back to Loki. "Fuck me. I can't believe that worked."

"The captain's never going to believe this," Loki declared as he turned and headed back to finish his work on the flooded turbine.

"Damn! This beats the hell outta jump-recharge-jump!" Josh declared.

* * *

"*Captain, Comms,*" Naralena called across the intercom on Nathan's desk. He stared at the intercom, not wanting to answer. Ten seconds later, the call repeated. "*Captain, Comms.*" Nathan continued to stall as if not answering would make everything better. Five more seconds passed, then seven, then nine. His hand instinctively shot out and tapped the comm-button. "Go ahead."

"*Sir, Helm reports we're ready for jump sixty-two.*"

"Very well," Nathan answered. "I'll be there in a moment."

"*Aye, sir.*"

Nathan's gaze turned to the hatch that led back to the bridge. How long could he wait? How much extra time should he give his crewmen, his friends, to return. A minute? An hour? A day? Each was too little and yet too long. What if there was nothing wrong with them? What if they were simply playing it safe, letting themselves get as far out of the Herculis system as possible before jumping away? He might be leaving them behind when they were just trying to do the best job possible.

He had considered leaving the jump shuttle behind to wait for them. Unfortunately, he had allowed Abby and the Takarans to use the shuttle to attempt to figure out how to make the mini-ZPEDs power the shuttle's mini-jump drive directly without the problems experienced when they had tried the same thing with the Aurora. It was currently in a state of disassembly, and it would take several days to make it flight-ready once again.

The hardest part was that, as captain, his decisions set a precedent. Whatever extra time he gave Josh and Loki he would be expected to give others. There was nothing wrong with giving them extra time. The ship was not in danger, and surely waiting another twenty minutes wouldn't put the Earth at considerably more risk. Of this he was quite sure. Yet he was still undecided.

A memory of Captain Roberts suddenly flashed through his mind. *What was it he said? Sometimes*

being captain is about making the call? Was that it?
Nathan decided that was it, and he rose from his
desk, straightened his uniform, and proceeded to
the bridge.

"As you were," he told the guard, cutting him off
before he could announce his entrance. "Report?"

"Jump drive is fully recharged," Mister Riley
reported. "We are approaching the jump point for
jump sixty-two. Time to jump is three minutes."

"Any sign of the Falcon?" Nathan asked the
tactical officer.

"No, sir," Mister Randeen answered.

"All our spacecraft are aboard?"

"All except the Falcon, sir. Flight reports ready to
set red deck on your order."

"Deep-space scans?"

"Negative contact, sir," Mister Navashee reported.

"Mister Chiles, recalculate jump sixty-two to
occur in jump time plus twenty minutes. Let's give
our boys a few extra minutes in case they're just
running late."

"Aye, sir," Mister Chiles answered. "Recalculating
jump sixty-two to jump plus twenty minutes.
Maintain present course and speed, sir?"

"That's correct." Nathan turned back around
and headed back to his ready room. "You have the
bridge, Mister Randeen."

"Aye, sir."

Nathan stepped back into his ready room,
closing the door behind him. His pulse was racing,
and he could feel a bead of sweat running down his
forehead. He could not understand why granting
them an extra twenty minutes had such an effect
on him. He had made far more difficult decisions in
the past, ones that had knowingly sent hundreds

of good men to their deaths. Yet none of them had caused such a reaction.

He was only two days from home, and he was still having to make such decisions, when all he wanted to was to hand the ship and all the responsibility that went with it over to someone else, someone more qualified than he. Was that really so much to ask?

* * *

Josh stood at the mouth of the cave, the mist from the nearby waterfall blowing across in front of him. He stared out through the flowing mist at the valley below. The sun was nearly down, and the entire valley was in a dark shadow cast by the opposing ridge. He could see the lights of at least four small cities twinkling through the trees as they swayed in the evening breeze.

Overhead, four Jung fighters continued to circle the area, no doubt scanning everything below while the investigators continued studying the debris at the crash site. They had been hiding in the cave for nearly two hours now, and the smoke from the fires at the crash site had long since disappeared.

The four circling fighters turned and headed east, their tails flashing bright as they kicked their engines up to full power. Josh tapped his comm-set. "The fighters just headed away. This may be it. Be ready to fire her up."

"I'm ready," Loki announced from the back seat. He had been strapped in and ready to go for the last fifteen minutes. His helmet was on, but his faceplate was up, his gloves lying in his lap.

Josh continued to watch impatiently, waiting for

the signal. Minutes passed. One minute became two, then four, then six. He watched the time display on the handheld visual scanner more so than he did the magnified display of the valley below, until there was a bright flash. It wasn't the one he was looking for, however. It was an explosion of some kind at the crash site. Then another one. He thought he heard the sound of distant gunfire, much like the projectile weapons that Jessica and the Aurora's original crew had used before they had run out of ammunition and had been forced to begin using energy weapons instead. As quickly as it had started, the sounds stopped. Josh lowered the visual scanner, watching the valley with his eyes only. Then it came, three red bolts of energy weapons fire, shooting directly up in the air. He tapped his comm-set. "Let's go!" he cried out as he turned and ran back to the Falcon.

Loki pressed the button on his console and initiated the rapid launch sequence. This sequence used the batteries to light the turbines rather than spinning up the fusion reactors first, thereby getting them in the air more quickly.

Josh clambered up the boarding ladder, crawling in through the busted out section of canopy just as the steps began to retract into the side of the ship. He could hear the whine of the turbines as he put his helmet on and snapped it securely into the mating collar around his neck.

"Ten seconds to full turbine power," Loki reported.

Josh pulled his flight harness over his shoulders and locked them in place, securing himself into his flight seat as the ship came to life. His flight status display flickered as the power being generated by the four air-breathing turbines began to reach them, bringing them to life even before the reactors were online.

"All four turbines are hot and ready. Spinning up the reactors," Loki announced.

"Here we go," Josh announced as he applied just enough lift and forward thrust to get the Falcon to slide forward along the cave floor. He didn't dare try to hover for fear they would smash into the ceiling and end their flight in a hurry. As the nose of the Falcon passed out of the cave, it dipped slightly. Josh applied more thrust to keep them from diving and sliding down the side of the mountain nose first. It was a bit too much thrust, however, and the rear of the ship slammed against the rocky overhang in a terrible crunching sound.

Warning lights began to flash on Loki's console as warning alarms sounded. "Jesus, Josh! Haven't you banged this ship up enough?"

"She's not responding correctly," he said, "but it's okay now; we're airborne. Josh struggled to keep them level as the spray from the waterfall and the winds coming through the canyon on their way out into the valley buffeted them about and threatened to topple them over and back into the cliff. Josh yawed the ship to port, hoping to put the wind at their backs. The wind was just enough to give them a little forward momentum. That was all he needed, as he was afraid to move the turbine nozzles away from straight vertical lift at this point. "How are we doing back there?"

"We're fucked!" Loki declared. "I've got all kinds of things going wrong! Systems are crashing all over the place, Josh!"

"What about the jump drive? Is it working?"

"I won't know until the reactors are online!"

"How long is that?"

"Thirty seconds." Loki looked at his tracking display as it, too, came to life. "Oh shit. Those fighters, they're turning around. I'm pretty sure they're coming back our way!"

"How far out are they?"

"A couple hundred kilometers, I think."

"What do you mean, you think?"

"I mean I'm not sure. If this thing is working right, then they're a couple hundred kilometers. Yup, they're headed back toward us now. ETA, one minute."

"How many seconds until the reactors..."

"Fifteen!"

"We're moving forward, so we're good. Tell me you've got a jump plot ready."

"Of course. Oh man!"

"Now what?"

"Switch to internal emergency suit life-support," Loki ordered.

"Don't tell me..."

"Life support is fried."

"What does that give us, ten minutes?"

"Reactors are hot, running jump drive diagnostics."

"Fuck the diagnostics, Loki! Just jump!"

"Remember what happens if some of the emitters don't work, Josh?" Loki yelled. "What if the half that gets left behind has the jump drive in it?"

"Fuck," Josh cursed as the ship nearly rolled over to starboard. "How long?"

"Diagnostics will be done in ten seconds!"

"And those fighters?"

"Thirty?"

"Will they be able to see us?"

"Not if we stay at this altitude!" Loki promised.

"Not until they are right on top of us!"

"Well, at least there's that!"

Garrett picked up the long-range visual scanning device off the dead Jung technician and raised it to his eyes. He scanned the cliffs near the waterfall until he located the Falcon. It struggled to stay in the air as it drifted slowly forward. As he activated the scanner's glare filters and reduced its brightness to its minimum setting, he couldn't help but think that what he was seeing was not that impressive. Then without warning, a brilliant blue-white light seemed to spread across the battered little spacecraft. In a split second, the tiny ship became a brilliant ball of blue-white light, brighter than any star Garrett had ever seen. It was brighter than the midday sun, and even after it was gone, it left a red dot in his field of vision. The Falcon was gone. There were no contrails, no signs of a crash, and no debris falling from the sky. Either the ship's reactors had overloaded and completely incinerated the ship, or their method of propulsion was just as impressive as they had led him to believe.

* * *

Nathan came out of his ready room and walked confidently to his command chair. "Time to jump?"

"Three minutes," Mister Riley reported.

"Tactical?"

"No contact with the Falcon, sir. Flight reports ready for red deck on your word."

"Comms?"

"Nothing, sir, nothing but the usual signals we've

been picking up from various core worlds for the last few jumps."

"Mister Navashee?"

"Nothing, sir."

"Very well. Red deck, Mister Randeen. Mister Riley, execute jump sixty-two on schedule."

"Aye, sir. Activating auto-nav. Jump sixty-two in one minute."

Nathan heard the sound of footsteps as someone entered the bridge. He rotated his chair slightly to the left to see Cameron and Lieutenant Yosef standing by the port auxiliary console near the exit. He could see the expression of concern on the lieutenant's face. She and Josh had been an item for several months now. Nathan looked her in the eyes, wanting her to know that he was aware of her pain. He looked at Cameron as well, although he wasn't sure why. Perhaps it was to show her how confident he was in his decisions, even though he knew it was a lie. He had never been less confident about any decision in his life. Yet he was making that decision anyway. He was making the call. He was being the captain.

"Jumping in thirty seconds," Mister Chiles updated.

Nathan looked to his left at Mister Navashee who he knew was currently scanning as far out as the Aurora's sensors could reach, hoping to catch a glimpse of the Falcon at the last moment. The look in the sensor operator's eyes answered his question and dashed all hope.

"Fifteen seconds."

Marcus sat in his small office along the port

wall of the hangar deck, looking out at the forward transfer airlock that connected the main hangar deck to the starboard fighter alley. The elevator pads in the forward transfer airlocks, besides going to the deck below like all the others, also traveled all the way up through the top of the Aurora's hull to act as launch and recovery pads. It was this pad from which Josh and Loki had departed in the Falcon over fifteen hours ago. At any moment, the alarm horn would sound telling everyone to clear the pad before it started its journey upward to recover the Falcon upon its return. He had been sitting there for hours, his door open the entire time, pretending to be reviewing reports on his data pad.

He remembered the day Josh's mother had died while working in the ore processing plants on Haven. It had been an accident, a stupid accident. But it had happened on his watch, which made it his responsibility. Because of that, he had taken it upon himself to pick up the woman's only child, little Joshua, from school. When he told Josh what had happened to his mother, the little boy had never cried. The only emotion he had ever shown was to look up into Marcus's eyes and ask him who would be taking care of him now. From that point on, Marcus had taken care of him. He had been a handful, going from a little snot running around the processing plant to a cocky, smart-ass hotshot pilot burning through a copilot a month, right up until Loki came to his left seat. From that point on, the two of them had been like brothers. Josh seemed the younger, crazier brother, and Loki the older, more responsible one that kept the younger brother from going too far. The boy had been a pain in Marcus's butt from day one, but he was the closest thing to family that Marcus had ever known.

Then it happened, a sharp pain shot through his teeth. At that moment, he knew that the Aurora had jumped, and Josh and Loki had not made it back in time. He stuck out his foot and pushed his office door closed so no one could see him.

CHAPTER NINE

"Captain?" Vladimir called from the ready room hatch.

"Yes?" Nathan responded without looking.

Vladimir entered the ready room and closed the hatch behind him.

Nathan continued looking at his data pad. "If you're going to ask me how I am, you needn't bother."

Vladimir moved over to the desk, taking a seat. "It's okay to be upset, Nathan. We all are. Having to leave Josh and Loki behind, well, it sucks."

"Yes, it does," Nathan said. "But in four more jumps we'll be home, and I can hand the keys to someone else. The 'suck' will be over."

"Sometimes, you do not make sense to me, Nathan," Vladimir said. "One moment you're the captain, larger than life and full of confidence; the next moment you're pouting like a spoiled, little boy that does not want to eat his vegetables. Do you really hate being captain that much?"

"Most of the time, yes," Nathan admitted. He looked up from his data pad. "It's great to have everyone look up to you, to salute you, to call all your own shots, and to be in charge of your own fate. But you see, there's a catch. You're in charge of everyone else's fate as well. Sometimes, you're even in charge of the fate of people you'll never know.

That's the part that sucks, Vlad."

"I was wrong; you're not like a spoiled, little boy," Vladimir said as he leaned back in his chair and put his feet on Nathan's desk. "You are more like a little girl. A whiny, crying, spoiled, little girl." A big smile appeared on Vladimir's face, his eyebrows shooting upward as if to say, 'What do you think of that?'

"Nice," Nathan responded. "Is that the way you talk to your captain?"

"To Captain *Plaxa*, yes."

"I'm not even going to ask what that means."

"It means crybaby. To me, you are Captain Crybaby."

"Great. Anybody ever tell you that you suck at pep talks?"

"Come on, Nathan," Vladimir begged. "You were a great captain. You defeated an entire empire! What happened to you?"

Nathan leaned back in his chair. "The closer we get to home, the more I realize how much I hate about being captain."

"Then hand command over to Cameron. She'd love that."

"Yeah, that would look really good on the old resume, wouldn't it? I can see the headlines now. Senator's son resigns command two days from port. That'll help my father's political career."

"Who cares about his political career? That's his problem, not yours."

"Tell him that."

"You make everything way too complicated, my friend." Vladimir dropped his feet to the floor. "Listen to me, Nathan, you cannot worry about what anyone thinks about you or your father. In the end, you only answer to yourself. You are a good man. Do what you think is right."

"I don't know, Vlad," Nathan disagreed. "I've done some very bad things."

"This is sometimes the role of men, especially leaders," Vladimir said as he rose from his seat. "My job here is done. Now I must return to my duties." Vladimir turned and headed for the exit, stopping and turning back around by the hatch. He rose his hand in mock salute. "Captain Plaxa."

Nathan offered a hand gesture of his own. It wasn't a salute.

* * *

"Jump complete!" Loki announced.

"Turbines have shut down!" Josh reported.

"That's because there's no air in space," Loki remarked.

"I know, I was just saying..."

"Fuck!" Loki shouted as another warning system began to flash. "Contact!"

Josh looked at his tracking display. "What is that?"

"It's a Jung warship! The one that was on its way out of the system!"

"Where are we?" Josh wondered.

"We're still in the system. We only jumped a few light hours out."

"What the hell, Loki?!"

"It's not like I had much control over the direction we were jumping, Josh!"

"You still could have jumped us farther!"

"The farther the jump, the more chance of error..."

"We weren't trying to hit a target, Loki!" Josh complained. "We were just trying to escape! How far out is he?" he asked as he pushed his throttles forward.

"Half a million kilometers, but I don't think he's seen us."

"I got no power, no maneuvering!"

"The spaceflight systems aren't online yet," Loki reminded him. He began the startup sequence for the main drive.

"Why the fuck not?"

"We did a rapid launch sequence, remember? Rapid launch on the ground doesn't include spaceflight systems. It assumes you'll fire those systems up as you climb out!"

"Shit!" Josh yelled in frustration. "Do we have any forward momentum?"

"A few meters per minute..."

"Jump us again!"

"By the time he gets anywhere near us..."

"He doesn't have to get near us, Loki!" Josh interrupted. "Even the Aurora's rail guns can reach half a million klicks, and we're barely moving!"

"How far do you want to jump?"

"The farther the better!"

"Scanning forward," Loki reported.

"Come on!" Josh begged. They were unarmed and adrift. Once the enemy ship spotted them, it would take little effort for them to target their weapons and blast them into oblivion.

"We've got a clear jump line," Loki announced as he locked in an emergency escape jump. "Jumping in three......"

Josh checked the status of the main drive. It would take another minute for it to spin up.

"Two......"

Maneuvering was ready, but Josh knew he

couldn't touch it until after the jump.

"One......jumping," Loki announced.

Josh closed his eyes as the ship jumped. A moment later, he looked down at his tracking display. It was clear, and the threat indicator light had turned off. "Where are we now?"

"Just outside the 72 Herculis system," Loki reported. "We'll have mains in forty seconds."

"How much time?"

"Fuck, I don't know," Loki admitted. "The systems are acting all screwy."

"What do you mean?"

"According to this, it's four o'clock tomorrow morning."

"Check your watch," Josh suggested.

"It's busted, shattered during the crash. What about yours?"

"I gave it to Garrett, remember?"

"What about the handheld visual scanner? That displays the time, doesn't it?"

"I left it in the cave," Josh admitted.

"Great, so we have no way of knowing if we're early or late."

"We jump to the rendezvous point," Josh said. "If they're still there, we're early. If not, we're late."

"Mains are coming online," Loki announced. "But take it slow, Josh. The inertial dampeners are offline."

"Got it." Josh pushed the throttles forward a tiny amount. Even then it was enough to push them back into their flight seats with considerable force.

"I said take it easy," Loki grunted.

"That was easy!" Josh argued. "It was only one percent."

"At this rate, it will take hours to get up to a

decent speed."

"So we just jump our way back to the Aurora. She can slow down to match us so we can land."

"You don't understand," Loki said. "At this speed, it will take ten times as many jumps to reach the Aurora."

"Then we do ten times as many jumps."

"We've only got ten minutes of oxygen left, Josh."

"So start jumping!"

"The rendezvous point is four light years away. We'll have to make—I don't know—forty jumps maybe? I can't plot and execute that many jumps in ten minutes, Josh!"

"Can't you just set it to dump the maximum amount of energy into the jump fields and keep pushing the button to repeat the same jump over and over again?"

"The upgrades!" Loki realized.

"What?"

"The upgrades! The Takarans made a bunch of upgrades to the jump drive software, like the auto-nav!"

"Don't remind me," Josh complained. "I hate that thing."

"They also added a multi-jump algorithm that allows us to perform several jumps in rapid succession. The idea was to use the ZPED to power the jumps, so the Aurora wouldn't have to recharge between jumps. If it had worked, she could've made the trip back to Earth in a few hours instead of a few weeks!"

"What does that have to do with us?"

"We make short jumps without recharging!"

"No shit!"

"They tested the algorithm with this ship!"

"Where were we?"

"The day we went down to Takara to visit Tug and Deliza," Loki explained as he began scrolling through the selections in the jump drive's sequencing computer. "It's in here!" Loki quickly calculated a course back to the rendezvous point and punched it into the flight computer. "I'm sending you the course for the rendezvous point! Get us on course and push the throttle as much as we can stand while I program the multi-jump algorithm."

"That I can do," Josh replied as he altered course. "How many jumps do you really think it will take?"

"It looks like thirty-six, give or take. We'll stop after thirty-four and get an accurate fix on our position."

"Will we make it in ten minutes?"

"We'll make it in three, Josh," Loki said confidently.

"Sounds good to me," Josh declared. "Throttling up another one percent." Again they felt the force of acceleration push them harder back into their seats.

"Fuck, Josh," Loki grunted. "I can barely breathe as it is!"

"Suck it up, Loki. We need the speed."

"I can barely punch in the numbers," Loki grunted as his arms strained against the acceleration.

"Stop complaining. You're wasting air."

"That should do it," Loki announced. "Thirty-four jumps at max power. That should put us within a jump or two of the rendezvous point."

"Let's do it," Josh groaned as he struggled against the force of acceleration pressing him into his flight seat.

"Drop both your sun visor and your auto-darkening visor," Loki said. "Close your eyes tight and keep them closed. We're going to be doing a jump every five seconds, and we have no canopy to help protect us."

"What are you saying?"

"I don't know what effect all those rapid jumps will have on us," Loki told him.

Josh swallowed hard as he dropped his visors. "I hadn't thought of that," he admitted. "I'm ready."

"Starting multi-jump sequencer," Loki announced as he closed his eyes and pushed the button. The first jump flash went off, sending a tingling sensation through his body. "Shit! Did you feel that?"

"The tingling?" Josh replied as the second jump flashed.

"Yeah!"

"Is that normal?" Josh asked as the third jump flashed.

"I don't know. Kind of scary though."

"Any idea if it's working?"

"Well, if we can feel it..." Loki said as the next jump flashed.

"I meant, are we jumping forward?"

"I don't know. I'm afraid to open my eyes and check." Another jump flashed.

"How many jumps was that?" Josh asked as the next jump flashed.

"Six or seven, I think."

"My head is starting to feel funny," Josh told him as he continued keeping his eyes shut tight.

"Lightheaded?"

"Yeah," Josh answered.

"Me, too."

"I kind of like it," Josh admitted.

"Not me."

"Try not to think about it," Josh told him. "A few

more jumps and the Aurora will be hailing us on comms."

"I hope you're right," Loki said. "I'm starting to get nauseated."

"How many jumps have we done?"

"I'm not sure; I lost count. Fifteen, maybe?"

Josh squinted his eyes even tighter, shaking his head to fight the increasing dizziness he was feeling. Flash after flash, the jumps kept occurring in five second intervals. He wondered if the effects might be less if the jumps were ten seconds apart. He was sure it would, as every time the jump occurred, his symptoms got worse. Then, just as they started to subside, the next jump would come. "This pretty much sucks," Josh said. Between the dizziness and the constant force of acceleration, he wasn't sure he was going to be able to remain conscious.

"I'm not going to make it," Loki called over the comms.

"Hang on, Lok!" Josh encouraged. "Just a few more jumps." Josh felt his stomach begin to churn. A wave of cold washed over him with the next jump flash, followed by a surge of nausea that became worse with each subsequent jump. "Oh, God! I'm gonna puke!"

"Hold it in!" Loki warned. "You've got to hold it in!"

"Fuck, stop it! Please! I can't take this!" Josh cried as his head began to throb. He began counting the seconds between each flash, hoping to distract himself from the discomfort, but all it did was make it worse. Then it was over.

"Oh thank God," Loki declared.

"Is that it?"

"Yeah, that's it," Loki answered as he opened his

eyes and checked the jump control console. "Thirty-four jumps in three minutes."

Josh opened his eyes and raised his visors. "Everything looks the same except for the blue-white blotches in front of my eyes."

"Yeah, I've got them, too. It worked though." Loki checked his suit levels. "Could you back off on the throttles a bit, Josh? I think we're using up our air faster than we should."

"No problem," Josh told him as he pulled back slightly on the throttles. He began to feel lighter as the thrust levels decreased. "I'll leave it at one G for now."

"That's better," Loki agreed. "One more jump should do it. Just give me a second."

"Take your time," Josh told him. "I'd like to get at least some of my color back before we land."

Loki smiled as he plotted the last jump. "Ready to jump."

"Let's do it," Josh said as he lowered his visors once more.

Loki placed his finger over the button and lowered his visors with his free hand. "Jumping."

One last flash washed over them, bringing back that same tingling sensation as the first one.

"They're not so bad when they're farther apart," Josh said. "Don't you think, Loki?" Josh waited for a response. "Loki?"

"She's not here," Loki mumbled.

"What did you say?"

"The Aurora's not here."

"Are we in the right spot?"

"We're only two thousand kilometers from the rendezvous point," Loki told him. "They should be right here."

"Maybe they're nearby," Josh said as he turned on his comm-set. "Mayday, mayday, mayday. Aurora, this is the Falcon. We are damaged and running out of oxygen. Requesting rendezvous. Repeating: mayday, mayday, mayday. Aurora, this is the Falcon. Do you copy?"

"It's no use, Josh. She's not out there."

"How can you be sure?"

"I've scanned in all directions. She's not there. We must be too late."

"Maybe we're just in the wrong spot."

"I've checked our location three times, Josh. We're in the right spot."

"Maybe we're early."

"Doubtful. We'd have to be seven hours early. The Aurora is already at the next layover."

"Fuck!" Josh screamed. "What are we going to do?"

"We keep jumping."

"They're ten light years away, Loki. What are we going to do, make another hundred jumps?"

"I'm thinking more like ninety."

"I don't think I can take ninety more jumps, not every five seconds."

"Actually, it would be every three and a half seconds this time. We've only got six minutes of oxygen left, and we need at least a minute or two to land, maybe more."

"Okay, it's official now. This officially sucks!"

"Wasting oxygen, Josh. Wasting oxygen."

"Fuck," he muttered. For the first time in his life, he felt hopeless. "Let's get this over with."

Loki finished punching the new parameters into the multi-jump sequencing algorithm. "Josh, if this doesn't work..."

"Shut up and push the button," Josh told him as he dropped his visors again.

"Better kill the mains first, just in case we pass out," Loki suggested.

"Good idea." He pulled the throttles back to zero. "At least we won't have to deal with that at the same time."

Loki dropped his visors once more. "Jumping in three......"

"Thanks for sticking with me, Lok," Josh said.

"Two......It was my pleasure......One......"

"Sorry for nearly getting you killed so many times."

"No, you're not."

The Falcon jumped, then again three and a half seconds later. She kept jumping over and over again. Josh felt the tingling sensation return, followed by the lightheaded feeling, the nausea, and the throbbing headache. It all built up so much faster this time. He quickly lost count of the jumps. "Loki! How are you doing back there?"

"Fuck!" Loki cried in anguish.

"Fuck!" Josh cried back as he squinted his eyes even tighter. He crossed his arms and grabbed tightly at his flight harness, pulling his head down as much as he could in his helmet, as if he were trying to touch his chin to his chest. He felt as if his head were about to explode, and his stomach was being twisted into a knot. A few flashes later, he felt his nose start to bleed. His mouth opened and his stomach emptied into his helmet... not once, but twice. The stench inside his helmet was awful. He thrashed his head about, trying to get the chunks of vomit to stick to either his head or the inside of his helmet so that he wouldn't suck them back into his lungs as he struggled to breathe. His eyes began to hurt. He felt like they were swelling up to enormous size. He screamed out in pain but couldn't hear himself over the sound of Loki's own screams coming over the comm-set in his helmet. Finally, Loki's screams stopped as he finally succumbed to the pain and passed out. Josh envied his friend, praying for unconsciousness to take him as well. Eventually, everything went dark, and there was nothing but the agony. A moment later, his wish was granted.

* * *

"We know we were ambushed in the Oort," Jessica said, from the couch in the captain's ready room, "so we know that the Jung at least suspect that the Earth is trying to develop a superior propulsion technology. The fact that they only had two gunboats waiting for us suggests they didn't know exactly what that propulsion technology was."

"Or that they simply didn't have any other ships in the area," Cameron said.

"No, she's right," Nathan said. "Just before our first jump, Captain Roberts said that the Jung had invaded the Alpha Centauri system six months prior. They must have had ships in that area for several months beforehand. Even their slowest ships can do ten times light, so it's only five and a half months to Sol."

"Those gunboats can do twenty light," Jessica pointed out. "Even their heavy cruisers can do fifteen. I don't think they knew exactly what we were up to, and that's why they didn't commit anything larger than a couple of gunboats. They were saving everything they had in the area for the invasion of Alpha Centauri. If that test jump had taken place a few months later, we might have been staring down a couple of Jung battle platforms."

"I thought those were just rumors," Nathan said.

"Nope, recon confirmed them," Jessica told him. "I saw them mentioned in the stuff that Fleet sent over for Captain Roberts, the stuff that was time and location locked."

"Then perhaps she is right," Nathan said to Cameron. "We need to recon the Alpha Centauri system on our way home."

"I hope you're not thinking about coasting through like the Falcon," Cameron said.

"I was thinking more along the lines of standing off and collecting images from outside the system. Maybe jump around the outer perimeter to get images from different angles."

"Still seems risky."

"Isn't risk part of our job?" Jessica asked.

"Of course," Cameron said. "It's just that we're so close to home."

"I, of all people, am anxious to get home and hand everything over to Fleet," Nathan reminded her. "I just keep thinking that if Captain Roberts were here, he'd reconnoiter every damn system he could before returning to Earth."

Cameron begrudgingly nodded her agreement. "I'll work up a mission profile and run it past you before the next jump."

"That's in what," Nathan looked at his watch, "three hours?"

"More like two and a half."

"Better get on it, then," Nathan told her.

"Aye, sir."

"I'll help you," Jessica offered, rising from her spot on the couch.

"*Captain, Tactical!*" Mister Randeen called over the intercom. "*Contact!*"

All three of them instantly charged out of the ready room and onto the bridge.

"It's the Falcon!" Mister Randeen reported. "She just jumped in about two million kilometers off our starboard beam."

"Comms!" Nathan called as he made his way to his command chair. "Any word?"

"No, sir. No answer to hails."

"We're picking up their telemetry now, sir," Mister Navashee reported. "She's badly damaged."

"Recommend general quarters, sir," Cameron urged. "They may have been followed."

"Sound general quarters," Nathan ordered. "Helm, turn into them and slow to two hundred thousand kilometers per minute."

"Turning into contact. Slowing to two hundred thousand KPH, aye," Mister Chiles answered.

"Let's get some fighter cover out there, Commander," Nathan told his XO.

"Green deck," Cameron ordered, "launch the alert fighters. Have them take up protective positions around the Falcon. Stand by the rescue teams and ready the deck for recovery."

Nathan felt the Aurora make her turn to starboard as her speed reduced.

"Captain, I've got their bio-monitor signals: rapid and irregular heart rates, low blood pressure, low respiratory tidal volume on Loki..." Mister Navashee suddenly turned his head toward the captain. "Josh isn't breathing at all, sir."

"Comms, alert medical."

Lieutenant Kakayee flashed his ready sign to the launch officer and grabbed the hand rails on either side of his cockpit. A moment later, the massive door in front of him dropped into the floor, and his fighter shot forward with incredible acceleration. Despite his inertial dampeners, he was thrown back in his seat as his tiny fighter hurtled down the launch tube. Two seconds later, he could see the outer door approaching him rapidly. His pulse raced and his breath quickened. He had gone through this launch cycle at least a dozen times on training flights over the last few days, but every time he wondered if that final door would open before he slammed into it.

The door fell away a moment later, opening the long launch tube to space, and the fighter shot out into the open, his main engines firing automatically as soon as he left the tube. "Talon One, airborne," he reported.

"*Talon Two, airborne,*" his wingman called out as well.

Lieutenant Kakayee glanced over his right shoulder. His wingman, Lieutenant Mallard, was just behind him and to his right, having launched from the neighboring tube. He listened as the other two fighters announced their departure from the Aurora's port launch tubes.

"*Talon One, Flight. Proceed to target,*" the flight controller instructed over the comms. "*Talon Three, establish outer perimeter and orbit.*"

"Talon One copies. Time on target: thirty seconds." Lieutenant Kakayee looked to his left as the Aurora slid past his port side. He could see the other two fighters now as they pulled up higher relative to his own flight path. They would circle the Falcon at varying angles in order to provide cover in case another, possibly hostile contact suddenly appeared. Meanwhile, he and his wingman would intercept the Falcon. He had never met the Falcon's flight crew, but he knew of them. Their actions at the battle of Answari had saved more than one of the lieutenant's friends.

"What's going on?" Marcus asked as he ran into the starboard fighter alley. He grabbed a deckhand that was running past him. "What's going on?"

"They launched the alert fighters," the deckhand answered.

"Why?"

"The Falcon, she's back, but I think something's wrong. I gotta go, Senior Chief."

Marcus let the deckhand go and made a dash for the forward ladder that led up to the observation rail and flight deck operations. After shooting up the ladder, he ran down the catwalk, bursting into the operations room.

Master Chief Montrose was the first to notice the senior chief and immediately moved over to intercept him. Flight Ops was busy, and the last thing they needed was for Marcus to get in the way. Worried though he might be, his place was not in Flight Ops; it was down on the deck.

"Marcus, you shouldn't be in here."

"What's going on?" he demanded. "What's wrong with the Falcon? Are they all right?"

"We don't know yet," the master chief told him. "It just appeared. They're not answering comms, and their life signs are very weak."

"Whattaya mean 'weak'?"

"We believe they are unconscious, and..."

"And what?"

"It appears Josh isn't breathing."

"What? Is he dead?"

"No, he's got a faint pulse, but if he's not breathing, that won't last long."

"Then get him down on the deck!" Marcus demanded.

"We're trying to figure out how to do that right now..."

"Whattaya mean 'trying to figure it out'? Activate the auto-flight system. It'll bring him right down onto the same pad he took off from!"

"They didn't have auto-flight systems in those old interceptors."

"No shit! I had to install one myself!"

"Wait," the master chief said, somewhat confused. "You installed an auto-flight system in the Falcon?"

"Yeah, back in Takara. It wasn't an easy job, either."

"I don't understand. If they have an auto-flight system, why hasn't it activated?"

"'Cuz that stupid, little shit hates auto-anything! He never turns the damn thing on. That's why I wired it for remote activation, so send the fucking code already!"

"What's the code?" the master chief asked.

"It's in the Falcon's maintenance logs!" Marcus bellowed. "Don't these stupid command types keep track of anything? It's all in the Falcon's spec sheets as well!"

"Stay here!" Master Chief Montrose ordered, pointing at Marcus. "I mean it."

"Sir, flight reports Talon One has visual on the Falcon," Naralena reported.

"Patch him through to me," Nathan ordered. A moment later, Naralena nodded that the channel was ready. "Talon One, Aurora Actual. What do you see?"

"It's the Falcon, sir, but she's pretty banged up. Lots of exterior damage. Looks like she crashed, maybe more than once. And her canopy is busted. Her cockpit is open to space. I repeat, her cockpit is open to space."

"Is there any movement?"

"No, sir. I can see the flight crew, but they are not moving."

"Captain, CAG!" Major Prechitt called.

"Talon One, Aurora Actual. Stand by one." Nathan quickly switched channels. "Go for Captain."

"Sir, the Falcon has auto-flight that can be remotely activated, but we need to be within close proximity to her in order to do so."

"Talon One is with her now."

"I know, sir. If the Falcon can still maneuver, we should get the Aurora as close to her and properly lined up as possible. Since we don't know the state of her flight systems, the less she has to maneuver, the better."

"Copy that," Nathan answered. "Mister Chiles," he called.

"On it, sir," the helmsman answered as he pushed the Aurora to the left to prepare to turn around and come up under the damaged Falcon.

"Major, we're swinging wide to come around up under the Falcon now. As soon as we're in position and close enough for you to activate her auto-flight, we'll signal you."

"Yes, sir. The Falcon launched from the starboard pad, so that's where her auto-flight will want to set her down again."

"Wouldn't it be easier to set her down on the flight apron?" Nathan wondered.

"Yes, sir, but we don't know the extent of her damage. If we start trying to remotely manipulate her, we might cause more problems. Safest bet is to let the auto-flight put her back on the starboard pad. Besides, we can get her into pressure faster that way."

"Understood. Tell your fighters to back off and give us room."

"Aye, sir."

"Maybe it would be best if you let the rescue team handle it," Master Chief Montrose told Marcus.

"What would be best would be for you to get the fuck outta my way unless you like having a broken nose," Marcus said in all sincerity.

The chief of the boat looked the senior chief in the eyes. He knew his threat was serious. He also knew he could kick the senior chief's ass without breaking a sweat. And he knew that if it was his kid, he'd feel the same way. "Very well, Marcus. Meet the rescue team on the gun deck. They're gonna intercept the Falcon as she passes."

"Thanks," Marcus grumbled.

"They know what they're doing, Senior Chief, so don't get in the team's way, or you could cost your boy his life."

Marcus didn't answer the master chief but turned and ran out the door on his way to the gun deck.

"Approaching the Falcon now, sir," Mister Riley reported. "We'll be in position in approximately fifteen seconds."

"Tell Flight Ops to stand by," Nathan told Naralena.

"Four hundred meters. Speed: one five zero," the navigator called out to his helmsman. "Target speed: one three eight."

The helmsman, Mister Chiles, never touched the joystick. Unlike Josh, he felt quite comfortable performing precise maneuvers from the console. In fact, he preferred it. Flight algorithms were far more precise than manual manipulation could possibly hope to be. Joysticks were for fighter pilots and hotshot show-offs, as far as he was concerned.

"Two hundred meters. Speed steady at one five zero. Stand by for braking in three seconds...... and......begin braking."

Mister Chiles touched a button and initiated the next programmed maneuvering sequence, telling the Aurora to match the Falcon's course and speed and to position herself directly below her.

"Speed decreasing. Range closing. Five seconds to position."

Nathan watched the main view screen. The view was set looking aft from the camera directly behind the missile turret housing, which sat atop the center of the ship's main section. The starboard launch and recovery pad was directly behind and slightly to starboard of that camera, so they had an excellent view of the Falcon as the Aurora slowly drifted into position. "She looks like she ran into the side of a mountain," he mumbled.

Cameron was also watching as she stood next

to Nathan. Jessica watched from beside the tactical station directly behind the captain's command chair.

"How the hell did they get that thing all the way back here?" she wondered.

"If I know Josh and Loki, by sheer determination," Nathan mumbled.

"In position, Captain."

Nathan gestured to Naralena, who immediately passed the signal on to Flight Ops. "Nicely done, gentlemen." He watched as the Falcon fired her thrusters and began to descend, moving closer to the Aurora.

"Why isn't she deploying her landing gear?" Cameron asked.

"Look at her gear bay doors," Nathan told her.

"They look like they're buckled inward," Cameron realized. "What the hell happened to them?"

"Fifty meters. Ten seconds," Mister Riley reported from the navigator's station.

"Is everybody in position?" Nathan asked.

"COB has rescue and medical teams waiting on the gun deck. They've already got the doors to the elevator shaft open. They'll jump in as she passes on her way down."

"Good."

"The senior chief's there as well," Cameron added.

Nathan looked at her. "That doesn't seem like a good idea."

"I suspect the senior chief didn't leave the COB much choice."

"I suspect not," Nathan agreed.

"Five seconds," Mister Riley reported.

Nathan watched as the Falcon settled onto the pad on its belly, listing slightly to port as the pad's artificial gravity came to life in order to hold the

Falcon against the pad's deck as it descended.

"Contact," Mister Riley reported.

Nathan watched the view screen, waiting for the pad to start its journey down into the ship. "Why isn't the pad coming down?"

"They have to safe the Falcon's engines first," Cameron reminded him.

"Pad is coming down," Mister Riley reported.

Nathan looked back up at the view screen to see the Falcon disappear into the top of the Aurora, the outer doors to the elevator tube closing over her so the tube could begin rapid repressurization. Nathan jumped from his seat, then paused to look at Cameron.

"Go," she told him. "I've got the bridge."

"I'll be in medical," he yelled as he ran out of the bridge.

"Follow us, Senior Chief," the rescue team leader instructed Marcus.

"Yeah, yeah, no problem!" Marcus yelled. The Aurora's gun deck was located two decks below her upper main hull and ran underneath the eight mini-rail gun pods that lined the perimeter of the ship's main section. Most of the deck was used to store rail gun ammunition in a series of automated hoppers that could be directed to any rail gun that needed them. In addition, much of the Aurora's forward environmental and life support systems were located here. The gun deck lacked the acoustical dampening properties of the ship's main habitation spaces; hence it was quite noisy.

Both the port and starboard forward elevator pads that led from the flight deck to the Aurora's topside were also used to move cargo and machinery from the cargo deck at the bottom of the ship up to the gun deck. The starboard access door had already been overridden and opened in order to access the elevator pad on its way down.

"They're not going to stop her on this floor, sir," the leader of the rescue team told Marcus. "They'll just slow it down a bit so we can jump on as it passes. That way, we can start extrication on the way down. With any luck, we'll have them out by the time we get to the hangar deck."

"Fifteen seconds," the officer in charge of the gun deck called out.

"She'll still be moving pretty fast, so be careful. Best thing to do is to just take a giant step out after she passes and let yourself fall straight down feet first. Bend your knees when you land; it's farther than it looks. But there's no roof above the pad so..."

"I'm chief of the deck, mister," Marcus reminded him. "I've ridden the elevator before."

"Yes, sir."

"Stand ready!" the officer of the deck ordered. The four rescue men and the four medical specialists stepped up to the edge of the massive open doorway. They spaced themselves apart evenly, with enough space between them for the gear they carried. Marcus stepped up to the end of the line as well. He looked out into the open elevator shaft. It was open all the way down to the hangar deck, and he could see more men standing six decks below on the hangar deck looking up at them.

Marcus looked up at the underside of the elevator shaft as it descended quickly toward them. Each of the men checked their positions to ensure they were not leaning into the doorway so much that they might be struck by the descending pad. Marcus did the same.

Finally, the massive elevator pad passed by his face. The pad, with all its support structures and motor compartments, was several meters thick in all, and it took several seconds for it to completely pass them by. As soon as it passed below their waists, all eight men tossed the rescue bags out onto the descending elevator pad. All sixteen bags fell in unison, and the row of men stepped off a moment later as the elevator passed their feet.

Marcus stepped off as well, only a moment later. Both rescue teams had obviously rehearsed this maneuver before, as they made it look as easy as skipping the bottom step on a staircase. The senior chief's landing was not as graceful, and he fell to one side as his feet touched. By the time he got up, the first two rescue men were already climbing up onto the Falcon, while the other two men began checking that her systems were properly shut down and there were no other fire, electrical, or chemical hazards that might threaten the safety of either the rescue teams or the flight crew they were there to rescue.

Marcus charged past the four medical specialists as they were unpacking their gear in preparation to begin treatment. He followed the first two rescue men up onto the starboard wing-body's leading edge. The rescue men had chosen to straddle the battered fuselage and slide forward from behind the cockpit, as there was no boarding ladder available to them at the moment.

Marcus knew what they were trying to do, as the canopy's manual release mechanism was located at the rear of the canopy on either side. He also knew that the canopy had a tendency to stick when you tried to slide it forward, as it was not originally designed to do. He used the two step wells built into the side of the fuselage a meter below the canopy alongside each flight seat. The wells were designed to give when kicked with the toe of a boot if the ship was in a pressurized environment. Marcus kicked the aft step well in, and the cover folded up and in nicely. He brought his leg over and stuck his left foot into the step well toe first, grabbed the edge of the broken canopy, and hoisted himself up and over.

"What are you doing, Senior Chief?" the rescue man on top of the fuselage yelled.

"Don't worry about me! Just get the canopy released!" Marcus replied as he kicked in the next step well alongside the forward seat position and inserted his right foot. In one smooth motion, he hoisted himself up and swung his right leg up over the nose of the Falcon, mounting it like a hover-bike.

At that moment, he looked inside the forward canopy windshield. He could not see Josh's face through his helmet's sun visor, as it was polarized to reflect sunlight, but he wasn't moving at all. No rise and fall of the chest, not even a twitch of a finger.

There was a loud pop as Marcus felt the canopy's broken frame vibrate.

"Canopy is released!" the rescue man called from aft of the canopy.

Marcus planted his feet against the small canards on either side of the Falcon's nose, standing slightly as he grabbed the leading edge of the canopy that now stuck out after being released from its aft rail locks. He lifted up as he pulled the canopy forward toward the ship's nose. "Push!" he ordered the rescue man at the rear of the canopy. The battered piece of metal and clear canopy resisted at first, then finally sprung free, gliding cleanly forward on its rollers. Marcus slid backwards, falling off the nose of the Falcon and landing hard on his backside on the elevator pad below. Luckily for him, the artificial gravity on the pad was only at three-quarters of the ship's normal gravity. Otherwise, the medical team might have been treating him as well.

The canopy screeched to a stop, not quite as far forward as it was designed to go. But it was enough to gain clear access to the Falcon's flight crew. "Adjust pad gravity to one-half normal!" the rescue man called over his comm-set.

Marcus could feel himself becoming lighter as the artificial gravity on the pad lessened.

Once the canopy had slid forward, the emergency boarding ladder dropped out of the starboard side of the Falcon. It was no more than two metal rungs hanging out of the side of the ship, but it was enough for the medical specialists to climb the side and reach the unconscious flight crew.

"Pop his face plate!" the medical specialist ordered as he reached for Josh's face plate. "They need air!" A moment later, both face plates were off, and their helmets were in the process of being removed.

"This one's breathing!" the rescue man called out. "Pass me some oxygen!"

"His name is Loki!" Marcus yelled in anger and frustration. "The other one is Josh!"

"This one's not!" the medical specialist reported as he handed the oxygen kit to the rescue man behind Loki. "Pass me another O2 kit and an intubation package," the medical specialist at Josh's side added. "And give me the suction bag; he's got puke everywhere!"

One of the other medical specialists passed the requested devices to the one attending to Josh. The man dropped them in Josh's lap and immediately began suctioning out Josh's mouth. Then he grabbed one of the other kits and pulled out a small device. He inserted the device and activated it, immediately connecting it to the oxygen bag sitting in Josh's lap. "Tube is in. Auto-respirator is running."

Marcus could hear the sound of the auto-respirator as it rhythmically filled Josh's lungs with oxygen.

"Tele-pack is connected," the medical specialist reported as he attached another device to Josh's suit electronics. "Toss me a pre-filled."

One of the medical specialists on the deck tossed a pneumo-jet up to the medical specialist attending Josh. He quickly injected something into Josh's neck. "Ph stabilizer on board." The medical specialist stepped back onto the starboard wing-body, making room for the two rescue men. "This one's ready for extrication," he announced as the elevator pad began to slow. The first rescue man moved forward and began unhooking Josh's flight harness in preparation to remove him from the spacecraft.

The elevator finally came to a stop at the hangar deck. A dozen rescue workers and deckhands rushed onto the platform, carrying additional gear and pushing boarding ladders.

"No gear!" one of the deckhands called out. "Bring in the shorties!" A moment later, the taller boarding ladders they had originally brought in were replaced by shorter models.

Marcus watched as half a dozen men worked

together to raise Josh out of the cockpit and carry him down the boarding ladder. His body was limp and lifeless, and his face was ashen and covered with blood and vomit. His blond hair was wet and matted. Marcus looked over one of the medical specialist's shoulders as he pulled open one of Josh's eyelids and shined a light in his eye.

"Pupils are dilated and sluggish!" the specialist reported. All Marcus could see was that Josh's eyes were terribly bloodshot.

Within minutes, Josh lay on a rescue gurney with tubes and monitoring leads connecting his body to the gurney's underside. Moments later, he was rushed away to medical, leaving Marcus standing there.

Master Chief Montrose came up and stood beside Marcus, putting his hand on his friend's shoulder in a show of support. As he did so, they rolled Loki past him as well. Loki's eyes were also bloodshot, but he was awake and looking right at Marcus as they rolled him past. For a moment, he could have sworn he saw a smile on Loki's face, but it was hard to tell under the oxygen mask.

"Come on," Master Chief Montrose told Marcus. "Let's get you over to medical."

* * *

The treatment room was empty of patients except for Josh and Loki. Marcus had sat between the two of them for the better part of the day. Nathan had come and gone, choosing to spend as much time in medical as possible. Lieutenant Yosef had spent most of her off-duty time at Josh's bedside as well but had insisted on working her normal shift.

Nathan, on the other hand, had been more than happy to let his XO cover him as much as she could. He had already authorized a change in course in order to recon the Alpha Centauri system before returning to Earth, and jump sixty-three had already been executed. Two more jumps would bring them just outside the Centauri system, after which, one more jump would finally get them home.

Nathan's first instinct had been to skip Alpha Centauri altogether and get back to Earth sooner rather than nearly a day later. One just naturally assumed that a hospital on Earth could provide better treatment than the medical department on a starship. However, in the case of the Aurora and her Corinairan medical staff, that was not the case. In fact, Josh and Loki probably could not be in better hands, short of being back in the Pentaurus cluster.

Over the hours, Nathan had come to know Senior Chief Taggart a lot better. He wasn't as gruff and unintelligent as some believed. In fact, he was quite wise, having a broad range of life experience. Underneath his loud, opinionated exterior beat the heart of a kind, old man. He just hid it well. Nathan found that he quite preferred such a person to the posturing, pompous, political types that he had grown up around. At least with Marcus, you knew what he truly thought, because he flat out told you so with no reservations. He was a brutally, but refreshingly, honest person.

Even Tug, a man whom Nathan had come to see as a mentor of sorts, had carried a hidden agenda of his own. He was a man of few, but carefully chosen, words—words that effectively placed in the listener's mind the thoughts Tug most wanted that person to have. He wished that his own father—the senator and possibly, by now, the president—would speak in such a masterful fashion. Like most politicians, he had a tendency to speak around a topic instead of about it.

Nathan felt a hand on his shoulder. He looked up and saw Cameron standing next to him. He rose from his chair and followed her out of the treatment room and into the corridor.

"How are they doing?" Cameron asked.

"They're stabilized for now," Nathan told her. "Loki was in and out of consciousness for a while. They sedated him so that the nanites could do their thing—something about them not being able to work on brain cells that were currently in use or something."

"They're both better off not being awake while the nanites are working. It was bad enough having them poking away at my insides. I can't imagine what it would feel like in my head. What about Josh?"

"He is worse off. Abby thinks it's because he was in the front seat. Most of the canopy around him was broken away, nothing but frames and a few shards of clear canopy. Loki, on the other hand, still had most of the canopy around him. Abby thinks that, because of this, Josh had more direct contact with the jump fields."

"And that's what injured him?"

"That, the cold of space, hypoxia, massive levels of CO_2. Think about how much energy is dumped into those jump fields. I'm surprised he's still alive."

"So am I. We just finished reviewing their flight records. They used the new multi-jump algorithm that the Takarans came up with. They made one hundred twenty-two jumps in an open cockpit in under ten minutes. The last series was eighty-seven jumps, all at three and a half second intervals. It's unbelievable."

Nathan's head dropped in shame. "I should have waited."

"Nathan, they were three hours late. How long were you supposed to wait? You had to think of the mission, the crew. Everyone knows that, even Josh and Loki."

"Perhaps." Nathan lifted his head, looking toward medical. "I wonder if Marcus knows it."

"I'm sure he does as well."

"Any idea why they were so late to begin with?" Nathan wondered.

"We haven't gotten that far back in the flight records yet."

Nathan sighed. "How long until our next jump?"

"Jump sixty-four took place a few hours ago," she said, checking her watch. "Sixty-five is a little over four hours away."

"And that will put us one jump from Centauri?"

"Correct. I think it would be wise for both of us to get some rest before then. We know there are Jung in that area, so we should be ready."

"I'd like a staff meeting before the next jump to review the ship's readiness before we jump into a potentially hostile area."

"I'll schedule one to take place an hour before the next jump. Maybe you should get some rest."

"No way I could sleep," Nathan told her, "not now."

"Maybe get something to eat then."

"I'll be fine, Cam," he assured her as he prepared to return to the treatment room. "I'll see you at the briefing."

Nathan left the corridor and returned to the

treatment area, again taking a seat across the room from Josh and Loki. He leaned back in his chair and watched as the Corinairan nanite specialist and his technician wheeled in the nanite control scanner and positioned it over Josh. Cameron had once described to him in great detail what it felt like to have the microscopic robots working to repair you on the inside. It had not sounded pleasant at all. He had to wonder why the Corinairan doctors were so insistent that one could not feel the nanites working inside when there was firsthand evidence to the contrary. Perhaps it was something unique to Terrans or to Commander Taylor herself.

Nathan closed his eyes to ease the burning. He had been awake for twenty hours now, and they had been stressful hours at that. He let his mind drift to other thoughts: to his family home in the hills outside Vancouver, to the lazy summer days playing with his friends, to weekend hockey games on the frozen ponds of his youth, and finally, to returning to everything he knew to be home.

CHAPTER TEN

"Loki should have a full recovery," Doctor Chen announced. "He will need nanite therapy for some time and, therefore, will require constant monitoring, but we are confident he will fully recover." Doctor Chen paused, looking around the briefing room. "Josh is in much worse condition. Due to his position in the cockpit, he was more exposed to the jump fields and suffered far more tissue degradation as a result. He has significant cerebral edema that has required constant management, and there is significant damage to the portion of his brain that controls voluntary motor control."

"What is his prognosis?" Nathan asked.

"He is breathing on his own again, which is a very good sign. But we are keeping him in an induced coma to allow the nanites to work on the damaged areas of his brain. He may have to stay that way for weeks. Until then, we can't be sure."

"Has Loki regained consciousness yet?" Nathan wondered.

"He had some semi-lucid moments as his sedation began to wear off, but we're keeping him sedated as much as possible as well, although not as deeply as Josh."

"When will he be able to remain conscious for longer periods? We'd like to hear what happened to them."

"A few days, I suspect."

"We have gone through all of their flight records for the 72 Herculis mission. Of course, they only tell us what maneuvers they performed and what damage they sustained. It doesn't tell us why," Major Prechitt explained. "We still have to go through the Falcon's video recordings and threat tracking logs. We should know a bit more after that."

"What do you think happened to them?" Nathan asked.

"Based on the flight records, it appears they were ambushed as they passed between the inhabited planet in the 72 Herculis system and one of her smaller, closer moons."

"How were they discovered?" Nathan wondered. "When she's running cold and dark, the Falcon is nearly impossible to detect."

"It appears they were forced to do a short burn in order to avoid an unforeseen moon. Based on the moon's orbit and speed, I don't think they were able to see it when they originally plotted their flight path through the system. Less than a minute after that burn, they dropped thermal decoys, performed some interesting maneuvers, went to full power, and made a run for it around the far side of the planet. I'm guessing they were trying to use the planet as a visual shield to hide their escape jump from their pursuers. However, they were forced to dive straight down into the planet's atmosphere as more enemy contacts rose from the planet's surface directly ahead of them. They managed to lose them in a series of canyons, but then things become somewhat confusing."

"How so?" Nathan asked.

"Well, they had a sudden dramatic loss in altitude that, quite frankly, doesn't match any aerodynamic forces or patterns that I'm familiar with. At the same time, they lost nearly all power in their turbines. Next, two of the turbines seemed to recover, while the other two kept threatening to fail."

"Were they hit?"

"No, sir. As best we can tell, the two turbines failed because they were full of water."

"A sudden rain storm?"

"That dumped large amounts of water in a single spot?" the CAG responded. "Unlikely."

"Maybe they skimmed a lake or a river or something," Cameron suggested.

"At the speed they were flying, I doubt they could have done that and remained airborne," the CAG told her. "Besides, while that might explain the water, it doesn't explain the sudden extreme loss of altitude. I did notice, however, that just before the sudden drop in altitude, Josh overrode the automatic thrust vectoring system, swung all four turbine ducts straight down, and brought them to full power."

"So whatever caused the sudden drop in altitude, he saw it coming and was trying to counter it," Nathan surmised.

"That's what I thought as well. I think something forced him downward suddenly, perhaps into a lake or river. This caused them to take on water quickly which led to a crash landing. There was a lot of damage to the top of the Falcon as well, so maybe another ship rammed him from above in an attempt to force him down."

"It does make you curious, doesn't it?" Nathan stated.

"A few hours later, they lifted off again and quickly jumped away. With very little emergency oxygen in their suits, they were forced to make two multi-jump sequences. The first one to get to the rendezvous point, the next to get to the Aurora's next layover point."

"Why don't those suits carry more oxygen?" Cameron asked.

"The Takaran flight suits were not designed to be used outside of the interceptor for long periods. They only carry enough oxygen to make an emergency transfer between two spacecraft in case they need to be rescued from a damaged ship. We looked at adapting the Corinari flight suits, but they require a much larger ejection seat that would not fit into the Falcon's cockpit."

"Thank you for your report, Doctor. Please keep us informed of their condition."

"Yes, sir," Doctor Chen assured him. "If you don't mind, I'd like to return to medical."

"Of course."

"Captain," Jessica began as the doctor left the briefing room, "I would like to point out that the Falcon's mission has provided us with an amazing amount of intelligence. We now have ground images of surface civilizations, combat footage, and real-time flight dynamics data on Jung fighters. We even have the optical and thermal signatures of three Jung warships, as well as the signatures of their radar sets. And that's just the tip of the iceberg. Fleet Intelligence is gonna flip when they see this stuff."

"I agree, Captain," Major Prechitt said. "My flight combat analysts are pouring over this stuff as well. Having never studied anything other than

Takaran battle tactics, they are truly enjoying the new challenge."

"Hopefully, the price of this intelligence won't end up being too high," Nathan commented solemnly. He turned to Vladimir, hoping to move the meeting along. "Lieutenant Commander, how are we doing with the upgrades to our weapons systems? Will we have the plasma cannon turret operational before we get back to Earth?"

"Doubtful," Vladimir said. "We didn't have enough power conduit available to run additional lines to power the weapon. Lieutenant Montgomery and his team are adapting one of the mini-ZPEDs to power the weapon directly. It should be ready for test firing by the time we reach Earth."

"What about the torpedo tube upgrades?"

"The port upgrade in tube two is complete. We still have to install the separating bulkhead in the starboard bay before we can use the plasma cannon in tube four at the same time as conventional torpedoes in tube three. We have yet to start on the conversion of tube six."

"And the rest of the weapons systems?"

"All rail guns are in proper working order."

"Major Prechitt," Nathan said, turning to his CAG next, "how go the training flights?"

"Quite well, sir," the major answered proudly. "Both our launch and recovery cycle times have improved, and my pilots have been developing both their intercept and dogfighting skills. We have also been developing numerous defensive tactics for protecting the Aurora against enemy fighters."

"What about attacking larger ships?" Cameron wondered.

"As the Talon fighters were originally designed

to intercept and harass larger ships in orbit over Corinair, our pilots are already well versed in such tactics."

"That's good to hear, Major," Nathan said. "It will be interesting to compare the flight tactics of the Corinari and EDF pilots."

"My staff is looking forward to the exchange."

"Commander Taylor, how is our propellant holding up?"

"With the emergency course change to rescue the Falcon, we've burned a bit more than anticipated. However, we should still arrive in Sol with more than enough to park her safely in orbit over Earth."

"How will our recon of the Alpha Centauri system affect our reserves?"

"We've already made the course change to intercept the Centauri system," Cameron explained. "The largest use of propellant, other than our final deceleration burn in Sol, will be when we leave Centauri. That requires a ninety degree turn. If the Falcon had not been damaged, we could've sent it in without altering our own course, thus saving considerable propellant."

"I don't suppose there's any chance it could be flight-ready in a few hours," Nathan asked.

"Not a chance," Vladimir answered.

"I thought ship captains were supposed to be able to ask for miracles from their chief engineers," Nathan teased.

"Only in the movies, sir," Vladimir responded.

"Captain, we'll be okay on propellant," Cameron assured him. "If we weren't, I'd let you know. We've come up with a flight plan around the Centauri system using a series of short jumps with small turns in between. In addition, since the jump to

Earth is only four and a half light years, we're going to perform a deceleration burn during each turn. By using a series of short, decelerating turns, we'll only use half the propellant compared to performing the maneuvers separately."

"That's good thinking, Commander."

"Of course, if we run into trouble and are forced to defend ourselves, it had better be a short engagement."

"Noted," Nathan said. "How long until we jump?"

"Jump sixty-five is scheduled for fifteen twenty."

Nathan looked at his watch. "That's in about forty minutes, people. Let's make sure everyone's ready. It's our last mission before we hand the ship back over to Fleet, so let's make it a good one."

* * *

"Jump sixty-five complete," Mister Riley reported.

"Verifying position," Mister Navashee reported from the sensor operator's station to port.

"Threat board is clear," Mister Randeen added.

"Position verified," Mister Navashee announced. "We're at the first turn, two light-months outside of the Alpha Centauri system."

"Begin the first recon series, Mister Navashee," Nathan ordered.

"Aye, sir, beginning passive thermal, radio, and optical scanning."

"Will the opticals be of any use from this distance?"

"Yes, sir. The Aurora had very good optical telescopes to begin with, but the digital enhancement the Takarans provided greatly increased its range. At this distance, we could pick out and ID a ship our size up to about four light-months."

"Impressive. Too bad we couldn't go farther, though," Nathan said. "I'd love to have a look back at how the Jung took the system nine months ago."

"Yes, sir."

"Comms, record all broadcasts emanating from the target," Nathan instructed Naralena at the comms station.

"Yes, sir," Naralena answered.

"Mister Willard," Nathan said, turning his attention to the usually unmanned electronic countermeasures station. "It's good to see you back."

"Thank you, Captain."

"How are the ECS algorithm experiments going?"

"Very well, sir. We may be ready for live testing soon."

"I'm sure the EC community at Fleet will be very interested in your proposals. Meanwhile, with radar and scanner signatures, I'd like you to monitor and collect any signals you think might be indicative of jamming or other countermeasures coming from the Alpha Centauri system. We've only encountered a few Jung ships since returning to space, so the more information we can collect about their electronic countermeasure capabilities, the better."

"Yes, sir."

"Time to full charge, Mister Riley?" Nathan asked.

"Sixty-five was only an eight light year jump, so about four hours to full recharge, sir. After that, each layover will only be an hour as we work our way around the system.

"How soon will we be starting our deceleration turns?"

"Not until the next jump, sir. Then we'll be doing a continuous deceleration turn as we work our way around the system, during all eight mini-jumps."

"Very well," Nathan stated as he sat down in his command chair. "Mister Randeen, put the system on the main view screen, maximum magnification."

"Aye, sir," Mister Randeen answered from the tactical station. "Using starboard camera number two."

The main view screen shifted its view thirty degrees to starboard and zoomed in on the Alpha Centauri system. Nathan could easily make out the primary and secondary stars in the binary system, shining far brighter than any other stars on the screen. "Where's Proxima?" he wondered.

"Proxima Centauri is currently passing behind the system's primary star," Mister Riley reported. "Besides, it's more than six light-months away from us, and it's not very bright, so I doubt we could pick it out clearly from this distance."

"Of course," Nathan said. "And Sol?"

"It's off our starboard beam right now."

Nathan took a deep breath, letting it out slowly. "Hard to believe we're almost home," he admitted.

"It must feel good, sir," Mister Riley commented.

"It does. I didn't realize how homesick I actually was until recently. Seems the closer we get to Earth, the more homesick I become. How about you, Mister Riley? Ever get homesick?"

"We've only been gone a few weeks, sir," Mister Riley answered. "I've made interplanetary runs that were longer."

"Are you looking forward to seeing Earth?"

"In as much as it is the birthplace of humanity, yes, I am."

"If you could go anywhere on Earth when you got there, where would that be?" Nathan asked.

"I'd like to see old Scotland, sir. The Celtic blood runs deep through the Corinairan people, so it's sort of a homeland for us—the birthplace of our culture. I think a lot of us would like to go there."

"I'll see what I can do to help get you all there," Nathan promised.

"Thank you, sir." Mister Riley turned his chair to face the captain. "Have you ever been there, sir?"

"No, I'm afraid not. But I hear it's beautiful. It's not a popular tourist attraction, however."

"Why is that?"

"It was completely wiped out by the plague: Scotland, England, Ireland, all the British Isles. Many escaped to the European mainland, but it was deserted for centuries. People only started migrating back a few hundred years ago, so it's not as heavily populated as the rest of Europe."

"A shame," Mister Riley stated.

"One of many, really." Nathan rose from his seat. "Mister Randeen, you have the bridge. I'll be in my ready room."

"Aye, sir," Mister Randeen reported.

"Let me know if you spot anything interesting, Mister Navashee."

* * *

Nathan walked into workshop number four in the Aurora's engineering department. It was the only shop space left on the ship that wasn't being used by Takarans working to upgrade different components on the Aurora. Of all his new crew, the Takarans seemed to be having the most fun. They greatly enjoyed taking the Aurora's antiquated technology and making it more efficient. Some of their solutions were so simple, it was embarrassing for Vladimir at first. He had begun avoiding working directly with them for this reason. Eventually, he got used to it.

In the middle of the room stood Mister Percival's custom, long-term stasis pod. Several panels had been removed, and a large section of its internal electronics had been pulled out while still connected in order to gain access to the various circuit boards.

"What is it you wanted to show me?" Nathan asked as he circled the stasis pod in search of Vladimir who was on the opposite side. He wore a special visor that was linked to the ship's computer system in order to help him identify various components of the pod.

"Ah, Nathan," Vladimir said. The special visor magnified his face from Nathan's perspective, making his eyes appear enormous. Vladimir lifted the visor as he spoke. "I've finished my analysis of Mister Percival's stasis pod. I must say, it was a very well-designed system. Very solidly constructed, which is not surprising considering its origin." Vladimir tossed a small circuit board to Nathan.

Nathan caught the circuit board and examined it. "Aren't these Cyrillic characters?" He looked at Vladimir, who smiled. "Let me guess; it was made in Russia?"

"Of course," Vladimir said with a shrug.

"Is that what you dragged me down here to show me?"

"Nyet. I wanted to show you this." Vladimir tossed another circuit board at him, this one even smaller.

"What's this?"

"Can you read?"

Nathan looked at it again. "It says *LOGMEM00517A-*

CHRONO-B." Nathan looked at Vladimir. "So?"

"It is a memory board for use in the stasis pod's log system. This one is specifically for keeping time records. It is the backup timelog memory chip from this pod."

"And?"

"Why is it not in Russian like everything else in this pod?"

"Because the Russian one was broken, so they replaced it with one from a country that spoke English?" Nathan tossed the circuit board back to Vladimir. "Seriously, Vlad."

"I checked the other pods, they were all made in the former United States, as was this memory board. I think someone replaced the previous memory board with this one. They probably pulled it from another pod, one that had been running for two hundred years."

"How do you know?"

"I don't," Vladimir admitted, "not positively. But there is one minute missing from the incremental log on this memory board. The missing minute occurred approximately eight hundred years ago."

"So you think someone changed the board to make it look like the occupant of the pod had been in stasis for the entire trip, instead of since the time that the colonists died."

Vladimir looked at Nathan with relief. "Finally."

"So Mister Percival was lying about being in stasis the entire time?"

"Or he is not Mister Percival." Vladimir picked up a data pad. "I was curious, so I borrowed this from Jessica."

"What is it?" Nathan wondered.

"It's the log from the Jasper colony," Vladimir

told him, "at least the portions that we were able to recover. It has several recordings of communications with the Jasper in the very early days of the colony, before the shuttle crash." Vladimir played the recording and held it up for Nathan to see.

Nathan watched the split screen recording. On the left was an image of one of the colonists, presumably the man placing the call. A moment later, Mister Percival's face appeared on the right side of the screen.

"Look familiar?" Vladimir asked.

"Mister Percival," Nathan realized. "Then he was awake when they arrived."

"But if you listen, they are not referring to him as Mister Percival."

Nathan listened as Vladimir turned up the volume and restarted the comm-log entry. Nathan's expression changed when he heard the colonist address the other man by his real name. "Captain Dubnyk?" Nathan said. "Percival is really Dubnyk?"

"Or Dubnyk was really Percival," Vladimir said. "We really have no way of knowing at this point."

"Who knows about this?"

"Other than you and I, only Mister Percival, or Captain Dubnyk, whoever he really is."

"What about Jessica?"

"I haven't told her yet."

"I'll tell her," Nathan said, "and Cameron as well. But nobody else, not just yet. I need to think this through."

"As you wish," Vladimir promised.

"Nice work, by the way."

"Of course," Vladimir smiled.

* * *

"Mister Sheehan," Nathan said as he stepped up to Loki's bed. "Nice to have you back."

"Thank you, sir." Loki's voice was raspy and weak. His body lay still with his arms at his sides, and he moved his head and mouth no more than was needed.

"How are you feeling?"

"Like my body has been turned inside out."

Nathan's face cringed. "Doesn't sound fun."

"No, sir." Loki's head rolled slightly toward his left, his eyes straining to see his friend in the bed next to his. "Is Josh going to be okay?"

"Don't you worry about Josh, Loki," Marcus assured him. "He'll be fine. Nine lives, that one has."

"Are you feeling up to a few questions?" Nathan asked, trying as best he could not to pressure the young man.

"Yes, sir."

"What happened?" Nathan asked, choosing to let Loki attempt to tell his story rather than bombarding him with direct questions. If necessary, such questions could come later.

"There was a fifth moon orbiting the fourth planet in 72 Herculis, the inhabited one. We didn't see it when we were plotting our course before jumping in, and it wasn't on the charts." Loki swallowed hard, his mouth dry. "When we were about halfway to the planet, the fifth moon came out from behind. That's when we saw it. It was small, more like a large asteroid than a moon, kind of irregularly shaped. At first, I thought it might be a captured one, like the Corinairans did—you know—to mine them in orbit. But we couldn't use active scanners to get a good read on it."

Nathan could see that Loki's mouth was dry and asked one of the medical staff to bring water. "Why the burn?" he asked Loki.

"We were going to pass too close to that moon," Loki answered. "We were afraid she was going to suck us in if we didn't do a small burn."

"Cold jets wouldn't do it?"

"No, sir, not strong enough." Loki took a few sips of water before continuing. "We tried to keep the burn low and short in the hopes that no one would notice, but as soon as we made the burn, we took fire: four missiles from the fifth moon we were passing by. There was a base of some sort down there. Josh pulled some fancy moves and evaded the missiles, but they launched fighters next, and we had to make a run for it."

"Why didn't you just jump?" Marcus asked.

"They'd see us," Loki answered. "They'd know."

Nathan nodded, showing Loki that they had made the right decision.

"Josh decided to try to run behind the planet. He figured we could jump away from the dark side. He tried to time it so those fighters would lose their line of sight on us so we could jump. We figured they'd think we went down to the surface. They launched more fighters from that base to try and cut us off coming around, but they didn't know we were planning to just disappear on them."

"So why didn't you?" Nathan asked.

"We were just about to when more fighters came up from the planet surface right in front of us. Josh dove us straight down, nearly burnt us up passing through the atmosphere, but he managed to shave off enough speed so we could maneuver down low. We lost them in the canyons, even took a few out.

Then we hit that waterfall..."

"Waterfall?" Marcus wondered.

"Just as we came around a bend in the canyon. It was just there, right in front of us. It was huge, spilling off the canyon wall on the left."

"Why didn't you maneuver around it?" Nathan asked.

"No chance. We were already swinging to port as we came around. Josh had no time. He barely managed to force the turbine nozzles to swing down before we went in. If he hadn't, we'd be at the bottom of that river right now."

"That kid and his crazy stunts..." Marcus complained.

"No, he did great, really. Two of the turbines got flooded and were quitting on us when we came out. He could barely keep us in the air. Ship wanted to flip over real bad. We needed to set down. Josh fired everything we had—missiles, drones, decoys—all into the valley ahead as a diversion."

"A diversion?" Nathan wondered.

"A fake crash site. Then he stuffed us into a small cave up high in the canyon wall next to the waterfall."

"How did he find it so quickly?"

"He saw it on the TFS as we came out of the falls, high on our port side. Problem was, it was kind of small. Couldn't use our gear."

"Is that when the canopy was damaged?"

"Probably, but it was cracked when we came out of the falls. The crash landing probably just finished the job."

"How did you get airborne again?" Marcus wondered.

"Nothing was wrong with the turbines," Loki

explained. "They were just flooded with water. We just cleaned them out best we could, and they fired up."

"So the fake crash site idea worked?" Nathan asked in disbelief.

"Sort of. I mean, it worked for a while, but they had fighters circling overhead, keeping an eye out. Garrett warned us that it was just a matter of time before they figured it out and started searching for us."

"Wait a minute," Nathan interrupted. "Who's Garrett?"

"Leader of one of the resistance cells on the planet."

Jessica had been standing back out of the way and listening to Loki's account of the events, not wanting to intrude. Now, her interest was piqued. "Captain, if I may..."

Nathan stepped aside to allow Jessica closer to Loki.

"Hi, Loki. Tell me about Garrett," Jessica persuaded.

"Big, scary looking, dirty. Beard, crazy hair and clothing, like he wanted to blend into the forest. They were all like that."

"What kind of weapons were they using?"

"Projectile, like the ones you used before you ran out of ammunition. Said the Jung could track the energy weapons and locate them. That's why they didn't use them."

"How did they find you?" Jessica asked.

"Said they used that cave as an observation post from time to time. They were going to watch the Jung activity around the crash site from there. They found us there by accident. We almost got into a shootout with them. Josh stared them down, gun to gun, got them to back away. Their leader got Josh to trust him enough to lower his weapon. Good thing, too. They created a diversion in the next valley and got those fighters to leave the area."

"Why did they agree to help you?" Jessica wondered.

"Josh fed him a line about how we were part of a powerful alliance," Loki explained, "that we were joining forces with the people of Earth to come save the core from the Jung. You know how Josh is."

"And he believed him?" Nathan asked with surprise.

"The boy can be quite convincing," Marcus said.

"He didn't at first," Loki said. "They believed the Earth was still infected. Garrett said it was off-limits, always had been."

"That explains a lot," Jessica mumbled.

"So they got rid of the fighters in the area," Nathan said.

"Yes, sir. Then they took out the Jung at the crash site. Once they did, we got in the air, barely, and jumped out from within the canyon."

"So they could see you?" Nathan asked.

"Yes, sir, the resistance, at least. Maybe a few people in the nearby towns and such as well. But the Jung were gone. As far as we know, they may still think we crashed in that valley. Garrett said they weren't too bright, that they stole all their tech from others."

Jessica's eyebrows went up. She was obviously pleased with even that little bit of intelligence.

Nathan could tell that Jessica had a million more questions she wanted to ask, but he could also tell that Loki was tired and in discomfort. He remembered

Cameron's dislike for the way the nanites felt inside of her when they were making repairs to her tissues. He wondered if Loki was going through the same thing right now. "That's enough for now, Loki," he said, putting his hand on Jessica's shoulder and stepping in front of her. "We figured out the rest from your flight recorder. You two did an amazing job." Nathan put his hand on Loki's shoulder. "Get some rest. We'll talk more later."

"Is Josh going to wake up soon?" Loki asked.

"He's in worse shape than you, Loki," Nathan admitted. "He was more exposed to the jump fields since he was sitting up front. The doctors are keeping him knocked out while the nanites work on his brain, so he doesn't feel it."

"I don't feel it."

"Count yourself lucky," Marcus grumbled. "I've heard stories."

"Get some rest," Nathan insisted. "Let me know if you need anything."

"Yes, sir," Loki said, closing his eyes.

Nathan stepped back from the bed and turned toward Jessica who had an anxious look on her face. He motioned to her to wait until they were out of the room.

"Captain," she started in hushed tones, unable to contain herself, "if there is an organized resistance, then that means that the people that the Jung rule over are not willing subjects. In fact, it takes a lot of hate to stir up a resistance."

"We only know of one man at this point," Nathan argued.

"Loki said 'they,' Nathan," Jessica pointed out as they entered the corridor. "*They* did this. *They* did that. And Loki used the term *cells* which implies a larger, more organized structure."

"Yeah, I got that," Nathan said. "But how does that help the Earth?"

"If nothing else, it means the Jung occupation of at least one world is opposed by some. If there is resistance, that means some of the Jung resources have to be dedicated to suppressing that resistance. That draws resources away from other campaigns..."

"Like the invasion of Earth," Nathan surmised.

"Exactly. And if there is a resistance on one Jung world, it stands to reason that there might be others on other Jung worlds."

Nathan knew she was right. Nearly every government entity in human history had met with some form of organized resistance, both violent and nonviolent.

"Captain, maybe we should think about putting an asset on the ground back there," Jessica urged.

"Someone?" Nathan asked, knowing full well who that *someone* was.

"Well, that is what I trained for back at the academy."

"Who's going to keep my ship secure?"

"We're four light years from home, Nathan. We're safer now than we've ever been."

"We don't have the propellant."

"Use the jump shuttle to drop me off. They can drop me in orbit on the night side and jump right out again. I've space-jumped before."

"It's still being used to test the ZPEDs with the jump drive. Besides, the answer would still be no."

"Nathan..."

"Taking a few hours to recon Alpha Centauri on the way home is one thing. Sending an asset behind enemy lines is completely different."

"How is it different?" Jessica argued.

"Wars have started for less," Nathan told her. Nathan could sense Jessica's frustration. This kind of mission was exactly what she had trained for, and it was exactly what she wanted to do. Being this close to a perfect opportunity had to be difficult.

"Nathan..."

"I'm sorry, Jess. The answer is no. The best I can do is recommend it to Fleet when we get back, for all the good that will do."

"Fine," she pouted as she stopped in the corridor while Nathan continued on, "but don't expect me to show up as a character witness at your court-martial."

"Funny," Nathan called back to her as he continued down the corridor.

* * *

"These are images of Kent," Jessica explained, "the primary inhabited moon orbiting the gas-giant Larelias in the Alpha Centauri A system."

Nathan sat at the conference table in the darkened briefing room, staring at the images as they flashed across the view screen on the far wall. He had seen pictures of the Earth-like moon before, from the Data Ark. "I remember this moon. It was the first extra-solar colony of Earth, late twenty-second century, I believe."

"As you can see from these atmospheric readings, it is an industrialized world. You can also make out several orbital platforms as well."

"How many people are living there?" Nathan wondered.

"On Kent, Fleet estimates were in the millions.

Remember, they had their own space defense fleet before the Jung invaded."

"What happened to them?" Cameron asked.

"They must have been destroyed. We were unable to find them in either the A or B systems," Jessica surmised. "However, we did find several Jung warships still in the area." Distant, fuzzy pictures of warships appeared on the view screen. "These appear to be cruiser-sized warships."

"How many of them did you find?"

"Two in the primary system and two more in the secondary, orbiting the terraformed planet, Bretang."

"So there are four warships in the system?" Major Prechitt counted. "Any idea about their fighter compliment?"

"We've never encountered such ships, so we really don't know," Jessica admitted. "However, they are twice the size of the Aurora, so it's reasonable to assume that they carry at least as many fighters as we do, if not more."

"Any way we can get more details on these ships?"

"We would need to loiter a lot longer in order to take longer exposure shots to compile," Cameron stated. "That would burn up a lot of propellant. Either that or send in a recon ship, which we don't have available at the moment."

"One other thing," Jessica said as the picture changed. "Another ship arrived in the B system during our last imaging. It was much larger than the others. I'm pretty sure it's a Jung battle platform."

"Battle platform?"

"Massive ships, lots of missiles, fighters, guns," Jessica explained. "Fleet believes they are designed to sit in the middle of a system and pound the crap out of anything. Right after we built the first FTL recon ships, Fleet found three of them: one in the Tau Ceti system, one in 82 Eridani, and the last one in the Omicron 2 Eridani system."

"All three of which are core worlds," Nathan noted for the benefit of Major Prechitt, who was still unfamiliar with the history of human space exploration outside of the Pentaurus cluster.

"Fleet believes the Jung park them in their most valuable systems in order to maintain control over those systems."

"A show of dominance," Nathan said.

"Precisely," Jessica agreed with a nod.

"So now they are parking one in the Centauri system?" Cameron asked.

"I believe so," Jessica said. "Either they will leave the battle platform in Centauri space and send one or more of the cruisers to invade Sol, or they will send the battle platform to Sol instead."

"Either one would be difficult for our Defender class ships to defeat," Nathan commented. "What would you do," he asked Jessica, "if you were planning the invasion of Earth?"

"From what Loki told us, the Earth has been considered off-limits ever since the plague for fear of reinfection. That would explain why they never invaded us."

"Perhaps we're just the farthest system away from them," Vladimir suggested.

"Possible," Jessica admitted, "but unlikely. Think about it. The Earth would be the crown jewel in their empire. Not only is it the birthplace of humanity, but even now, it's still the best place for humans to live. Everywhere else we either have to adapt to the planet or adapt the planet to us. We evolved on Earth, and it's perfect for us. Even terraformed worlds have their problems. I believe they didn't consider invading Earth until they realized that it was no longer infected."

"How did they figure out it was safe?" Cameron asked.

"Recon flights? Spies?" Jessica said. "It could've been as simple as picking up media broadcasts once again. We've been beaming them out into space for two hundred years now."

"Assuming you're right, and they're preparing to send either the battle platform or the cruisers to attack Sol, how long do we have?"

"We still don't know their top speeds," Jessica stated, "but a reasonable assumption would be about two months for the cruisers and about six months for the battle platform."

"Then Fleet's original estimates were not that far off," Cameron said.

"Apparently not," Nathan agreed. "We need to get this information back to Fleet. Once the public learns how real the Jung threat is, Fleet will have all the support it needs."

Major Prechitt looked confused. "Support? Your defense forces are lacking support?"

"Political support," Nathan explained. "Many people in the Earth's various governments believe it would be in our best interests to seek a peaceful resolution through negotiations, and that in order to do so, we must ease up on our military growth, especially in space, as a sign of good intent."

"Then this should change their minds," Major Prechitt said.

"Let's hope," Nathan said. "How long until we're ready to jump home?"

"We're at fifty percent charge right now, so we can jump any time."

"We'll wait an hour before we jump to ensure we have a bit left over for an emergency jump, just in case."

* * *

"Jump seventy-four plotted and locked in, sir," Mister Riley announced. "Jump drive is at sixty-eight percent charge. With a jump distance of four point four light years, we'll still have a few light years of jump distance available to us on arrival."

Nathan looked at Cameron standing next to him on the bridge. "There was a time when I didn't think we'd ever make it."

"It does feel good," Cameron said.

Nathan took a deep breath and exhaled. "Mister Riley, execute jump seventy-four."

"Aye, sir," the navigator answered. "Activating auto-nav. Jump seventy-four in ten seconds."

Nathan watched as the auto-nav made tiny adjustments to the ship's course and speed in order to increase the timing and accuracy of their jump.

"Five seconds," Mister Riley reported.

Nathan turned and looked at Jessica. She stood by Mister Randeen at the tactical station, about to relieve him. She, too, had a smile on her face.

"Three......two......one......jump."

The blue-white jump flash filled the bridge, disappearing a moment later.

"Jump seventy-four complete," Mister Riley reported.

"Verifying position," Mister Navashee announced from the sensor station.

"Threat board is clear," Mister Randeen reported from tactical.

"Position verified," Mister Navashee reported. "We are just outside the Sol system, sixteen point three light hours from Earth."

Nathan stared at the forward view screen. In the center, directly ahead of them, was a small, slightly yellowish dot. It was only fractionally brighter than the stars around it, yet it shown like a beacon to Nathan. It was their sun, the sun that lit their very existence. They had been gone for only four months, but it felt like a lifetime.

"Captain?" Cameron said. "Orders?"

Nathan snapped out of his daydream. "Right." He looked at Cameron, unsure of what to do next. They had discussed this at length during the last briefing, but it had all suddenly slipped his mind. "Scans," Nathan remembered. "Mister Navashee, perform a full passive scan of the Sol system: radio, thermal, optical, the works."

"Yes, sir."

"Tactical, anything in the optical scans that looks even remotely threatening?"

"No, sir," Mister Randeen answered. "I see no evidence of any traffic whatsoever."

Nathan's brow furrowed somewhat. "None?"

"None, sir."

"Odd."

"We wouldn't pick up any of the patrols on the fringe of the system with a low-power sweep," Cameron reminded him.

"But there's always one ship deep in the system," Nathan said. "That's standard operational policy, even if they're just coming or going."

"They could be transiting behind Jupiter, or

Saturn, or any of the gas-giants, relative to us that is," Cameron said.

"What are the odds?"

"For most people? A trillion to one," Cameron stated. "For us, not so high."

"Is that what I think it is?" Abby asked as she walked onto the bridge.

"That's Sol," Nathan confirmed. He could see tears in the physicist's eyes.

"How long before we jump in?" Abby asked.

"Don't worry, Abby," Nathan answered. "We'll be jumping in soon enough. We're just checking things out first. We don't want to have an accident on our last jump."

Abby smiled briefly. "I'm sorry, Captain."

"Don't be. I know how you feel." It was one of the most truthful statements he had ever made, and he was sure that every Terran aboard felt the same way. A simple shakedown flight four months ago had turned into an unannounced test of a top secret, experimental propulsion system, one that was believed to be the best hope for the defense of Earth against the Jung. That first test jump had turned into a battle, one that resulted in their being thrown across the galaxy, where they were forced to fight to survive and eventually return home. Now, they were back, flying through the same Oort cloud where their adventure had begun. One more jump and the adventure would be over. Nothing but endless reports, interviews, and investigations awaited them. Endless reports had never looked so good.

"Captain, I'm not picking up any transmissions on Fleet channels," Naralena reported.

"What about civilian space traffic?" Nathan

asked.

"No, sir. I'm picking up media broadcasts, but no comm traffic other than some low-power, civilian radio comm chatter. But that's all local, planet-side stuff, not space traffic."

"Jess, take a listen to those broadcasts, and tell me what you think," Nathan instructed.

"I'm on it," Jessica answered as she moved toward the comm stations at the back of the bridge.

"Not even from the mining operations in the belt?" Cameron wondered.

"No, sir."

"What about the beacon from the orbital assembly platform?" Nathan asked.

"No, sir, nothing."

"Mister Navashee, concentrate opticals on Earth. I want to see the OAP."

"Aye, sir," Mister Navashee answered. "Locking optical telescopes on Earth."

"Could they be purposefully reducing their transmissions?" Cameron asked. "To appear less prepared, less threatening?"

"We wouldn't fall for that," Jessica said, "so I doubt the Jung would."

"That's a lot of traffic to keep quiet," Nathan commented. "How do you continue to operate without comms and navigational beacons?"

"Lasers?" Cameron suggested. "All ships have laser comm systems in order to broadcast and receive targeted comm beams instead of sending out omnidirectional broadcasts."

"If the Earth were trying to keep a low profile, that would certainly help," Jessica said, as she continued to listen to various media broadcasts from Earth through her comm-set.

"Perhaps," Nathan said, pondering the idea. "That would make sense, especially if they already know about the buildup in the Alpha Centauri system."

"Fleet still has the small FTL recon ships. After what happened to the Centauri, they'd probably be keeping a close watch on the system."

"But how often could they receive updates?" Nathan wondered.

"The recon ships were only capable of eight times light," Cameron said. "Unless they were upgraded while we were gone, the most they might have gotten was one, maybe two updates since Alpha Centauri was first attacked."

"Captain," Jessica called, "these are all just standard multimedia broadcasts: entertainment, music, news, sports, the usual stuff."

"Any of it sound abnormal?"

"No, sir," Jessica answered. "From what I can tell, it just sounds like a typical day on Earth. Maybe if we spent some time analyzing it, we might find out more."

"Captain, I believe I've located the orbital assembly platform," Mister Navashee reported. "I'm putting it up now."

Nathan and Cameron watched as a still image of the OAP appeared on the main view screen. The image was slightly out of focus but appeared to be of similar size and shape. Nathan squinted his eyes slightly and cocked his head, examining the image. "Are you sure that's the OAP? It looks different somehow." He turned to Cameron. "Does it look different to you, or is it just because the image is fuzzy?"

"The size and configuration are similar," Cameron stated. "Is there any way to enhance the image quality?"

"This is a very short exposure, sir," Mister Navashee reported. "I only had enough time for this one shot, as the OAP was about to slip behind the planet. I can get a better picture when it comes back around in about an hour and a half."

"Give us another low-power sweep, Mister Randeen," Nathan ordered.

"Aye, sir."

"What do you think?" Nathan asked Cameron.

"Not what I expected," Cameron admitted. "However, it all does make sense when you think about it, assuming the system is on a war footing, that is."

"They have every reason to be; that's for sure," Nathan agreed.

"Still no contacts, Captain," Mister Randeen reported.

Nathan stared at the main view screen, the tiny yellowish star beckoning to him. "Recommendations?"

"We could transmit a message via laser comm and wait for a response," Cameron suggested.

"It would take sixteen hours for the initial hail to reach them. With encryption, ID challenges, and the time it takes while some comm officer in Fleet operations runs around yelling, 'The Aurora is alive. The Aurora is alive,' it could take days to get instructions out of them." Nathan shook his head. "No. The Earth is a mere sixteen light hour jump away, and the system is clear. Mister Riley, plot jump seventy-five to Earth. Put us a few minutes from orbital insertion."

"Plotting jump seventy-five to Earth, aye," the navigator reported.

Nathan felt a chill go down his spine. "I guess

this is it," he told Cameron and Abby. "We're finally home."

Abby looked at Nathan with gratitude in her eyes. "Thank you, Captain," she whispered.

"Jump seventy-five plotted and locked," Mister Riley reported.

Nathan looked at the faces of each and every person on the bridge at that moment, the key personnel with whom he dealt daily: the auxiliary technicians working in the background in supporting roles, most of whose names he never knew; his executive officer and his chief of security, both whom were good and trusted friends; then there was the physicist whose father's genius had completely changed the course of humanity from the moment the first jump had been initiated. These people and this ship had been his world for the last four months. They had been his sole reason for both living and dying, day in and day out. Now, it was all about to come to an end. For months, he had longed for this moment, the moment when the enormous burden and responsibility of command would be taken from his shoulders, and he could stop pretending to be captain. A small part of him was sorry to see it end.

"Comms, ship-wide," Nathan ordered. He cleared his throat and waited for Naralena to signal that the ship-wide address channel was active. "Attention all hands. This is your captain. We are about to execute the final jump in our voyage back to Earth. For those of you who are from Earth, I welcome you home, and I thank you for your tireless efforts in getting us back to the place of our birth. To those of you who joined us in the Pentaurus cluster, I welcome you to the birthplace of humanity, the home of your ancestors. I thank each of you as well, for without your willingness to leave your homes, we never would have made it back to ours. Again, I thank you all for your service. You have all earned your place in history. The crew of the UES Aurora will never be forgotten. That is all." Nathan gestured for Naralena to close the channel.

"Ship-wide closed," she reported quietly.

Nathan took a breath. "Mister Riley, you may execute jump seventy-five when ready."

"Aye, sir," Mister Riley reported. "Activating auto-nav. Executing jump seventy-five in twenty seconds. Auto-correcting course and speed."

Nathan again felt the ship move slightly as the auto-navigation system made the final course and speed corrections before jumping the ship to her final destination. A lot had happened over the months. Many had died, but many had survived. The Aurora, a ship only partially completed at the time of their first flight, was now not only finished but was vastly improved. He and his crew had good reason to be proud.

Cameron moved to stand directly beside Nathan. "You surprised me, Nathan," she said in a hushed tone so that only he would hear her.

"How so?"

"You were a fine captain."

"Jumping in five seconds," Mister Riley reported.

"Thanks," Nathan answered. "You're lying, but thanks anyway."

"Three......two......one......jump."

The bridge filled once again with the blue-white jump flash. When it cleared, the familiar sight of the Earth sat in the middle of the view screen. She appeared as a quarter crescent, beautiful and blue, with white clouds partially obscuring her land masses. Even her dark side was stunning, bathed in the faint light reflected from her only moon.

Nathan felt his heartbeat quicken and his hands and feet become cold. Excitement washed over him like a cool breeze. This was a familiar sight, one that he had seen in pictures as a child and again as an adult as a member of the fleet. He had seen it from this perspective before as a cadet during flight training and from the Aurora's aft cameras as they had pulled away on their first flight.

"Jump seventy-five complete," Mister Riley reported.

"Verifying position," Mister Navashee announced, although it was obvious to everyone that they had arrived precisely where they had intended.

"Position verified," Mister Navashee reported. "We have arrived at Earth."

"Five minutes from orbital insertion," Mister Riley added.

"Comms, prepare to transmit a message to Fleet," Nathan ordered. "Standard encryption, all Fleet comm frequencies. Message reads, 'Aurora returning. Orbit in four minutes. Requesting instructions.'"

"Aye, sir," Naralena answered.

"Is it true?" Vladimir asked as he entered the bridge. "*Bozhe moi,*" he exclaimed as he stopped dead in his tracks, staring at the main view screen. "It's true; we are home."

"Shouldn't you be in engineering?" Cameron asked.

"I had to see it for myself," he said. "I've never seen it from this far out, only from orbit. Who knows if I'll ever get another opportunity?"

"Why wouldn't you?" Cameron asked.

"With all the amazing repairs I've made, and my work with Corinairan and Takaran technologies, I'm sure Fleet will move me to special projects."

"You don't think they're going to do that with all of us, do you?" Cameron wondered.

"Don't worry, Commander," Nathan said. "You and I are going to be tied up with reports and investigations for months. After that, I'm sure you'll get a shipboard assignment."

"One minute to orbital insertion," Mister Riley reported.

"Reply from Fleet," Naralena announced. "Message reads, 'Welcome home. Clear for orbit. Proceed to OAP and make port.'"

"That's it?" Cameron asked. "No 'Where have you been?' No 'You're supposed to be dead'? Just 'Welcome home. Park it over there'?"

"What did you expect, Commander?" Nathan said. "They're probably running around yelling and bumping into each other trying to figure out how we're still alive."

"It's probably just a standard response from some young comm officer," Jessica added. "Word probably hasn't even reached the brass yet."

"We left four months ago, stocked for a day trip," Cameron said. "You would think they would at least ask if we needed assistance."

"Perhaps our disappearance is still classified," Vladimir suggested.

"Now that would make sense," Nathan agreed, pointing at his friend.

"He is correct," Abby agreed. "Security around the project was frighteningly tight. As far as I know, only two people outside of the project knew of its existence."

"Well, it doesn't matter now," Nathan said. "We just appeared out of nowhere right in front of the Earth and everybody on her."

"You're just begging for that court-martial, aren't you?" Cameron said.

"Well, if that doesn't do it, nothing will."

"Entering Earth orbit," Mister Riley announced.

"OAP on the horizon," Mister Navashee reported.

"Take us in, Mister Chiles," Nathan ordered.

"Aye, sir, taking her into port," the helmsman answered.

"Sir, I have a contact coming up from behind the planet," Mister Randeen reported from tactical.

"What is it?" Nathan asked.

Mister Randeen looked at his display, his expression suddenly changing. "I'm sorry, sir. I lost it. It went to FTL as it came over the horizon."

"A recon ship?" Jessica suggested. "Headed out to Alpha Centauri, no doubt."

"If they had just waited a few more minutes, we could have saved them the trouble," Nathan bragged.

"We'll make port in ten minutes, Captain," Mister Riley reported.

"Very good." Nathan turned to Cameron and the others. "I guess it's time to start packing."

"Time for you to find an attorney," Jessica teased.

"At least that will come to an end," Nathan said, pointing at her.

"Captain," Naralena called, "I'm picking up a transmission from the surface."

"From Fleet?" Nathan asked.

"No, sir, at least, it's not through any Fleet comm channels. It's in the clear, no encryption."

"From who?"

"No caller ID. Just the message," Naralena

reported.

"How do you know it's for us?"

"They called us by name... Aurora." Naralena looked back at her console. "It's repeating, sir."

"Put it on speaker."

"*...a trap! Aurora! Aurora! It's a trap! Aurora! Aurora! It's...*" The message was suddenly interrupted, replaced by a high-pitched, whiny static.

"What happened? Why did it stop?" Cameron asked, frowning.

"The message stopped, Captain." Naralena spun around and looked at the captain again. "They just stopped transmitting."

Nathan looked at Cameron, his expression sinking and his face turning pale. He then turned to Jessica. "General quarters," he ordered.

"General quarters, aye," Jessica responded.

"Helm, break orbit and make for open space," Nathan ordered. "All ahead, one quarter. Steer toward the sun."

"Breaking orbit, aye. All ahead, one quarter. Making way toward the sun," Mister Chiles reported.

"Mister Riley, keep an updated combat escape jump," Nathan ordered. "One light minute out." Nathan turned to Cameron. "Get to combat, Commander."

"What is going on?" Abby cried out.

"Vlad!" Nathan called.

"I've got her," Vladimir answered as he wrapped his arms around Abby. "Come on, Abby. We've got to go."

"Wait! What's happening?" she cried again in anguish.

Vladimir led Abby toward the exit, handing her off to one of the newly arriving guards, as the bridge detail was increased during the alert. "Get her out of here," he ordered the guard.

"Aye, sir."

"Nathan, I'll be in engineering!" Vladimir yelled as he left the bridge.

Nathan waved his acknowledgment as he continued giving orders. "Tactical, alert flight to be ready for combat ops as soon as the deck goes green, and spin up the rail guns for point-defense."

"Aye, sir."

"Mister Willard," Nathan called out as Mister Willard took his station at the electronic countermeasures console. "Start jamming all frequencies, comms, target acquisition, radar, the works!"

"Aye, Captain," Mister Willard answered.

"Contacts," Mister Navashee announced. "Coming up from the surface fast. I count fifteen, maybe more. Transferring tracks to tactical."

"I've got them," Mister Randeen responded. "Attempting to ID," he announced, but Jessica beat him to it. "Jung fighters, Captain! Count eighteen."

"Helm, steady as you go. Kill the mains and stand by."

"Steady as she goes. Mains at zero, Captain."

"Green deck, launch fighters!" Nathan ordered.

"Green deck, aye," Mister Randeen answered.

"*Nathan!*" Cameron's voice came over the comms. Nathan could tell she was running by the sound of her voice. "*Keep a close eye on your propellant levels!*"

"Copy that," Nathan answered.

"*I'll be in combat in thirty seconds.*"

"First four fighters are airborne, sir. Vectoring towards contacts."

"Comms, tell flight to keep them high and not to dive down on the contacts until they reach max range."

"Yes, sir."

"Tactical, deploy the quads through our underside and sweep those contacts before our birds get there. Let's see if we can thin them out a bit."

"Aye, sir. Deploying quads."

"You run the guns. I'll take tactical," Jessica told Mister Randeen as she stepped in beside him.

"Yes, sir," he answered, relieved to have some help.

"Second wave is airborne," Naralena reported.

"Jamming on all frequencies."

"Commander Taylor reports she's in combat, Captain," Naralena reported. "Chief of the boat is in damage control. All battle stations report manned and ready."

"Two more contacts," Mister Navashee reported. "They just came out of FTL on the far side of Venus."

"Jung cruisers," Jessica reported. "They're still ten minutes out at present speed."

"Quads are online," Mister Randeen reported. "Targeting approaching Jung fighters."

"Fire when ready," Nathan ordered.

Along the underside of the Aurora at her midship, all four quad-rail gun turrets spun around to point back at the Earth as she slowly fell away. Bright, electrical flashes ran up the gun rails as fragmentation projectiles leapt out of the Aurora's largest guns. The rounds streaked through space, heating up slightly as they penetrated the upper atmosphere of the Earth on their way to the Jung fighters. Just before they reached their targets, the rounds burst apart into hundreds of smaller pieces, each piece carrying tremendous, kinetic energy that tore through the small fighters as they struck. Several fighters exploded instantly, while others spun out of control and began falling back toward the Earth.

"Five contacts down," Mister Randeen reported. "Six, seven, eight…"

"The first four Talons are approaching max range, sir," Mister Navashee reported.

"Cease fire!"

"Holding fire on the quads, sir," Mister Randeen answered.

"Tell flight their birds are clear to engage," Nathan instructed.

"Aye, sir," Naralena answered.

"Jess, let's send some missiles toward those cruisers. No reason to let them walk in unimpeded."

"How many would you like?"

"How about four each to start," Nathan ordered.

"Aye, sir," Jessica answered. "Launching missiles."

"Contact!" Mister Navashee exclaimed. "Just beyond the orbit of Mars. Just came out of FTL as well."

"Another cruiser," Jessica reported, "maybe a battleship. It's bigger than the others."

"A battle platform, maybe?" Nathan wondered.

"Not big enough."

"How did they all know?"

"That contact that went to FTL as it came over the horizon," Mister Randeen said, "it must have been a messenger."

"They must have had ships sitting just outside

the system," Jessica surmised. "Just far enough out that we wouldn't find them, but close enough that they could FTL to them and recall them quickly."

"Shit," Nathan exclaimed as the first round of missiles streaked away from them on the main view screen toward their Jung targets. "We don't have the propellant for this."

"Flight reports fourth wave is airborne," Naralena announced.

"That makes twelve of our fighters to ten of theirs," Jessica advised.

Nathan looked at Jessica. "Tell flight to hold off launching any more for now."

"Aye, sir."

"But have them ready in the tubes just in case."

"I expect the major will have them there whether we tell him or not," Jessica commented.

"Combat, Bridge," Nathan called over the comm-set.

"*Go for Combat,*" Cameron answered.

"Commander, give me a call on the current tactical situation. Do we have enough propellant to engage all three ships using the same jump-shoot-jump tactics we used against the Ta'Akar?"

"*I'll get back to you in a moment, sir.*"

"The first two cruisers are firing missiles," Jessica reported. "Spread of twelve. Time to impact: five minutes."

"Keep an eye on them, Mister Randeen. Start your point-defense fire when they get in range."

"Aye, sir."

"*Bridge, Combat,*" Cameron called over the comms.

"Go ahead," Nathan answered.

"*Captain, we can engage all three and still have*

enough propellant to cut and run or achieve Earth orbit again, but only if we get them in the first pass or two. More than that and we risk running dry."

"Understood." Nathan stared at the tactical map displayed on the main view screen.

"Orders, sir?" Jessica asked.

"Charge the plasma cannon in tube two. Load nukes in tubes one, three, five, and six."

"Aye, sir," Jessica answered.

"Comms, I need to know how soon those Talons can finish off those Jung fighters."

"Aye, sir."

"Mister Riley, plot a jump. I want to come out one hundred thousand kilometers in front of those two cruisers, equidistant between their flight paths."

"Aye, sir."

"Mister Chiles, when we come out of our jump, you're going to yaw to port just enough to bring our tubes to bear on the first cruiser. As soon as we fire, you'll yaw back to starboard and put our tubes on the second cruiser," Nathan explained.

"Understood, sir."

"Once we fire on the second cruiser, bring the nose back on course, fire up the mains, and pitch down so we can jump clear before the nukes go off."

"Yes, sir," Mister Chiles answered.

"Flight reports five minutes, sir," Naralena announced.

"Jump plotted and locked," Mister Chiles reported. "Updating as we fly."

"Port plasma cannon charged and ready," Jessica reported. "All tubes loaded with nukes and ready for snap shots."

"Mister Randeen, I need you to clear us a path through those missiles before we can jump in and attack. Use the quads if you have to."

"Yes, sir," Mister Randeen answered. "Recommend we reset the quads to the topside and show our uppers to the targets. We can get more guns on those missiles that way."

"Very well," Nathan said. "Helm, pitch down ninety degrees."

"Pitching down ninety, aye," Mister Chiles answered.

"Missiles will be in range in ten seconds," Jessica reported.

"Comms, let flight know we'll swing back to pick up our fighters after the first pass on those cruisers."

"Yes, sir."

"Mister Riley, after our first strike, I want to jump just past the targets. Another hundred thousand kilometers should do it. We'll put another torpedo into their backsides on our way out."

"Aye, sir," Mister Riley answered.

"We'll use the same yaw maneuver with the aft tubes, Mister Chiles."

"Yes, sir."

"Firing point-defense. Firing quads," Mister Randeen reported.

All sixteen mini-rails guns located around the Aurora's perimeter opened fire at once, sending thousands of fragmenting point-defense rounds per second toward the incoming Jung missiles. At the same time, the Aurora's four larger quad-rail guns also began firing, sending much larger frag rounds toward the targets at an even greater velocity.

One by one, the icons representing the incoming missiles disappeared from Jessica's threat board.

"It's working, sir. Our path will be clear any moment."

"What about our missiles?" Nathan asked.

"They're shooting them down at the same time," Jessica reported.

"Figured that."

"All twelve incoming missiles have been destroyed," Jessica reported.

"Hold your fire, Mister Randeen," Nathan ordered.

"Point-defense and quads are cold," Mister Randeen reported.

"Helm, bring our nose back up and prepare to jump."

"Pitching up," Mister Chiles reported.

"Ready to jump in five seconds," Mister Riley added.

"Stand by forward tubes," Nathan told Jessica. He turned his chair around partway to face her and added, "Feel free to take a few shots with our new plasma cannon, if you get the chance."

Jessica turned to Mister Randeen. "Would you like the honors?"

"Hell yes."

"Jumping in three......two......one......"

The bridge filled with the blue-white flash. A moment later, the flash cleared.

"Jump complete."

"Yawing to port," Mister Chiles reported.

"Full magnification," Nathan ordered. "Keep the camera on the targets."

A moment later, the view screen zoomed in. Nathan could barely make out the two gray and red blobs at the center of the screen, but they were rapidly growing larger as the Aurora raced toward them.

"Our nose is on the port target," Mister Chiles

reported.

"Fire tube one!" Nathan ordered.

Jessica pressed the button on the tactical console to fire the first torpedo. At the same time, Mister Randeen fired the plasma cannon in tube two.

Bright red balls of plasma energy streaked across the magnified view screen, lighting up the entire bridge as they streaked ahead of the first torpedo.

"Jesus," Nathan exclaimed, surprised by the intensity of the plasma shots as a dozen of them streaked toward the first cruiser.

"Torpedo away," Jessica announced.

"Yawing to starboard," Mister Chiles reported from the helm.

"Direct hits all across the port target's bow, sir!" Mister Navashee reported. "Her forward shields are gone, damage to her forward sections, forward missile battery, rail guns... Damn! She's hurt! She's venting atmosphere!"

"On the second target," Mister Chiles reported.

"Fire tube three!" Nathan ordered.

Once again, a dozen balls of red plasma energy streaked over the upper left side of the screen toward the ever-enlarging targets in the distance.

"Torpedo away!" Jessica announced.

"Bringing her back to course and pitching down," Mister Chiles reported.

"Second target is taking damage as well!" Mister Navashee reported. "Shields, hull damage, just like the first target, sir!"

"Five seconds to first torpedo impact!" Jessica reported.

"Let's get out of here," Nathan urged.

"Clear jump line coming up," Mister Chiles reported from the helm.

"Jumping in three..." Mister Riley announced, "...two......one......"

The jump flash came and went, and the two targets that had been growing in the center of their view screen were gone.

"Jump complete," Mister Riley reported.

"Yawing to starboard..."

"Belay that," Nathan ordered. "Steady as she goes."

"Holding steady," Mister Chiles answered.

"Torpedo one impact!" Mister Navashee reported.

"Aft view, Jess," Nathan ordered.

Jessica quickly put up the view from the Aurora's aft camera and zoomed in on the targets as the first torpedo's detonation flashed brightly. The explosion tore the cruiser on the right into several large pieces. The secondary explosions that followed broke the doomed cruiser up even further.

"Target destroyed!" Jessica yelled. "Torpedo two in three seconds."

Nathan watched the screen and waited, the second flash coming a few seconds later. The second cruiser did not break apart like the first one, but she was visibly damaged with secondary explosion blowing sections off her outer hull.

"Second target is hit. She's lost all power," Mister Navashee reported. "She's out of the fight for now."

"I'm not taking any chances," Nathan said. "Jess, put a spread of missiles into her."

"Captain, she's not..."

"They were waiting for us, Jess," Nathan snapped. "That means they've already invaded the Earth. Who knows how many people have died. And where are all our ships?" He stared at her directly. "Fire the goddamned missiles and finish that bastard off."

"Aye, sir," Jessica answered.

"Helm, prepare to come about as soon as the target is destroyed. We'll jump back to Earth and pick up our fighters before we engage the last ship."

"Yes, sir," Mister Chiles answered, exchanging glances with his navigator.

"Missiles loaded and ready," Jessica reported.

"Fire," Nathan ordered calmly.

Jessica hesitated for a moment, then pressed the button. On the view screen, four missiles streaked overhead on their way to the target.

"Missiles away," Jessica reported. "Ten seconds to impact."

The bridge remained quiet as the missiles traversed the hundred thousand kilometers between the Aurora and the crippled Jung cruiser. Finally, there were four bright flashes of light, and the cruiser exploded.

"Target destroyed," Jessica reported.

"Helm, come about," Nathan ordered.

"Coming about, aye."

"Mister Chiles, jump us back to high Earth orbit as soon as we finish our turn. Then prepare to jump out to engage the next target."

"Aye, sir."

"Captain, another wave of fighters is coming up from Earth to engage our Talons in orbit."

"Time to jump?"

"One minute," Mister Chiles reported.

"Mister Navashee?"

"The second wave of contacts will reach our Talons in five minutes, sir."

"Comms, alert flight. Ready the deck. We'll be picking up our fighters in less than two minutes."

"Yes, sir."

"How are we doing on propellant?"

"Down to four percent," Mister Chiles reported. "I'm using as little as possible in my maneuvers."

"I know," Nathan assured him.

"Turn complete."

"Jump."

The bridge filled momentarily with the jump flash, and the Aurora arrived back in high Earth orbit.

"Jump complete."

"Green deck," Nathan ordered. "Let's get our birds on board."

"Green deck, aye," Jessica answered. "Recovering fighters."

"Prepare our next combat jump, Mister Chiles," Nathan ordered. "Same as before, one hundred thousand kilometers out. We'll launch two nukes, then hold on target long enough for Mister Randeen to get even more plasma shots off before we pitch down and jump under. We'll put two more in her from behind if necessary."

"Yes, sir."

"Captain, maybe we should..."

Nathan raised his hand, cutting Jessica off in mid-sentence. He had only one thing on his mind; he wanted the Jung out of Sol and off the Earth, and he would do whatever was necessary to accomplish his goal.

"Flight reports all fighters are on board," Naralena reported.

"Very good. Red deck. Helm, break orbit and set course for our next combat jump."

"Red deck, aye," Jessica answered.

"Breaking orbit," Mister Chiles acknowledged.

"Load nukes in tubes one and three. Stand by

on the plasma cannon, and ready another round of missiles," Nathan ordered.

"Aye, Captain," Jessica responded. "Loading nukes in tubes one and three. Plasma cannon standing by. Readying missiles."

"Jump point in ten seconds," Mister Riley reported.

Nathan could feel his rage growing by the moment. He wondered how long the Jung had been in his system, how long it had been since they had invaded the Earth and destroyed her defenses. Had it happened yesterday? A week ago? A month ago? What if it were recently? If so, if he had gotten back sooner, could the Aurora have made the difference? While they were fighting the Ta'Akar, were people back on Earth being slaughtered the way the Corinairans had been?

"Contacts!" Mister Navashee reported.

"More fighters?" Nathan wondered.

"No, sir, two more contacts coming in from behind the moon."

"What?" Nathan asked. "How is that possible?"

"They must have come in by FTL like the others, sir."

"More cruisers," Jessica reported.

"Another contact!" Mister Navashee reported. "Coming out from behind the sun."

"She's too obscured by the sun to ID," Jessica said, "but she's big, bigger than the others."

"Contacts by the moon are launching fighters!" Mister Navashee reported. "Thirty, maybe forty contacts!"

"Time to attack range?"

"Five on the fighters, ten on the ships," Jessica reported. "The one by the sun is a few hours away

410

unless she goes to FTL."

"*Bridge, Combat!*" Cameron called over comms.

"Go, Commander," Nathan said, although he already knew what she was going to say.

"*We don't have the propellant for this, sir.*"

"We can still take out the third ship," Nathan argued.

"*Every drop counts here, Captain. We're it. We're all the Earth's got left. We're going to need all the propellant we've got just to find more. We try anything else, and we're guaranteed to lose. If not now, very soon.*"

Nathan stood there silently, staring at the screen, anger and frustration boiling up inside him.

"*Captain?*" Cameron called over the comm-set.

"Sir?" Jessica urged.

"*Nathan,*" Cameron called, "*you know I'm right, damn it! If you don't break off and jump out now, I will!*"

Nathan turned and looked at Jessica. His eyes were pleading and full of pain. He knew he had no choice; he had to run.

"To fight another day, sir," Jessica told him.

The slightest of smiles formed at the corner of his mouth, if only for a moment. "Secure all weapons. Mister Riley, jump us out of the system."

"Securing all weapons," Jessica answered.

"Where to, sir?" Mister Riley asked.

"Where to?" Nathan wondered. "Anywhere. Just jump us clear of the system, a few light years maybe. Just leave us enough in the energy banks for another one light year jump."

"Two light years out, then?" Mister Riley asked. "That should put us off any obvious transit routes between core worlds."

"Very well," Nathan agreed. "Execute when ready."

"Aye, sir. Jumping in five seconds."

"Aft view," Nathan ordered. He watched as the view screen switched back to the aft facing camera. The Earth was slowly shrinking as they pulled away from her. A few seconds later, the jump flash came and went, and the view screen was empty, showing only the stars behind them.

"Jump complete," Mister Riley reported.

"Threat board is clear," Jessica announced.

"Stand down from general quarters," Nathan ordered.

"Standing down from general quarters," Naralena acknowledged.

Nathan turned and walked past Jessica at the tactical station on his way toward the exit. "Tell the XO to report to the bridge," he instructed as he passed.

"Nathan," Jessica started.

"Until she gets here, you have the bridge."

"Where are you going?"

"I'll be in my quarters."

The bridge was silent as Nathan walked to the exit and left.

"Captain off the bridge," the guard at the hatch announced.

Jessica sighed. "Tactical is yours again, Mister Randeen."

"Yes, sir."

Jessica moved toward the command chair. "Mister Navashee, full passive scans, three hundred sixty degrees. Nothing approaches us without our knowing: not a ship, not a rock, not a grain of dust. Understood?"

"Yes, sir."

"And start thinking of where we might find some propellant," she added as she plopped down in the command chair. She looked at Mister Chiles and Mister Riley sitting in front of her at the helm. "What are you two looking at?" she snapped. Both men immediately turned back around to face forward without saying a word.

* * *

Nathan lay motionless on his bed. The room was dark, and his eyes were closed, just as they had been for several hours. As usual, sleep eluded him. He had considered going to Doctor Chen and asking for something to knock him out for a few days, but his desire to avoid all contact with the crew was greater than his need for sleep.

The buzzer at his door sounded. He continued to lie there, ignoring the buzzer as it repeated its obnoxious call. "Go away," he mumbled to himself as the buzzer continued to sound. Eventually, it stopped. "Thank you." Nathan continued his attempts to force sleep to come. This time, it was his comm-set, lying on the nightstand. The small light on the side of the comm-set flashed, casting an intermittent green hue across the room. He could hear a faint voice calling to him through the ear piece.

"*I know you're awake, Nathan.*"

It was Cameron, and apparently she was determined to speak with him.

"*Open the door, or I'll have Jessica override it, and we'll come in anyway.*"

Great, there are two of them, he thought as he

rose from his bed and headed toward the main room. Nathan walked lazily across the main room. "I'm never going to be able to sleep again," he moaned as he opened the door. Standing before him were Cameron and Jessica. Directly behind them were Vladimir and the chief of the boat, Master Chief Montrose. "I don't remember calling a meeting."

"I called it," Cameron stated as she pushed past him and entered. "Can we turn on some lights?"

Nathan stood aside as the others followed Cameron past him into the main room. The lights came on without warning, causing Nathan to squint. "Bright."

"What? Have you been sleeping the whole time?" Cameron wondered.

"Trying? Yes. Actually sleeping? Not so much."

"For six hours?" Cameron asked, surprise on her face.

"Maybe you should see the doctor, sir," Master Chief Montrose said.

"When I can't sleep, I drink," Jessica stated. A moment later, she realized everyone was looking at her. "I mean, when I'm off... Okay, fine. I know a guy who knows a guy who has a still, okay? Come on. Tell me none of you has ever wanted to throw a few back and unwind."

"Why have you not shared this with us?" Vladimir asked.

"Is that why you're all here?" Nathan wondered. "To get me drunk?"

"No, sir," Cameron answered.

"Too bad," Nathan said as he plopped down on the couch.

"Maybe later," Jessica added as she plopped down next to him, "if you're a good boy."

Master Chief Montrose watched as Cameron and Vladimir also took seats. "Terrans have very unusual military protocols."

"Take a seat, Master Chief," Nathan said. "That's an order."

"As you wish."

"We want to know what the plan is," Cameron said.

"The plan? Other than trying to get some sleep, I don't have any plans. Although, Jessica's sounds like a good one. How much booze does your friend of a friend have on hand?"

"We're serious, Nathan," Cameron insisted. "We need a plan."

Nathan sighed. "I've been trying not to think about it."

"And how has *that* been going?" Cameron asked.

"Lousy. In fact, I'm pretty sure that's why I can't sleep."

"Then surely you must have run a few ideas through your head, especially if you've been trying for six hours."

"A few scenarios have run through my mind, yes," Nathan admitted. "Unfortunately, they all suck."

"Why?"

"They all end with me getting us all killed, or getting millions of people on Earth killed, or cracking a planet in half." Nathan looked at Cameron, then at the others. "To be honest, I just don't think I have it in me."

"What are you talking about?" Vladimir asked in shock. "Of course you do."

"No, I don't, Vlad, and you know it. You all know it. I've been playing the part of captain for months now. I hated it, but in the back of my mind, I knew that, once we got home, it would all be over, and I could get back to my old life. But now, that's no longer an option. I'm stuck here, and I don't think I can handle it anymore. I'm just not the right man for the job."

"And which of us is?" Master Chief Montrose asked. Nathan looked at him funny. "Seriously, Captain, which one of us is more qualified than you?"

Nathan pointed to Cameron. "She is."

"How am I more qualified?"

"You're smarter, you scored higher, you know the regs inside and out..."

"That just means I'm more disciplined than you are," Cameron said. "Okay, I am smarter, but I am not better qualified."

"How are you not more qualified than me?"

"Than I," Cameron corrected.

"See?"

"Yes, I scored higher, and yes, I know the regs better," Cameron admitted.

"You even know the ship better than I do," Nathan declared.

"Yes, that's true as well. But right now, Nathan, you're probably the most experienced starship captain in the history of Earth. You've logged more light years, fought more battles, destroyed more ships... Hell, you even negotiated an interstellar alliance! One of questionable legality, yes, but you still did it."

"There you go," Jessica said. "There's your silver lining."

"What?" Nathan looked confused.

"Now you don't have to worry about a court-martial."

Nathan rolled his eyes.

"Look, Nathan, I'll admit that when we first met, I thought I had you all figured out. I thought you were a spoiled, little, rich boy who was playing soldier just to piss off his father. I decided that was who you were and would always be, but you changed. You faced up to your responsibilities and accepted the consequences of your actions. And you did the right thing, even when others were telling you to do something different. That's what a captain does; he makes the call. Don't you see, Nathan? You *are* the captain of the Aurora. You may not have been handed your command by some brass hat, but you've earned it nonetheless. With every command you've given, with every shot you've fired, with every life you've defended, with every death that has resulted from your decisions. But also with every victory, and with every sleepless night. You *are* the captain. You're *our* captain, more so than Captain Roberts ever was."

"It doesn't matter who is captain," Nathan said. "We're still screwed. The Earth is screwed. I screwed her."

"What are you talking about?" Vladimir wondered.

"I should have gotten us back sooner. I should have headed home as soon as we escaped from Haven. Millions of people on Corinair would still be alive."

"And we would still be under the rule of the Ta'Akar," Master Chief Montrose said, defiance in his voice. "Our demise would have come either way. Without Na-Tan, eventually we would have been destroyed, our world remade to meet the needs of the Ta'Akar."

"Nathan, when we left Haven, we didn't have the

propellant, the food, or the crew to make it home," Cameron insisted. "Sure, we might have made it back in five or six months, maybe. But our chances were extremely poor. Believe me; if I had thought otherwise, I would have made a bigger issue of it."

"She's right about that," Jessica agreed. "She would have."

"You made that call because that is what captains do; they make the call. Right or wrong, they make things happen. And you did get us back, Nathan. It may have taken four months, but we made it. And we got back in better shape than we were when we departed."

Nathan shook his head. "It doesn't matter. We are still screwed. There's nothing we can do."

"We can fight," Jessica declared. "At least, that's what the people of Earth are doing."

"How so?" Nathan asked.

"They sent us a message," Jessica told him. "Someone risked their life to warn us, someone who knew who we were. They sent that warning because they knew that, as long as there was one ship out there fighting the Jung on their behalf, there was hope."

"We have to give them that hope, Nathan," Cameron insisted.

Nathan looked at her. "This isn't going to be like it was in the Pentaurus cluster, Cam. The Jung are not the Ta'Akar. The Ta'Akar controlled maybe ten worlds and had a fleet of less than twenty ships. The Jung may control more than fifty worlds, at least half of which are probably industrialized." Nathan laughed nervously. "Hell, to the Jung, twenty ships is not a fleet; it's a battle group. No matter how you look at it, we are no match for the Jung. We have almost no propellant, limited ordnance, limited food, and limited crew. We're limited in everything."

"We have a jump drive," Jessica stated.

"And a captain who knows how to use it," Cameron added.

"And lots of cool advanced technology," Vladimir declared. "And people smarter than us who know how to use it," he added with a laugh.

Nathan looked at Cameron. She had been a thorn in his side since day one, always competing for his job, a job he had never really wanted in the first place. Over the months, she, too, had changed. He could no longer feel her nipping at his heels, looking for a way to show him up. She had become his trusted XO, his friend, and one of his biggest supporters. Without her, he knew he could not have accomplished anything.

He looked at Jessica. Her strength and courage in the face of danger always amazed him. She could jump into the fires of hell, all the while believing she could beat the devil himself and return unscathed.

Then there was Vladimir, his closest friend and loyal confidant. He once bragged that he could fix anything. Thus far, he had proven that to be true. His sense of humor was sometimes all that kept Nathan together.

"And what of the Corinari?" Nathan asked, looking at Master Chief Montrose.

"The crew will follow their captain," Master Chief Montrose said, "without hesitation or regret."

"Why?"

"Because you *are* the one. You *are* Na-Tan."

"No, I'm not," Nathan disagreed. He had used that moniker in order to gain the support of the Corinairan people to battle the Ta'Akar. But it was something he had never felt good about. He had only been able to live with his actions because he knew it was necessary. It was the Corinairans he was defending at the time.

"It is not for you to decide whether or not you are Na-Tan," Master Chief Montrose explained. "Fate will decide that for you." The master chief stood. "Order us to fight for the people of Earth, and the Corinari will do so, Captain."

Nathan looked at the master chief. He was a good man and a fine example for his people. He looked at his friends, each of them, one at a time. The look on their faces as they waited for him to make a decision pulled at his heart, leaving him little choice. "One hour," he finally said. "Senior staff in the command briefing room. We need to figure out our next move."

"Yes, sir," Cameron answered happily as she stood as well.

"Now everyone get out of here so I can take a shower and get dressed," Nathan said, pulling at his robe. "This isn't exactly regulation."

Jessica and Vladimir stood and followed Cameron and Master Chief Montrose to the door. Vladimir, who was last in line, stopped and turned back toward his friend, his captain. He raised his right hand, formed a perfect military salute, and held it.

Nathan looked at Vladimir who had sworn never to salute him. It had been in jest, a bit of good-natured fun between friends, and Nathan understood the significance of Vladimir's gesture on this day.

Jessica joined Vladimir, coming to attention beside him and raising her hand in salute as well.

Cameron turned back, noticing Jessica and Vladimir's gesture. She tapped the master chief on the arm to get his attention as she, too, fell in line and saluted.

"I will *never* understand your military," the master chief mumbled as he joined the line and saluted.

Nathan rose to his feet and straightened his robe, his eyes locked on Vladimir's as the big, Russian engineer cracked a smile out of the corner of his mouth. Nathan returned the salute. Today, he truly became the captain of the Aurora.

Thank you for reading this story.
(*A review would be greatly appreciated!*)

COMING SOON

"CELESTIA: CV-02"
Episode 8
of
The Frontiers Saga

Want to be notified when
new episodes are published?
Join our mailing list!
Simply send an email to:

mailinglist@frontierssaga.com

(Put "Join Mailing List" in subject.)
You will continue to receive notifications
until you ask to be removed from the list.

Made in the USA
San Bernardino, CA
11 September 2017